SAFE HAVEN

SAFE HAVEN

Patricia MacDonald

This first world edition published 2018
in Great Britain and 2019 in the USA by
SEVERN HOUSE PUBLISHERS LTD of
Eardley House, 4 Uxbridge Street, London W8 7SY.
Trade paperback edition first published
in Great Britain and the USA 2019 by
SEVERN HOUSE PUBLISHERS LTD.

British Library Cataloguing in Publication Data
A CIP catalogue record for this title is available from the British Library.

ISBN-13: 978-0-7278-8848-8 (cased)
ISBN-13: 978-1-84751-972-6 (trade paper)
ISBN-13: 978-1-4483-0181-2 (e-book)

Typeset by Palimpsest Book Production Ltd.,
Falkirk, Stirlingshire, Scotland.

ONE

Rain pelted the windows of La Petite Auberge, and the twinkling white lights threaded through the trees along the cobbled driveway seemed to hover, a floating strand of wavery nimbi, in the prismatic streaks on the glass. The rambling fieldstone and stucco house overlooking the river, so characteristic of this part of Bucks County, Pennsylvania, had been cleverly, expertly transformed to resemble a rustic French farmhouse. Of course, it was a farmhouse with upholstered fruitwood chairs at every table, and cascades of gorgeous flowers. In the large, timbered vestibule was a fireplace, now crackling, and, in one cozy corner, a gleaming, baby grand piano.

Dena Russell stared out into the darkness from between the dark blue millefleur-patterned drapes which flanked the front doors of the cavernous firelit foyer. In the rain-spattered glass, her reflection might have been that of a child. She was small-boned and had a heart-shaped face with bangs and chin-length hair. Everything about her was delicate and petite – everything except the large belly under her dark green knit jumper which heralded the baby that was due in less than two months.

The headlights of a car appeared at the end of the long drive and Dena glanced at her watch, wondering if it might finally be Brian. Although the dinner guests at the restaurant were just beginning to arrive, Dena's work as the assistant pastry chef was done for the day. Tonight, she and Brian were supposed to be attending Lamaze class at the Monroe County Hospital, and she did not want to be late.

A voice at Dena's ear said, 'Where the hell is he?' Dena jumped, startled, as if someone were reading her thoughts. She turned and saw Albert Gelman, who, with his longtime companion, Eric Schultz, had created La Petite Auberge, standing at her elbow, frowning into the darkness. 'What?' she asked.

'Peter,' said Albert impatiently, waving a well-manicured hand at the gleaming black baby grand piano, crowned with a spectacular arrangement of fresh flowers. 'Our patrons pay for the ambiance,' he said. 'That includes the piano player.'

Albert was referring to Peter Ward, a young widower who was raising two girls on his own, and was often late these days as he tried to cope with the recent departure of his upstairs neighbor who doubled as his regular baby-sitter. During the overlapping segments of their shifts, Peter had aired his troubles to Dena.

'I'm sure he'll be here soon,' said Dena. 'He's had a lot of problems lately.'

'I have my own problems,' said Albert. 'I don't have time for his.'

Albert had spared no expense to create this restaurant, a French fantasy transported to this historic Pennsylvania town on the far outskirts of suburban Philadelphia. He wanted a setting that would be worthy of Eric's cooking, which he had learned in the Burgundy region of France. Both men vacationed in France every year, and always brought back treasures to add to the already exquisite decor. Albert's expensive taste was evident in every detail, and indeed, now in its third year of operation, La Petite Auberge attracted guests from as far away as New York. Although he seemed to be fussy and hypercritical, Dena knew, after working for him for the last six months, that Albert was fair and had a kind heart.

'He'll be here,' she reassured him. At that moment the door opened and a bearded man with longish brown hair flecked with gray came in. He was wearing a black turtleneck, a tailored gray tweed jacket, and a trench coat. He shook the rain off his umbrella and put it in the faience porcelain stand by the door. Albert walked over and lifted the wet raincoat off Peter's shoulders with the tips of his fingers, holding it at arm's length from his own bespoke gray suit. 'You,' he growled, 'are late.'

'I'm sorry, Albert. My little one was feeling kind of needy. She wouldn't let me go until I read to her, and brought her juice and all . . .'

'Puh-leeze,' said Albert. 'Enough. Go. Sit. Play.'

Peter gave Dena a conspiratorial grin as he headed for the piano bench. They both knew that Albert, kindhearted though he was, had no frame of reference for children. Their ways and needs were a mystery to him. Dena smiled back at the harried parent.

Albert hung up Peter's coat as Peter sat down, pushed open the lid to the keyboard, and played an arpeggio that drew a pleased murmur from the cluster of couples in the dining room. Albert sighed. 'I don't know why I keep him.'

Dena smiled. 'Because you're a sweetheart, Albert.'

He pointed a finger at her. 'Don't you believe it,' he warned. Albert turned away. 'I have a restaurant to run.'

Dena made a gesture that indicated she was erasing her smile, as Albert disappeared around the corner. For a moment her gaze fell on Peter, as he began to play a melancholy Francis Lai song. Albert insisted on a strictly French repertoire at the piano, and dictated Peter's wardrobe as if he were an actor in a play. The sophisticated, fashionable clothes did not exactly suit Peter's sturdy, all-American frame, but Peter always insisted that he didn't mind. He said that Albert had better taste than he did.

Dena and Peter often chatted in the moments when their paths crossed, and Dena had to admire him. He seemed utterly devoted to his two small daughters, and it couldn't be easy, raising them alone. As if he could feel her gaze on him, Peter looked up from the keys. He had keen, gray-green eyes that were unmistakably intelligent, though often sad. There was a worried, distracted look in his eyes tonight that made her look at him questioningly. He glanced around, as if to make sure that Albert was nowhere in sight, and then inclined his head slightly as if to call her over to the piano.

Dena took another look out the window. She was getting seriously worried about the time. There was still no sign of Brian's truck. It had been difficult enough to convince him to attend the class with her. The first two series of classes that she'd wanted to attend, he had insisted that he couldn't manage it. Trying to be understanding, she had put it off. Now, it was too late to put it off any longer. The baby was due in less than two months.

She turned away from the window and walked over to the piano, leaning against it and looking at Peter inquiringly. 'What's up?' she asked.

'Something I wanted to tell you,' he said, his soft voice barely audible over the notes he was playing.

'I can hardly hear you,' she said.

He patted the seat on the piano bench beside him, but she was unwilling to sit there. After all, she was expecting Brian, and she knew he would take it the wrong way. At the same moment, she felt weary of having to think that way. She leaned over the piano, as far as her large belly would allow. 'What is it?' she asked.

'I haven't said anything to Albert yet,' he said.

Immediately, she felt her heart begin to sink, knowing before he said it what this was going to be about. 'Are you leaving?' she asked.

Peter gazed at his music intently and nodded.

'Oh, Peter, no,' she said. She suddenly had a sense of how much she was going to miss him. He was always interesting to talk to, always considerate of her, especially in this late stage of her pregnancy. 'Who will I talk to?' she asked.

'Talk to Brian,' he said.

'Yeah, right.'

He glanced up at her, and she realized how she was slumping against the shining piano. She forced herself to straighten up.

'Things aren't going well?' he asked.

Dena sighed, and pressed her lips together. Last year, she was living in Chicago, and had come to New York for a master class in artisan bread-baking. While she was in New York, she decided to take a quick trip to Monroe to attend her tenth high school reunion, and had run into Brian Riley, a guy she scarcely knew, but had had a crush on in high school. To her amazement, the attraction had been mutual this time, and they had begun a long-distance romance that resulted in her unplanned pregnancy. When she came back to Monroe, at his insistence, to live with him, she scarcely knew him, but she had been full of hope. Now, six months later, that hope had all but disappeared. 'You might say that,' she sighed.

Peter frowned. 'Anything I can do?'

'No,' she shook her head. 'I've got to figure this one out myself. But, tell me about you. Why are you leaving? Where are you going?'

Peter looked around again nervously as he finished his song, and reached up to change his sheet music. He began to play again. 'I got an offer for a job out in Minneapolis. I'm from there, originally. It's more money, and the hours are better for the girls. They'll both be in school, and I need to be home at night.'

Dena squeezed the sleeve of his jacket. 'You're a great dad,' she said. 'You always put them first.'

He shook his head, as if to brush off the compliment. 'I'm going to hate telling Albert. He's not going to take it well.'

Dena nodded in agreement. 'You've got that right.'

'He's been good to us. It isn't that. But, you know, circumstances change.'

'I know,' said Dena. How well I know, she thought. She and Brian had seemed so well suited to one another when they only saw each other on occasional weekends. But not long after she moved back here to live with him, she began to see another side of him – a much different side. Brian's father had had a stroke and was in a nursing home, and it was true that Brian worked long hours maintaining his father's horse barn and was often tired and stressed out. Dena could be understanding about that. But he was also possessive and jealous, unwilling to see, or let her see other people. After six months of living here, she didn't know a soul outside of work. She felt isolated at the farm, and if she suggested that they have any other friends, he would question her suspiciously. He didn't seem to trust her at all. Although for a while she had tried to tell herself that their relationship would improve, her hopes were all but gone.

'Do you think you and Brian will get married?' Peter asked.

Dena started. Marriage was the farthest thing from her mind these days. Not so long ago, she had wanted a marriage and a family so much. She had taken her pregnancy, which happened in spite of her precautions, as a sign that this was meant to be. That Brian was the one. But, it didn't seem that way any more. 'I don't think so,' she said truthfully.

'Well, whatever happens,' he said, 'you'll have your baby. There's nothing more wonderful in the world.'

His words made her feel oddly lonely. 'Peter, I hate it that you're going,' she said. 'I'm going to miss you so much.'

'Dena,' demanded a familiar voice coldly.

Dena turned and saw Brian, still in his boots and dirty jeans, from the barn, standing behind her. She was struck, as always, by the sight of him. Despite his disheveled clothes, he was one of the handsomest men she had ever seen. He had black, curly hair and long eyelashes, and he still had the physique of an athlete, thanks to years of working at his father's barn.

'Hi,' she said. He must have heard her. She could see he was angry, but she refused to be ashamed of a kind word to an acquaintance. Deliberately, she turned back to Peter. 'I've got to go.'

Peter smiled at her briefly, and then looked up at a matron in a red suit who had approached the piano. 'Can you play "Music of the Night"?' the woman asked.

'I'm sorry, I don't know that one,' Peter lied smoothly. 'How about "La Vie en Rose"?'

'But that's so old,' the woman protested.

'Like women, and fine wine, it improves with age,' said Peter gallantly. The middle-aged woman giggled flirtatiously before returning to her table.

Brian did not wait for Dena but turned on his heel and stalked out of the restaurant. Dena followed him. His pick-up truck was parked at the entrance to the restaurant. Dena opened the door and clambered awkwardly into the cab beside him. Brian did not glance at her. He was watching the rear- and side-view mirrors as he pulled away from the curb.

Dena glanced at her watch but decided not to protest about the time. It wouldn't do any good now. 'Nasty night,' said Dena.

Brian did not reply. The silent treatment, she thought. Not again. 'How was your day?' she asked.

'Not as interesting as yours,' he said sarcastically.

'Brian,' she said wearily.

'My day was shit,' he said. 'I've got two sick horses and the owners are blaming it on the barn.'

Dena tried to be sympathetic. She knew how difficult his life had become. At the barn, Matthew Riley boarded about a dozen horses and trained them for competition.

Before the accident, he would routinely take a caravan of horse trailers to faraway competitions. Matthew had been a somewhat domineering man, who had never really ceded any of the responsibility of the business to his son. Brian's initiation had been overnight, and traumatic. So far, he had met with nothing but loss. He had been forced to sell part of the farm, including his own little house and the property it stood on, just to avoid bankruptcy.

'I'm sorry,' she said automatically.

'Me too,' he said abruptly. 'I'm exhausted and I'm strung out. And now we have to go to this thing tonight.'

'This thing,' she repeated, bristling. 'You mean the Lamaze class.'

'Yeah, right.'

'Look, if you don't want to come, then don't.'

'Would you rather I didn't?' he asked.

'I would rather you did it willingly,' she said, her own temper flaring.

'I'm sorry. I'm not sensitive enough to enjoy these things, like your boyfriend from work.'

'Oh, for God's sake,' said Dena.

'If all I had to do was sit around playing the piano all day . . .'

'At least Peter is a man who sees a baby as a wonderful thing, not some millstone around his neck,' she snapped.

'Ah,' Brian said, as if satisfied. 'The ideal man.'

Dena shook her head. She felt as if she had been walking on a razor's edge for months now. She struggled to control her anger. 'Brian, I don't want to fight with you. I'm just trying to make a point. You know very well Peter's nothing but a friend to me. In fact, he was just telling me that he's leaving. He got another job.'

'You must be heartbroken.'

'Oh, stop it Brian.'

'Stop it, Brian,' he mimicked her.

Dena felt furious, but she told herself to calm down. This couldn't be good for the baby, to constantly be angry and on edge. But he twisted everything she said. When this had started, she made excuses for him, and tried to understand. But she found that these days she didn't really care any more why he did it. All she could think of was how much more of it could she stand. She stared out the window and refused to take the bait.

They rode in silence until they reached the sign for the Monroe General Hospital. The front of the hospital had a circular drive that curved under a wide, brightly lit arch that covered a walkway. Brian pulled up under the portico.

The hospital was fairly quiet on this rainy night. There was another couple approaching the main doors. The woman had long, chestnut-colored hair, and with one hand she gently pressed her distended belly. The man beside her was holding an umbrella over both of them. He had graying hair, and wore a suit and tie. His arm was curled protectively around his wife, and they were smiling. Dena watched the couple wistfully as they came up the walkway. They looked the way you were supposed to look with a baby on the way – excited, happy, tender.

All of a sudden, Dena realized that she recognized the woman. It was a close friend from high school, Jennifer Smith, who didn't, as far as Dena knew, live here any more. She rolled down the window and leaned out.

'Jennifer,' she called.

The woman looked up, mildly curious at the sound of her name, and their eyes met. At first, the woman looked confused, and then the confusion in her face cleared. She walked up to the window of the cab and put her white hands on Dena's. 'Dena,' she exclaimed, 'what a nice surprise! What are you doing here?'

'Lamaze class. What are you doing here?'

'Me too!' Jennifer exclaimed happily. 'I didn't know you—'

'You either. It's been years,' Dena cried. 'I thought you lived in Boston, or somewhere.'

'I did,' said Jennifer. 'My mom just died a few months ago and we're just back here to be closer to my dad. To help him out.'

'I'm sorry,' said Dena. 'She was a lovely person.' Dena remembered Jennifer's parents well. They owned an elegant old hotel and Dena's mother had worked there when they lived in Monroe.

'Thanks,' said Jennifer. 'Oh, and this is my husband, Ron Hubbell,' she said proudly. The graying man in the suit came up and bent his head to say hi. Dena shook his hand.

'But when did you come back here?' Jennifer asked.

'Oh,' said Dena, slightly flustered. 'About six months ago. Well, I'd like you to meet,' she turned and looked at Brian. His jaw was clenched, and his eyes were hard and angry as he gripped the wheel of the truck. He did not look at her. Dena licked her lips nervously. 'This is Brian Riley. We're . . . living together,' she said with a false brightness.

Jennifer straightened up and backed away from the truck, as if she had been slapped. The color drained from her face. Her friendly smile vanished and she clutched her husband's hand, whose genial expression had also become closed and wary.

'Get out,' said Brian. 'I'll park the car.'

Taken aback, Dena hesitated. She could feel her own face redden.

'Get out,' he growled. Dena gathered up her purse, opened the door and clambered out, adjusting her coat around her. Jennifer and her husband had backed away from the curb. 'Can I walk in with you?' Dena asked. Jennifer nodded without speaking.

Dena glanced inside the cab at Brian. 'So, I'll see you in there?' she said. As if in reply, the passenger window rolled silently up, covering the dark interior of the truck with a convex glass surface that showed her an ugly, distorted image of her own wary face.

TWO

'OK,' said the teacher, who wore a flowing, broomstick-pleated skirt, chandelier earrings and was named Mariah. 'Next week, we're going to work on timing our breathing. Coaches, very important lesson for you.' The men in the classroom shifted or straightened in their seats, their faces reflecting a cheerful humility at their standby position in this childbirthing endeavor.

Dena's face flamed, but she sat silently in the folding chair, staring straight ahead at the teacher. She could feel Jennifer glancing at her sympathetically from time to time, but she pretended not to notice. Dena had stopped looking around for Brian about half an hour into the class. She had been relieved when the teacher showed a film, so that no one could stare at her in the dark. She imagined all those couples looking at her, feeling sorry for her that she was here all alone. She wanted to say, I'm not alone, but even as she thought that, she knew it wasn't true. She was alone. Brian had never come in, never even bothered to stop in the back to explain. Dena wondered if it had something to do with the obviously unwelcome encounter with Jennifer and her husband. She and Jennifer had not had a chance to talk, since the class was already starting when they walked in.

Oh, what difference does it make? Dena thought. Any excuse would do for Brian.

She tried to concentrate on the class, on the film which showed a woman in natural childbirth, surrounded by her loving husband and a midwife. It had seemed as if the class would never end.

'See you all next time,' said Mariah. 'Be good to yourselves.'

Before Jennifer could ask her any questions, Dena was up and out of the room. She looked around the quiet corridors of the hospital, but Brian was nowhere to be seen. Why didn't I bring my own car? she thought. She rummaged in her purse for her phone. Her hands trembled as she called the cab company. She managed to keep her voice steady as she gave the dispatcher her information. Hanging up the phone, Dena started to walk across the lobby. Jennifer was standing down near the door of the Ryman room, chatting with another woman from the class, a stocky blonde with her hair twisted up in a barrette, wearing a rain slicker. Dena tried to pass them unobtrusively, hoping not to be noticed. But Jennifer excused herself and hailed Dena with a wave of her hand.

'What happened to Brian?' Jennifer demanded.

Obviously, Dena thought, there is some bad blood between them. Although, on one hand, she was curious, mostly she didn't want to know what it was. 'I don't know. I called a cab,' she said.

'Let us drive you,' said Jennifer.

Dena had known that offer was coming. That's why she had made such a hasty exit. She just couldn't bear to talk about it. She didn't want to have to explain why Brian had never come in. Why he hadn't come back to pick her up; why she was left alone this way. 'Really, it's OK,' said Dena.

'Is everything all right with you?' Jennifer asked, and Dena could hear the genuine concern in her voice. 'I'm worried about you.'

A lie came instantly to her lips, along with the desire to save face, but the look in Jennifer's clear, hazel eyes was so grave that Dena just shook her head. 'We're . . . having some problems,' she admitted.

Jennifer reached out and squeezed her hand. 'Why don't you come home with me? We're living on Chestnut Street. We bought the Morgans' old house. Do you remember it?'

Dena nodded. 'Thanks. But I'm tired. Not tonight,' she said.

'Dena . . .' Jennifer began. 'Listen to me. I'm very concerned about you. Please come with us.'

'We wish you would,' said Ron.

Dena appreciated their concern, but found it troubling at the same time. 'Thanks,' said Dena. 'I mean it. But not tonight. I'll call you. I promise.'

Jennifer reached out for Dena's phone and entered her information. Then she handed the phone back. 'Now I'm in your phone,' she said. 'I want you to remember that . . . you have a friend here.'

Dena glanced out and saw the cab pulling up under the portico. 'My taxi's arrived,' she said, putting her phone back in her purse. She began to put on her raincoat and Ron hurried to help her. She and Jennifer exchanged a brief embrace, and Jennifer seemed unwilling to let go of her hand. Dena pulled away, went out and got into the car, giving the address as if she were in a dream.

She looked back to see Jennifer and Ron standing behind the plate-glass doors, Ron's arm protectively wrapped around his wife, as they watched her go.

Nothing seemed real to Dena. Mercifully, the cabby was not talkative, so Dena was able to collect her thoughts in the dark back seat of the cab on her way back to the Rileys' horse farm.

There was no escaping the crudeness of this latest slight. How much more of this are you going to take? she asked herself. She had been making excuses for Brian for months. Of course he was depressed, worried about his father, and oppressed by his financial woes. It would be unreasonable to expect him to be anything but depressed. She had even made excuses for his drinking. Told herself it would pass, it was just a way of coping. She had told herself all these things and more. Anything, but face the reality of her situation.

Her own father had died when she was six years old, and she always thought of her life in two parts – the years before his death had a glow of happiness in her memory. And then . . . Her mother had done the very best she could, supported Dena and her older sister, Marcia, and always told them they could have the life they wanted. Watching her mother's struggle to keep a roof over their heads, Dena had grown up knowing that a woman needed to be able to support herself. She had never been a great student, though she had forced herself to go to college. But it was not until she attended an adult ed class on cake decorating that she found the work she was looking for. After that, it had been easy to make her career. She had attended the most difficult classes she could find on pastry making. She had even spent six months studying in France. Now, she had a profession, and it was well-paid, satisfying work. She had become the kind of self-sufficient woman her mother had always urged her to be. But, secretly, the life she wanted for herself was very different from her mother's. She wanted a husband and children. She wanted that glow back. She had just about given up hope when she met Brian, and then it had all seemed possible.

Dena looked out the taxi window at the rainy back roads of Monroe. She had pictured a childhood for her baby that would be different from her own. She had always felt self-conscious about being without a father. When she realized she was pregnant, and her romance with Brian was blossoming, she had thought it could happen. She had come back here on an impulse, and now, perhaps it was time to admit she had made a mistake.

Is this what you want for this baby? she asked herself as the cab whizzed through the drizzly night. Parents who can't get along, and a house full of tension and misery? Compared to that, wasn't it better for a child to have a single parent and a home full of love? Isn't that what your mother would do if she were still here? Her mother had always spoken of her late father in the most admiring way. She never dated after he died. No one seemed to measure up to his memory. Dena had prayed that a man would come along for herself who would be equal to his memory. Maybe she had sabotaged her own chances by expecting too much. But this was definitely not enough, and she had to face it. You can do it alone, she told herself, as angry tears sprang to her eyes. It wasn't what you hoped for, but you can do it.

'Where's the entrance?' asked the driver, slowing down on the dark highway that circumscribed the town. Once upon a time, when Dena was in high school, all the land back here had been rural, but now, most of it was built up with condo developments or private homes on large lots, and much of the sleepy, rustic charm of this colonial-era town had been lost to progress.

'There,' said Dena. 'Between those lampposts there's a break in the stone wall.' The driver nodded, and turned into the Rileys' farm. In the darkness the taxi rolled slowly down the gentle incline over the gravelly driveway, high beams illuminating the wooden gates of paddocks on either side of the road. Dena had pictured her baby, her child with Brian, growing up to swing on those gates, ride the horses, live close to nature in a way that was all but gone these days. She tried to dismiss the thought from her mind. Face it, she thought. It was all part of a dream.

The taxi pulled up in front of a ranch-style house with an ancient fieldstone stable and a barn just beyond it. She and Brian had been living in the house since Brian had been forced to sell his land and his mobile home to pay the bills. She had tried to make the best of it, to cheer him up, by keeping it neat, and putting flowers around. But, gradually, she had lost the desire to pick up Brian's beer bottles, bus his dishes, and treat the place like home. These days, the ranch house seemed almost forbidding to her.

Dena paid the driver and got out of the car. She rubbed her back for a minute where it was sore and stood outside, beside her car and Brian's pick-up, reluctant to go in. The house was dim, but she could tell there was a light on in the kitchen. She could also see the cold, silvery glow of the TV on in the living room. All right, she thought, taking a deep breath. Pull yourself together. You have to think of your baby now.

She opened the door of the ranch house and went in, and looked around. The house was comfortable in an old-fashioned, masculine way. There was a plaid sofa, and a recliner, and a rocker, braided rugs on the floor, and a magazine rack stuffed with hunting and fishing magazines. But the appliances in the kitchen were ancient, and the house still had a landline. Brian's parents had been divorced for years, and his mother lived in California. There were few reminders of her in the house. All of Matthew Riley's belongings were still there, however, although the doctors had told Brian it was unlikely that his father would ever be coming home.

The air in the room was stale, and smelled of beer. Brian was slumped in a recliner in front of the television. Empty beer cans were piled up beside the chair. He was staring at the television but the sound was off. He looked up at Dena with narrowed eyes. Then he looked back at the TV.

No apology. Nothing. All right, she thought. Let's do it that way. She set her pocketbook down on the scarred dining table and hung her coat up on a hook by the front door. She knew that he expected her to say something, to scold or berate him. She was not about to give him the satisfaction. Without a word, she passed through the living room and walked down the hall to the dark bedroom. She snapped on a stiff, frilly bedside lamp, and picked up her book, which sat on the bedside table. With a sigh, she tossed it onto the quilted polyester bedspread with its indistinct pattern of water lilies. There was a closet with louvered doors at the other end of the room. Dena walked over to it and opened the doors. The scent of a potpourri sachet wafted out into the room. She stretched up on tiptoes and wrestled her suitcase down from the top shelf.

As she threw the suitcase on the bed, she heard his footsteps start down the hallway, then hesitate. Then, he strode to the door of the room and stood in the doorway, wobbling slightly as he stared at her.

Dena could feel his gaze on her but she ignored him, picking up her paperback and tossing it into the open suitcase. Then she walked over to the dresser near the bathroom door and pulled open the top drawer.

'What are you doing?' he said.

Dena still did not look at him. 'What does it look like I'm doing?' She lifted her underwear carefully from the drawer and placed it into the open suitcase.

Brian stared at the suitcase as if he didn't know what it was. She glanced at his handsome face, now slack from too much beer, his keen blue eyes glazed over. Part of her felt sorry for him. Somewhere inside of him was that rugged, earnest man who had wooed her. The first month or two, when she moved here, had been promising. But even then, there were signs. Signs she ignored. The idea of her pregnancy took some adjustment, but they were managing. And he did drink more than she had realized, but it didn't really worry her. Not then. Not till later. Not until she realized how insecure he could be, how possessive. At first it had seemed flattering. But then . . . He even seemed to see the coming baby as a rival for her love. You should have seen it coming, she berated herself. Oh, what's the difference, she thought. There was no use in placing blame. She could only think of her baby now.

'Where do you think you're going?' he said in a slurred voice and, for a moment, Dena felt a little shiver of fear. No, she thought. He's not dangerous. He's just drunk. More drunk than she had ever seen him, she had to admit. But that was all it was.

'Brian,' she said, as briskly as she could. 'This isn't working. I think it would be best if I moved out of here.'

'What isn't working?' he demanded, his eyes narrowed.

'This,' she cried, throwing her arms out. 'This . . . us. You, drinking all the time. Your jealousy. You never even showed up at the class tonight. Look, I'm sure I'm partly to blame. I've been preoccupied with the baby. And you have a lot on your mind. Whatever. I have a baby to think of. If you don't care about your own baby, well . . . I'm not going to try to make you care. But somebody has to think about it. I have to think about it.'

'How do I know it even is my baby?' he said.

Dena's eyes widened in disbelief. She tried to respond, but she couldn't even form the words. She shook her head. 'That's beyond . . . That's pathetic, Brian. I can't believe you said that.'

Brian rubbed his hand over his hair, and for a moment a vaguely sheepish look wavered in his eye. Then he walked unsteadily over to the bed, and lifted up a piece of lacy underwear out of the suitcase. Dena bent down and picked up her slippers from beside the bed, holding them in front of her protruding belly. She watched him warily. Brian rubbed the silky lingerie between his fingers and nodded. Then he tossed it back into the suitcase.

'Going off with your new boyfriend?' he asked, an ugly leer distorting his handsome features.

'Oh, for God sakes, Brian,' she said. She put her slippers into the suitcase and then reached for a pile of shirts in the drawer. 'You are unbelievable. I don't have a boyfriend.' Then she looked at him ruefully. 'Any boyfriend,' she said.

She walked over to the closet and began to slide clothes off the hangers. 'Don't you turn your back on me,' he warned.

She tried to ignore the menacing sound of his words, and keep her voice even. 'Look, Brian. I'm not going to talk about this right now because you're drunk. If you want to talk to me tomorrow . . .' She started to think about where. She didn't even know where she was going. I'll go to the hotel, she thought. There was one hotel in town, the Endicott. It was a stately old place, the one owned by Jennifer's parents . . . by her dad now. She could go there for the night. Tomorrow she would think about what to do next. She turned to place her last shirt into the suitcase but, before she could put it down, Brian grabbed the handle of the open bag and hurled it across the room. Dena's clothes flew everywhere as the suitcase hit the wall and landed with a thud on the floor.

Dena stared at him in shock. Brian looked at the bag crumpled on the floor and then looked back at Dena with a kind of malevolent satisfaction in his eyes. 'Tell your boyfriend to come pick it up,' he said.

Dena's heart was hammering, and sweat popped out in her palms, on her hairline. 'You . . . you . . .' she sputtered. 'You stinking drunk . . .' She felt almost blind with hatred for him now, but she knew there was fear in her eyes as well. He had never acted like this before. Never . . .

Calm down, she told herself. Think. What's important. The clothes are not important. You just need to get out of here. She had left her purse on the dining table as she went by. Her car keys and her phone were in there. She tried to talk to herself in a rational, sensible way. Go downstairs, get your purse with phone and your keys and just leave. Don't argue about the clothes.

She let the plastic hanger she was holding slip from her hands. Her fingers were icy. She started for the door of the bedroom but he slipped into her path.

'Excuse me,' she said, trying to get by him, but he moved, so that she couldn't. 'I'm not kidding, Brian,' she said in a low voice. 'Get out of my way.'

For a moment he hesitated, and she was sure he would back down, step away from the door and let her go. But instead, he extended a hand against the doorframe and blocked her exit.

No, she thought. This isn't possible. She couldn't match his strength. If he wouldn't move, she was trapped. 'I'm warning you,' she said, trying to sound determined, but she could hear the quiver of anxiety in her voice.

Brian gazed at her, sensing her fear, and seemed to find it somehow exhilarating. 'Don't you warn me . . .' he muttered. 'I'll say who goes where and I'll say when . . .'

'Oh, that does it,' said Dena. More outraged than afraid, she did not try to push past him, but turned, strode around the bed and reached for the receiver of the cordless phone on the night table. 'That does it.'

Before she realized what was happening, he lunged across the bed, and grabbed her arm, trying to jerk the phone out of her hand. Stymied by the sinking of the mattress, he missed her arm and grabbed the strap of her jumper, jerking her forward and down, so that her knees buckled. With his free hand he reached up and smacked her across the face, and she felt warm blood trickle from her nose, run over her lip.

Stunned, Dena touched her lip and then, as he scrambled up, she raised the receiver of the phone and smashed it as hard as she could across his knuckles. The battery cover popped off the phone and flew across the room. The battery pack hung by a red wire. Dena smashed the plastic receiver down again on his hand, and, when he let go with a cry, she ran to the bathroom, slammed the door shut and locked it, her hands shaking, still clutching the dismantled receiver.

Outside the door, Brian roared and began to pound on it with his fists. Dena saw her face in the medicine cabinet mirror, dead white, with a rivulet of blood running down her upper lip and her chin. 'Open this door, Dena,' he shouted. 'I'm warning you. I'll break it down.'

Do something, she thought. She was shivering, her fingers icy. It sounded as if the door was going to give way at any minute. With numb trembling fingers she pushed the battery pack back into its compartment, praying the phone would still work despite the fact that she had used it to escape him. She felt her heart hammering as the batteries clicked into place, and then she pressed the button for phone. Over the sound of his shouts and his hammering on the door, she heard the blessed buzz of a dial tone in her ears. It took her two tries, but then she managed. She dialed 911, and pressed the receiver to her face, as tears ran down her cheeks and mixed with the blood on her chin.

THREE

The ranch house was almost dark, and ominously quiet, as Sergeant Tyrell Watkins and Patrol Officer Ken McCarthy rolled up in their cruiser, their radio squawking. Sergeant Watkins rubbed the mustache on his upper lip absently and shifted in his seat to look around at the dark farm, the quiet barn.

'It's so quiet,' said Ken anxiously. Like all police officers, he knew that the most volatile situation you could encounter on the job was a domestic violence call.

'Too quiet,' Tyrell agreed grimly. 'But, maybe our boy has left the scene. Until we're sure, keep a sharp eye out.'

'Count on it,' said Ken.

'All right,' Tyrell said. 'Let's go in.'

The two men got out of the car, the leather of their jackets creaking, and approached the house. Tyrell drew his gun. 'Police,' he called out, rapping on the door. 'Open up.'

There was no answer from inside the house. The officers looked warily at one another, and then Tyrell, still holding his gun, pushed open the door and stepped in.

The television was still running in the living room, and a clutter of beer cans was scattered like a miniature obstacle course around the living room, but there was no one in the room. Tyrell walked toward the light in the kitchen and Ken followed, his heart hammering. It didn't take long for Tyrell to scope out the kitchen.

'Clear,' he said.

The young patrolman let out a little sigh and then steeled himself again. The sergeant started down the dark hallway with the patrol officer following him.

'Police,' Tyrell called out in his soft drawl. There was no reply. Tyrell looked into each room, throwing the light switches as he made his way down the hall to the last bedroom, where a light was already burning. He walked in, pointing his gun, and looked around. Clothes were scattered everywhere around the room, and Tyrell nearly tripped over a suitcase which lay in a heap beside the door. The closet door was open, and clothes hung off their hangers at crazy angles. But the room was quiet. Tyrell walked over to the closed door on the other side of the bed. The wood in the door was splintered. The 911 caller had said she was trapped in the bathroom.

Tyrell tried the doorknob, but it was locked. 'Police, ma'am. Are you in there? You can unlock the door now. He seems to be gone now.'

Ken McCarthy, who stood in the bedroom doorway, one leg jiggling nervously, was not so sure of that. He kept looking down the hallway, expecting some enraged, cleaver-wielding husband to burst out and come charging at him. Ken wondered if he'd be able to shoot. He'd never had to shoot a gun in his brief tenure as a Monroe patrolman, but there was always a first time. He glanced back at Tyrell, who was waiting patiently outside the battered door. He always seemed so cool. As if nothing ever bothered him. I'll be like that someday, Ken thought, if I keep doing this long enough.

'It's all right, ma'am,' said Tyrell. 'You can open up the door now.'

Inside the bathroom, Dena sat shivering on the floor tiles in the corner, between the toilet and the bathtub, where she had sunk down to wait for help. Brian's pounding had stopped after a while, and she had heard the sound of the pick-up's engine roaring in the driveway, but she was not about to get up and unlock the door. She sat in the corner, shivering and waiting.

Now, at the sound of the officer's voice outside, she forced herself to move. Her legs ached, and felt stiff and cold from resting on the tile. She could tell, without looking, that they were bruised. She used the lid of the toilet and the side of the tub to lever herself to her feet. She walked the few steps to the door on unsteady legs, and unlocked it, pulling the door open and looking out blankly.

A black police officer with a mustache and a smooth, tense-looking face stared back at her. He looked down at her pregnant belly and then back at the blood dried on her face and his expression flickered, but only slightly. He was trying not to let her see how surprised he had been when she opened the door. At first glance, he thought he was looking at a child.

'Are you all right, ma'am?' he asked politely.

Dena nodded. 'Is he gone?' she asked.

'He seems to be,' said the officer. He holstered his gun, and offered her an arm.

Dena reached out and grasped the sleeve of his leather jacket as she emerged from the bathroom into the clothing-strewn bedroom.

'You'd better sit down,' said Tyrell.

Dena did as she was told, sitting down in a wicker chair with a ruffled cushion in the corner by the closet. The sergeant walked over to his officer, and spoke quietly to him for a moment. Ken nodded back and then walked down the hallway.

'Mrs . . . um.'

'Miss,' said Dena, 'Russell.'

'Miss Russell, we're gonna get you over to the hospital, first off.'

'I'm all right,' said Dena dully.

'Well, I think we better let the doctors determine that.'

Dena started to argue and then decided against it. 'Maybe, you're right,' she said.

'Can you walk?' he asked her.

'Yes,' she said, pushing herself up from the chair seat.

'You'd better take some things,' he advised. 'You may not be coming back here for a while.'

'Sounds like you've done this once or twice,' said Dena.

The sergeant nodded, unsmiling, and began to pick up the clothing off the floor.

Dena put it hastily back into the bag she had started packing.

'Miss Russell, what kind of a car is your husband driving? We're going to have to pick him up and talk to him about this.'

Dena wanted to protest, to explain, to talk about it, but at the moment there was only one thing she could think to say. 'He's not my husband,' she corrected the sergeant. 'Thank God.'

*   *   *

Dena sat at the edge of an examining table of the Emergency Room waiting for the doctor to return with her test results. Sergeant Watkins was at the nurses' station talking quietly on the phone. Officer McCarthy had disappeared after they left the Riley farm, but she knew that Sergeant Watkins had spoken to him several times since then.

Dena closed her eyes, but when she did the pounding in her head seemed to increase. All of a sudden, the woman doctor who had treated her earlier came through the swinging doors, carrying a chart and walked up beside her, patting her on the knee.

Seeing the doctor, Sergeant Watkins finished up his phone call and stood by, at a discreet distance.

'Everything checks out, Miss Russell,' said the doctor. 'You're all right, and the baby's all right.'

Dena sighed and managed a weak smile.

'Just be careful for the next twenty-four hours, watch for any signs of bleeding.'

'I will,' said Dena.

'Your face may be a little sore, but nothing's broken.'

Dena nodded, too ashamed to look the doctor in the eye.

'You should make sure someone is with you tonight, just in case of bleeding.'

Dena nodded.

The doctor looked at the sergeant with raised eyebrows. 'OK,' she said. 'We're finished here.'

Dena slid off the table and straightened out her jumper. Tyrell held the door open for her and she walked out into the waiting area. She was acutely conscious of the other people, looking up at her curiously, a very pregnant woman with a bruised face, accompanied by a police officer. Dena could hardly believe this was happening to her.

This was the kind of thing that happened to people on those crazy, true-crime videos on TV. Not to normal people. I'm a college graduate, she wanted to shout. I understand French, and I once decorated a cake that was served to Oprah Winfrey. As if it mattered. It was laughable, she thought, if it weren't so sad. The doors opened out automatically, and Dena stood hesitantly under the halogen lights, looking out at the dark parking lot.

'What happens now?' she asked.

'Well, I'll drive you to wherever you want to stay tonight.'

'I guess I'll go to the Endicott Hotel,' she said.

'You heard the doctor, ma'am. You should not be alone.'

Dena did not reply, and Tyrell had the distinct impression that she had nowhere to go. Then she sighed.

She remembered Jennifer's insistent invitation, tendered as she had entered her number into Dena's phone.

She didn't know what else to do. 'I'll go to my friend's,' she said in a small voice. 'She'll let me stay.'

They walked over to the patrol car, and Tyrell opened the door for her. Dena slid awkwardly onto the front seat and waited for him to come around the other side. The radio was squawking unintelligibly. She stared out into the darkness, feeling numb.

Tyrell got into the car. 'Where does your friend live?' he asked.

Dena hesitated, then remembered. The Morgans' old house. 'Chestnut Street,' she said.

The officer's face was impassive as he started the car. 'So I don't have to go to the police station,' Dena said.

'Not tonight,' said Tyrell. 'Tomorrow, we'll need you to swear out a complaint. You have a couple of options,' he said, reciting the possibilities of prosecution, relocation, counseling or restraining orders.

Dena listened in silence. Then she said, 'I don't want to press charges,' she said.

Tyrell did his best not to sigh as the patrol car negotiated the quiet streets of Monroe. These women were all alike. It was hard to feel sorry for them. 'I'm afraid that's not up to you, Miss Russell,' he explained. 'We are compelled to investigate, even if the victim is reluctant to testify.'

Dena rested her forehead against the cold glass of the passenger side window. 'I just want this to be over,' she said.

Tyrell shook his head slightly. How often had he heard this, or some variation of it? It irked him that he and his men had to go out, and risk their safety, to confront these violent household tyrants, just to have their beat-up wives and girlfriends turn around and go right back home to them.

Dena straightened up and looked over at him. 'I appreciate your coming out to help me, tonight, Sergeant Watkins.'

Tyrell Watkins nodded politely, his face a blank mask. 'No problem, ma'am.'

'He never did anything like that before,' said Dena. 'It was a complete shock,' she said. 'I wouldn't have thought it was possible.'

Another perfect relationship hits the skids, Tyrell thought cynically. Surprise. 'That's the house – up there,' Dena said. 'The cottage with all the windows.'

'Here,' said Jennifer Hubbell, carefully handing her husband, Ron, a bowl of vegetable soup. 'Be careful, it's hot.'

Ron took the bowl gratefully and placed it on a magazine that sat atop the coffee table in front of him. 'Thanks, honey,' he said. 'I didn't get a chance to grab anything before I got on the train tonight. And then we had the class . . .'

'And that rain was kind of chilling,' she agreed, settling herself down into the sofa cushions beside him.

Ron was instantly concerned. 'Are you chilled? You'd better change those clothes if they're wet.'

'I'm OK,' she said, rubbing her hands together. 'That's not why I'm shivering.'

Ron gazed at her solemnly. 'I know, honey,' he said. Ever since they'd arrived home, his wife had been upset.

'I just can't believe it, Ron,' she said. 'I knew he had another girlfriend. Well, it wouldn't matter who it was, but knowing that it's Dena. A friend.'

'Take it easy, honey,' he said. 'You can't afford to get too worked up.' He blew on his soup and ate a spoonful with some crackers. 'Aren't you having some?' he asked.

'I'll try a little later,' she said, making a face. She'd been nauseous for much of her pregnancy so far, although she rarely complained about it.

'She doesn't realize . . . She doesn't know what he did,' said Jennifer.

Ron sipped his soup thoughtfully. 'Well, I have a feeling she will call you. Although you have to be careful what you tell her.'

'What I tell her?' Jennifer yelped. 'I'm going to tell her the truth. That's what I'm going to tell her.

'Jenn . . .' he warned.

'She has to know, Ron.'

'Babe, there is such a thing as slander.'

'It's not slander. It's the truth,' she cried.

'He was never arrested. He was never charged . . .'

'Are you taking his side?' she demanded.

'You know I'm not,' he said. 'I feel exactly the same way you do.' He had never met Jennifer's sister, Tanya. She had died long before he'd even met Jennifer. Tanya was five years younger than Jennifer, and had moved in with Brian Riley right out of high school. Less than nine months later, she was dead. Brian Riley claimed she had slipped, and cracked her head in the shower. Officially, Tanya's death was ruled accidental. But Jennifer never believed it. Tanya would call her often in tears over his jealousy, his temper, the way he treated her. But no matter how often Jennifer urged her to do so, Tanya never called the police.

'I think he's a menace,' said Ron vehemently. 'And I don't think you're overreacting.'

Jennifer regarded her husband seriously. 'It's too bad not all men are as good as you.'

Ron smiled and rubbed her knee. 'I think you should talk to Dena. I have a feeling she'll be receptive. Obviously, that relationship is not going well.'

'That's what I'm afraid of,' said Jennifer. 'I mean, he was happy with Tanya for a while too. It wasn't till after things started going bad that I started getting those phone calls.'

'It's not too late,' he said. 'I'll help you any way I can.'

'I know,' she said. He was twelve years older than her, and it showed in the gray around his temples. His first marriage had been childless, and ended in divorce. His first wife, Anita, had changed, and wanted her freedom. Her loss, thought Jennifer. She felt like the luckiest woman in the world to have found him. They'd been married less than a year, but it had been an extremely happy year for them both.

Ron cast his new wife a glance and saw her gazing fondly at him. 'What?' he said.

'Nothing. Eat your soup before it gets cold,' she said, smiling at him. She heard the sound of her ring tone from the kitchen. 'I better get that,' she said.

He watched her disappear into the darkness of the dining room, thinking about how he had been given a second chance. More than a second chance. He heard the murmur of her voice from the kitchen and then he heard Jennifer squeal with delight. She came out of the kitchen, cheerfully waving the iPhone. 'Laura and Skip are getting married,' she announced, beaming.

'That's great,' Ron cried. Laura was Jennifer's best friend in Boston, and Skip was Ron's college roommate. Though Laura and

Skip worked in the same hospital, they didn't know each other until Ron and Jennifer had introduced them.

'They want us to stand up for them at the wedding,' Jennifer exclaimed. Ron grinned, tickled by his wife's delight.

'I don't know,' Ron teased her. 'What do you think?'

'Of course we will,' Jennifer cried.

Ron nodded. 'Of course,' he said.

He thought, for a minute, about the expense of going up to Boston, spending the weekend, renting a tux, and a new dress for Jenn. Then he chided himself for being a cheapskate. He hated it that his first thought was about money at the announcement of such good news. Nobody deserved a break more than Skip and Laura. Skip, a diabetic since childhood, had struggled most of his life with ill-health. He'd become a doctor with a true sense of compassion for his patients. Laura was a nurse who had endured the world's bitterest divorce and the loss of her kids to her vindictive ex-husband. Finally, after so many years of disappointment and misery, they had found some happiness together. He could not help feeling a little proud that he and Jennifer had helped to bring it about.

Ron loosened his tie, picked up the remote and switched on the TV as Jennifer returned to the kitchen. He might as well watch something. This conversation with Laura was bound to be long. Ron began to surf the channels, looking for something to catch his interest. Something short. He couldn't get involved in watching a movie. That commute to Philly from here was over an hour so he had to get to bed a little earlier. He didn't mind though. So far, it was working out all right, even though, when he transferred down here, he had a lot fewer clients than he'd had in Boston. He was just a little edgy because today he'd heard a troubling rumor. There was talk in the office that the Philadelphia branch was going to be closed. He hadn't been able to get confirmation on it yet. He only prayed it was idle gossip. How could he ever tell Jenn? She was so happy to be back in her old home town, in their new house. He didn't want to disappoint her. She always seemed to see him as if he was some kind of a hero.

The channel changer reached a football game, well in progress. It was the Patriots, and it was the third quarter. Great, he thought. My old team. He pushed his soup bowl to one side and settled back. From the kitchen he could hear the pleasant murmur of his wife's voice. Ron slid off his shoes and burrowed into the sofa cushions, losing himself in the progress of the game.

All of a sudden, his comfort was interrupted by the sound of a knock at the door.

Ron looked at his watch and frowned. Who the heck would be arriving at this hour? With a disgruntled sigh, he slid his shoes back on and stood up. He walked over to the door and opened it, peering out into the drizzly night.

Dena Russell stood on the doorstep, her face white except for a purplish bruise on the side of her face. On the curb, in front of their house, was a police cruiser, a police officer leaning against it with his arms folded across his chest.

'Dena?' Ron asked.

'I'm sorry to bother you, Ron,' she said.

'What is it? What happened? Come in,' he said.

Dena remained on the doorstep. 'This is horribly embarrassing,' she said. 'I've . . . there's been . . . some trouble . . . I don't know anyone here any more. I just didn't know where else to go.'

'No, you were right to come here,' he said.

Ron could feel Jennifer come up behind him. She edged up beside her husband, staring at her friend on the doorstep. 'Dena, what in the world?'

Dena looked back at her girlhood friend. 'Brian hit me,' she said baldly. 'I had to call the police. I need a place to stay tonight.'

Jennifer held her cell phone to her ear, 'Laura, I'll have to call you back, honey.' She put the phone in her pocket and extended a hand to Dena. 'I don't believe it,' she said, shaking her head. 'That bastard. You get in here right now,' she said, pulling her inside the house. 'You'll stay with us.'

FOUR

Tyrell Watkins pushed open the door of the squat, red-brick building that was the Monroe police station and went inside. He greeted Peg, the dispatcher, who pointed to an open tin of cookies on her desk and mouthed the words, 'Have one,' as she worked the call board. Tyrell took a cookie and began to chew on it gratefully. He was always hungry at this time of night. Only a skeleton crew manned the station in the evenings, although several patrol cars were out and about. Tyrell started toward his desk to begin his paperwork on this call when, to his surprise, he saw Ken McCarthy emerging from the men's room.

'Hey man,' he said. 'What's up? Did you find our boy?'

An uneasy expression crossed the young officer's face and he avoided the sergeant's gaze. 'Yeah, we found him all right.'

'You couldn't have processed him already,' Tyrell said.

Ken shook his head and sighed. 'No, we didn't,' he said.

'Well, why not? Where is he?'

Before Ken could reply, the door of Chief Lou Potter's office opened, and a handsome, dark-haired young man emerged, and walked toward them. He was dressed in dirty jeans and a barn jacket and a pair of cowboy boots. He did not look up at anyone as he walked by.

Tyrell peered at the man curiously for a moment and then called out, 'Hey . . . Boots.'

Brian Riley looked up in surprise and then his gaze settled on Tyrell. His face broke into a smile and the two men moved to greet each other. They clasped hands, shifted fingers like a lock tumbling, and renewed their grip. 'Hey man,' said Brian. 'I didn't know you were a cop. It's been a long time.'

'Got that right,' said Tyrell, chuckling. 'Since high school, isn't it?' As he recalled, they'd only played together one year on their high school football team. Boots was a few years younger. He played linebacker – or was it a free safety? The one thing Tyrell would never forget was that Saturday afternoon in the parking lot after the game when a bunch of disgruntled fans hadn't liked the fact that the wide receiver had dropped two balls in a losing effort. Their insults, most of them racial epithets, still stung when he thought about it. Only Boots, so called for his ever-present cowboy footgear, had stood shoulder to shoulder with him that day.

'What are you doing here, man?' Tyrell asked.

Brian smiled sheepishly. 'Ahhh, I got into a little trouble tonight.'

Tyrell nodded. He could smell the alcohol on the other man's breath. 'Can I help?' he asked. It was a favor that had been years in the returning.

Brian shook his head. 'It's been settled.'

At that moment, Chief Potter emerged from his office, rubbing his face with a meaty hand. He was dressed in civvies – chinos and a corduroy shirt and a pair of suede Rockport shoes. Lou Potter was a widower – his wife, Hattie, had died of breast cancer two years ago. Lou was in his mid-sixties, nearing retirement and suffering from heart problems himself. He lived now with his daughter, Kim, her husband and two kids.

He'd hired Tyrell at the rank of sergeant straight out of the service, giving him credit for his military duty over the objections of Heath Van Brunt, who had come up through the ranks and regarded this decision as heresy. Chief Potter looked around the station and then gestured for Tyrell to come into his office. 'Sergeant. Can I see you in here a minute?'

Tyrell turned back to his old teammate. 'Hey, I gotta split man. Take it easy.'

Brian gave him a casual salute. 'Good to see you again, Tyrell.'

Ken, who had been watching their exchange with a strange look on his face, shook his head and returned to his desk. Tyrell frowned at him. 'What's with you?'

'That's him,' Ken said.

'Who?'

Tyrell did not appreciate the cryptic whisper. 'The boyfriend. Brian Riley.'

Tyrell turned to see Boots heading out the door of the station house into the night.

He walked into the chief's office. 'Close the door,' said Lou Potter.

Tyrell frowned, but obliged. Lou Potter fell heavily into his chair and indicated another chair for Tyrell. 'Have a seat, Tyrell,' he said.

'What's going on? What are you doing here at this hour, Chief?'

Lou Potter rubbed his face again. 'I know all about the 911,' he said. 'Brian called me when they brought him in.'

Tyrell heard the familiarity in the way the chief spoke the name, and he understood what was coming.

'Look, I've known that boy all his life, Tyrell. His dad and I go back a long way. A long way.'

Tyrell understood. His late grandfather, Reggie Brown, had also 'gone back a long way' with the chief. They used to go fishing together, which was another reason that Tyrell was a sergeant on the force. Lou Potter was nothing if not loyal.

'How's the girlfriend?' Lou asked.

'She's OK,' Tyrell admitted. 'Some bruises.'

'Ken told me she's a "reluctant" vic.'

Tyrell nodded.

'Now, look, Tyrell. You know and I know, these domestic things are not all equal. There was no weapon, right? The kid's got no record.'

'No. No weapon.'

'I'm not excusing him, mind you, but this boy has been through hell lately. Believe me. A while back, my friend Matt, Brian's dad, had a stroke at the wheel of his car, and crashed it. They've had lawsuits, medical bills, Brian's dad is still in the hospital . . .'

Tyrell grimaced sympathetically but the chief did not notice and plowed on. 'The girlfriend was pregnant – she just moved in, on top of all Brian has to worry about. Matt Riley can't eat, he can't talk. It's pitiful, Tyrell. It breaks your heart.'

Tyrell nodded. He knew the chief often visited an old friend at the nursing home. Now that he put it together, he understood. 'Terrible,' agreed the sergeant.

'And you know how these things go,' said the chief earnestly. 'I'm talking to you as a friend here. The kid is trying to help out his father, run his business, the baby is on the way, and he's been stressed out. So you know what happens. The girlfriend's feeling neglected, and she's got all the pregnancy hormones bouncing off the wall, so she's bugging him night and day. He's been having a few beers too many, just to try to relax, and before you know it – boom, this happens.'

'Oh yeah,' said Tyrell.

'I know what you're thinking, Sergeant. And believe me, I came down here when he called me tonight, and I read him the riot act. I told him I was sorry for all his trouble, but hitting women was not the way a man coped with this kind of thing. I told him I never wanted to see him in here again – never. He's a good kid, basically, Tyrell. He was crying when I got through with him.'

'Listen, Chief . . .'

'I know. I know. What good is it gonna do to lock him up? The girlfriend's not gonna testify. There's no weapons charge. He's already got so much weighing him down. I mean, I know all about the new protocols and all that . . . But I'm talking to you man to man here . . .'

Tyrell held up a hand. 'Chief, stop. It's OK. I know Boots.'

'Boots?'

'Brian . . . Riley. I just didn't recognize the name when we got the call. We played football together in high school. He's a good man. And I owe him one from way back.'

Lou Potter sighed. 'He *is* a good man. You know how circumstances can build up on a person?'

Tyrell nodded. He knew. He also knew, as did the chief, that there had been times when Tyrell sent a friend on his way with a warning when, technically, by the book, he should have been cuffing him and reading him his rights. 'I just hope he'll cool it now,' Tyrell said.

'Tyrell, there's not gonna be a next time. I'd stake my life on it. But listen, why don't we just keep this between us? No need to get Heath involved in this.'

Tyrell understood exactly what the old man was saying. Heath Van Brunt, who was away at a conference in Rhode Island on Forensics in Law Enforcement, did everything by the book. He would never allow this kind of leeway on his watch.

'Sometimes a chief just has to use his judgment,' said Lou.

For a guilty instant, Tyrell thought of the girlfriend, cowering in the bathroom.

Then he dismissed it. 'You're right,' he said. 'No big deal. Boots has learned his lesson.'

Tyrell saw the doubt and worry flicker in the chief's eyes. 'I'm sure,' Chief Potter said. 'One hundred per cent.'

Although he also had his doubts, Tyrell nodded in agreement.

Jennifer closed the door to her bedroom and climbed into bed beside her husband.

Ron reached out and put his arms around her, holding her close. He could feel her quivering.

'Did you tell her?' he asked.

Jennifer shook her head. 'I found I couldn't just blurt it right out. She could tell I had bad feelings about him. I told her he had a history . . . a reputation for treating women badly.'

'I'm a little surprised you didn't give her the whole gory story.'

'I thought about what you said. Something just made me hold back. She's just so upset tonight. I felt like she just needed a friend to talk to tonight. She told me about their relationship. It was all too familiar.' Jennifer freed herself from his embrace and sat up in bed, her flowered, flannel nightgown tenting around her. 'I told her she should press charges, but she says she won't.'

'Why not?' Ron asked, although he had a good idea of why. It was understandable to him that Dena might not want to get involved in a long, legal process over this. Bad enough to have endured it – she might not want to subject herself to the humiliation of recounting it again and again. Still, there was no point in saying that to Jennifer. She had an unswerving sense of right and wrong. And her experience with Tanya had made her adamant on this subject.

Jennifer shook her head. 'She says she just wants to be done with him. She says she's known for a while that they weren't going to make it together. She wants out. A clean break.'

'That may not be what he wants,' Ron observed. 'Especially with a baby on the way.'

'I know. The baby adds another risk to the whole thing,' Jennifer cried. 'Babies can really up the ante when it comes to these types. Talk about cruel and vindictive. I told you about Clifford.'

It took Ron a second to place the name. Then he nodded. Clifford was her friend Laura's ex-husband. He'd never met him, but he'd heard the stories. In fact, Jennifer and Laura had met in a support group in Boston for abuse victims and their families after Tanya died. 'Look at it this way, honey. If she was thinking about leaving him already, this may just give her the push she needs. You know?'

Jennifer nodded. 'It'd better.'

'And if she needs an additional kick in the pants, it's time to tell her about Tanya.'

'That's what I figured,' said Jennifer.

'I'll ride out there tomorrow and pick up her stuff if she wants.'

'I'll go with you,' said Jennifer.

'Jenn . . .' he warned.

'You wouldn't deny me that pleasure, would you?'

'We'll see tomorrow,' he said.

'And she can stay here as long as she needs to.'

Ron nodded. He wasn't thrilled with the prospect of an open-ended houseguest, but he wasn't about to argue with Jennifer on this. He knew the guilt she had suffered for not doing more for Tanya. For not insisting that she leave. For not physically coming and taking her away. She would never abandon a friend in this situation. 'Sure,' he said. 'Now you, little lady, have got to get some rest. We have our own baby to think about.'

Jennifer smiled at him. 'I'm so lucky to have you,' she said. Ron pulled her back into his embrace. 'I'm the lucky one,' he said.

Dena sat in a yellow-flowered slipper chair by the guest-room window and stared out into the darkness. Monroe, the sleepy little town she'd once called home, was asleep now, breathing peacefully. Dena felt anything but peaceful.

Jennifer had been a perfect friend. She had let Dena talk, and not berated her for her mistakes. She'd been adamant about Brian – that he was a man to be avoided – and Dena could tell, there was something personal in her obvious contempt and dislike for him. But she hadn't said, and Dena almost didn't want to know. They talked for a while, but finally Jennifer had gone back to her room, back to her waiting husband.

Dena felt grateful to her old friend, for taking her in so readily. Not everyone would do that, but Jennifer had always been generous that way. When you were her friend, you knew it. She was lucky to have found such a great husband as Ron. She deserved it, Dena thought, if anyone did. But, at the same time, it was impossible not to envy their happiness a little. This house, so sweet, so ready to welcome a new baby. She had glanced into the nursery as they walked down the hall to the guest room and felt a pang of longing that nearly doubled her over. Where would she bring her own baby, when the time came? She didn't know now.

Dena often wished that her own mother was still alive, but never more so than tonight. She remembered the years when they had lived here in Monroe, when Dena was in junior high and high school. Her mom worked long hours to support them but, still, they had had good times here. Her mother had never been too tired for a trip to the movies, or a late-night talk.

If only I could talk to you now, Dena thought longingly. But she didn't need to wonder what her mother would say. When Dena first began dating, her mother said, never let a man strike you, for any reason. Arguing is one thing. Everybody has arguments. You could resolve an argument. But a man who hits you . . . Your father and I never hit you. Why would you allow someone else to hit you? Especially someone who said they loved you.

I won't go back, Mom, Dena thought. I'll never go back to him. She rubbed a hand absently over her swollen belly as she thought of all the dreams she had had that now were lost. She thought back to that weekend of the high-school reunion, when Brian had monopolized her at the party, and then took her back to his ranch to show her the stars. Those romantic, long-distance weekends that followed. The pregnancy, despite their precautions. It had seemed like fate, that they were meant to be together. Her cheeks flamed with shame at how willingly she had overlooked her doubts and dived in. Now, you have to pay for it, she thought, rubbing her belly, apologizing to her baby. No, that was no way to think, she chided herself. I've made my mistakes, she thought, but you weren't one of them. I will take care of you. I will protect you, she promised.

We'll manage together. Just like Mom managed. That thought was comforting somehow. Soothing, but not soothing enough to make her want to sleep. She stared out the window and watched the starless night.

FIVE

The next morning dawned cool and gray. Dena, who had fallen asleep around five, felt exhausted as she walked up the stone pathway to La Petite Auberge, thinking about the next step in her life. She needed a plan. Her car and her belongings were still out at the Riley farm. At breakfast Ron and Jennifer had offered to go out there to get her things this afternoon and, despite the fact that it felt precipitous, and she felt as if she wasn't ready for it, she knew in her head that there was no reason to wait. 'Then, it's settled,' Ron had said as he dropped her off at work, and she realized, with a heavy heart, that indeed, it was.

As she rounded the vine-covered trellis that shielded the entrance, she saw a sudden movement out of the corner of her eye. 'Dena,' a voice said urgently.

Dena whirled, stifling a cry, and stared. Brian's face seemed to float in the shadows. His eyes were red and surrounded by dark circles, as if he had not slept either. And what a hangover you must have, Dena thought, without an ounce of pity. In his left hand he held a bouquet of red roses tied in a magenta ribbon, which he thrust toward her. Dena shook her head, refusing them. 'I don't want them. What are you doing here?' She could hear the tremor in her voice and she willed herself to control it. 'Please,' he said. 'Please. I've been waiting. Your boss said I could wait out here,' he explained, indicating a rush-seated Normandy bench beside the trellis. 'I told him we had a misunderstanding . . .'

A misunderstanding, she thought? I understood it perfectly. 'Did you tell him you hit me?' she demanded.

Brian averted his gaze, and pursed his lips. For a minute she thought he was going to erupt again, but instead he said nothing.

'I doubt he would have been so agreeable if you told him that.'

'I'm sorry about that,' he muttered. 'I was . . . I had too much to drink.'

Dena just shook her head.

'Haven't you ever made a mistake?' he asked.

Dena felt a cold, rueful determination in the pit of her stomach that refused to be guilt-tripped over this. 'The cops said they were going to arrest you,' she said coldly.

'They brought me down to the station,' he admitted. 'They didn't keep me, though.'

Dena didn't know whether to be indignant or relieved. She didn't want to get involved in some kind of court battle. But still, they had said they would prosecute him whether she pressed charges or not. 'What did you tell them – that it was my fault?' she asked.

This time she saw a definite flash of anger in his eyes, and it made her courage waver. But his words were conciliatory. 'I didn't come here to argue,' he said. 'I want you to come home.'

'That's not my home,' she said.

'Not that house, no,' he admitted. 'That's just a place we're staying, temporarily. I mean, I want you to come back to me. We have a baby coming. We need to be together.'

'I'm fine where I am,' she said grimly.

'And where is that?' he demanded. 'I tried to find you last night. I looked everywhere I could think of.'

'You might as well know. I'm not going to hide from you. I'm staying with Jennifer and her husband. The people from the Lamaze class. And don't pretend you don't know her. I can tell she knows a lot about you.'

His expression, vaguely wheedling and apologetic, suddenly changed. His eyes became hard. 'What lies has she told you?' he said.

Dena did not reply.

'I want to know what she said,' he demanded, shouting.

Dena turned on him angrily. 'Stop that,' she said. 'Stop shouting. She said you have a bad reputation with women and you certainly deserve it.'

'I don't want you listening to her lies,' he said. 'She's a harpy. She's evil and she's bent on ruining me.'

'Oh God,' said Dena disgustedly. 'I don't know why I'm even talking to you.' Her disgust seemed to bring him up short. Immediately, he was contrite.

'Because you love me. Dena, I was out of my mind last night. I don't know why I acted like such a maniac, but all I can say is, I was wrong. I've been stressed out and I did the wrong thing. I'm pleading with you to forget what I did. Remember how much I love you. I need to be with you. We need to be together. You've got to believe me, baby. Please . . .'

His words filled her with a queasy distress. In a way, his pleading was flattering. A while ago, she would have been grateful for it. But after last night . . . 'I can't forget what happened,' she said.

'Oh baby,' he said softly, and she was shocked to see tears welling in his eyes. 'I'll make it up to you. I promise you. It will never happen again. I'm not going to drink any more. I decided that last night. And I'll never, never do that to you again. I'm not asking you to forget it. Just forgive me and we'll start over.'

Forgiveness, she thought. It was what you were supposed to do. The Christian thing. The right thing. A person was supposed to be allowed to make a mistake. One mistake.

'Please, baby,' he whispered, and he began to come toward her in that way he did when he wanted to make love to her. That look of need in his eyes always melted her, and she could feel it now, licking at her, like a flame. She felt as if her head was full of conflicting voices – her mother, warning her never to be with a man who hit her; Jennifer, so indignant on her behalf; her own deep determination to give him up. But against it all was Brian's face, now tear-stained, his eyes pleading and promising. And there was the baby. Without Brian, it would have no father. It would grow up just like she did, wishing for her dad.

She couldn't hear her own thoughts this way, with his sad eyes entreating her.

She had to have some room to think. 'I can't talk about this now, Brian. I have to go in,' she said.

'No, baby, don't go,' he said, reaching out and grabbing her arm.

His hand clamped around her upper arm, riveting her like an electric shock. In that instant, it all came back to her. She saw herself, trapped in the bedroom, his hand raised against her. Oh no, she thought hopelessly. There was no going back. She remembered why she had decided against him.

'Let me go,' she said through clenched teeth. She tried to shake her arm free but he tightened his grip.

'Dena, what can I do to convince you?'

'You can let go of her right now,' said an angry voice. Dena turned, and blushed, as Peter Ward strode up to where they were standing.

'Stay out of this,' said Brian in a menacing voice.

Peter stared at the bruise on Dena's face. 'Did he do this?' he asked. He turned on Brian. 'You son of a bitch.'

'Stop it, both of you,' said Dena. 'Brian, let me go. I have to go to work.'

Still glaring at Peter, Brian released her arm. She wanted to rub it, but she didn't. She didn't want Peter to see that Brian's grip had hurt her. She didn't want to make it seem that she was choosing Peter over him. Brian extended the roses to her once again, and this time, she took them without a word. She didn't want to get into an argument over the flowers. She didn't want to get into an argument at all. Her mind was made up. Soon enough, he would have to realize it.

'I'll see you later,' Brian said. Clearly, he hoped he had convinced her. Peter watched him go with narrowed eyes.

Dena turned away from both of them and went into the darkened foyer of the restaurant. Not wanting Peter to follow her, she went directly to the ladies' room. The lovely anteroom had a comfortable chair, a gilded vanity and a pale green wooden wastebasket with a decoupage of pink roses on the side. How appropriate, she thought, and she dumped the bouquet, blossoms down, into the basket. She went through to the lavatory, and ran some cold water in the ivory porcelain sink. Cupping her hands under the stream of water, she patted it on her face, examining the discolored bruise on her face that was her souvenir. She patted her face dry gingerly and then went out into the anteroom and sat down in the comfortable, toile-covered bergère chair in the corner, resting her head back against the carved wood of the frame. She stayed that way for about ten minutes, until Nanette, the youngest sous-chef in the kitchen, came through the door, and started at the sight of her there.

'Oh hi,' said Nanette. 'René is looking for you.'

'I was just resting,' said Dena faintly.

Nanette looked sympathetically at Dena's protruding belly. Just then Nanette noticed the stems of the roses sticking out of the wastebasket. Dena saw her flirt with the temptation to pull them out, but then she looked knowingly at Dena. 'Wait for me,' she said. 'I'll walk back with you.'

'I was planning on it,' said Dena.

When they emerged from the ladies' room, talking to one another, Dena noticed Peter seated at the keyboard, studying some sheet music. He did not look up as they walked by, and Dena exhaled with relief. She didn't want to talk about it with Peter, or anyone else. She just wanted to get to work and be left alone.

Vanessa Pittinger sneezed, and wiped her nose on the sleeve of her flannel shirt. Wrangler, the horse she was currying, turned his head and whinnied softly, as if to say, *Gesundheit*. Vanessa smiled, and laid her face briefly against his shining, walnut-colored neck. 'What a good boy you are,' she murmured softly. Every day, after she got off the bus from middle school, Vanessa changed into her barn clothes and ran the short distance from her huge house in Thornfield Crossing, to the Riley farm.

Vanessa's parents had built the house four years ago, when Vanessa was ten, and everybody who saw it always carried on about how fabulous it was. But Vanessa hated being alone there after school. The rooms were huge and seemed silent. The wall-to-wall carpeting throughout the house muted the sound, and there was never even the hum of a car passing outside to break the silence. Thornfield Crossing, an enclave of mansions built on the land which was once a truck farm sold to developers, was pretty much deserted during the day, and most people got home late from their big, important jobs, and never socialized. Everyone knew the identities of their neighbors, and how they made their money, but there was no getting together for supper or anything.

At Christmas, they usually had a Thornfield Crossing cocktail party, which was just an excuse for the hosts to deck the halls better than anybody else's house, and you had to dress up and eat gross food and be totally bored the entire time.

No, to Vanessa's mind, the Riley farm, with its ramshackle little ranch house and gloomy stone barn, was a paradise. She loved all animals, but horses most of all. And even more than horses, she loved Brian Riley. Her parents knew how much she loved the horses but, so far, she'd managed to keep her crush on Brian a secret between her and her diary. Not that they were likely to care. Both of them worked killer hours at big jobs. They never even came over to the barn. Still, her mother was always saying how dangerous horseback riding was, and reminding her of Christopher Reeve. If I could be there when you were riding, her mother said, it might be different. But I don't want you going over there and jumping on a horse anytime you feel like it when I can't supervise. And whose fault is it, Vanessa thought dramatically, that her mother was never around to supervise? Vanessa sighed. For now, she had to settle for volunteering in the barn and being around the horses. And around Brian . . .

The office door banged open and seven sets of large, liquid equine eyes, as well as one set of curious, lovesick teenaged eyes, turned to look as Brian Riley appeared and began to haul a bucket of grain down the length of the cold cement floor of the barn.

Brian jostled the shining flank of Rajah, who was cross-tied between the stalls for grooming, and the stallion snorted and shook his huge head.

'Vanessa,' Brian barked. 'Are you in here?'

'I'm working on Wrangler,' she called out in her light, girlish voice.

'What is Rajah doing out here?' Brian asked.

'His owner came to ride him and wanted me to groom him. I told him I'd do it after I finished Wrangler. So I tied him up out there.'

'Oh,' Brian said gruffly. 'Well, don't take all day with Wrangler.'

Vanessa did not reply. Sometimes she felt so tongue-tied around him. There was something about him that reminded her of those guys in romance novels, like Heathcliff in Wuthering Heights. She loved it when he teased her, but other days he was gloomy and ignored her. It all depended on his mood. Today seemed to be a gloomy day. She watched out of the corner of her eye as he poured the grain into the stationary buckets in the hayracks. Then he went back and got the wheelbarrow down by the hay bales, and a large pitchfork. He wheeled the barrow down to Rajah's stall and went inside, muttering to himself. He shoved the pitchfork under the closest pile of manure and lifted it, and the surrounding hay, into the wheelbarrow.

Vanessa finished with Wrangler, and then walked out to where Rajah was tied, patting his shining flanks as she gazed in at Brian, mucking the stalls. Brian looked up at her unexpectedly, and she blushed furiously. She had to get her mind back on her duties. She began to undo Rajah's tack, wondering, as she did so, how anybody could be so lazy as to own a horse as beautiful as Rajah, take him out, and not even bother to put him up when they were done riding. Actually, she knew the woman who owned him. She lived in Thornfield Crossing. Figures, thought Vanessa disgustedly. As she was hauling Rajah's saddle back to the tackroom, a man appeared in the doorway to the barn, looking lost. He had grayish hair and was wearing a suit and a trench coat. Really lost, Vanessa thought.

'Can I help you?' she said.

'I'm looking for Brian Riley,' the man said.

At the sound of his name, Brian came out of Rajah's stall, still holding a pitchfork full of manure. The man saw him but didn't smile or look pleased. 'Brian, I'm Ron Hubbell,' he said. 'We met last night.'

'What do you want?' said Brian coldly.

'I came to get Dena's car and a couple of her things.'

Vanessa's eyes widened. Where was Dena, she wondered. Despite the fact that Dena was Brian's girlfriend, Vanessa kind of liked her, the little she knew of her. She seemed nice and she was going to have Brian's baby any day now, even though they weren't married. In a way, Vanessa looked at Dena in awe. How could she be around Brian all the time and not just faint at the sight of him? Talk to him about household things in a normal voice like her parents did, as if Brian was just an ordinary guy? In fact, Dena didn't even seem particularly thrilled to be with him most of the time. And now, there was this strange new development. Vanessa tried to pretend she wasn't listening.

Brian threw down the pitchfork and stalked over to where the man stood. He gave him a steely look, and then looked out at the driveway in front of the barn. 'Is that her there, in your car?'

'No,' said Ron. 'That's Jennifer. She will drive Dena's car back.'

'This is Jennifer's idea, isn't it,' said Brian.

'Dena asked us to come,' said Ron.

'I don't think so,' said Brian. 'I think you've got things a little confused.'

'I didn't come here to argue, Brian. Dena gave me the car keys, and told me what to get. I just don't want to go into your house without your permission.'

'Well, you don't have my permission,' said Brian angrily. 'I know your wife is telling her all kinds of lies about her sister, trying to get Dena to leave me . . .'

Ron voice rose. 'Look you . . . You'd better keep your mouth shut about my wife's sister. If you know what's good for you . . .'

'Threats?' Brian asked.

It took all of Ron's will not to reply.

'I've got news for you, buddy. Dena is coming back to me.'

'I don't believe you,' said Ron, but his heart sank. This was what happened, all too often. Jennifer was so sure Dena was going to stay strong. She would be so upset.

'I don't care what you believe,' Brian said. 'That's private. Personal. So why don't the two of you butt out of our business?'

Ron nodded, as if he understood. 'All right. If you won't let me go into the house, I'll leave her stuff here. I'm sure there's nothing here she can't do without.'

Brian jammed the pitchfork into a hay bale, and leaned his forehead against the handle. Then, with a great effort, he spoke more evenly. 'Look,' he said. 'I know you don't believe this right now, but what happened last night was just . . . an error in judgment.'

What happened last night, Vanessa wondered? She saw the other man's face turn stony at Brian's words. 'I'm taking the car, now,' he said. 'If she wants to come back to you, she'll have to drive herself.'

The man turned and left the barn without another word. Brian followed him out, and Vanessa tiptoed up to the door of the barn and peeked around it. The man in the trench coat spoke to someone in the passenger side of the Honda Accord. Then he opened the car door and a woman with long, coppery hair that caught the rays of sunset got out, took a set of keys from his hand, and climbed into Dena's dark green Camry, looking furiously at Brian, and then slamming the car door.

For a minute, Vanessa thought Brian was going to grab the pitchfork and charge at them. He was glowering at them like an enraged bull. But when he turned away he looked tragic, as if he was going to break down crying. Vanessa's heart seemed to swell up in her narrow chest, as if it was ready to burst. She wanted to go to him and comfort him. If Dena couldn't appreciate what kind of a man she had, well, Vanessa could. She imagined touching that curly black hair, smoothing it, like you would a horse's mane, and murmuring words of reassurance into the curve of his neck. She imagined his tears, falling on her hands, soft as rain, and she would gently, carefully wipe them away and say something that would make him start to smile again, and he would thank her, and look at her quizzically, as if he had never really seen her before.

The two cars rattled up the rutted driveway, sending up dust. Brian watched them go and then turned back toward the barn, kicking gravel with the toes of his worn old boots. Vanessa ducked back inside, and resumed currying Rajah, pretending not to have seen anything, trying to make herself invisible.

SIX

Dena stuck an arm through the sleeve of her jacket, and then felt someone behind her lift the jacket up and over her shoulders. She didn't have to turn around to see who it was. She could smell the Roger Gallet cologne that Albert insisted Peter wear to work.

'Thanks, Peter,' she said.

Peter put on his own topcoat. 'Hey,' he said offhandedly. 'I'm going home to have dinner with the girls. Why don't you join us?'

Dena knew that Albert always let Peter go home between the lunch and dinner sets to eat with his children. 'Thanks,' she said, 'that's nice of you, but I don't think so.' What if Brian were out there waiting, she thought. That's all he'd need to see.

'Oh, come on,' he said. 'It would be fun. My girls would enjoy meeting you.'

Dena eyed him suspiciously. 'I know what you're doing, Peter. And it's very nice of you, but it's not necessary.'

'What am I doing?' he asked innocently.

Dena raised her fingertips to the bruise on her face. 'You're being nice because you feel sorry for me.'

'Well, if you got that the way I think you did . . .'

'I don't want to talk about it,' she said.

'OK, we don't have to talk about it,' he said. 'Besides, with my older one around, you won't get a word in edgewise anyway.'

Dena frowned. Why should she care what Brian thought? He had no business stalking her. Besides, Jennifer and Ron were being so good to her, but she didn't want to be a third wheel, hanging around their house. They needed some time to themselves.

'I couldn't stay long,' she demurred.

'Hey, me neither. I have to get back here. I can drop you off on my way back. Where are you staying?' he asked in a casual tone.

'It was that obvious?' she said.

'Well,' Peter admitted, 'he did seem to be trying to get you to come back.'

'I'm staying at the home of an old friend from high school – but I don't want to discuss it,' she insisted.

'All right,' he said. 'Let's just go eat.'

Dena smiled. 'All right,' she conceded. 'That sounds good.'

Peter parked the car in front of a yellow frame house that had seen better days in a quiet cul-de-sac called Bigelow Street. 'Home sweet home,' he said.

'It's a good-sized house,' said Dena.

'It's a two-family house,' he said. 'We live on the first floor. The woman who used to baby-sit for me lived in that second-floor apartment before she moved.'

'Oh,' said Dena, nodding. 'That was convenient.'

Peter nodded ruefully. 'More than you know.'

They walked into the house and Dena looked around the open kitchen and family room. Everything about it was neat and tidy. Except for the colorful drawings hanging on the refrigerator, you would never know that two children lived here. Peter went over to the refrigerator and opened it.

'Do you want something to drink? I have all kinds of juices.'

Dena noticed that he didn't even offer her alcohol. It wasn't the first pregnancy he'd been around. Come to think of it, she had never noticed him drinking any alcohol himself. 'Nothing, thanks. I'll wait. Where are the girls?'

'Oh, these days they're at a neighbor's house after school. She'll drop them off any minute. Let me just get a few things ready,' he said, turning on the stove and rummaging in the refrigerator.

'Can I help?' she asked.

'No, just relax,' he told her.

'How come your baby-sitter left?'

Peter took a carton of milk and a Pyrex dish out of the refrigerator and set it on the counter. 'Her daughter is going through a messy divorce, and had to get a full-time job. She needed Brenda to care for the grandchildren.'

'Ah,' said Dena.

'Make yourself at home,' he said. 'Sit down. You must be tired after all you've been through.'

There it was again. Her opening to tell him about her situation – what had happened with Brian. She didn't blame him for being curious, but she didn't even want to think about it, never mind discuss it. 'I'm fine,' she said firmly. Change the subject, she thought. Make him talk about himself. 'I like your house. How do you keep it so neat?'

'It's not easy,' he admitted. 'You have to have a system. Of course, that will all go to hell in a handbasket when we move again.'

'Moving's tough,' Dena agreed with a sigh.

'You giving it any thought?' he asked.

She started to bristle at the question, but then she simply shook her head. 'I haven't decided. But, yes,' she said truthfully.

His interest made her feel restless. She got up and walked over to the bookcase, thinking how you could get to know someone by looking at their things. Peter's bookcase held mostly children's books.

'Where did you live before you came here?' she asked.

'Florida actually,' he said, putting one dish in the microwave and another in the oven. 'I was working at a hotel in Miami.'

'How did you end up here?' she asked, resuming her seat on the sofa.

'Albert and Eric visited the hotel for a gourmet show. They heard me play and offered me a job. They promised to work around my schedule with the girls.'

'You play very well,' Dena said.

Peter shrugged. 'It used to be a hobby. I had a regular job before my wife died. But then, afterwards, the girls needed me,' he said simply. As he mentioned his wife, he gestured to a framed photograph on the fireplace mantel. A lovely, laughing woman with blonde hair blowing around her head was pictured there.

Dena got up and went over to the mantel. 'Was that your wife?' Dena asked gently, picking up the photo.

'Yeah,' said Peter.

'She's lovely.' She glanced up at him, but could not read the expression on his face. 'What did she die of?'

'Brain tumor,' he said shortly. 'It was all over, start to finish, in three months.'

'Oh God,' said Dena. 'I'm so sorry.'

Peter nodded. 'Thanks.' The tone of his voice indicated that he wanted to dismiss the subject. Obviously, he had still not recovered. We've both got things we'd rather not discuss, Dena thought. An awkward silence fell between them.

'Can I set the table?' she asked brightly.

'That's Tory's job,' he said.

At that moment the front door opened and two girls came in, both blonde, both dark-eyed. The taller one was thin, with shoulder-length straight hair. The smaller child was chubby, with curls.

'Daddy!' Tory cried, and started to run to him. Then she saw Dena and stopped short. The younger one, Megan, stood behind her, peering around at Dena fearfully. 'Who's that?' Tory demanded.

'This is Dena Russell, someone I work with. Dena, this is Tory, and behind her is Megan.'

Dena smiled. 'Nice to meet you.'

Tory frowned at her father, who came over and gave her stiffened body a hug.

Avoiding Dena's smile, Megan buried her face in Tory's side.

Tory looked at her sister, and then at Dena. 'She's afraid of people,' said Tory.

Dena nodded. 'I understand. I was shy when I was little. How was your school today?' Dena asked Tory.

'Good,' said the child. 'Dad, guess what. I got one hundred on my spelling test.'

'You'd better have. We drilled those words,' said Peter. 'I've almost got supper ready here. Tory, you better set the table.'

Immediately the child set to the task, while Megan ran around behind an armchair where she thought Dena couldn't see her.

'Megan, how was your day?' Dena asked.

Megan hunched herself up into as small and still a ball as possible.

'She hardly ever talks,' Tory explained, distributing silverware. 'The pre-school teacher told Dad she was . . . morgidly shy.'

'Morbidly?' said Dena.

'No, I think it was morgidly.'

Dena glanced over at Peter. He was working busily, slicing something on a cutting board, but she could tell he was listening as he worked.

'There,' said Tory. 'Dad, do I have time to read to Megan before supper?'

'One story,' he said.

'Good. Come on, Megan,' she said. She grabbed a book off an end table and climbed up in the chair which was Megan's hideout. 'It's Ratty and Mole,' she said, dangling this information in a singsong voice.

Megan sidled out from behind the chair and, avoiding Dena's gaze, clambered up beside her sister.

'What are you reading?' Dena asked.

'*Wind in the Willows*,' Tory said gravely. 'She likes to hear about Ratty and Mole having their picnic on the river bank.'

'I don't know that one,' said Dena apologetically.

'Daddy read it to me when I was little, and now I'm reading it to Megan.'

Dena nodded, wondering how he had managed it. When she looked around the tidy house, it had less clutter than she and Brian made, all by themselves. This was a tight ship, all right.

'Didn't your dad read to you?' Tory asked.

Dena shook her head. 'I don't remember. He died when I was about your age. But my mom read to me all the time. Did your mom read to you too?'

'My mom's dead,' said Tory coldly.

'Well, I know,' said Dena gently. 'I just meant, it wasn't so long ago. Maybe you remembered . . .'

'I don't remember,' Tory said angrily.

'Supper,' said Peter. 'Everybody wash your hands.'

The sound of a police siren wailing nearby made Dena jump. Tory looked up at her father with fearful eyes.

'It's nothing,' said Peter sharply. 'Go get your hands washed.' Megan began to whimper. Peter picked her up and patted her back. 'Megan, stop that,' he said. Peter looked at Dena apologetically. 'We had to call the ambulance a number of times when their mother was ill. I think they still have bad memories of that.'

'That's not true, Dad,' Tory protested. 'We don't remember it at all.'

Peter set Megan down on the ground. 'Hurry up,' he said. 'It will get cold.'

'What are we having?' Tory demanded.

'Chicken and broccoli,' he replied.

'Oh goody,' said Tory.

'These girls eat broccoli?' Dena asked in a shocked tone.

'We love broccoli,' Tory announced.

Dena looked up at Peter, who was distributing food on the plates. 'How'd you do that?' she asked.

'Do what?' Peter looked at her blankly.

'Well, a lot of kids don't like vegetables,' she said. 'I didn't. Did you?'

'I never had them,' he said. 'My mother's idea of a meal was to sit me in front of the television with a box of cold cereal. It's a miracle I didn't have rickets.' Looking into the past, his eyes turned as cold as gray sea.

'You're right,' said Dena quickly. 'It's what they should eat. But broccoli?'

'Children eat what they're given,' he said, pointing at her belly wedged up against the table. 'You'll see.'

The teenaged baby-sitter showed up shortly after dinner, and Peter had a quiet word with her while Dena said goodbye to the girls.

'Thanks for letting me come over,' she said to Tory.

'Thanks for coming,' said Tory. 'No one ever comes over.'

Dena smiled. 'You girls going to get in your pjs and watch your favorite shows now?'

Tory frowned. 'What do you mean?'

'On TV,' said Dena.

'We don't watch TV,' said Tory. 'It's not good for you.'

'Dena,' Peter called, 'I've got to go.'

Impulsively, Dena gave Tory a hug. Tory did not resist it, but

Megan scampered away, out of range of any possible affection. 'It was nice to meet you,' she said.

'Come again,' Tory entreated her.

Dena smiled and waved, and followed Peter out the door. As he shut the door behind him, and waited to hear that it was locked, he pointed to the staircase in the hallway. 'Mrs Kelly's apartment is up those stairs,' he said. 'Nobody's rented it yet. It's furnished. Not lavishly, but it's adequate.'

Dena understood what he was getting at. 'I don't know what I'm going to do yet,' she said.

'I hope you're not thinking of going back to him,' Peter said sternly. 'That would be a terrible mistake.'

She felt immediately resentful of his advice, and yet, she knew it was kindly meant. 'Spoken like a father,' she observed ruefully.

'Well, I can't help it. I take it very seriously. You have a child to think of now. If you won't leave him for your own sake, you have to at least think of the child,' he said defensively as they walked down the path to the car.

'I think of little else,' she said quietly.

He opened the car door for her. 'Of course you do.'

She forced herself to smile as she jockeyed into the passenger seat. 'I know you're only saying it because you care.'

He slammed the door and walked around to the other side of the car. When he got in she said, 'Thank you for dinner, Peter. That was fun. Your children are lovely.'

'Children are the most important thing in the world,' he said vehemently. 'No sacrifice is too great.'

His words made Dena feel suddenly alone and adrift again. Why couldn't I have found a man who believed that, she thought? It didn't bear thinking about.

Peter followed her directions to Jennifer's house and let her out at the curb.

'See you tomorrow,' she said, and then she amended it. 'No, I won't. I'm off tomorrow. You working lunch?'

'Just dinner,' he said.

'Well, thanks again.'

He waved, and pulled away from the curb. Dena started up the steps to the brightly lit house. She stopped when she saw her car, sitting in the driveway. Ron must have gone to get it. She sighed, both relieved and sad to see it there. I'm starting all over again, she thought.

Just then a shadowy figure emerged from behind a tree near the driveway and approached her.

She cried out in alarm.

'Don't scream,' he said. 'It's just me.'

'Brian, stop it. Stop lurking around. My God, you scared the life out of me.'

'Where were you?' he asked. She saw him staring suspiciously at the departing car. 'You were with him, weren't you? Probably having a quick fuck after work.'

'You're disgusting. Leave me alone,' she said angrily.

'You told me you were coming back to me.'

Dena looked at him in disbelief. 'I did no such thing.'

'Is this his baby?' he demanded.

'You're out of your mind.' She started back up the steps. Brian rushed up to her and she could see him in the porch light. There was a wild look in his eyes.

'Stop it, Brian,' she said. 'I'm warning you.'

'They came and took your car. They said you wanted your things.'

'I do want my things.'

'Why? What do you need them for? Why aren't you willing to give me another chance? How long are you going to punish me? I mean, how much more punishment do I have to take?' His voice was growing strident.

'I'm not punishing you, Brian,' she said, trying to quiet him down. 'And there's no other man. This just isn't going to work. I have to . . . to start over on my own . . .'

'I can't let you do that,' he said.

His words sent a chill through her.

Suddenly, the door opened, and Jennifer appeared on the front porch. She smiled quizzically at Dena and then she saw Brian. She looked at Brian and the expression on her face underwent a terrible transformation. She gazed at him with undiluted hatred in her eyes.

'You. How dare you come here? To my house.' Her voice was venomous. Brian took a step toward her and Dena suddenly felt scared. 'Brian, don't.'

At that moment Ron came up behind his wife. 'What's going on out here?' he said. 'I heard voices.'

Over Jennifer's shoulder he saw Dena and smiled, and then he saw Brian, starting up the steps.

'Have you been with him all this time?' Jennifer demanded of Dena.

'No. I had dinner with a . . . friend. He was waiting here for me,' Dena explained apologetically.

Ron went down the steps to meet him. 'All right, that's it. You are not going to come near this house,' he fumed. 'You are trespassing. Now, get the hell out of here, or I'll call the police.'

'Brian, go away. Please,' Dena pleaded She turned her back on him and started to walk inside. Ron lingered a moment on the step, but then he followed the women into the house.

Once inside, Jennifer locked, bolted the door and chained the door with trembling hands.

'I'm sorry about that,' said Dena. 'I don't think he'll try to get in.'

'You don't know him,' said Jennifer, avoiding her gaze.

For a second, Dena was a little insulted. She was, after all, carrying the man's baby. But Jennifer's face was chalky, and before she could form a reply, Dena sensed that there was something going on which she did not understand.

'What do you know, Jenn?' Dena asked. 'What do you know about Brian that I don't?'

Jennifer looked as though she was struggling to speak, and then she looked at Ron. who was eyeing her warily. She drew herself up and took a deep breath. 'We got your car for you,' she said evenly. 'He wouldn't let us have your clothes and your belongings.'

'Thanks for trying. Why am I not surprised?' Dena sat down wearily on a chair in the living room. A little fire danced in the fireplace. Dena gazed into its flames for a moment. The she looked back at her friend. 'Jenn, what is it you're not telling me about Brian?'

Jennifer and Ron exchanged a glance. Whatever it was, Dena thought, Ron knew about it too.

'Look, whatever it is,' said Dena, 'it's not going to change my mind one way or the other. I'm not going back to him. I mean, I've known for a long time that this was . . . that it wasn't going to work out. The only thing that kept me there this long was the baby. I kept thinking if I tried harder . . . In a way, I'm glad he hit me. It was just what I needed to make up my mind about him. About this relationship. Baby or no baby.'

Jennifer stared at her, and Dena could see that she was trying to decide something. She looked at her husband, but Ron seemed to be concentrating on gently rearranging the small chunks of wood with the fireplace poker. Jennifer took a deep breath.

'My sister was involved with him,' she said.

Dena searched her memory. 'Tanya?' she asked. Jennifer nodded. 'About six years ago.'

'She had trouble with him,' Dena said flatly. 'He hit her, too.' Jennifer did not reply.

'I see. No wonder you feel this way.' Jennifer must feel self-conscious, she thought, to be bringing this up. There was no need, Dena thought. She did not feel possessive about Brian. Quite the opposite. 'Did it go on for a long time?' Dena asked.

'Too long,' said Jennifer.

'I should talk to her,' Dena mused.

'That won't be possible,' Jennifer said in a shaking voice.

Dena frowned, wondering if Tanya had moved away. Dena stared at her friend, puzzled, and saw that her eyes were bright with tears. And then a chill stole over Dena, in spite of the cheerful fire, as she suddenly realized what Jennifer was trying to say.

SEVEN

All night, Dena slept fitfully, dreaming that he was still outside and waking with a start. Several times she went to the window to look, but the street was quiet, and there was no sign of him. Early in the morning her phone rang. It was Albert, asking if she could come in to work after all. Dena got up and got dressed. She was exhausted, but determined. The long night had helped her to come to a decision. She came downstairs to find Jennifer, seated in the breakfast nook of her newly painted kitchen, still in her bathrobe, yawning and scrolling down her phone.

Dena made herself a cup of coffee, toasted a bagel, and joined Jennifer at the table. They glanced quickly at one another and then away. Neither one mentioned the revelations of the night before. But it loomed, like a third party, at the table.

'Aren't you eating breakfast?' Dena asked as she swallowed down a vitamin with her coffee, and began to chew on the bagel. 'Oh, I can't,' said Jennifer, making a face. 'Morning sickness. Actually, I don't know why they call it morning sickness. Everything makes me sick.'

Dena grimaced sympathetically. 'I had it for a few weeks. Not that badly though.'

'I don't mind,' said Jennifer, smiling. 'It's worth it.' Dena nodded but did not smile.

'So, what are you up to today?' Jennifer asked.

'My boss needs me to come in. So, I'll do that. And then I have some arrangements to make,' said Dena.

'What kind of arrangements?' Jennifer asked.

'I've decided to call my sister in Chicago. See if I can stay with her until the baby is born. I can't drive out in this condition, so I'll need to see about having my car shipped. There's a lot to think about . . .'

Jennifer reached over and touched her hand. 'I'm so relieved, Dena.'

'Have I been that bad a guest?' Dena asked, trying to tease her a little.

'You know it's not that,' Jennifer said seriously.

Dena smiled. 'I know it. I think the best thing is just to get away from here, ASAP.'

'Believe me, I agree,' said Jennifer. 'I just hope he doesn't follow you.'

'I don't think he can, realistically. He has so many obligations here.'

'He's not going to like it,' Jennifer warned.

'He has nothing to say about it,' Dena replied tartly. 'That's the point. My mind's made up. It's over. And I don't want to keep running into him. Popping up everywhere I go. It's over and it's time for me to get away from here.'

'Good for you,' said Jennifer. 'I really believe you should.'

Dena got up and rinsed her coffee mug in the sink.

'Are you and your sister close these days?' Jennifer asked.

Dena leaned back against the sink and thought about Marcia. Marcia was settled, with two kids and a husband, and she had always regarded her younger sister as something of a vagabond, even though Dena had a job and an apartment. Sometimes, in the past, Dena thought Marcia might secretly envy the freedom she had, the chances she had taken. Dena knew she would have to endure Marcia's disapproval, but she needed her older sister's stability right now. 'We're close in spite of our differences,' Dena explained. 'I mean, she's my sister. Last night I was thinking about that Robert Frost poem. You know, home is the place where, when you have to go there, they have to take you in . . .'

Jennifer smiled sadly. 'I'll miss you. If things were different, we could have raised our kids together.'

'I'll miss you, too,' said Dena warmly.

Jennifer's phone rang and she answered it. A look of surprise, and then a smile crossed her face. 'I'll be out this morning, but I'll be here all afternoon. OK, thanks.'

'Who was that?' Dena asked, noting her pleased expression.

'The florist. It seems my husband has ordered me flowers.'

'For no reason?'

Jennifer shook her head, and her auburn hair glistened. 'It's my anniversary today. We've been married for one year today.'

Dena smiled at her. 'Congratulations. It seems like you really found the right guy.'

'I did,' said Jennifer. 'I can't help it, I just have to admit it.'

'You guys going out tonight?' Dena asked, drying off her plate and replacing it in the cabinet.

Jennifer shook her head. 'I can't keep anything down. It would be a waste to go out to dinner. I think we'll just stay in, have a quiet evening. I'll pick up something he likes at the store.'

'Well, I better get going,' said Dena. 'I've got an appointment to show wedding cakes at the restaurant. What about you?'

'I've got a doctor's appointment, a couple of errands,' said Jennifer, yawning again. 'If I can just wake up.'

Dena came over and put an affectionate arm around her friend. 'I'll never be able to thank you for taking me in like this. You always were a good pal. All these years later, you haven't changed a bit that way.'

Jennifer smiled and squeezed her hand.

'Where are my car keys?' Dena asked.

Jennifer pointed to a basket on the counter. Dena picked them up and jingled the bunch. 'I'm on my way,' she said.

*   *   *

A few hours later, in a darkened room, Jennifer lay on an examining table, waiting for the technician and trying not to think about anything but her baby. But she kept on thinking about Dena and all that had happened. At least Dena would get away from Brian, and have a chance at a normal life. If only she had been as insistent with Tanya . . .

The door to the examining room opened and the technician and a nurse bustled in. In a few minutes, Jennifer was staring at the moving image on the monitor beside her as the technician moved the microphone-sized instrument across the cold gel on her abdomen.

'Everything looks good,' he said brightly, as a broad smile wreathed Jennifer's face. 'Five months, right?'

Jennifer nodded, nervously toying with the hair barrette in her hand as she gazed at the screen.

'He's sleeping at the moment, but he's doing fine. Everything looks perfect. I'll make you a picture of him to take home to your husband.'

'He?' Jennifer exclaimed.

'Figure of speech,' said the technician, reaching back to turn off the machine.

Jennifer hated to see the image disappear. Reluctantly, she turned away from the darkened screen. The nurse, standing by the examining table, began to wipe the gel off Jennifer's abdomen and then pulled the sheet up over her. 'We call them all "he" until further notice,' the nurse explained, smiling. 'Doesn't mean a thing.'

'Oh, OK,' said Jennifer, not sure if she felt relieved or disappointed. They had decided not to find out the baby's sex beforehand, but if she just happened to find out . . . Jennifer pulled herself up to a sitting position. All of a sudden she shook her head and let out a weak exclamation.

'What's the matter?' asked the nurse, switching on the lights and turning around. 'Whoa, I just felt really dizzy,' said Jennifer with a shaky laugh.

The nurse automatically reached for her wrist and checked her pulse. Then she put a blood-pressure cuff on her arm and pumped the bulb. 'Did you eat this morning?' she asked.

'Not really. Nothing stays down very long these days,' Jennifer admitted.

The nurse nodded and tore off the cuff. 'Your blood pressure is a little on the low side. It's not unusual.' She reached in a cabinet and fished out a plastic-wrapped packet of saltines. 'Here, eat a couple of these before you leave.'

'I will,' she said obediently. She clutched the packet in the same hand as her barrette.

'Be careful getting off the table,' said the nurse.

Jennifer nodded, and reached up to replace the barrette in her long, auburn hair. Her arms felt a little weak.

The technician held out a grainy black-and-white printout from the sonogram and Jennifer reached for it eagerly. 'Thank you,' she said sincerely, gazing at the printout.

'You can get dressed now,' said the nurse. 'The bathroom is that door on the right.'

Jennifer thanked the nurse too. Her bladder was ready to burst from all the liquid they had made her drink before the sonogram, but she could not immediately get herself to stop gazing happily at the picture. Wait until Ron sees you, she thought. He'll be over the moon.

When they left her alone in the room, Jennifer put the picture and her package of saltines carefully in her satchel and wadded up her clothes to take into the bathroom. She pulled on her T-shirt and her black stretch pants, then sat down on the toilet to relieve her bladder. As she stood up again, she felt that woozy sensation sweep over her. She noticed the light beginning to disappear around her like a shutter closing around a camera's lens, and then, as her knees began to buckle, she actually saw a starburst twinkling in the blackness before her eyes. You do see stars, she thought, and it was her last thought as her arms splayed out and she crumpled to the floor.

The next thing she was aware of was her cheek, smushed against the cold floor of the bathroom. Wow, she thought, pulling herself up with a feeling of amazement and rubbing her cheek. I really went down for the count. She tried, unsuccessfully, not to feel a little scared by it. It happened so fast – what if she had been out in the middle of the road somewhere? As it was, this bathroom was a pretty dangerous place to topple over. She felt an immediate sense of gratitude that she had not cracked her head open on the sink.

I should have eaten those crackers right away when the nurse gave them to me. She reached into the satchel which was on the floor beside her, rummaged inside for the saltines and broke open the package. She stuffed the dry crackers into her mouth. I'd better be careful on the ladder, she thought. She still had some stenciling of borders on the wall left to do in the baby's room. If she told Ron about this, he'd probably forbid her to finish. He was paranoid about anything happening to her, or the baby.

I'll keep it to myself, she thought, rising unsteadily to her feet. She gathered up her bag and opened the door to the examining room. The nurse came in. 'What's the matter?' she said. 'You still in here?'

'I passed out,' Jennifer admitted.

'Come with me,' said the nurse sternly. She pressed her arm under Jennifer's and propelled her out the door. 'Did you eat those crackers I gave you?' she demanded.

'Just now,' said Jennifer meekly.

Jennifer allowed herself to be led out into a little area off the waiting room. There the nurse made her sit, and checked her blood pressure again.

'All right,' she said. 'Now listen, if you feel that woozy feeling again, stop whatever you're doing and put your head between your knees. And no jumping up quickly. Now lean back and just relax for a few minutes.'

'OK, thanks,' said Jennifer. She sat in the little anteroom, watching people pass by the door. One woman met her gaze as she walked by, and waved shyly at her. Who is that, Jennifer wondered. Do I know her? It was an all too common experience for her these days, since she'd moved back here to her home town. People were always hailing her, and starting conversations, while Jennifer tried to make small talk and not let on that she had no earthly idea who it was. She would try to say innocuous things while she did a frantic brain search, trying to match the person by age, sex and level of familiarity to some part of her past – the school, the neighborhood, the church. It was embarrassing how often it occurred. When she moved away from Monroe to go to college in Boston, she had let go of the past, thinking she would never need it again. And now, she was trying to reassemble it, like a broken mosaic, before her old friends and neighbors realized how careless with their memory she had been.

'OK,' said the nurse, bustling in. 'You can go. But for goodness' sake, find something you can keep down in the morning. And take it easy this afternoon. No stress.'

Jennifer thanked her again, and went to collect her bag and

coat. She still felt shaky, although, thank God, there was nothing wrong with the baby. That would be the worst, Jennifer thought. This should be the happiest time of a woman's life, she thought. But obviously it wasn't, not for everyone. She couldn't help but think of Dena, all alone when she should be sharing her happiness with a loving husband. Well, better to be alone than with Brian. The thought of Brian filled her with the customary fury. Oh Tanya, she thought. You've had no justice. He broke you like a toy. Stop, she told herself. Stop it. The nurse said, no stress.

Jennifer rode down the elevator and walked out to her car. It was parked in the small lot in front of the medical building. That was the beauty of living in Monroe again. A small town where you could always park, and people had time to stop and talk. Of course, that was also the problem, when you couldn't recognize them, she thought wryly. She got into her car and drove down the tree-lined streets toward their new home.

Jennifer parked the car in front of the house on Chestnut Street. It was a street of older, well-kept homes with lovingly tended gardens and dappled sunlight on the pavement. She got out of the car and imagined them, walking the baby in a carriage here. Someday that baby would grow up, and ride his bicycle over these uneven slate sidewalks.

Jennifer picked up the empty recycling can beside the car and carried it back toward the house, her shoes crunching on the gravel driveway as she walked. As she returned to the front of the house, a woman wearing a headset jogged past her on the sidewalk and smiled. Across the street, the mailman waved as he paused to push some envelopes through a brass door slot. Two blocks down, a man was pulling a child in a red wagon. Jennifer sighed at the peacefulness of it all. She opened the back door of the car, took out a bag of groceries and Ron's dry cleaning from the back seat, and then climbed the steps to the front door.

The multi-paned enclosed porch was warm with the morning sun. Jennifer opened the door and called out, 'Dena?' but she didn't expect an answer. There was no sign of her friend's car in the street. Jennifer picked up the mail from the floor and then walked back to the kitchen, placing her satchel on a pine chair. Then she picked up her phone to call her husband. His secretary reported that he had gone to a meeting with one of his clients.

'No problem,' Jennifer said. 'I'll talk to him when he gets home.'

She hung up, feeling wistful, and filled with longing for him. Ron was so absolutely the right man for her, that it was hard to remember now how panicky she had become before she met him, thinking perhaps she would never find someone. She'd joined clubs, gone on blind dates, even tried internet dating. And then, when she'd given up all hope, she'd met Ron.

The phone rang at her elbow, and Jennifer jumped, half expecting it to be her husband. They were so close they had ESP sometimes. 'Hello,' she said eagerly.

'Hello, Jennifer, this is Mariah. Your Lamaze instructor.'

'Oh hi,' said Jennifer, a little disappointed.

'Listen, I'm going out of town next week so I'm scheduling an extra class this week. Tomorrow night. Can you make it?'

Jennifer looked at the kitchen calendar and nodded. 'Yeah, I think we can do that. No problem. And I'll tell Dena Russell if you'd like.'

'Would you? That'd be great. Save me a call. See you then.'

Jennifer made a note and posted it on the refrigerator under a bunch of bananas magnet. Then, she posted her sonogram under an apple. A wave of anxiety swept over her as she thought of Dena again, so alone and vulnerable, despite the brave front she was keeping up. But at least she had made up her mind to leave. Not to be a victim. That was the important thing now.

Jennifer took out a bottle of fruit juice from the refrigerator door and took a swig, remembering the nurse's warning. If only Ron were home. The thought of him brought unexpected tears to her eyes. He was so strong, such a rock. She had never known she needed a rock until she met him. She took a deep breath and closed the refrigerator door. Stop it, she told herself. Don't get all weepy. You've got teddy bears and duckies to paint.

At that moment, she heard a noise from the front of the house. She thought she heard her husband, calling for her. Was it someone at the front door? 'Ron?' she called out. Maybe he had come home after all. Read her mind, and decided to surprise her.

But there was no reply. The feelings of apprehension returned, stronger than ever. Stop it, she chided herself. It is broad daylight in Monroe. What in the world is there to be afraid of? Ever since you got pregnant, you've become a wimp, she chided herself.

She left her cheery, disorganized kitchen, and walked out to see who could be waiting at her door.

EIGHT

Dena finished piping rosettes of whipped cream onto a tray of éclairs, washed her hands and indicated to René that she was going to use the phone. She had put her phone in the pocket of her smock when she'd arrived at work, but this was the first break she'd had. She went over to the quiet room where René had his desk, and sat down. She punched in her sister's number and waited for someone to pick up. A child's lisping voice answered.

''lo?'

'Candy? This is Aunt Dena.'

There was a silence on the other end of the phone as the four-year-old contemplated this information.

'Candy, is Mommy there?'

'Uh huh . . .'

'Can I talk to her?'

There was a thunk as the phone was dropped on a countertop. 'Mo-o--o-m . . .' Dena waited, sighing anxiously.

'Hello,' said a familiar, distant voice. Marcia always answered the phone in a hurried tone, as if she were being interrupted from something important.

'Maree, it's me.'

'Dena?'

'How are you?'

'Oh, frazzled. Grant is out on the boat.' Grant was a commercial fisherman and when he went out to fish on Lake Michigan, Marcia was left to cope with the two kids alone. 'How are you?'

Dena tried to sound upbeat. 'Good. I feel OK. Was that Candy?'

'Yeah, my helper. I'm amazed she didn't hang up on you,' Marcia said affably. 'How are you doing, anyway? You must be big as a house by now.'

Dena looked down at her voluminous smock. 'I'm pretty large.'

'What's the matter?' Marcia asked suspiciously.

Dena sighed. They were not much alike, but they *were* sisters.

Marcia could always read her voice. 'Things have gotten . . . complicated around here.'

'Complicated how? Candy, put that down. *This instant.*'

'I'm thinking about leaving here.'

'The boyfriend. I knew it.'

'You don't even know him,' Dena said defensively.

'Yeah, neither did you. That's how I knew it was a bad idea.' *I told you so.* It was like being mocked, as a child. But, of course, she was right this time.

'What happened?' Marcia demanded.

'We just don't get along,' Dena said.

'Well, don't you think you ought to try? For the baby's sake?'

For a minute Dena wondered why she had bothered to call. 'I have tried,' she said.

Marcia sighed noisily. 'You know, it's not easy. It's not like marriage is always a bed of roses.'

Dena had hoped to avoid the bald fact of it, but there was no other way to cut short her sister's litany of advice. 'He hit me,' she said bluntly.

'Oh my God,' said Marcia, instantly aghast. 'Are you all right? Is the baby all right?'

'We're all right. But, I can't stay with him.'

'Well no, of course not. Lord, Dena, how did you get mixed up with a guy like that?'

Dena shook her head. 'What do you think? I advertised in the paper for a guy who would hit me. What else? Look, forget I called.'

'No, honey, wait. I'm sorry. Look, I don't want you being all alone. You come here and stay with us, as long as you need to. Have your baby here. I'll help you any way I can.'

In spite of everything, Dena thought, we are sisters. Marcia had anticipated her question. She hadn't even needed to ask. Relief washed over Dena like a wave. At the same time, she thought of Jennifer. And Tanya. The sister she no longer had to rely on. 'I thought I might,' Dena admitted. 'Just until the baby comes.'

'And then what?' Marcia demanded, as if the post-baby situation was hopeless.

'I'll move back into the city. Maybe get my old job back. I only sublet my apartment.'

'You know you can't go gallivanting around like some kind of free spirit with a baby.'

'Marcia, are you going to lecture me the whole time I'm with you? Because, if you are . . .'

'No, no, I'm sorry. Look honey, I'd come and get you myself but with Grant gone . . .'

'Don't worry, I can get there.'

'Don't try driving here by yourself. Not in your condition.'

'I'll fly. Don't worry.'

'No, no. Don't fly.'

'Don't fly? How am I supposed to get there? Dogsled? What's wrong with flying?'

'Oh Dena, it's dangerous for the baby. Don't you know that? One of my girlfriends was eight months along and she lost the baby after a plane flight. It has something to do with the change in cabin pressure.'

More like an old wives' tale, Dena thought. 'I've never heard of that.'

'I'm not lying. Ask your doctor. Please, humor me. Take the train. I'll pick you up in Chicago. When will you come?'

'Soon. I'll call you.'

'OK. You can have Candy's room. I'll put her in with Christie. It'll be fun. You'll see.'

'Right,' said Dena sadly, thinking of how she had imagined her baby's birth. She hadn't planned to be holding her sister's hand. But, she reminded herself that she was lucky to have a sister. She thought of Tanya again, and the regrets that had poured out of Jennifer last night. That she had not stepped in, been more insistent, that Tanya leave and come to her. Take care of each other, Dena's mother had said, when she knew her own death was near. Up until now, it hadn't been necessary. Dena saw René gesturing to her from across the room. 'OK, thanks Maree. I've got to go . . .'

'And Dee, don't worry. Everything will work out OK.'

Dena said goodbye and hurried over to René, who informed her in French that the wedding cake customers were upstairs waiting for her. Dena grabbed the sample book and rang for the service elevator.

As she emerged from the elevator dressed in her chefs' whites and carrying the loose-leaf photo album of wedding cake confections, she blinked at the brightness in the restaurant. Sunlight streamed into the busy dining room and gleamed off the copper molds and pans against the walls, interspersed with bookshelves and faience pottery that made up the insouciant decor, its simplicity belied by the extravagant flower arrangements. Waiters dressed in black pants, white shirts, black bow ties and long, white linen aprons moved smoothly through the murmuring lunch crowd. Albert appeared in the corridor, having heard the service elevator doors open, and hailed Dena. 'They're in there,' said Albert in a stage whisper. 'You can get started.' As they entered the light-filled dining room, Albert started at the sight of her face. 'What happened to you?' he cried, pulling her back by the arm.

Dena's hand went automatically to her bruise, realizing that he had not seen her yesterday because he hadn't been in the kitchen while she was working. 'I walked into a closet door,' she lied. From the appalled look on his face, she thought he must be worrying about what the clients would think. But she had under-estimated him, as people sometimes did.

'The hell you did. Is this why he was waiting for you outside with the roses yesterday? I should have sent him packing. Oh, I'd like to get my hands on him.'

'It's all right, Albert. They're looking at us,' she reminded him.

Albert turned his attention to the well-groomed middle-aged matron and her lissome, self-conscious daughter, dressed in black, who waited anxiously at a corner table. Dena sat down and Albert introduced Mrs Wolcott and her daughter, Carol. Dena greeted them pleasantly. They both glanced at her bruised face and distended belly, but neither one mentioned it. Albert sat down beside Dena, and began to explain, in a low voice, why the restaurant preferred to provide the cake, rather than rely on an outside bakery.

'Frankly,' Albert said, in a tone that brooked no dissent, 'there's no one in the area who can match the kind of work that René and Dena are capable of. We don't want to serve your guests a brilliant meal, and follow it with an inferior cake.'

Dena blushed. She had been dreading telling Albert she was going to be leaving. He had been so kind to her. But he would understand. And René was really the irreplaceable one. He was taking lessons in English, so he could deal directly with the customers.

Mother and daughter glanced at each other and nodded meekly. 'I agree completely,' said Mrs Wolcott.

At a nod from Albert, Dena lifted the notebook onto the tabletop and opened it. Mrs Wolcott and her daughter bent their heads so that only their coiffures, one stiff and bleached, one a shining, artless chignon, showed over the pages of the notebook. The cakes pictured were fairy-tale confections of spun sugar doves and cascading flowers in fondant, fashioned in shades of white and ivory, or the blushing tints of spring.

Dena answered all their questions patiently, and enjoyed the oohs and ahhs as they studied the photos. It took her mind off . . . everything else. She was proud of the work she had done here with René. She had learned a lot at his elbow. But now, her mind wandered to the future. She knew her old boss in Chicago would want her back. But the hours were long there. If she was going to have to support her baby, maybe she could start a home business of making wedding cakes, at least while the baby was young. After all, she was not going to have anyone to help her.

'This one, definitely,' said the bride-to-be, in the tone of one unused to asserting herself. She pointed to a photo of a white cake, with cascading violets and lily of the valley.

Dena nodded. 'I love that one myself. And the flavor?'

'Chocolate,' said Carol Wolcott.

'Chocolate?' her mother protested.

'Hal likes chocolate,' the soon-to-be-wife said firmly.

Mrs Wolcott, who repeatedly admired a lemon-flavored cake topped by a crown of white roses, reluctantly agreed, and the choice was made.

'All right,' said Dena. 'I'll convey your wishes to René with all the particulars, and Mr Gelman will take care of the rest.'

More relaxed now, the mother leaned back and smiled at Dena. 'They are all so beautiful, it's hard to choose.'

'I know,' said Dena. She stood up with some degree of difficulty.

'Did you bake one of these for your own wedding?' Mrs Wolcott asked, and Dena saw a warning look in the eyes of Albert Gelman.

It's an innocent question, Dena reminded herself. A woman of her generation would naturally assume that Dena was married. She was just being friendly, making conversation, Dena told herself. She wondered why answering was so painful. Get used to it, she thought. This is your life, from now on. 'No, I didn't,' she said, and before the woman could inquire further, she picked up the notebook and was gone.

*   *   *

Vanessa Pittinger lay in bed, wearing a headset attached to her CD player, staring at some show on the Discovery channel about snow leopards in Asia. Fluffy clusters of used Kleenex surrounded her, and tumbled off the quilt, drifting to the floor. Occasionally she would toss one into the wastebasket beside the bed, but usually she didn't bother. Vanessa dunked her finger into a jar of cold cream her mother had given her before she left for work, and gingerly applied a dollop around her reddened nostrils. Then she slid down under the quilt and began to cough. She coughed and coughed until she gagged, never taking her eyes off the TV. The cough medicine and spoon that her mother had left on the night table remained unused.

On the bedspread her phone began to ring, but Vanessa didn't hear it, because she had the volume turned up so high on the Alanis Morrissette CD. At the other end of the line, Vanessa's mother, Pam, was waiting, hoping no one in the office would see her making a personal call. She worked in a brokerage firm in Philadelphia, and it was a high-pressure environment. She waited as the phone rang eight times, and then gave up. She wasn't worried about Vanessa's whereabouts – she'd rarely seen her daughter feeling as punky in all her fourteen years as she had this morning. Of course, she could scare herself into thinking that an axe-murderer had invaded their house and found the sick girl alone there. But Pam tried to avoid those kinds of thoughts. No, it was the headset. She knew it.

She'd try again later. But she felt a pang of guilt at leaving her sick child home to fend for herself. When Vanessa was a little girl, Pam used to bring her to the office on sick days, or sometimes Dick would stay home with her if he had a lot of paperwork from his accounting firm piled up. Now, Vanessa was a teenager, and could be left alone, which made life easier. Still, it would have been nice to stay there and feed her chicken soup. Her own phone rang at her elbow, and Pam sprang back into her broker mode.

Vanessa, meanwhile, took a slurp of her soda, and found it completely flat. As little as she wanted to get out of bed, a fresh Coke was one thing she would get up for. Blowing her nose again, she took off her headset, got out of bed and walked, barefoot, without a bathrobe, out of her room and down the stairs.

Vanessa went into the kitchen, noticing how cold she was when her bare feet hit the tiled floor, and opened the refrigerator. She stared impassively at the contents of the fridge until she found another Coke and pulled it out. As she was looking in the dishwasher for a clean glass, she suddenly noticed something odd. She was smelling something.

She hadn't thought she could smell anything with this cold, but she was smelling it now, and it made her skinny little body rigid. She sniffed again, to be sure. There it was. Smoke. She never thought much about being left alone. She was used to it, and liked to think of herself as almost an adult. But when that acrid smell penetrated her senses she was instantly a child again, feeling totally alone and vulnerable. Her first impulse was to grab the phone and dial 911, as she'd been taught in all those grade-school trips to the firehouse. But then she thought, no, don't be lame. You'll look like a doofus if it's a false alarm. And it obviously wasn't in the house. They had fire alarms in every room. She went to the windows looked out. At first she saw nothing. Then, all at once, there it was. A gray plume rising over the hill. Coming from the direction of Riley's farm.

The barn, she thought, and her heart seemed to stop. What if the barn had caught fire? What if Brian wasn't there, and didn't know about it? There was nobody else around here. Nobody who could take the horses out of there. She thought lovingly of each one of them, her heart fixating, in particular, on Wrangler. She had to do something.

She looked at her barn clothes hanging on a hook in the laundry room. My mother will kill me if I leave the house while I'm sick, she thought. That was forbidden – unless there was a fire. But there is a fire, she reminded herself. I can't stand here thinking about it. Those animals are helpless in there. She could see it in her mind's eye, leading them through the blaze, out to the safety of the pasture. Everyone would be so proud of her that they wouldn't care that she had gone out while she was sick. Brian would be so grateful. And then, at the thought of Brian, another possibility occurred to her. What if he was in the barn, trapped by the flames? With no one to save him but Vanessa.

That did it. She pulled on her dirty jeans, barn coat and boots over her nightshirt and hurried for the door. She let herself out looking around everywhere. There was nobody else to see it in this ghost-town of a development, she thought. But the plume of smoke was still there. She began to run, up, over the hill.

*   *   *

Ron Hubbell had thought about calling from the train station for a ride but, the truth was, he wasn't quite ready to face Jennifer, so he had walked the half a mile home to his house. As he turned the corner onto Chestnut Street, he saw Jennifer's car parked in front of the house. He sighed, dreading what was to come. She would be so surprised to see him. Surprised and pleased, no doubt. She would think he was coming home early, in honor of their anniversary.

Their anniversary. Their first year as man and wife. He could still picture her as she'd looked on their wedding day, her face lit like a candle, her long auburn hair caught up in coils interspersed with little white flowers. He had a picture of her looking like that on his desk at work. It was his favorite. He had planned to put one beside it, of her and the baby. Except that, when the baby came, he wouldn't have a desk to put it on.

He had found out in the morning, and all he could think about was how he was going to tell her. He told his secretary he was going out to lunch with a client, but the truth was, he couldn't do any business today. His mind seemed to be spinning in circles of anxiety. They would have to sell the house, and probably take a loss on it. And Jennifer wouldn't want to leave Monroe and her dad. But Ron had to work. If he was lucky he'd get his old job back in Boston. But of course, everybody in the Philadelphia office was going to want to be relocated. What if they didn't want him back in Boston? He was too old to start looking for a whole new company. And, in the meantime, the baby would be coming. And the baby would need so many new things. On the already strained credit card.

A couple of kids passed him rollerblading down the street. One of these days, he thought. Maybe I'll learn when the kid learns, he thought, trying to cheer himself up, but today it was no use. By the time the kid was ready to rollerblade, he'd be fifty years old.

He noticed all the leaves on his lawn as he came up to the steps, and he had to admit to himself that raking was pretty low on his list of things to do these days.

Although he probably should put an hour or two in over the weekend. There were so many other jobs left to do on the house. But were they worth doing, now that he knew they might have to move? And then, at the thought of moving, he chided himself for his bad mood. After all, he had Jennifer and the baby. When they moved, they would move as a family. And what else really mattered? Every time he thought of Dena today, and Brian Riley, he reminded himself to count his blessings.

He opened the porch door and walked into the house. He noticed that not a single light was burning. For a minute it made him feel uneasy. Jennifer was the queen of lamplighting, whether you were in a room or not. She never shut them off till bedtime.

Usually, if he mentioned the electric bill, she teased him. But he had been complaining a little lately about all the bills. Maybe she'd decided to become economical all of a sudden.

He steeled himself, wishing he could avoid telling her this news which could no longer be avoided. He didn't want to see the disappointment in her eyes. She would be all happy and excited about their anniversary, and then she would see the look on his face. She would read it in his eyes and she would know. She was clever that way. She always seemed to know when something was bothering him. Well, he was going to put a positive face on it. She relied on him for that. She always said he was her rock. Today he felt more like a pebble. It seemed as if the house was watching him silently, waiting for something. That's stupid, he told himself. What could a house be waiting for? He opened the inside door to the living room. 'Happy anniversary, Jenn,' he called. 'It's me.'

NINE

'Chief, can you come up here for a minute . . .?'

Chief Potter called out, 'Right away,' and followed the voice upstairs in the house where the first homicide in Monroe in twenty years had taken place. From the anxious sound of his officer's voice, Lou felt a glimmer of hope. Maybe someone had found something they could use to identify the killer. Lou had plenty of experience with crime over his long career in the police department, and he'd seen his share of blood and battery. But murder was something foreign to him. He was trying not to show how out of his depth he felt to the victim's distraught husband and father.

'Where are you, Tyrell?' he called out.

The sergeant stuck his head out of one of the doors down the hallway. 'In here,' he said.

Lou walked to the room where Tyrell Watkins was waiting. He walked in and looked around. The room was painted white, but the ceiling was a pale blue, with fluffy white clouds and a couple of kites painted on it. All the furniture in the room was white – the crib, the dresser, the changing table. A bright yellow rug, hooked in a Mother Goose pattern, covered the shiny pine floorboards in the middle of the room. An unopened package of newborn diapers sat on the changing table.

'I'm guessing she was pregnant,' said Tyrell.

Lou pressed his lips together sadly and nodded. 'Oh God,' he said.

Lou knew who Jennifer Hubbell was. She and her sister had grown up in Monroe. Jennifer had gone away to college in Boston and had lived there ever since – until three weeks ago. But Lou hadn't recognized her when he saw the body. Of course, even if he saw her every day, he wouldn't have known her. The slim, fully clad body had been sprawled on the floor between the dining room and the kitchen. The walls were spattered with red, as if someone had dropped a brick into a bucket of scarlet paint. She'd been beaten mercilessly about the head with the fireplace poker. Lou had seen people who had gone through windshields who weren't that badly broken up. But he never would have known by looking at her that she was pregnant.

'It might have been wishful thinking,' Tyrell suggested.

Lou shook his head. 'No. I'm betting on your first guess.'

Tyrell Watkins folded his arms across his broad chest. 'Maybe he didn't want a baby.'

Lou knew whom his officer was referring to. Ron Hubbell had found his wife's body when he got home, so he said, from work. It had been his frantic call to 911 which had summoned them. Even without a lot of hands-on experience, Lou knew that their prime suspect was the husband. Add to that the time-honored maxim, known to all cops – whether homicide was routine or foreign to them – that the one who finds the body is most likely the killer, and he knew he had to bear down on Ron Hubbard about his story. But he wasn't looking forward to it. 'I'm going to see if the doc is finished with him yet,' said Lou. 'Anything else of interest up here?'

Lou saw a strange expression cross Tyrell's broad, dark, even-featured face. 'What?' he said.

Tyrell narrowed his eyes as if he was about to speak, and then he shook his head slightly. 'Nothing,' he said. 'We're still looking.'

'Well, keep after it,' said Lou. He returned to the stairwell, ducked his head, and went back down to the first floor. At the foot of the stairs he encountered Gwendolyn Holmes, the local MD, who was pulling on her coat, preparing to leave.

'Oh, Chief Potter,' she said.

'Dr Holmes. Can I talk to him now?'

Gwendolyn Holmes glanced over her shoulder. 'I wish you wouldn't. He is really in rough shape. Can't it wait until tomorrow?'

Lou Potter shook his head grimly. 'I'm afraid not.'

'Well, I gave him a sedative. Jennifer's father is being stoic, although he looks like a stroke waiting to happen. Anyway, the husband may not be able to answer your questions. Don't expect too much of him.'

Lou Potter nodded and walked into the living room. Two technicians from the county were quietly dusting the overturned furniture for fingerprints, and a yellow tape sectioned off the room which was considered to be the crime scene. There was a cop taking photographs all around where the body had been. Lou went the long way around into the kitchen, where the two men huddled. One light burned over the sink.

In the midst of the commotion in his house, Ron Hubbell sat in a chair, his elbows resting on the kitchen table, his head in his hands. His tie was askew and the white shirt that he wore was splotched with scarlet. Even from across the room, Lou could see that his body was shaking. His father-in-law stood at the sink, staring out into a pitch-black backyard. Lou knew the girl's father. Jake Smith owned the only hotel in town, the Endicott, where the Policeman's Ball was held every year. And, of course, Lou remembered him from that business about the other daughter. The one who fell in the shower and cracked her head. Jake Smith was so red in the face that Lou could see why Dr Holmes was worried about him. Lou dreaded this interview. Taking a deep breath, he approached the grieving men.

'Excuse me,' he said. 'We need to ask Mr Hubbell some questions.' Lou did not say: you're a suspect in the murder of your wife. Right now he was the only suspect. But, Ron Hubbell looked up at Lou with such total despair and grief in his eyes that Lou was tempted to just squeeze the man's hands, turn around and walk out. Lou may not have had a lot of experience with murder, but he knew people. This man was totally devastated.

Jake Smith turned away from the sink and came and stood behind the chair where Ron sat, putting his large, worn hands on his son-in-law's shoulders. 'Can't you see he's too upset to talk,' he said grimly. He held onto Ron's shoulders like a man trying to hold down a tent in a tornado.

Lou ignored the father's anger. What else could you do in a situation like this but be angry? 'Ron,' Lou said. 'I've got to get some information so we can find out who did this.'

Ron wiped his eyes and tried to inhale a deep breath. Lou wondered what he had been like before the sedation, if this was afterward. Lou pulled out a chair and it scraped across the wooden floor. He faced the weeping man and took out his pad and pen. 'Now Ron,' he asked, 'how long were you and Jennifer married?'

Ron glanced up at the wall clock, as if he were trying to figure it out to the minute. 'Today was our anniversary – one year.'

Lou winced. He hated to bring up the next subject. 'And she was expecting a baby.'

Ron nodded, and did not seem surprised that he knew. 'She was five months' pregnant. The baby was due . . .' He dissolved into sobs again.

'It's all right son, we can figure it out,' said Lou.

'April,' Ron whispered.

'OK,' said Lou. 'When was the last time you saw your wife alive?'

'This morning,' Ron whispered. 'Before I left for work. Oh my God, was that only this morning?' he cried.

Lou cleared his throat and looked down at his pad. 'We know she went to the supermarket and the dry cleaner's. We found her packages, still out on the table.'

'She was on her way to the doctor's,' said Ron. He opened his hand and revealed a crumpled piece of paper in it. 'To get this,' he said. 'I found it on the refrigerator, under a magnet.'

Lou frowned, took the paper from him, and flattened it out. On the paper was a black and white image that resembled the shadowy arc of a windshield wiper. Inside the grainy arc it looked like a fish in a fishbowl. They hadn't had these when Hattie was pregnant, but Lou's daughter had showed him one when she was having her first. Lou realized what it was. 'The baby,' he said. 'I'm so sorry.' 'My grandchild,' said Jake. 'They killed my child and my grandchild.'

The atmosphere in the room was tense, and Jake Smith looked as if he was about to throw a punch at the nearest target. 'I need to talk to Mr Hubbell alone,' Lou said firmly. Lou indicated that Ken McCarthy should escort the father from the room.

Reluctantly, looking back at his son-in-law, Jake accompanied the officer out.

'OK Ron,' said Lou, in a matter-of-fact tone, 'I need to know. Were there any problems between you and Jennifer? Money problems or . . . uh . . . sexual problems of any sort?'

Ron did not protest. He just shook his head. 'None. None at all. We were so happy. We were looking forward to being parents.'

'Your wife was . . .' He looked at his notes. 'Thirty years old?'

'That's right.'

'Did she have any other children? Previous marriages?'

'No. None,' he said. 'Neither one.'

'What about you? Ever married before?'

Ron nodded. 'Once.'

'Divorced?' Lou asked bluntly.

Ron nodded.

'Any children?'

'She didn't want children,' said Ron bleakly.

Lou nodded. 'I'll need her name and address.'

Ron did not appear to hear him.

'I'm just looking at my notes here, Ron. I mean. This seems odd . . . I mean, Jennifer comes back here to live after being away for . . . how long?'

'Twelve . . . thirteen years,' said Ron, with a sob.

'Thirteen years later she comes back, and in three weeks, she's murdered.'

Ron buried his head in his hands. 'We should never have come here,' he moaned.'

'Why do you say that, Ron?' Lou doggedly continued. 'Did Jennifer have any enemies? Was there anybody in town that she was wary of . . . or didn't want to see? Did she ever say anything to you?'

Ron started to protest and then he stopped, and his eyes widened.

'Did you think of something?' Lou asked.

'Yes,' said Ron. 'There is someone.'

At that moment, Officer Ken McCarthy appeared in the doorway, shepherding a very pregnant woman with a dazed expression in her eyes.

'Who's this?' the chief demanded.

Tyrell Watkins came up behind them and entered the kitchen, looking anxiously at the chief. 'This is the Hubbell's houseguest,' Tyrell said. 'Miss Dena Russell. She just got home.'

Dena looked at Ron in bewilderment. 'What happened?' she asked. 'What happened to Jennifer?'

Ron was looking at her now as if the sight of her face was reviving a nightmare. 'Miss Russell was staying with the Hubbells,' said Tyrell, his gaze locked on the chief's. 'She had some problems with her boyfriend the other night. Mr Brian Riley.'

A hot flush flooded Lou's body, pulsing at his pressure points. He knew exactly why Tyrell's eyes were wide in his mocha-colored face. With difficulty, Lou managed not to betray his own feelings to the people in the room.

'Come in, Miss Russell,' he drawled. 'We'll need to talk to you.'

TEN

Dena looked around in confusion. She had just passed Jennifer's father, looking devastated, and now, here was Ron, white as paste, his clothes splotched with blood.

Five minutes ago, when she had pulled up to the house, panicked by the sight of all the police cars, Sergeant Watkins had met her at the door, saying only, 'I wondered if you were still here.' She tried to question him, but he had ignored her queries, indicating only that the young policeman should lead her around to the kitchen. Now her gaze fastened on the bloodstained shirt which Ron was wearing. 'Ron? What happened? Are you hurt? Where is Jennifer?'

The police chief stared at her. 'Were you a friend of Mrs Hubbell's?' he asked.

It took a moment for the question to register. 'Were?' she repeated faintly.

The police chief stared back at her, and then she knew. Dena felt the world falling out from under her. She grabbed the back of a painted kitchen chair and swayed slightly. With military efficiency, Tyrell pulled the chair out and pressed her down onto it before her legs gave out.

Dena's fingers and cheeks felt numb, as if she'd been frostbitten. 'Is Jennifer . . .?'

'Yes,' Lou said. 'Someone . . . she was . . . murdered.'

'It's impossible,' Dena said. 'No.'

Lou Potter looked at his pad and then gazed at her angrily, as if she were somehow to blame. 'What are you doing here, Miss Russell?'

'I've been staying here. They took me in,' Dena said faintly.

Ron seemed to come to life. 'Her boyfriend came looking for her. He acted crazy,' said Ron angrily. 'That's who I'm talking about. Brian Riley. Jennifer hated him. He was here last night and we threw him out.'

'All right, let's call a halt to this for the moment,' said Lou, standing up abruptly. 'This is not a group discussion. Miss Russell, I'll talk to you at the station. First, I have to finish with Mr Hubbell.'

He walked out into the hallway, where Jake Smith waited anxiously 'I think you should try to get some rest right now. I'm sure I'll have more questions for you tomorrow. But I promise you . . . I promise you we will find whoever did this to Jennifer. We will find him and we will put him away forever, all right? We won't let you down.'

'They're all gone,' Jake said. The look in his eyes said that the horror was just beginning to register. 'All my girls.'

Lou looked at the shattered man with compassion. 'Is there someone here who can help you . . .?'

'There are some friends outside,' Tyrell said. 'I'll call them.'

Lou met the worried gaze of his sergeant calmly. 'Good. See that you get him safely dispatched. I'll talk to Miss Russell alone,' he said. 'After I finish with the husband.' He inclined his head back toward the kitchen. He spoke quietly into Tyrell's ear. 'We need to establish the husband's movements around the time of death. Get started questioning the neighbors. Find out if anybody saw him on the train or coming home. Also, we need to check his finances, insurance . . .'

Tyrell peered into the kitchen at the disconsolate man in the bloody shirt slumped over the table. 'You think this might be an act?'

'I don't know anything about that,' said Lou carefully. 'There's such a thing as regret or remorse. It can look a lot like grief.'

'Looks real to me,' said Tyrell.

'Sergeant,' Lou said in a warning voice.

Tyrell turned to Jake Smith and offered to escort him out to his friends who were waiting behind the police barricade. Jake acceded, in a daze. Lou went back into the kitchen and put an arm under Dena's elbow, lifting her from the chair.

'This can't be happening,' said Dena. Tears had begun to run down her face.

'Take it easy, now, Miss Russell. Everything will be all right. You go along with Officer McCarthy. I'll see you back at the station.'

Dena sat in a chair in the chief's office for what seemed like an hour until he was able to sit down across from her. The interruptions had been constant – the phone, reporters, police with paperwork to show him. Dena spent the time sipping a cup of water which the dispatcher, a sympathetic woman named Peg, had brought to her, and studying the photos of the chief and his family which were clustered on the windowsill behind his desk. Every few minutes her thoughts would return to Ron, sitting in that bloody shirt at the table – all his dreams shattered. She thought about the fact that she had stopped to eat before she headed to the Hubbells' house. She hadn't wanted to disturb their anniversary dinner, so she had stopped at a coffee house for a sandwich, picturing Ron and Jennifer toasting their happiness by candlelight. And all the while . . . It was agonizing to think of it. While she ate her lonely sandwich, she had envied them.

Dena wiped the tears away again. Her face was puffy with weeping. She tried not to think about how this had happened to Jennifer. Because, when she did, her thoughts kept circling back to the same horrible possibility.

Chief Potter came into the room, and shut the door. Dena jumped at the sound. 'Sorry to startle you,' he said. He sat down and folded his hands on his desk.

'Now, Miss Russell,' he said. 'I'm sorry to keep you waiting.'

'That's all right,' Dena said automatically.

'How long were you a guest in the Hubbells' home?'

'Not long,' she said dully. 'A couple of days.'

'But you did have an opportunity to observe them together.'

Dena was a little surprised. She had assumed the questions would be about Brian. 'Yes, I . . . I saw them, of course.'

'I realize that you were grateful to them, for taking you in, and you were distracted by your own problems,' he said.

'That's for sure,' Dena agreed. She took another sip from her cup of water.

The chief spread his hands wide. 'Did you notice any discord, any arguing that went on . . .'

'No, none,' said Dena. 'They got along so well . . .'

'Any exchanges between them that made you think perhaps everything wasn't as it should be.'

Dena sat up in her chair and stared at him. 'No. What are you implying?'

'I'm just asking you a question,' he said blandly.

'They were very happy together. They had a new house and a baby on the way. They loved each other . . .'

'Sometimes people only let the world see a small corner of their relationship,' he said.

'That's true,' Dena conceded. How well she knew. 'But, if they were trying to hide something, they did a pretty good job.'

'Did you know that Mr Hubbell was married before?' the chief asked.

Dena nodded. 'Jennifer mentioned it. Lots of people are married more than once.'

'Do you know why his first marriage ended?'

Dena looked at him ruefully. 'No. What difference does that make?'

The chief ignored her angry tone. 'You were close friends with Mrs Hubbell?

Dena hesitated, wanting to be clear. 'We were old friends, from high school. I hadn't seen her in years. We met again at our Lamaze class.'

'Oh yes. The baby,' he said.

'Chief Potter, I feel as if I have to say . . .' She didn't want to be the one to bring Brian's name into this. But surely the police had to be told about the animosity between Jennifer and Brian. 'Before her . . . death, Mrs . . . Jennifer told me some things about the man I was living with that were terribly disturbing. I don't know if you realize that she had certain suspicions—'

The chief cut her off. 'I'm not interested in your domestic squabbles. I think that will be all for right now, Miss Russell. I just want to make it clear that we don't want you going anywhere for a while. I want you right here until we make an arrest in this case.'

'But I can't stay here,' Dena protested. 'I'm planning on leaving Monroe. The things Jennifer told me have made me very uncomfortable about being here any longer . . .'

'Uncomfortable?' he asked incredulously. 'This is a homicide investigation, Miss Russell. We will have further questions for you. You are not free to go. Is that clear?' The phone lying on his desk rang and he picked it up, gesturing toward the door.

Dismissed, Dena left the office feeling stunned and confused. She could hardly believe it. He hadn't asked her one thing about Brian. He didn't seem to want to hear about it. And while she didn't want to think that maybe Brian . . . They couldn't possibly think that Ron would kill Jennifer. She remembered how outraged he had been that Brian had struck her. How Ron had defended her.

'You done with that?' Peg the dispatcher asked, approaching her, and pointing to the cup. Dena felt as if this was a suggestion that she should be moving along. But moving along to where, she wondered. She looked at the station clock over the fire exit. She couldn't go to the hotel – it belonged to Jennifer's dad. For all she knew, he might blame her for what happened tonight. She put her arms around her belly, cradling the baby who waited there. Where can we rest, she thought?

'Yes,' she said, handing her back the cup. 'Thank you.' She hesitated for a moment. She hated dragging anyone else into this. But her options were limited. She reached into her bag and pulled out her phone.

Albert picked up on the first ring. 'La Petite Auberge,' he sang.

'Albert, it's Dena.'

'Hi, sweetie. What's all that racket?'

'I'm at the police station.'

'What?' Albert cried. 'Oh no, not again. How dare he lay a hand on you . . .'

'It's not that. I'll tell you all about it. The thing is, I don't have a place to stay again. Do you and Eric have room . . .'

'Oh God,' Albert cried, exasperated. 'There isn't a square inch of the carriage house that's not covered with sheetrock and sanders. We're renovating, you know. The only place that's even habitable is our bedroom. And I don't really see us in a ménage à trois.'

Dena managed a weak smile. 'I understand . . .'

'Wait a minute, wait a minute, don't hang up . . .' She heard Albert's muffled voice as he spoke to someone in the background. She wanted to stop him, to say 'never mind', but he wasn't listening to her. In a minute or two he was back on the line. 'OK, it's settled,' he said. 'I just spoke to Peter about the apartment above his. It's available and he has the keys. Don't worry about the landlord. He's a friend of mine. That's how I got the place for Peter. I'll square everything with him. It's furnished. It'll be fine for you for the time being.'

'No, Albert,' she protested. Brian was sure to find out she was living in the same house as Peter. It would be asking for trouble, and she didn't want to provoke him.

'You'll be in an apartment upstairs from Peter. In fact, I just told him to knock off for the night and come get you.'

'Albert, I don't think it's wise. I'm afraid Brian might misinterpret—'

'The hell with Brian. It's his fault you're in this predicament. If he hadn't been such a pig you'd still be living there. Now, do as I say and I'll talk to you tomorrow. Watch at the door. Peter will be pulling up outside any minute.' He hung up before she could protest further.

She knew Albert was trying to help, but she couldn't help feeling uneasy about this solution. He hadn't seen the look in Brian's eyes last night. Or heard about Tanya Smith. Stop it, she told herself. You're still letting Brian run your life. She went out in the vestibule to wait. She wasn't there a minute before the other doors opened and Tyrell Watkins came in, looking distracted and grim. Dena almost hoped he wouldn't notice her, but of course, he did. Tyrell nodded. 'Miss Russell. Trouble seems to follow you around,' he said. And then, as if chastened by the sight of her pale, drawn face, he said, 'I'm sorry about your friend.'

'Thank you. She was a wonderful person. I hope you will find whoever did this to her. To them,' she said deliberately.

Tyrell wasn't about to discuss it with her. 'We will. Excuse me, it's late and I have a lot of work to do.'

Dena turned back to the door and stared out, her face flaming at the obvious contempt with which the sergeant regarded her. I must seem like a pathetic statistic to him – an unmarried woman, pregnant and knocked around by her boyfriend. It isn't true, she wanted to cry out. I'm not like that. This time last year I had my life in order. Now, it seemed, she was just trying to keep her wits about her in a maelstrom.

Out of the darkness, Peter's kindly, bearded face appeared. Dena heaved a sigh of relief at the sight of him and pushed open the door.

'Well, hello there,' he said. 'I hear we're going to be neighbors.'

Tyrell knocked on the chief's door and heard him mutter something from inside which he took to mean 'enter'. He pushed the door open and walked in.

Lou was talking on the phone, but he indicated a seat and Tyrell sat down. The chief finished his call and replaced his receiver. Then he folded his hands in front of him on the desk. 'That was Van Brunt,' he said. 'He wanted to leave the conference and come right back.'

Tyrell nodded. He had no particular affection for the captain, Heath Van Brunt. He would be at his officious worst in a murder investigation.

'But I figured,' the chief went on, 'he's already up there in Rhode Island. I told him to see about renting a car tomorrow and checking things out in Boston. Talk to some people who knew Hubbell during his first marriage. The ex-wife.'

'Good idea,' said Tyrell.

'He thought so too. He's getting on it in the morning. Now, what have you come up with?'

Tyrell pulled his pad from his jacket pocket and consulted it. 'I spoke to the husband's secretary. He left for lunch at eleven o'clock and never came back. He cancelled with the client he was supposed to be meeting. We're trying to locate somebody who saw him where he claimed to be during those hours. Or on the train, or walking home from the train. We've talked to all the neighbors except for one old lady, who either wasn't home or was sleeping like the dead. The neighbors said she sometimes goes to stay with her daughter for the night. I'll try her again tomorrow. Anyway, nobody saw anything, but then again, nobody was home. Most of the families in the neighborhood have two people working. Those houses are empty during the day.'

'It's that way everywhere these days,' the chief observed. 'Well, maybe the old lady will know something. Those old gals can be nosy.'

'I'm waiting to hear back about the insurance coverage, and I'll know more about their finances when the bank opens tomorrow.'

The chief nodded.

'But I'll tell you one interesting thing. The secretary told me that the official word came down today that they are closing the company's Philadelphia office.'

Lou frowned. 'He just transferred here. They just bought that house.'

Tyrell raised an eyebrow. 'Stressful, wouldn't you say?'

'It bears some looking at . . .' the chief agreed. He picked up a pencil and doodled on his blotter. 'Definitely.' Then he looked up at Tyrell. 'That's good work for tonight.'

'We'll have the test results tomorrow. Blood types, all that . . . As for fingerprints, the poker was clean.'

Chief Potter nodded.

'There's one other thing I was thinking about, though.'

'What's that,' Lou asked quietly.

'Did you ask the Russell woman about Brian Riley?'

Lou shook his head. 'What for?'

'Lou,' Tyrell said. 'It just makes me nervous. We had him here, and we just let him walk out . . .'

'What's that got to do with the price of oranges . . .?'

Tyrell raised an eyebrow. 'The husband said they were at odds.'

'Why would he kill her?' Lou Potter cried. 'He had no reason to kill this woman.'

'Well, the husband indicated that she was angry at Brian Riley. Did he say why?'

'Just taking her friend's side in the argument, I imagine,' said Lou. 'Women sticking together. You know the drill.'

'I got the feeling it was more than that,' Tyrell persisted.

Lou sighed and hesitated. Then he spoke. 'All right, Tyrell, you're going to hear all this anyway, so let me just lay it out for you. Some years back, the dead woman's younger sister was living with Brian. A real romance, as far as I know. The usual lovers' spats, I imagine, but no real trouble. We never heard boo from her. Anyway the girl fell down in the shower and cracked her head open. A terrible accident. But, you know how it is. People have trouble accepting that accidents happen. They feel better if they can blame someone. So they blamed Brian. They tried to get us to arrest him but there was simply no evidence against him. Not a thing.'

'I see,' said Tyrell.

'So, naturally, Jennifer Hubbell was eager to take in the Russell woman. Try to turn it into an international incident.'

'Yes, but now we know that Riley is capable of violence . . .'

'Violence,' the chief scoffed. 'Miss Russell looked fine to me when she was in here a few minutes ago. Look, every lover's quarrel is not abuse. Every black and blue does not mean somebody was abused.'

'Hey, I know,' said Tyrell. 'I'm not saying he busted her all up. But, by the same token, you know how these things go down. Maybe Jennifer told Brian his girlfriend wasn't there and he thought she was lying to him. Maybe he got pissed off because he thought they were shielding her from him. You know – nobody comes between me and my woman.'

'He's not that kind of kid,' Lou insisted. 'That's number one. And number two, the one he's after . . . the one he's interested in is the girlfriend . . .'

Tyrell shook his head. 'They're not going to be satisfied . . .'

'Look, I'll question him. Don't worry,' said Lou. 'But it doesn't pay to have too many theories. Even Van Brunt, when I talked to him, liked the husband. Right away. These things aren't all that complicated. This wasn't random. There was no break-in, no sexual assault. No weapon carried in. This was an impulse that got out of hand. An argument, perhaps, that escalated . . . In a case like that, it's always the family. The husband. You know I'm right.'

'True,' the sergeant said doubtfully. 'That's usually the case.'

'We're just going to proceed in an orderly manner. Our first line of inquiry has got to be the husband. If we find out something else – fine. Now, it's late. Maybe you should head home and get some sleep. It's going to be a long day tomorrow.'

Tyrell took the hint and stood up. Then he shifted his weight and looked back at his boss. 'I just want to get whoever killed her, same as you,' he said gently. 'I don't guess I'll ever forget the sight of that poor girl.'

'Nope,' Lou sighed, and he squinted his eyes as if to ward off the memory. 'I know I never will.'

ELEVEN

Dena closed the door to Peter's apartment behind her and tiptoed in. Peter stood up and laid his book down on the table.

'Are the girls asleep?' Dena whispered.

Peter smiled. 'You don't have to whisper. It would take an earthquake to wake those two up.'

Still wearing her coat, Dena sat down on the chair beside his, holding her pocketbook in front of her.

'How did you like the place?' he asked.

Dena tried to smile. She had climbed the stairs and used the key Peter gave her.

The little apartment was technically furnished, although it was strictly a rudimentary collection of table, chairs and a bed. The places on the wall where the former tenant had hung pictures were dark rectangles of unfaded wallpaper. Still, there were clean sheets in the closet, and all the utilities were turned on. 'The place is fine,' she said.

Peter made a face. 'It looks a little bleak up there.'

'It's not that,' she said. 'I'm only looking for something very temporary. I'm just really worried that . . . Brian is horribly jealous, you know. It's completely irrational. He asked me if you were the father of my baby. Which would be quite a trick since I was pregnant when I moved here. Pregnant when I met you.'

'I assume you told him that we are not—'

'Of course, I told him,' said Dena wearily. 'He doesn't hear it. I'm a little worried that he might take his anger out on you, or . . . God forbid . . . the children.'

'He doesn't scare me,' said Peter. 'I can protect my children.'

'I hate to put this burden on you. I swear I'd leave this town tonight if I could. I'd already made up my mind to go to my sister's. She's expecting me. But now the police say that I have to stay here until they know who killed Jennifer.'

Peter frowned. 'Oh, well, we'll make the best of it. How about a cup of tea?' he said, walking over to the sink and filling the teakettle. 'I was just going to make myself one. It's herbal,' he said. 'It will be relaxing.'

'I'm going to go up,' she said.

'It won't take long,' he said.

Dena leaned back in the chair. 'OK thanks. Just for a few minutes.'

He turned on a burner and set the teakettle atop it. Then he began to rummage around in the cupboards. 'You've had quite a night,' he said.

'It was horrible,' she said, staring blankly ahead, thinking of Jennifer.

'Did you know this woman for a long time?' Peter asked. 'The one that was killed?'

'I knew her a long time ago,' said Dena. 'When we were in high school together. She was a wonderful person.' She glanced up at Peter, who was arranging mugs and tea bags on the counter.

'Well, it's a shame,' he said, in the tone of a person trying to display interest in a stranger.

'It's a nightmare,' Dena said. 'I keep thinking about her poor husband. And her father. Jennifer's mother died this past year. And her sister was killed—'

'Killed?' Peter asked.

Dena thought about telling him the whole story. Tanya's tumultuous history with Brian and her suspicious death. Not tonight, she thought. All she could think of was Jenn tonight. 'She died in an accident,' Dena said.

'That's too bad. What did the police want to know from you?' he asked.

Dena sighed. 'They wanted to know about Ron and Jennifer's relationship,' she said. 'If they argued.'

'Do they think *he* did it?' Peter asked.

'I told them it was impossible. They were happy together.'

'Although you did say you hardly knew them,' Peter observed.

'I knew enough,' Dena insisted. 'It wasn't Ron. They're wasting their time trying to blame it on Ron.' She thought again of Jennifer, telling her about Tanya's death. Her suspicions about

Brian. 'I have a terrible feeling that this goes back to something that happened a long time ago . . .' she said.

'Dammit,' he cried, shaking his hand and jumping away from the stove.

'What happened?' she asked, getting up. She felt suddenly self-conscious for having maundered on about Jennifer. Most men, she reminded herself, weren't interested in stories about your old friends.

Peter shook his head. 'I picked up the teakettle without a potholder. Damn.' He put his fingers under the cold water tap.

'Are you OK?' she asked. She came over and picked up his hand, which was trembling under the cold, rushing water of the faucet. She examined his fingers. There were red streaks on his fingers. 'You're going to have some blisters, all right,' she said. 'I'll put something on it.'

She turned the burner off under the kettle and went down the hall, passing a doorway with a paper cutout of a ballerina taped to it. Inside, by the nightlight, she saw two blonde heads resting on the pillows of the twin beds, although one of them was moaning and flopping around in her sleep. Dena smiled at the sight of them. Finding the bathroom, she collected Band-Aids, antibiotic ointment, and Tylenol from the medicine cabinet. When she returned to the kitchen, Peter was gingerly drying his hands on a towel.

'Here, sit down,' she said. 'I'm used to this. I work in a kitchen. This happens all the time. Take these,' she said, handing him two tablets and a glass of water. 'It's good for the pain.'

Peter swallowed the tablets without water, and sat silent as she applied the ointment and a couple of Band-Aids to his fingers.

'There,' she said. 'I hope that's not going to keep you from playing the piano.'

Peter flexed his fingers, frowning at them. 'No, I'll be all right.'

'Do you want that tea now?' Dena asked, lifting the kettle with a potholder.

Peter nodded. 'I'm sorry. I interrupted you. You were talking about your friend.'

Dena shook her head. 'No, never mind.'

'I didn't mean to cut you off like that. It just hurt,' he said.

Dena shook her head. 'I was just rambling on,' she apologized.

Dena set his steaming mug down on the counter. She had lost her own taste for tea. And company. 'Maybe I'd better go up to my . . . new digs,' she said grimly.

'You know,' he said, obviously trying to dissuade her. 'I've been thinking about the baby.'

'My baby?' she asked.

'Your baby, of course,' he said. 'I don't think people pay enough attention to the months prior to a baby's birth. I mean, it's a living creature. It can feel the stresses and sorrows of its mother. I really believe that.'

'I do, too,' said Dena, feeling guilty. How much stress had her baby felt already? How much sorrow? This pregnancy had been far from idyllic.

'Well,' he said, tapping his mug, 'by the same token, I think the baby can benefit from things that are soothing, and uplifting. Like music, or . . . herbal tea,' he said.

Dena smiled and nodded, although she really didn't care for the floral fragrance of the brew.

'Or poetry. I often read poetry to my girls before they were born.'

'What a nice thing to do,' Dena said.

'So, I'd be honored if you'd let me do the same thing for your baby. Just a little poetry now and then, to soothe you.'

Dena shook her head. 'That's not really necessary.'

'Come on,' he said. 'I'd enjoy it.'

'I really should go up,' she protested. But she could see the slight disappointment on his face, and she was, in truth, in no hurry to go to bed in the cheerless apartment above. Besides, she would probably only lie awake, thinking about Jennifer.

'Come on,' he said. 'It won't take long.'

'I could use something soothing tonight,' she admitted. She put her hand gently on her belly. 'We both could.'

Peter led her to her chair and sat her down. She looked up at him gratefully.

'You must have had wonderful parents, to be so caring.'

'Not at all,' he said, tucking an afghan around her legs. 'A sheer disaster. But, it taught me something valuable. I made up my mind that when I had children I would do everything differently. I would do what was best for my children. No matter what.' Peter sat down on the floor beside her and picked up his book off the end table. He cleared his throat.

'But how do you know what's best for them?' she wondered.

Peter shrugged, and found the poem he was seeking. 'You make a world where nothing can hurt them.'

'There is no such thing,' she said sadly. 'No one can guarantee that.'

'I didn't say it was easy,' he said. 'But it's what you have to do.'

Tyrell Watkins pulled up outside the pink and white bungalow where he lived with his grandmother, Ella Brown, and his younger half-brother, Cletus. He knew his grandmother would already be in bed. She went to bed earlier and earlier, ever since his grandfather died, and a lot of evenings Tyrell never saw her. But, despite the fact that his grandmother was probably trying to sleep, the insistent, thudding beat of some rap group was shaking the house. Cletus was home.

Tyrell wearily got out of his car and trudged up to the back door, opening it with his key. They never left the door unlocked. When Ella and Reggie Brown had first bought this house, way back when, it had been a nice, neat, family neighborhood. That was before drugs seeped into the lives of the people here, chipping away at their children's futures, turning a nice neighborhood into one where you had to bring your plants in at night for fear that some crackhead would steal them and sell them for a pipeful. Ella and Reggie had raised four kids in this house. Three of them were upstanding citizens – one of them was a college graduate. Drugs had only stolen one of their children – it happened to be Tyrell and Cletus's mother, Gerry. Twelve years had elapsed between the birth of Gerry's two sons. She was back on drugs within months of both of their births, and had deposited them with her parents to raise.

The back door opened into the kitchen, which was well-worn but spotless. There was a light on over the stove, and a plate covered with aluminum foil on the counter. His dinner.

Tyrell smiled, thinking about his old grandmother. He had quit the Marines to come back here because Cletus was a teenager and Ella fretted that she couldn't handle him. And secretly, he knew, she had been a little bit alarmed by the changes in the neighborhood. So, he had come back to his home and joined the police. Tyrell figured as long as he was here, she was perfectly safe, and the truth was that most of their neighbors were good, churchgoing people he'd known most of his life. Anyway, he felt at ease in this neighborhood, and he didn't much like the idea of living in some brand-new condo where nobody spoke to you from one week to the next.

Tyrell peeked under the foil and saw greens and cornbread on the plate. Good, he thought. I could eat a plate of that. Then went down the hall to the bathroom to wash up. As he walked past Cletus's room, he pounded on the door. Cletus opened it after a moment. He was smaller than his older brother, and darker-skinned. He wore short dreads and steel-rimmed glasses. On and off, Cletus attended the community college, and worked in the supermarket part time. At work he work a neat uniform, but the rest of time he favored his baggy, hip-hop clothes that he was wearing now. As far as Tyrell knew, he was no druggie, but that didn't mean he was out of danger. He was still a kid. Tyrell didn't dare to trust him, and didn't much care for some of the friends that came around looking for him.

Cletus looked impassively at his older brother through a narrow space in the door. 'What?' he said.

'You really need to ask me what?' Tyrell said. 'Grandma's trying to sleep. I can hear that music two blocks down.'

'Hey man, Grandma don't mind. She turns off her hearing aid and she doesn't even hear it. Besides, she goes to bed at eight o'clock.'

'Well I don't want to hear it,' said Tyrell. 'So turn it down.'

Tyrell went down the hall to the bathroom, and washed his face. He heard the thundering beat diminish. As he straightened up and was drying his face on a towel, Cletus appeared in the doorway, leaning against the frame. His clothes were as drab as rags, but Tyrell knew for a fact that the sneakers he was wearing cost nearly a hundred dollars.

'So,' said Cletus. 'What's shakin'?'

Tyrell shook his head. 'Long day,' he said.

'Hey, I heard some white girl got whacked in town.'

'That's right,' said Tyrell. Tyrell started down the hall toward the kitchen and Cletus followed him. Cletus opened the refrigerator and stared into it while Tyrell took the foil off his plate and put the plate in the microwave he'd bought his grandmother three Christmases ago. For the first year, she never would use it. But she was beginning to find it useful. While the food heated up, Tyrell flicked on the TV suspended above the refrigerator that he had installed for her. He found a basketball game and muted the sound.

Cletus took two beers from the refrigerator and set one down

at the table for his brother. Then he straddled the back of a chair.
'So you had a murder?' he said admiringly.
'We had a murder.' Tyrell could not deny the feeling of
importance it gave him to intone those words.

Then, despite the gratifying effect of his brother's admiration, he
remembered the image of that poor girl on the floor, beaten up like
that. His look of satisfaction faded as he sat down with his plate.
'Who was it? What happened?'
'White girl. Pregnant. About thirty. Nice house on Chestnut
Street, all ready for the baby. Somebody came in and beat her to
a pulp.'
Cletus grimaced. 'Robbery?' he said.
Tyrell understood the grimace. Everybody knew that most
robberies these days were for drugs, and robbery suspect could
be a code word for black man. Everyday life was tough enough
without that. Tyrell, who was wolfing down his food, hardly tasting
it, shook his head. 'I don't think so. No break-in. No sexual assault.'
'No break-in. That's good.' Cletus sucked down some beer and
tapped the bottleneck against his perfect white teeth. 'So, who
iced her? Her old man?'
Tyrell paused to take a drink of beer himself. He sighed, taking
in the offhanded way his brother said it. It wasn't real to him. It
was just like a TV show. He hadn't seen that poor girl, lying on
the floor with the blood everywhere. 'I can't say,' said Tyrell,
staring up at the players who were zooming up and down the
basketball court. 'It's too soon to say yet.'
'It's always the old man,' said Cletus knowledgeably.
Tyrell raised an eyebrow. 'You're an expert?'
Cletus shrugged. 'Everybody knows that.'
Tyrell swigged his beer and wondered. Naturally the husband
would lie, and pretend to be broken up if he did it. And, of course,
Cletus was right. The husband was always the prime suspect. Even
if he was halfway around the world at the time she was killed,
they'd still be looking at the husband. But he couldn't help thinking
it was kind of strange – that story Lou told about the victim's
sister and Brian Riley. Lou didn't seem to think that connection
meant anything. But Tyrell wondered.
'So you gonna do the Sherlock Holmes thing, bro?'
Tyrell stifled a smile. 'Oh yeah,' he said. He had to admit that
it was pleasant to sit there in the dim light of the kitchen, having

a beer and a conversation with his brother. They were at odds so often these days. When he'd been a child, Cletus had admired his older brother. Then, as he grew to adolescence, his attitude began to get worse and worse. They had trouble finding a common ground these days. The subject of a murder in town was of general interest, and Tyrell allowed himself to enjoy the companionable moment. But before he had even finished the beer he was drinking, he knew he was going to spoil it. He couldn't help himself.

'You go to classes today?' Tyrell asked. 'Or were you out hanging with the homies?' Cletus was smart – everybody knew it. He got a scholarship for his first year at college. But he didn't much care for school.

'No, man, I was not hangin'. I had extra hours at work today.' Cletus was already rising from his seat on the backwards chair. 'And you best stop talking to me like I'm twelve years old.'

'You gonna end up in that grocery store as the world's oldest stockboy if you don't start showin' up for those classes.'

'I'm not going to end up in no grocery store,' said Cletus. 'I'm gonna do just fine for myself.'

'Not if you don't get that diploma, you won't.'

'You don't have no diploma,' Cletus reminded him.

'We're not talking about me,' said Tyrell. 'I'm not the one we got to worry about.'

Cletus shook his head. 'Big Daddy's home,' he muttered.

'Where you goin?' Tyrell demanded, as Cletus walked over to the back door and pulled his oversized, zippered sweatshirt off a hook.

'I think I'll go find me some homies to hang with,' said Cletus sarcastically.

Tyrell fumed, and pushed his plate away. He didn't want to be his brother's keeper. But he had to do it. Somebody had to do it. His grandfather was gone and his grandmother was getting old. And nobody knew better than a cop how much trouble you could get into out there. He tried to remind himself that he had been young once, and had had an attitude himself. But tonight he felt old. Real old. He looked up at the young men on the television, playing their game. He knew it was work, but man, it looked like fun. To be flying across that shining floor, with nothing on your mind but speed, and the basket.

TWELVE

Heath Van Brunt eased his rented Lincoln Town Car up to the curb outside the elegant brick townhouse on Beacon Hill, and parked it with a sigh. This was his kind of a car. Roomy, luxurious and quiet. The drive from Providence had been a guilty pleasure, since he had exceeded the speed limit most of the way. But the ride was so smooth that you were over the limit before you even realized it. He'd had drivers say that very same thing to him when he was a traffic officer, but it had never prevented him from writing out a ticket. He was just lucky today to have evaded the radar.

Beside him on the caramel leather seat was a copy of the notes he'd taken over the phone from Lou Potter. Nothing unusual on the face of it. A divorce, no children, no obvious animosity between the parties. He was going to have to dig to find anything here. Heath started up the walkway to the house, aware of the attractive figure he cut.

He was fifty, but looked less than forty when he examined himself critically in the mirror. He'd jogged this morning before breakfast. His blue suit fit him closely, his shoes were shined, his reddish-blonde hair neatly trimmed. It was fortunate, he thought, that he happened to be in this vicinity at this particular moment. The idea of being far from Monroe, working on a murder investigation, gave him a sense of gravity and satisfaction that sometimes eluded him in the mundaneness of much of the work which came his way.

Heath rang the doorbell and stood back, folding his hands calmly in front of him. The door opened to reveal a fortyish woman with short, dyed-blonde hair and glasses. She was wearing a blue chambray shirt, sweat pants and running shoes. He looked past her into the foyer of the elegant old building, and realized it was not an apartment building, but a private home. He wondered, briefly, if Ron Hubbell had to support her in this fashion as a result of their divorce.

'Mrs Hubbell?' he asked.

'Are you Captain Van Brunt?'

Heath extended a well-manicured hand and she shook it un-enthusiastically and invited him in. He followed her into a Victorian living room and took the seat she indicated on an uncomfortable velvet settee. The house had been decorated in an authentic Victorian style, which included heavy, depressing window treatments, complete with swags and tassels. A laptop computer stood open on a massive mahogany desk, and there was a cup of coffee beside it, which she walked over and retrieved. She offered him a cup of coffee but he declined. She sat down opposite him with a sigh, in a tufted armchair, and crossed her leg in a fashion he found mannish, with her sweat-socked ankle resting on her knee. Behind her glasses, her gaze was level and unflinching. She did not seem to intend to speak first.

'Mrs Hubbell . . .' he began.

'Actually it's Edgerton.'

'You're remarried?' he asked.

'I use my maiden name,' she said.

'OK. Miss Edgerton. I guess you've heard about your ex-husband's wife being murdered. His new wife.'

'Well, when you called me,' she said.

'No mutual friends or relations called . . .?' he asked.

'We've gone our separate ways,' she said, shifting around in the chair, but keeping her cool gaze leveled on Heath.

'You knew your husband remarried, I assume.'

Anita Edgerton nodded. 'He called to tell me.'

'Did that bother you at all?'

She looked vaguely irritated, but her tone remained civil. 'Not at all. I was pleased for him.'

'Your divorce was amicable?'

'Yes, and long ago,' she said impatiently.

'But you have not remarried,' he said.

'No,' she said.

He looked around at the plush fabrics and antiques in the room. 'This is a very nice home you have here. Expensive, I should think.'

'We like it,' she said.

'We . . . being?'

'My partner and I. Look, Detective, what is it you want to know?'

Heath felt slightly offended and at the same time embarrassed at the implication that he was slow, in more ways than one. 'We're trying to determine if there was any reason Mr Hubbell might have had for . . .'

'Killing his wife? None that I could imagine,' she said. 'He is a perfectly nice man. And it seemed that he was delighted in his choice of a new wife.'

'Perfectly nice, but . . .'

'But what?'

'Well, you two obviously didn't get along.'

Anita Edgerton sighed. 'All right. I don't see any reason to dance around this. My partner, the person I live with, is a woman, Mr . . .?'

'Captain,' Heath said.

'Captain Van Brunt. Does that make things clearer?'

Heath did not intend to look like a country bumpkin in this woman's eyes. Small-town cop or not, he'd been around. He'd half guessed it already. She seemed like a dyke from the minute he set eyes on her. 'Were you seeing this woman while you were married?' he asked.

'No,' she said. 'I just . . . realized the marriage was a mistake.'

'Was your husband, Mr Hubbell, very angry when you apprised him of this realization?'

'Yes, he was angry. Did he go crazy and wave a baseball bat at my head? No. He is not that sort of man.'

Heath felt a dislike for this woman that made it difficult to be pleasant. But, he was here on a mission, so he continued. 'What sort of man is he, when he's angry? Have you ever known him to be violent?'

'No,' she said.

Heath folded his hands close to his diaphragm and licked his lips. 'Miss Edgerton, you seem to feel that I am imposing on you here. I would appreciate answers of more than one syllable, since we have a woman beaten to death in our town, and your ex-husband is the prime suspect.'

Anita took off her glasses and wiped a hand over her face. Heath could see the vestiges of a pretty woman there. She put her glasses back on, obscuring the view.

'You're right,' she said. 'I don't mean to be . . . rude.'

Heath waited, a prim look of rectitude on his face.

'I would say he is the kind of man who keeps his feelings pretty much . . . bottled up inside. Even when he's angry, he keeps it pretty well to himself. It's not so odd really. A common trait among us New Englanders.'

'I see. Was there anything in particular that would set him off. That you remember? Have you ever known him to snap out for any reason?' He could see her starting to reply without thinking. 'I'd appreciate it if you'd give this some thought. I don't want a glib answer, Ms Edgerton.'

She looked at him with narrowed eyes. Then she put her head back and examined the ceiling. She looked back at him. 'No,' she said.

'Surely you had arguments.'

'I would say we argued most often about money. He didn't care for credit cards, or bills piling up. Sometimes he was bothered about my spending. Even then, it was hard for him to actually say anything. He would brood until I insisted on knowing what his problem was. Sometimes, at tax time, we didn't talk to each other for several days at a time. Did he ever snap out? No.'

There was a sound of the front door opening, and a minute later, Heath caught a glimpse of a woman with longish hair and brightly colored scarves breezing past the doorway.

'Hi, it's me,' she called out.

'Hi hon,' said Anita Edgerton.

Heath felt like he wanted to throw up. That cheerful, intimate tone between them felt like fingernails down a blackboard on his nerves. Lezzies, he thought disgustedly. It's a wonder Hubbell didn't kill this one too.

The theme music marking the end of Matthew Riley's favorite morning TV program began to play, and the credits rolled over it. Matt made a noise of approval and shifted his gaze to his son, Brian, who sat in a slat-backed wooden chair, beside his wheelchair, his hands crushed together in his lap.

'Guh . . .' Matthew tried to speak. His handsome, leathery face was now slack on one side.

Brian nodded, as if he understood what the older man was trying to say, and patted him on the hand. 'You ready to go back now?' he asked.

Matt made another guttural noise and Brian responded, 'OK. We'll go back.'

He got up and came around behind the wheelchair.

Lou Potter, standing in the doorway to the TV lounge in the nursing home, watched them, his heart overflowing. He and Matt Riley had been boys together, playing cowboys and Indians in the woods. They had graduated from high school together, entered the service on the same day. Lou came home and married Hattie. Matt was on the horse circuit out West until he met Janine. How well Lou remembered the snowy winter's day when Matt introduced him to his wife.

Brian buttoned up Matt's shapeless cardigan and pulled it up across his lap so that it wouldn't catch in the wheels. Watching Brian, Lou felt proud of him. He was the right kind of a kid, treating Matt with such care and tenderness. He understood that Jennifer Hubbell's family was hurting, but that was no excuse for trying to blame it on Brian. And it didn't help that Brian's girlfriend was ready to jump right on the bandwagon. She was probably just mad that Brian didn't have the energy to cater to her, run out and buy her pickles and milkshakes in the middle of the night. Lou had no respect for women who expected everything given to them on a platter. He and Hattie had stuck together through some tough times. Some bitter disappointments. Hattie knew how to forgive without always reminding you about it. What happened to hanging in there when things got tough? As far as Lou was concerned, Brian was better off without that Russell woman.

Brian guided the wheelchair through the wide doorway and saw Lou standing there. He did not seem surprised to see him. Lou came often to see his old friend.

'Hey, Chief,' said Brian.

Lou squeezed Brian's shoulder. 'Hey son,' he said. Then he crouched down beside Matt's wheelchair and took his old friend's limp hand in his. Matt looked at him and tears came to his eyes. It wasn't unusual – this rock of a man now seemed to tear up at the drop of a hat these days – but it shook Lou every time he saw it. 'How's my buddy?' he said, trying to smile and ignore the tears.

Matt tried to reply. Lou could see that everything was functioning behind those eyes. All of Matt's intelligence and spirit were still there, but the body just wasn't cooperating. The frustration of it all was probably what made him cry, Lou thought.

'This isn't your usual time for a visit,' said Brian.

'Actually, I was looking for you,' Lou said, looking up at him. 'Matt, I have to talk to Brian for a minute. I'm on duty right now but I'll come back and see you later, OK?'

Matt frowned, as if perplexed and upset, and once again Lou cursed the duty that had brought him here this morning. A heavyset, middle-aged woman with glasses came down the hall looking at a chart.

'Lucy,' said Brian. 'Could you take my father back to his room?' The woman smiled benignly. 'The handsomest guy in the place. Of course I could. It's time for your medication anyway, Matt,' she said, assuming Brian's place behind the chair. 'See you later.'

Lou looked around and saw a quiet sitting area across from the nurse's station.

'Let's sit down, son,' he said. Brian followed him and they both sat down stiffly in a pair of turquoise blue armchairs beside a blonde-wood coffee table covered with unread newspapers, neatly arranged.

Brian sat at the edge of the chair. Lou couldn't help gazing at him for a moment.

He was a handsome young man, with that black curly hair and broad shoulders. Lou ran his hand through his own grizzled gray hair, remembering what it was like to be young, and handsome, like Brian. Before Lou could speak, Brian blurted out, 'Look, I know you told me to stay away from Dena, but I didn't do anything except try to talk to her—'

'It's not about that,' said Lou. 'Well, not directly, anyway. Have you heard the news this morning?'

Brian shook his head warily. 'After I finished in the barn I came right over here.'

'Jennifer Hubbell, the woman whose house your friend is staying at, was killed yesterday.'

Brian stared at him. For a second something flashed in his eyes that Lou could not exactly pinpoint. Almost a kind of . . . triumph, and then it was gone and Lou could not have sworn that he saw it. 'Killed? What happened to her?' Brian asked.

'She was murdered. Somebody beat her to death with a fireplace tool. Do you know anything about it, Brian?' Lou watched Brian's face carefully, out of long habit.

'What would I know about it?' Brian bristled.

'Hey, I'm not saying you do. I'm just asking you a question.'

'Nothing,' said Brian. 'I had nothing to do with it.'

'I'm not saying you did,' Lou protested.

'Yeah,' said Brian, 'but you know they have it in for me.'

'Who's they?' Lou asked.

'Come on, Lou. You know who I'm talking about. Tanya's family.'

Lou shrugged. 'I'd be lying if I said there were no hard feelings.'

Brian shook his head. 'They can believe what they want to believe. She fell. She hit her head. It happens. It's not my fault.'

'I know that, Brian. I closed the investigation, remember?'

Brian gave him a fleeting smile that felt like a reward. 'I know that,' he said.

'Still, I have to ask, son. Where were you yesterday afternoon?'

'In the barn. Working. Where else?'

'These are routine questions,' said Lou in a soothing tone. 'Now look, we know you were at the house the night before. You had an argument with the victim. What was that all about?'

Brian sagged in his chair. 'I knew it,' he said. Then he looked up. 'She was trying to convince Dena to leave me. She did a damn fine job of it too.'

Lou nodded. 'Well, you'd better know who your friends are in this thing.'

Brian frowned at him. 'What does that mean? Where is Dena now? She can't still be at that house after something like that.'

Lou found his question oddly inappropriate. 'I don't know. Some fellow from work found her a place. The information is at the station.'

Brian's eyes became hard. 'Who was it? What was his name?' he demanded.

'Who?'

'The guy from work. Was it Peter Ward?'

'Brian,' Lou said impatiently, 'I have no idea. I told her to call us with her information and I assume she did. That's not why I am here.'

'Why are you here?' Brian asked warily.

'Brian, the husband is . . . um . . . well, naturally he's looking for someone to blame.'

'Yeah,' Brian said sarcastically. 'Let me guess . . .'

'Well, he told us you had words over your . . . Dena staying there.'

'That was nothing. I was just . . . pissed at Dena'

'I know, I know. But it's how it looks, Brian.'

'How does it look?' Brian cried, running his hand through his dark hair.

'Her husband said you were angry about them taking Dena in.'

'They were interfering,' he said. 'Yes, I was angry about them interfering in my private business.'

'Did you ever threaten her? Mrs Hubbell?'

Brian glanced up at him and then looked away. 'What? No way! Who said that?' For a second, Lou had the unpleasant sensation that Brian was hiding something from him.

'The husband claimed you were very angry. Out of control.'

'No. I told you. No.' Brian looked around the little lounge as if he were trapped there. 'I don't know what you're talking about. I was working at the barn yesterday afternoon. You know I would never do that. You know me, Chief.'

'I'm sorry, Brian. I have to ask. There are going to be a lot of questions, not just from me.'

'I didn't go there,' Brian cried. 'No. No. *No.*'

'OK, son, OK,' said Lou. 'Take it easy. You know I don't suspect you. You're a good kid. You're . . . like a son to me,' he mumbled.

'I don't believe this,' Brian muttered.

'Look, your girlfriend was staying at their house. We're questioning everyone who was involved with these people. We need to find out who did this.'

'What about the husband?' said Brian. 'Maybe he's trying to blame me to cover his own butt.'

'We're checking him out,' Lou insisted, patting him awkwardly on the forearm. 'Don't worry.'

A frail, white-haired woman, her gnarled hands wrapped around the edge of her walker, stumped into the sitting area, looking at the two men indignantly. 'Where's my pocketbook?' she demanded. 'How do I get out of here?'

Lou and Brian exchanged a glance. There was something faintly comical about it, but neither one of them smiled.

Tyrell Watkins knocked on the door of the house three doors down from the Hubbells'. This door, once a shiny green, was dull, and there were flakes of green paint either missing or about to go missing. The whole house had a faded look, as if the owner had given up caring about it.

The peeling green door opened slightly, and a pair of rheumy eyes looked up at him in alarm, from behind the chained door.

Tyrell quickly held up his badge. 'Monroe police, ma'am,' he said, before the wary homeowner could slam the door in his face. 'We're asking questions about the murder of your neighbor, Mrs Hubbell.'

'You're a policeman?' a cracked old voice said doubtfully.

'Yes, ma'am. Officer Tyrell Watkins. Here's my ID.' Tyrell patiently held up his photo ID of himself in uniform. He couldn't blame anyone for being cautious – not after what had happened on this street. But he also felt pretty sure that if he was some freckle-faced white boy, they wouldn't be half so suspicious. Well, it didn't bear thinking about, he told himself, as the slice of face behind the door studied the badge and the ID he was holding.

'All right, young man,' the old person behind the door said, and the tone of voice made Tyrell relax slightly. It sounded just like what his grandmother would say, calling him 'young man' in that faintly reproving tone while she fumbled with the door chain. The door opened and revealed a very elderly woman, small and stooped, with an unruly fluff of white hair and arthritic hands that held a little, pilled-up cardigan sweater closed at the neck. 'Come on in, then,' she said.

Tyrell followed her into the stuffy, tidy house. The furniture in the living room must have been new in 1955. Everything matched, but was worn and faded. Family photos were framed on every available surface, and there were a number of prayers, embroidered and framed, which hung on the walls. A chenille bedspread was draped over the couch, and tucked neatly into the cushions.

She indicated an armchair for Tyrell, and lowered herself carefully down onto the couch cushions. A large, console television blared in the corner. Daytime talk shows.

The woman didn't even seem to notice it.

Tyrell consulted his pad. 'You're Mrs Drinkwater?' he asked.

'That's right. My husband Cyrus died nearly fifteen years ago. I live here by myself. I manage. It's not easy but I manage. Do you want a piece of candy?'

Tyrell glanced at the dish of Hershey's kisses, wrapped in red and green foil. He doubted she had stocked up early for Christmas.

More likely they were left over from last Christmas. 'No, thanks,' he said.

'Go ahead,' she said. 'They're good.'

'No, I try not to eat candy,' he said, and he patted his jacket, indicating his waist. He was rewarded with a peal of delighted laughter from the old lady on the couch.

'Oh, candy doesn't make you fat,' she said. 'Look at me. I'm skinny as a straw, and I eat candy every day.'

That's probably all you eat, Tyrell thought sympathetically. She was a gentle, cheerful soul, despite her obvious pain. 'Mrs Drinkwater, we knocked on your door last night . . .'

'Oh, I was probably asleep. I go to bed at seven thirty every night. I sleep like a baby. That's how come I lived so long.'

Tyrell mused that there might be truth in that. His own sleep was often fitful. 'We're wondering if you might have seen Mr Hubbell coming home yesterday.'

Mrs Drinkwater peered at her front windows, clean but discolored, covered by venetian blinds. 'Nope, but I wasn't looking.'

'Did you notice anything else? Strange people. Unfamiliar cars. Something like that.'

'Everybody around here is strange to me,' she said. 'I don't know anybody who lives here anymore. All the people I used to know on this street are gone now. Most of them are dead. Some of them moved to Florida. When Cyrus and I were raising our family here, we knew everybody. We'd all visit one another. The children would play together. Now, nobody's home all day long. All the mothers are off working. The kids don't get home till dark . . .'

'Yes, we noticed,' said Tyrell.

'Most days, I'm the only one here, it seems like.'

'Yesterday?' he prodded, seeing that her attention was wandering.

'Yesterday.' Her eyes had a faraway look.

Tyrell was clicking his pen shut, and preparing to close his notebook when she said, 'There was a green van.'

'A green van?' he repeated. 'New? Old?'

'Oh heavens, I wouldn't know.'

'Any logo?'

'Pardon?'

'Anything written on the side?'

'I didn't see anything.'

'How come you noticed it in the first place?' he asked.

'Well, there's a lot of workmen coming and going over there since they moved in. They're fixing up the place. I keep meaning to walk over there and ask one of them to take a look at my ceiling upstairs. I think I've got a leak in the roof. I told my son about it half a dozen times but he's been too busy to get by and I'm starting to worry about the water damage.'

Tyrell nodded, thinking guiltily of the household maintenance he sometimes neglected, even when he promised his grandmother he'd take care of it. 'What time was this? That you saw the van?'

The old lady knitted her eyebrows together in concentration and then shrugged. 'I don't know. Afternoon. Two o'clock. Two thirty, maybe.'

Time of death, he thought, his pulse quickening as he remembered the coroner's estimate. 'So, did you go over?' he asked.

'No,' she admitted. 'I got interested in my programs and I forgot to.'

'You didn't notice the license plate by any chance?'

'No,' she scoffed. 'Of course not.' Then she said more seriously, 'I wish I did. That poor child. How could anyone do such a thing?'

Tyrell stood up. 'I'm afraid we're still a ways from knowing that yet. But if you think of anything else . . .'

The old lady walked him to the door. 'I'll call you,' she promised.

'You put that chain on after I leave,' he said. 'And don't go offering those Hershey kisses to any old guy with a truck who looks like a carpenter.'

The old lady laughed again, cheerfully sheepish about his warning. 'I'll be careful, officer,' she said.

Tyrell stood on her doorstep and looked up and down the peaceful little street.

The old lady's observation had his thoughts racing. He had wondered about the husband. But what could turn a loving husband, even one coming home with bad news, into a raging killer? Could Jennifer Hubbell have been entertaining a visitor when her husband came home early from work, he wondered? A visitor who shouldn't have been there? A visitor who was driving a green van?

THIRTEEN

Dena unpacked a muffin and a cup of tea from the plastic convenience store bag, and set it out on the scarred surface of the painted gate-leg table. Then she put away the few groceries she had bought in the old refrigerator which had no light. Dena rummaged in a kitchen drawer for a spoon and a knife and sat down to her breakfast.

She had earned it. She'd been awake, on and off, for most of the night. Before dawn she was up, searching under the kitchen sink for cleaning supplies, washing and waxing every surface in the apartment. Even when a surface was clean, she found herself going back and wiping it again.

It felt crazy to her to be cleaning this way, wearing herself out before morning even broke. But it was better than lying in that bed. It prevented her from thinking. She knew, somehow, that Peter would be disappointed to learn that she had spent a miserable, restless night in the tiny apartment, despite his poetry reading and the herbal tea. It would take more than that to dispel the horror of yesterday's news. The thought of Jennifer and Ron, and their baby that now would never be born . . . The fear that maybe Brian was somehow involved . . .

Dena rubbed her own stomach protectively and sniffed, swallowing back the sobs that wanted to start again. She forced herself to breathe deeply, and then she placed the muffin on a faded flowered plate. Eat, she told herself, though she had no appetite.

Think of the baby. Despite the suspicions of the police, despite her own suspicions, she told herself it had to have been random. Blind chance. She herself might have been the victim, had she stayed home that day and been the one who had answered the door. The thought of that was no comfort. It made her feel slightly light-headed with anxiety.

The morning light shone weakly through the dormer windows, illuminating the meager furnishings of the apartment. It was a dreary little place but at least she was safe here. Brian didn't know where she was staying, and now that Albert knew better than to let him come around the restaurant, he had no way to contact her. How long will I be here? she wondered. Hopefully, not too long. But still there were a few things she would have to buy to make the place livable in, no matter how short a time she stayed. A reading lamp by the bed, a new shower curtain, a light bulb for the refrigerator. You can start today, she told herself, trying to think positively about feathering this temporary nest. Albert had told her not to come in today, so she could go to the hardware store and make a beginning. She was not going out to collect her things at Brian's. She was sure about that.

Dena chewed on her muffin without interest and burned her tongue on the first sip of hot tea. She was exhausted from the events of the last few days. Only a few days ago she had still been living with Brian, still trying to tell herself that maybe they could work out problems and be a family. And now, here she was, in these gloomy top-floor rooms with no mate and virtually no possessions. Don't look at it that way, she told herself. It's only for a little while. They're bound to find Jennifer's killer, and then you can get out of here. Go to Marcia's and wait for the baby. Start your new life as a single mom. The thought saddened her, as it always did, but she was beginning to get used to the idea.

Lots of women are single mothers. I can do it, she thought. My mother did it and I can do it. What choice did she have? Stop looking back, and regretting what might have been. Start planning the life you are going to have when you put this part behind you, she told herself.

She tapped absently on her phone. This afternoon, she would call Marcia and explain the delay. She dreaded the call, though. There was no way to explain other than to tell her that Jennifer had been murdered, and the word would send Marcia into a tailspin. Somehow she would manage to construe this as some sort of carelessness on Dena's part, that she'd had a friend who was murdered. Dena could so easily predict her sister's reactions. Still, she wasn't eager to get into it with her. Besides, there were other things to do. Dena struggled up from her chair, and pulled the magnetic pad off the refrigerator. Make a list, she told herself. Write it down and get started.

Now that the little apartment was clean, it was the best way she could think of to banish all the demons that assailed her when she just allowed herself to sit and think. Start to plan.

Dena wrote down, 'Linen outlet, hardware store,' and then, underneath that, 'Call Marcia.' It was a slim plan for a new life, she thought. But the very act of starting a list was comforting. She was just about to write down a fourth item when suddenly her phone on the tabletop beside her started to ring.

Dena jumped. The number was not one of her contacts. Then she shook her head. Telemarketer, she thought. Or maybe Peter. Wanting to know how she liked her new place. She wondered how she was going to work up any enthusiasm, so he wouldn't be too disappointed. She picked up the phone and took a deep breath. 'Hello,' she said.

There was a silence at the other end. At first, she thought it might be that automated delay, before the click and the phone solicitor kicked in with his spiel. 'Hello,' she said again, impatiently.

Silence again. And then, unmistakably, a breath at the other end.

'Who is it?' she demanded, although she knew there would be no answer. She heard the breath again, softer.

'Don't call me again,' she snapped, and slammed the phone back down on the table.

She snatched up her list and tried to study it. But she was distracted. Get a grip, she told herself. It was just some kids, fooling around. Or some bored idiot with nothing else to do. She took a deep breath. Just get back to your list. She put a hand to her forehead and closed her eyes.

Tomorrow was the funeral. She had to have something to wear. It made her furious to think that Brian had all her things. Holding them hostage. Well, she wasn't about to negotiate. He could keep them. Forget it, she thought. Don't even think about it. How could I have ever thought I loved him? 'Black dress,' she wrote, and then she put her hands over her stinging eyes.

The phone began to ring again.

When Tyrell arrived back at the police station, he had to push his way through a crowd of reporters to get inside. Lou Potter was already there, talking on the phone to Captain Van Brunt.

'All right,' said Lou, as he put the phone down, 'I'm afraid there's not much to go on.' He relayed to Tyrell the substance of Heath's conversation with Anita Edgerton and Tyrell told the chief about the green van.

'Well, it's a start,' said Lou, trying to sound optimistic. 'It all depends on how you look at it. I mean, the ex-wife says he worries about money. We know he has a baby on the way, and that he's losing his job. It could have led to quite an argument.'

Tyrell made a face. 'It's possible, but . . .'

'But what?' Lou demanded.

'But aren't we overlooking the obvious?'

'The obvious being . . .' Lou said coldly.

'Lou, I know the Riley kid is a friend of yours. But when you're talking motive . . .'

'I spoke to him, and he is not involved. Now, I think we need to have another conversation with Mr Hubbell,' said Lou. 'He's at the crime scene right now. He wanted permission to go into the house to pick out some stuff for the wife's funeral.'

Tyrell stood up. 'All right. Let's roll,' he said. He and the chief started toward the door.

'You drive,' said Lou.

The two men went out the back way, to where the squad cars were parked, but there were media people lying in wait there as well and they began to clamor at the sight of the chief.

'OK, OK,' Lou shouted over the din. 'I've told the others and I'll tell you. Tonight, at six, there will be a press conference over at the town council meeting room. Now, please, let us do our job.' Reluctantly, the crowd parted and Lou was able to get into the car beside Tyrell.

Tyrell took the wheel of the squad car as he was bidden, and the two rode in silence out to the Hubbells' stone cottage on Chestnut Street. As he parked behind Ron's car, Tyrell looked up at the sun glinting off the multi-paned windows in the porch of the house. Yellow tape was draped on stakes around the yard, marking the area as forbidden to trespassers. A patrolman stood guard at the door.

'What the hell's he doing outside?' said Lou in exasperation as they got out of the car. He marched up the steps to the patrolman, who greeted him respectfully.

'Why aren't you inside with Hubbell?' Lou barked. 'He could be destroying evidence while you stand around out here.'

The patrolman, who was little more than a boy, looked at his chief anxiously. 'He wanted a little privacy,' he said.

'Well, he can't have privacy,' Lou snapped. 'This is a murder investigation.' He brushed past the young man and opened the door to the front porch. He peered through into the bleak living room, opening the inner door and calling out, 'Mr Hubbell.' There was no answer. He indicated to Tyrell that he was going upstairs and the sergeant followed him, looking back at the spot where the body had been found. As they reached the top of the stairs, an older woman came out into the hall.

'Who are you?' Lou demanded.

'Ron's mother,' she said.

'Oh,' said Lou. He didn't have the heart to bark at her.

She pulled her sweater tightly around her, although it was warm in the house. 'Come in. We're going through my daughter-in-law's things.'

The two police officers followed the woman into the bedroom at the end of the hall. It was a cheery room, sun streaming in over the louvered shutters in the bottom half of the windows.

The double bed had a brass frame, and a quilt with flowers embroidered on it. The quilt was strewn with dresses and shoes. Ron Hubbell stood at the closet door, looking in with a blank expression on his face.

He turned and looked at the officers. His eyes were like sunken holes in his face. 'We're getting her clothes. For the funeral,' he said.

'You're not supposed to be up here alone, Mr Hubbell,' said Lou, and Tyrell was glad that he hadn't been the one to have to say it. He didn't know if he would have had the heart. There was something unbearably pitiful about the sight of him. It could be regret, Tyrell reminded himself, not devastation.

Rhonda Hubbell, who had followed them in, walked over to the dresses on the bed. 'This one, then?' she asked her son, holding up a pale blue knit dress with long sleeves.

Ron stared at the dress as if he could see his wife still wearing it.

'And the blue shoes, I think,' she said gently, tears sliding down her face.

Ron looked away and nodded, as if it didn't matter any more. Rhonda began to carefully fold the clothes and place them in a small bag.

'Mr Hubbell, can we talk to you downstairs?' Lou asked.

Ron nodded, and led the way to the staircase. He clutched the banister with both hands, as if he were a ninety-year-old man who needed it for support. He stopped in the living room, where an outline of his wife's body was still drawn on the floor. Turning away, he walked out onto the porch. It was a sunny space which could have been a lovely place to sit, but they had obviously not gotten that far in their work on the house. There were a couple of pieces of mismatched wicker furniture on the bare floor. Ron sat down heavily and stared straight ahead. Lou and Tyrell sat down on either side of him.

'Mr Hubbell,' said Lou. 'We need a little more information. We've had a report that someone saw a green van outside your home yesterday. Around the time of your wife's death. Was Jennifer . . . were you expecting anyone to be working here on the house yesterday?'

Ron looked surprised, almost excited for a minute, and then he sank back into lassitude. 'I don't think so. Sometimes people turn up, out of the blue, to finish up a job.'

'Anyone who drives a green van?'

Ron shook his head. Then he said, 'Maybe. I think the guys from Ranger . . . the electricians. They had a green van . . .'

'Could you give us a list of the people who were working on the house for you?' Lou said.

Ron thought about it for a moment. 'I guess so. Sure.' He made no move to get up.

'I'd like that list as soon as we're through here.'

'OK,' said Ron.

'Also, we still have a little problem with your whereabouts yesterday during the afternoon hours.'

'I told you,' he said dully. 'I came home early. On the one thirty train from Philly. I walked home from the station.'

'Did you see anyone you knew?' Lou asked.

'I don't know anyone here. We just moved here.'

'No one?'

'I saw some boys skateboarding.'

'Did you recognize them?'

'No,' Ron said.

'Would you know them if you saw them again?'

'No. I wasn't paying any attention.'

Lou shifted in his seat, his expression pained. 'How was everything at work yesterday, Mr Hubbell?'

Ron wiped tears from his eyes but made no sound.

'Anything unusual happen?'

Ron looked at him bitterly. 'You already know, don't you?'

'I'd like you to tell me,' said Lou.

'All right. I found out the office was closing. And, before you ask, yes, I was dreading telling my wife.'

Lou looked at his notes, though he had no need of them. 'That would have meant quite an upheaval for you and Jennifer. After you bought this new house, sank so much money into it . . .'

Ron looked at the walls around him. 'We didn't have time to even live here,' he said. 'We were never meant to live here.'

'. . . And everything is so much more difficult with a baby.'

Ron did not reply.

'Your ex-wife told one of our officers this morning that you had a tendency to get very upset about money.'

Ron stiffened, and then turned to glare at him. 'She said that? Anita said that?' Ron closed his eyes and his skin grew waxy, as if he was going to be sick. Lou and Tyrell exchanged a glance.

'Why are you doing this?' Ron whispered. 'I didn't kill Jennifer. Why don't you arrest Brian Riley? He was the one. He was responsible for the death of my wife's sister. He was over here ranting and raving about his girlfriend . . .'

'We have talked to him,' said Lou stubbornly. 'Now, we're talking to you.'

'I can't believe this,' said Ron. He swallowed hard. 'Why is that you are here badgering me while Riley is free to go about his business?'

'Mr Riley had no reason to kill your wife, Mr Hubbell. No matter what your wife may have thought, he had nothing to do with the death of her sister,' Lou said sternly.

Ron sank back into his chair 'I don't care what you do,' he said.

Lou stood up and Tyrell followed his lead. 'We are trying to track down your wife's killer,' Lou said. 'Can we have that list now?'

'What list?' Ron asked, confused.

'Of the guys who were on your job.'

Ron got slowly out of the chair. 'It's in the computer,' he said. 'I'll print it out for you.'

FOURTEEN

The light of day was fading and Peter's car was not in the driveway when Dena got home. Probably out with the girls, she thought. He was such a caring father. The kind of father any woman would want for her child. Dena put the thought out of her mind and popped the lid on the trunk of her car. She got out and went around to the back to collect her packages. She looked into the well of the trunk at her assortment of plastic shopping bags. She'd gotten a lot accomplished, considering how drained she felt and how little she had wanted to even leave the safety of her dreary rooms.

Her phone continued to ring and no one was there. Twice more she had answered it only to be met with silence, before she silenced the ringer. Let him call all day, she thought. But her defiance was shaky. The thought of him pursuing her on the phone made her feel lonely and vulnerable. She forced herself not to think about Brian. She tried to focus on the items she had crossed off her list. At least now she would have the basic necessities to make life livable in the apartment.

As she gathered the bags up in her arms, she wished that she could forget all this and just get on a plane to Chicago. Then, in spite of herself, she thought of Marcia's warning about airplane trips. Why did people say things like that? Even when they were being alarmists, it had a tendency to stick in your mind. All right. The train then, she bargained with herself. Whatever it took to get away from this place. Why did the police insist she stay here? She didn't know anything more about Jennifer's death. But at the same time, she felt guilty, feeling sorry for herself when the person who was hurting the most was Ron. Losing his wife, and being a suspect at the same time. It was too much to bear. Especially when it was so obvious that he was not to blame. While the police were ignoring . . . No, she thought. No. It couldn't be.

Laden with shopping bags, Dena walked up to the front door and reached down to open it. As her fingers touched the doorknob, the door swung open and she saw it. The pane of glass nearest the lock had been smashed out. Inside the dimly lit vestibule, she could see the shards of glass still glittering on the floor. She saw the little half-round table with mail on it, the closed door to Peter's apartment, and the foot of the stairs. The inside of the house was quiet. She looked around in the street, but there was no one else in sight. There were cars in a few neighboring driveways, but no people, anywhere.

Dena's heart started to race. She took a cautious step into the foyer. 'Who is it?' she demanded. 'Anybody here?' There was no answer.

She held the front door open with her foot and tried to look up the staircase to her own doorway. It got darker as the stairs went up, and she could not see her own landing for the gloom. She summoned her angriest voice. 'Brian, is that you?'

Once again, there was no answer. He wouldn't just stand there in the dark, not answering. Even Brian wouldn't do that, she told herself. And then she thought about Jennifer. Who had been lying in wait for her? Someone was out there. Someone as yet unknown to the police. Dena hesitated, and looked back at her car. Maybe I should go out and get in my car and drive away. Someone had broken that window and unlocked the door. They might still be inside.

Her arms were trembling, and she felt as if she could not hold her bags a moment longer. She set them down, propping the door open, and then, remembering her trip to the hardware store, rummaged in the Truvalue bag and pulled out the hammer and set of screwdrivers she had bought on impulse, waiting in line. She weighed them in her hands, and tossed the screwdrivers back in the bag. Gripping the hammer, she felt instantly more in control. She hesitated at the propped-open door, trying to decide.

He was trying to scare her. To unnerve her and keep her off-balance. The thought of him coming after her, breaking into her building, did scare her. But, at the same time, the idea of him trying to intimidate her was infuriating. She'd been single for years, and never been afraid to walk into her apartment building, even in the dark. Now, because of her baby's father, she was hesitating at her own doorstep, unable to go in to her own place and sit down, after a weary day. You bastard, she thought. I know it's you. And I'm not going to let you ruin my life. She hefted the hammer, and thought, for a moment, that she hoped he *was* still

there. The thought of whacking him with it was almost tempting.
All right, get it together, girl, she chided herself. You can't let him
win. You have to be able to go into your apartment without someone
holding your hand. There's not going to be anyone to hold your
hand.

She left her bags at the door and then, deliberately, Dena began
to hum, and mount the stairs, her grip damp on the handle of the
hammer. With every step she glanced up, and the landing became
clearer and more visible. She frowned when she saw that, indeed,
there was something at her door, but it wasn't a person. It was
some sort of squatty, oblong *thing*.

As she neared the landing, she recognized it. For a moment she
felt weak with relief. And then, in the next instant, furious. Brian
had been here all right. The object on the landing was her gym
bag. Nothing else. No other suitcases. A white envelope that said
'Dena' rested between the straps. Dena exhaled a noisy sigh. She
quickly unlocked her door and tossed the zippered bag inside. It
was light, as if it had almost nothing in it. The thought of him
choosing a few items to return to her was humiliating somehow.
Oh well, at this point she'd take what she could get, she thought.
She was grateful that Sergeant Watkins had had the presence of
mind to pack up that one bag for her on the night she left Brian.
Otherwise, she'd be shopping for underwear over at Goodwill.

Wearily, she went back down, gathered up her packages,
slammed the door shut behind her and locked it. She remounted
the stairs and went inside.

Humble as it was, Dena was glad to be back in the little apartment. She sat for a minute, collecting her thoughts, and then went
into the kitchen and put on the kettle for a cup of tea. Slowly,
deliberately, she went about opening and emptying the bags she
had bought while she waited for the water to boil, ignoring the
gym bag and the note which seemed to shout her name. She
distributed the little comforts around the house – put up the new
shower curtain and laid out the bathmat, hooked up the reading
lamp and arranged the new toiletries she'd bought. At one point
she thought she heard a faint, unfamiliar scratching sound,
but when she stopped to listen, she didn't hear it anymore. She
went back to her housekeeping, throwing out the scraps of old
soap, and wiping off the soap dishes for the fresh bars. She
unwrapped the flawed, but perfectly serviceable new sheets she'd

picked up at the linen outlet and went to the empty closet and
hung up the black, knit dress she had managed to find at the Kmart.
She left the hammer on the table.

The teakettle whistled and she went in and poured herself a
cup. Then, she sat down at the dinette table and pulled the gym
bag over to her. She smiled at her own naiveté, remembering,
when she moved here, that she had vowed to work out right up
until the day she gave birth. That resolve had faded as her girth
expanded. Maybe I'll start again, she thought. Go back to the gym.
She tossed the envelope off the bag and opened the zipper.

At first, she thought it was empty. She could see nothing in the
dark recesses of the bag except for something that looked like a
hairbrush. You bastard, she thought. I want my stuff back. She
started to reach inside, to lift out the brush, when all of a sudden,
the hairbrush moved of its own volition. Something scrambled in
the bag. Not a hairbrush. Fur. Coarse, bristly fur.

She screamed, and dropped the bag. The pointy snout, and agitated
black eyes of a barn rat protruded between the zipper teeth.

'Oh my God,' she cried, 'oh my God.' She was covered with
gooseflesh and her heart was beating wildly. She clapped her hands
over her mouth to keep from screaming as the creature scrambled
out of the bag and darted across the floor, its long tail vibrating.
The rat scurried frantically along the molding, its clawed feet
scrabbling against the floorboards, until it suddenly dove into a
dark, narrow space in one corner and disappeared into the wall.

Dena's stomach was turning over and, for a minute, she thought
she was going to vomit. She hugged herself, and shuddered. It
was in the wall. Her wall. She'd seen it go in there. Oh my God,
she thought. For a second she huddled there, too terrified to move.
Then, she realized she had to act quickly. You can't let it come
back in. Pull yourself together. Cover up that space. With what,
she thought, looking around frantically? Under the sink. She went
over and opened the cabinet door with trembling hands. There
were some rags in a pile, next to the cleaning items. She picked
up a handful of rags, went over and squatted down, stuffing the
rags in the hole. Then she looked around the room, her eyes darting
from one corner to the next. Anything that looked like a hole was
stuffed with a rag.

She looked around and saw, with sense of revulsion, her gym
bag, still gaping open on the floor. I will never use this again, she

thought. I don't even want it around me. She reached down and picked up the bag. With one swift motion she zippered it up, and quickly shoved it into one of her empty shopping bags, so that she would not even have to touch it. Holding the shopping bag at arm's length, she opened the apartment door and looked around outside. The hall was quiet. She went downstairs, and took the bag out to the trash cans behind the house. She picked up a lid and dropped the whole thing inside, holding her breath against the smell of the garbage. She jammed the plastic lid back down and ran back into the house, shivering. She mounted the stairs, went back into the apartment, slammed the door and locked it.

The white envelope with her name on it was lying on the floor in front of her. She bent down, picked it up and tore it open, her hands trembling. There was one sheet in the envelope and, on it, he had written only one sentence. 'You cannot do this to me,' it said.

Dena crushed the paper in her fist and threw it across the room. The crinkled ball of paper landed only a few feet away from her. She sat back down in the chair, her eyes suddenly brimming with tears, staring at the piece of paper on the floor as if it were alive.

The phone rang, and she jumped, muffling a shriek. She stared at the ringing phone with hatred, as if the person at the other end could see the animosity in her gaze. After about ten rings, echoing in the silent apartment, it stopped. Dena looked again at the wadded up note on the floor. She could still picture the words on the page. *You cannot do this to me.* Oh Brian, she thought. How could I have been so wrong about you? And her next question, the one she didn't even want to consider was, what are you capable of? Are you completely crazy? Was it you whom Jennifer found when she opened the door the other day? She realized that the possibility of it was paralyzing. She was afraid to even get up from her chair.

Then she set her jaw. No, she thought. Whatever you are, you cannot do this to *me.* She pushed herself out of the chair, picked up her phone and pressed a contact number.

A woman answered. 'Monroe police department,' she said.

'I'd . . . I'd like to report a break-in,' she said.

'Is this an emergency?' the dispatcher asked. 'Do you have reason to believe that the intruder is still on the premises?'

Dena looked around the dreary little apartment. 'No,' she said. 'No. He's gone. It was my old . . . boyfriend, but he's gone.'

'Oh,' said the dispatcher. 'OK. Well, give me the information.

I'll send a car around. We're shorthanded right now. They're having a press conference.'

'OK,' said Dena, obediently supplying the information.

'Will someone be there to let us in?' asked the dispatcher.

Dena felt her heart sink, as she looked around the apartment. 'Yes,' she said.

'We'll get somebody over there as soon as possible.'

'Thank you,' Dena whispered. She could not stop shivering. She put her coat back on. It made no difference. In the bedroom, on the sagging twin bed, she saw the blanket and an old quilt. She went in and crawled up on the bed, her back against the headboard, the blankets wrapped around her. Her teeth were chattering, and her fingers which clutched the blankets, were like ice.

The room in the Town Hall where the city council met every Tuesday was a modestly sized ochre-colored auditorium with a wall of windows that looked out on the gray beauty of the Delaware River rolling sluggishly by. The proscenium was outfitted with a horseshoe-shaped table with a microphone at each place, and the floor of the auditorium held rows of seats, supplemented today by folding metal chairs, which were normally set out only for meetings regarding the most controversial of local issues.

This evening, the room was crowded, and wires crisscrossed the worn wood floor like black snakes. Reporters and video-cam operators from Philadelphia, Trenton and even New York stations had converged for the police press conference regarding the brutal murder of Jennifer Hubbell. It wasn't that murder itself was so unusual – these reporters had a murder or more a day to choose from in their home cities. No, it was the contrast between a savage murder and the idyllic environs of Monroe which made for compelling footage on the evening news. Monroe was the kind of town where people flocked on three-day weekends, filling up the quaint inns and bed and breakfasts, strolling by the river, antiquing in the shops. The image of a girl, battered and left for dead in the charming little cottage on these idyllic streets, was worth the trip out of town.

Chief Lou Potter, the mayor, Tyrell Watkins and two other city council members were conversing, sotto voce, in preparation to taking their seats. A young man who worked at the high-school audiovisual department was tapping on the live microphones in preparation for the briefing. Reporters for the local weekly news-paper and the radio station, long-haired and dressed in jeans, regarded the big city reporters, clad in expensive blazers and perfect hair, with a combination of contempt and excitement. It was unde-niably heady to be in on a story that could summon this kind of firepower, and to have the inside track. On the other hand, it was embarrassing to be called on and have to announce the name of a paper or a station's call letters with a zero recognition factor.

The high-school kid at the microphone said, 'Testing,' and the sound boomed out across the room. The middle-aged news director at the local radio station announced in a loud voice, 'Well, if everybody would shut up, maybe we could get started. Some of us have a station to run. We can't sit here all day.'

As if in answer to this complaint, Lou Potter took a seat at the center of the dais, and the others began to seat themselves on either side of him. 'Good evening,' said Lou into the microphone, and the volume made everybody jump. Lou frowned at the hapless technician from the high school, who quickly made some adjust-ments. Lou waited patiently and then, when the young man had withdrawn, Lou leaned over the mike again.

'I have a brief statement to make and then I'll take questions.' He began, in a modulated voice, to recite the facts of the case as they were known to the police. Before he could even finish, questions were being shouted from the floor. Lou tried to answer them as they seemed relevant.

'No, we don't have a suspect in custody and yes, at the present time, the victim's husband is cooperating fully with our investigation.'

'Is it true that the victim was pregnant?' asked a reporter.

'Sadly, yes,' said Lou.

'What about the battered woman that was staying there?' shouted a man in a trench coat whom Lou had never set eyes on before. Lou glanced over at Tyrell with an incredulous expression, as if to say, how do they get this information? Tyrell looked down at his folded hands and shook his head. Like Lou, he was amazed that strangers could descend on the town and seem to know more than they did, overnight.

'The Hubbells did have a houseguest at the time of the murder. The woman was at work when this happened. Naturally, we're questioning everyone in the household.'

A loud buzz erupted in the room and Lou pointed to a female

reporter from Philly who was standing near the back. Beside her, the back door opened, and Captain Van Brunt slipped into the auditorium. 'Chief, what about reports that you are looking for a workman who might have been there on a job?' the pretty, no-nonsense reporter asked in a loud voice.

Lou cleared his throat. 'We are trying to locate anyone who might have information about Mrs Hubbell's death. I have no other comment on that at this time,' he said. 'When we have any more information, we will pass it along to you. That's all.'

Abruptly, Lou stood up. Tyrell, still seated, looked up and saw that Heath Van Brunt, dressed in a three-piece suit, was cruising in their direction. Lou, who was swarmed by reporters, did not see his captain approaching, so Tyrell came down off the dais to greet him.

'Hello, Captain,' he said. They shook hands perfunctorily. 'Did you just get in?'

Heath looked around at the mob of newspeople and his eyes shone with excitement. 'About ten minutes ago. Good to be back,' he said.

Tyrell knew that he should say, Good to have you back, but he wasn't that accomplished a liar. 'How was your trip?' he asked.

Heath tugged at the hem of his vest in a gesture Tyrell found irritating. 'Interesting. The conference was extremely informative. My interviews in Boston didn't prove especially illuminating, however. I guess you heard about my visit with the ex-wife.'

Tyrell nodded. 'We already spoke to him about it.'

'Everybody I talked to up there was knocking themselves out trying to tell me what a nice guy he was,' Heath complained.

'He still has no alibi,' Tyrell said.

'Well, that's something,' Heath said hopefully.

'He seems genuinely broken up,' Tyrell admitted.

'What's this bit about the workman?' Heath asked. He leaned toward Tyrell and Tyrell could smell garlic on his breath. 'I heard somebody asking about that when I came in.'

'Something I got from a neighbor,' said Tyrell. 'She saw a green van parked outside there at the approximate time of death.'

'Really?' Heath considered this with interest.

'We're checking on the workmen who were involved in their renovation. I thought maybe the husband surprised her in a tryst when he came home early. You know, some guy that had been around, working on the house . . .' Proud of his theory, Tyrell was quick to share it. 'Even the nicest guy might flip out over that.'

'Oh, when it comes to wives, it wouldn't take all that much,' said Van Brunt dismissively. Then he laughed. 'That's right. You're not married. How would you know?'

His tone was insulting, but Tyrell refused to let his irritation show. 'We're going to try and locate the van.'

The captain did not seem enthusiastic. 'Any luck so far?'

'It looks like the only green van belonged to Ranger Electric. I'll go over there and talk to them tomorrow. See who had it out.'

'See who had keys,' Heath corrected him importantly. 'Ranger Electric. I know that outfit. They did some work for Bev and me. They've got a black kid working for them who has a juvvie record. I recognized him when he came to the house. I can tell you I kept my eye on him while he was working there.'

Tyrell stiffened. 'Really,' he said coldly.

Heath shrugged. 'It could be important. It could have been a robbery that went south.'

'There wasn't any break-in. Nothing stolen.'

'Maybe she let him in. Maybe she knew him from having been there before. Let him in, and then caught him trying to palm something. Check it out.'

Tyrell felt his temper rising, and reminded himself that he was outranked. 'Yessir,' he said. Yessir, you'd love that, wouldn't you? That would fit right in with your preferred profile. A violent, senseless killing? All you had to say in this country was 'black man' and everybody nodded knowingly. The all-purpose villain.

Sometimes Tyrell wondered how he was ever going to work for Van Brunt when Lou retired. Tyrell had been a soldier, and he was used to answering to people he did not especially admire, but there was consolation in the fact that those people had to answer to others higher up than them. This was different. Chief of police in Monroe was the top of the food chain. A virtual dictatorship.

Van Brunt finally saw his chance to reach the chief and he sidled over, close to Lou's ear. Tyrell looked at Lou's tired face, the dark circles under his eyes, and, even more than usual, he worried about the chief's health. Van Brunt, by contrast, after a long road trip, looked relaxed and healthy. As if he could go on forever. Apparently conscious of the sergeant's eyes on him, Van Brunt turned and winked at Tyrell in a conspiratorial manner. Tyrell was unable to smile.

FIFTEEN

A sudden thump on her bed woke Dena from a dreamless chasm. Her heart leapt to her throat and she tried, in vain, to scream. All that came out was a strangled squawk. Confused by the darkness in the room, and her own awkward position, slumped against the headboard, she struggled up to a sitting position and looked around wildly, trying to get her bearings. Her eyes locked with another pair of eyes watching her from the end of the bed. She gasped, and then recognized the intruder.

'Tory, my God,' Dena cried, groping about until she found the switch of her new lamp and turned it on. The soft light scattered the shadows.

'What?' The child, wearing a flowered T-shirt and jeans, knelt at the end of the bed.

Dena tried to catch her breath. Her heart was thudding like a jackhammer. 'You scared me. How did you get in here?'

Tory held up a key. 'We used to come up here all the time when Miss Kay lived here.'

Dena leaned forward, hampered by her large stomach. 'You shouldn't have done that,' she said angrily. 'Give me that key.'

The child looked abashed and handed it to her. 'I'm sorry,' she said in a small voice. 'I wanted to surprise you.'

'You surprised me all right.' Dena rubbed her face and looked around. 'You scared me half to death.' Dena couldn't believe she had fallen asleep. Since about the third month of her pregnancy she could almost fall asleep standing up. But she wouldn't have thought it was possible after . . . The last thing she remembered was sitting there shivering in her blankets.

Tory curled up in a ball, as if to hide. Dena saw the contrite look on the girl's face and took a deep breath. 'Oh, it's all right,' she said irritably. 'Just don't ever do that again.'

The child glanced at her warily, and Dena smiled. 'It's OK. Really.' Dena looked at the clock. 'What time is it?'

'After supper,' said the child.

'Where's your dad?' Dena asked.

'He's downstairs, fixing the window,' she said.

'Oh. Oh no,' said Dena, frowning. She wanted to show it to the police. 'Somebody broke it,' said Tory. 'He had to fix it.'

'I know,' said Dena. 'I know.'

'I got an A in social studies, today,' said Tory.

'That's great,' said Dena, distracted. 'Did the policeman come yet?'

'What policeman?' Tory asked.

'Never mind,' said Dena. 'What were you saying?'

Tory frowned, as if disappointed. Then she gave Dena a sidelong glance. 'Why are you wearing your coat?' she asked.

Dena sighed, remembering. 'I was cold,' she said. 'I didn't want my baby to be shivering.'

'Is that it, in your tummy?'

Kids don't believe in the stork anymore, she thought. In answer to Tory's question, Dena nodded and rubbed her stomach.

'Can I touch it?' Tory asked.

Dena was a little taken aback, and her first impulse was to say no. But really, she chided herself, there isn't any harm in it. 'All right. Come here.'

Tory slipped off the end of the bed and came up beside Dena, who sat up on the edge. 'Here,' she said, placing the child's hand on her corduroy jumper. 'He moves around a lot. Can you feel it?'

The child frowned, and stared down at the scatter rug beside the bed, trying to discern some sign of movement under her small palm. All of a sudden she jumped away from Dena, and grabbed her hand as if it had been burned.

'I felt it,' she cried, her eyes wide with surprise. Dena laughed, delighted at the child's reaction.

'Tory,' Peter's voice cried out.

Dena and Tory exchanged a glance. The child looked alarmed.

'She's up here with me, Peter,' Dena shouted.

She wasn't sure if he heard, but in a moment she heard the muffled sound of footsteps on the stairs. He tapped at the open door and came into the apartment. 'Tory, what are you doing up here?'

The child looked up at her father. 'I felt the baby moving around. Inside her tummy. She let me.'

Peter frowned. 'You're bothering Dena.'

'She's not bothering me,' said Dena. 'She was just curious. I hope you don't mind,' she added quickly, suddenly realizing that Peter might not want his second grader to know that much about unborn babies. 'She asked me if the baby was in my tummy, and could she feel it . . .'

Peter's frown faded, and then he smiled. 'That's such an incredible sensation, to feel a baby moving like that.'

'It was doing a cartwheel, Dad,' Tory announced.

Peter held his palm up and pointed toward Dena's stomach. 'Could I feel it?'

Dena was startled by his question. 'Well . . .' she said, uncertainly.

'I remember when my wife was carrying the girls, how wonderful it was to feel that new life. I guess I would just like to experience that again . . .' he explained.

It's fine if it's your own wife, your own children, Dena thought. She wondered if she was being overly sensitive or prudish or something. It wasn't as if it was a sexual thing. All he wanted to do was feel a baby's movements.

She didn't know how to refuse without sounding uptight. Or, worse, making the child feel that her father had committed some kind of inappropriate gaffe.

'I guess so,' she said unwillingly.

He walked over and knelt down beside the bed like a communicant at an altar rail. 'Can I feel it again, Dad?' Tory asked in a hushed voice.

Peter looked up into Dena's face. 'Can she?'

Dena was suddenly struck by the innocence of it all. Here were two people who were awed by the fact of her baby's life. She was ashamed of her own hesitation. I'm just not used to the attention, she thought. I'm used to having this baby ignored.

'Sure,' she said.

'Come here,' he said to Tory, gesturing for her to join him. The child came up beside him and he took her small hand and placed it gently beside his own.

They both waited, smiling at each other and at Dena. Then, obligingly, the baby did something that felt like a somersault in the womb. Tory's face lit up again, and Peter let out an exclamation of delight. He gazed admiringly at Dena. 'That's an athlete,' he said enthusiastically.

Dena blushed, but was pleased. 'I hope so,' she said.

'I'm sure of it,' he said. He rose to his feet as Tory said, 'Let's wait, Dad. Maybe he'll do it again.'

'Oh no, miss. Let's get going. I left Megan alone downstairs to come looking for you.'

'OK,' said the child reluctantly, and slid off the bed. As she started for the door, she turned to see if her father was following her.

'I'll be right along,' he said. Then he turned to Dena. 'I replaced the broken pane of glass. Did you forget your key?' he asked wryly.

Dena shook her head and hoisted herself off the bed. 'It was Brian,' she said. 'I'm sorry, Peter.'

Peter shook his head. 'I thought so.'

'That wasn't all,' she said.

Peter frowned. 'What?'

'Don't tell the girls.'

'What happened?'

'He put a . . . rat . . . a barn rat in my gym bag,' she shuddered again at the thought.

Peter screwed up his face in disgust. 'What happened to it?'

'When I opened the bag it jumped out and ran into the wall.' She pointed to the mounds of rags in the corners of the room. 'I put those around so it couldn't get out. But I'm worried about your place. The children.'

He shook his head. 'Don't worry. More likely it made its way down the wall and is long gone by now. Those shingles out there are like Swiss cheese. You wouldn't want to spend the winter here.'

'I hope you're right,' said Dena. 'You'll check around, won't you?'

'Oh, sure.' His gaze was steely. 'He's dangerous, you know.'

'Yes,' she said faintly. 'I know.'

'Dad,' Tory screamed from downstairs. 'Police.' Peter's eyes widened.

Dena could hear footsteps mounting the stairs. 'I called them,' she said.

'Well, I'll just get out of the way,' he said, ducking out the door.

'Thanks Peter,' she called after him.

'Don't mention it,' he said. He sidestepped Tyrell who had arrived at the door.

'Sergeant Watkins,' said Dena, somewhat relieved to see his familiar face.

Tyrell watched Peter descend the steps and then looked around with a frown at the dingy little apartment, and Dena, standing in her rumpled jumper by the stove. She didn't look natural in this setting, he thought. She was pretty in a quiet way. Despite her huge belly she looked fragile, refined. This run-down house didn't suit her at all. 'I'm told you had a break-in,' he said calmly, as if he didn't recognize her.

She handed him the note. 'He broke the glass so he could let himself in and deliver this.'

Tyrell read the note without comment and handed it back to her.

'It came with a small present,' she said bitterly. 'A rat.'

Tyrell maintained a blank expression, although he felt secretly shocked at her announcement about the rat. He thought of the young man he knew, Boots, who had always been kind of friendly, and even-tempered. Tyrell had trouble trying to picture him doing something so . . . bizarre. Of course, these spurned lovers could be crazy. He looked over at her. 'When you say *he* . . .'

'You know who I mean,' she said, annoyed at his obtuseness. 'Brian Riley. The man who hit me the other night. He's been calling me on the phone repeatedly. Just breathing into the phone.'

'You sure it's him?'

'Who else would it be?'

'You say he broke the glass?'

'Yes, and let himself in.'

'Looked fine down there,' said Tyrell.

'Well, my neighbor fixed it when he got home.'

'He should have left it,' said Tyrell. 'How long ago did this happen?'

'I don't know. I got home a couple of hours ago.' Tyrell sighed and Dena saw him shift his weight. 'Please, sit down,' she said politely.

'You should have called us right then,' he said, refusing the chair.

'I called, soon afterwards,' Dena protested. 'Look, why are you acting like this is my fault?' she said. 'A man broke in my house. I'm . . . I'm making a complaint.'

'Did he enter your apartment, or just the vestibule?' Tyrell said.

'Just the vestibule?' she said in disbelief. 'Does he have to be hiding in my closet before you'll do something about this?'

Tyrell pursed his lips and then he set one long, graceful hand down on the back of a chair. 'Can I change my mind?' he asked.

Dena nodded curtly.

Tyrell removed his hat, sat down and tapped his long fingers on the tabletop. 'Miss Russell. You say Riley called you on the phone but you don't *know* that it was him. All right, he left you a note, unsigned . . .' he smacked the paper deprecatingly with the back of his hand, 'but it doesn't constitute a *threat*, per se. You say he broke a window, but I don't see a broken window . . .'

'My neighbor will testify about the window,' Dena cried. 'And, he put a rat in my gym bag and left it at my door.'

'And where is this rat now?'

'It ran into the wall and I blocked up the hole. Pardon me for not keeping it here in the apartment. Are you saying you don't believe me? Why would I make this up?'

Tyrell held up a hand to silence her. 'You say you're afraid of this man, but you saw the broken window and, instead of calling the police, you entered the premises by yourself.'

'I didn't want to give him the satisfaction,' Dena said defensively.

Tyrell gazed up at her with skeptical brown eyes. 'Of what?'

'Of . . . ruining my life. Destroying my peace of mind.' Dena sank into the chair across from him and stared at the note on the table. 'Look, I don't want to have to look around every corner. I don't want him hounding me. I just want him to stop,' she said. 'You can make him stop, can't you? Isn't it against the law to do things like this? Can't I get a court order or something? The other night you told me I could.'

Tyrell leaned forward and gazed at his steepled fingers. 'Well, the other night you probably could have. But, you didn't press charges, so the other incident . . . you can't take it to court.' He deliberately made it sound as if it were her fault. He didn't mention the fact that the chief had made sure there was no record of a complaint. He didn't tell her that they were officially required to pursue domestic violence complaints – with or without the cooperation of the victim.

And he didn't tell her that when her call tonight was reported, the chief made sure Tyrell was the one to answer it. Tyrell avoided her gaze and tapped on the note. 'And while this was an ugly thing to do, no judge is gonna issue a restraining order 'cause of this.'

Dena folded her arms over her chest, resting them on her belly. 'So you're saying there's nothing I can do?'

'We'll fill out the paperwork on this,' he said. 'I'll file it. The next time something happens, you call the police right away. You don't go take a bath and have supper and then decide to give us a jingle.'

Dena felt her face flame at this suggestion of her own culpability. 'I didn't take a bath. I called for help and you were all too busy to come.'

'We're a little preoccupied,' he said, 'with trying to find out who killed your girlfriend.'

'I know,' said Dena, chastened. 'Look, Sergeant. This is not some kind of . . . game I'm playing with Brian. I don't provoke him. I don't want any more to do with him. I wouldn't even be here in this town any longer if it weren't for the murder investigation. The chief told me not to leave town, so I am stuck here.'

Tyrell stood up, avoiding her angry gaze. 'I'll speak to Mr Riley about this – see if we can't get him to understand how he needs to clean up his act.'

'I doubt he'll listen,' said Dena, but nonetheless she felt somewhat relieved. 'But I'd appreciate it.'

'No problem,' he said.

'Any news about Jennifer's murder?' she asked.

Tyrell shook his head, and then looked at her curiously. 'You spoke to her that day. Did she mention any work she was having done? We're trying to figure out if she may have hired someone to do some work on the house that day.'

Dena shook her head hopelessly. 'No. I don't think so. She was doing some errands that day. Going for a sonogram. I still can't believe it. I can't believe it's her funeral tomorrow.'

'If you think of anything,' he said. He handed her a card with his cell phone and his beeper number on it. 'And if you have any further problems with Mr Riley . . .'

'I will. I'll call you. And thank you, Sergeant.'

'Just doing my job,' he said defensively. He didn't want her to thank him. It made him feel guilty. Guilty and worried. He'd been trying to trust that the chief's instincts were right about Brian Riley. Why else would he dismiss such a promising suspect? But if the truth were known, he thought, as he clattered down the stairs of the seedy duplex where Dena was trying to live and mind her own business, he hadn't exactly been working on her side.

SIXTEEN

The next morning Tyrell did not want to get out of bed. When the alarm went off he was deep asleep, dreaming about a river, and a boat that was caught in some tangled branches at the edge. He was trying to set the boat free, and the sun was warm on his back through the trees. When the buzzer sounded, and he opened one eye to look out at the gray day, he gave some serious thought to just turning over. The habit of being dutiful forced him to his feet and he dressed and ate the breakfast his grandmother had fixed for him in a fog. He was halfway to the station house when he remembered his promise to Dena Russell. He considered letting it ride, but the memory of her sitting there, with that heart-shaped little face and that big belly made him feel guilty again. So he detoured away from the center of town and headed for the rural area of Monroe.

It was drizzling when Tyrell pulled up on the gravel drive next to the Riley farm. He would speak to Riley, and get it over with. He pounded on the back door of the house and heard a cranky voice from inside telling him to wait. The door opened and Boots stood there, bleary-eyed and still in his stocking feet. His scowling, unshaven face broke into a boyish smile at the sight of Tyrell.

'Hey man,' he said. 'What are you doing waking me up?'

'Did I wake you?' Tyrell asked, surprised.

Brian waved at him cheerfully. 'Nah, I'm eatin' breakfast. Come on in.'

Tyrell followed him into the ranch house. The house smelled of stale beer, and there was an empty Johnny Walker bottle lying on its side on the plaid couch. Tyrell remembered the beer smell from his last visit here – the night of the 911 call. Tyrell followed Brian through the house. The TV was on in the living room, some morning news show playing, but the only light came from the kitchen. The house was visibly messier than it had been the other night. The woman's touch was definitely absent.

Newspapers were piled up, the garbage can was overflowing, and there was a pile of dishes in the sink. In spite of himself, Tyrell found himself thinking about Tanya Smith, Jennifer's sister. Was this the house where she died? Slipped in the bathroom and cracked her skull. Slipped. Fell.

There was a half-eaten bowl of cereal on the table, and a box of Pop-Tarts. Brian noticed the expression of disapproval on Tyrell's face and waved his hand around dismissively. 'The place is a mess. I'm not used to being a bachelor again,' he said. 'You married?'

Tyrell shook his head and took the seat that Brian indicated. 'No.'

'How'd you escape it all this time?' Brian asked with a dimpled smile. 'Handsome guy like you.'

'I was in the Marines, up till two years ago,' said Tyrell.

Brian nodded. 'So that's why I haven't seen you around all these years. I figured I would have run into you one way or another by now. You hungry, man?' Brian asked, as he resumed his seat behind his cereal bowl.

'No, you go ahead, Boots. My old granny got up with me this morning. Made me eggs.'

Brian hooted as he picked up his spoon. 'Boots. Shit, man. Nobody's called me Boots in ten years.' He began to dig into his cereal. He was pale, and his eyes were red-rimmed. 'Well, Boots is all right. But don't say eggs, man. I don't even want to think about eggs.'

Tyrell smiled, knowing the feeling. 'Tough night,' he said.

'Oh, yeah,' said Brian. He peered at his former teammate through bloodshot eyes. 'You mean to tell me you live with your granny?'

Tyrell smiled self-consciously. 'I finally left the service to help her out with my younger brother. He's a handful.'

'You lived with her back in high school,' said Brian.

'You got a good memory,' said Tyrell.

'Well, I remember some things,' said Brian, pointing a milk-edged spoon at him. 'I remember you were a pretty fair wide receiver. I remember you and I stood up to a bunch of thugs in the parking lot one Saturday.'

Tyrell shifted uneasily in his seat. Somehow, even though it was his most vivid memory of their acquaintance, he didn't like Boots being the one to bring it up. It made him feel vaguely . . . leaned on. 'I remember that too,' he said.

'So what brings you out here,' Brian said casually.

Tyrell frowned. 'Business.'

'Oh?' said Brian innocently.

'Your girlfriend called us last night.'

Brian pushed his bowl away and leaned back in his chair. He ran a hand through his curly black hair and sighed. 'Oh God, I'm sorry. I don't know what I was thinking, man. I've just been so pissed off at her.'

'Well, she's getting plenty pissed off at you. You got to back off, man. They've got laws against this sort of thing. Stalking. Harassment.'

Brian looked pained. 'You're right. I know it. I just, I just . . .' He threw his hands out and looked helplessly around the messy kitchen. 'I just can't believe what she's doing to me.'

In spite of himself, Tyrell had a sudden image of Dena, cowering in the bathroom the night of the 911 call, with that bruise darkening on her pale face. 'What do you expect? You hit her, man. You hit a pregnant woman right in the face.'

'I know. I'm ashamed of that. I had too much to drink. But man, what would you do if you found out your woman was cheating on you? I'm not even sure anymore that that baby is mine. And then, she moves in with him, right under my nose, all the time telling me that she's not sleeping with him. It's . . . it's killing me, you know.' Brian's voice broke, and Tyrell was embarrassed to see tears in the other man's eyes.

'She has her own place, you know,' Tyrell said gently. 'She's not living in his apartment. She lives upstairs from him.'

'Right. And that means they're not fucking,' Brian said hopelessly.

'Look, I know it's not easy, man,' Tyrell said. 'But, I'm telling you that you can't be breaking into her house and sending her a bag of rats or you're going to find yourself in a world of shit.'

'I didn't mean anything by it,' Brian protested. 'I meant it as kind of a joke.'

Tyrell was trying to be sympathetic but this word jarred him. 'A joke?' he repeated.

'Not like a funny joke,' Brian said quickly. 'More like . . . I
don't know. I just wanted to get her attention. She's treating me
like some kind of a . . . a rat. She's making me feel so low. I can't
reason with her. She doesn't listen.'

'Look man, I realize you're hurting. But you can't do this any
more. The chief told you. Now I'm telling you. Whether she's
involved with this other guy or not, she's breaking it off with you.
Breaking up is tough, everybody knows, but you got to accept it.
Get on with your life.'

'She doesn't mean it,' said Brian.

Once again, Tyrell found himself imagining Tanya Smith. He
pictured her as having long auburn hair, just like her sister, Jennifer.
He wondered if she had been trying to break it off with Brian
Riley too.

'She does mean it,' he snapped, more angrily than he had
intended. 'You've got to get that through your head.'

'You're right,' said Brian miserably. 'I'm sorry. I wasn't thinking
straight.'

Tyrell stood up, towering over the man at the table. 'Now look,
I'm warning you. Cool it. Do you understand? Just back off.'

Brian looked up at him and nodded. He looked like a child,
Tyrell thought, with his messy hair, a spoonful of Cheerios halfway
to his mouth, tears standing in his eyes. Just like a little wounded
boy.

The McGrath-Lewin Funeral Home sat on top of a slight rise just
three blocks out of the center of Monroe. It was a big, ungainly
house, renovated within the last twenty years for the express
purpose of catering to the bereaved. Thus, it was a house with
four living rooms of varying sizes, although it was a rare and bleak
day in Monroe when all the rooms were in use at once.

On this drizzly gray morning, Terry McGrath, the funeral
director, had taken the drastic step of hiring a valet for the parking
lot. This young man, in an ill-fitting navy blue suit and an umbrella,
was rushing around trying to keep up with the crush of arriving
cars. Lou Potter waved off his attentions, pointing to his ID stuffed
under the visor on the driver's side of his sedan. Then he pulled
up and parked it on the far side of Terry McGrath's car.

Lou got out of the car and adjusted his trench coat over
his sports jacket and his slacks. He had thought about wearing his

uniform, but he was afraid it might upset the family. Besides, he didn't want to stick out as a policeman. He wanted to be able to observe the people here discreetly. A solemn-faced man whom he did not recognize opened the door to the funeral home for him and stood back saying, 'Hi, Chief.' So much for discretion, Lou thought.

He nodded, and rubbed his palms together nervously. Taking a deep breath, he walked up the wheelchair ramp and into the vestibule. 'Will you sign the guest book, please, for the family,' asked another, dark-suited employee of McGrath's.

Lou took the pen and signed, glancing at the other names there. Then he handed back the pen and looked around, taking in the scene.

Lou had been to a lot of funerals in his life, many of them here at McGrath's. He had buried Hattie from here two years ago. The painful memories were like a corkscrew in his chest. But, he reminded himself, most of the funerals he'd attended were for the elderly parents of friends, or relatives who had passed on. Lately a few had been for his contemporaries, men in their sixties. But there was a vast difference between occasions like that, and the one he was present at today. There were always more than enough seats to go around when the dear departed was old. Although there were always tears, there were also frequent smiles, swapped stories, and exclamations of surprise at the funeral of one who had enjoyed a long life, well lived. There was a certain relaxed atmosphere at the services for the very old, especially after long illnesses. People gathered to say goodbye, but also to share in the relief of pain ended. People took solace in the hope that married partners, often long separated, were now together in the next life, old friends reunited in a better place. People often wore soft colors and cheerful patterns, as if they were off to an Easter service at church.

The crush of people here today, however, was in an entirely different mood. There were angry murmurs, and anguish was thick in the atmosphere. The sounds of sobs, not sniffling, rent the air as Lou pressed his way into the crowded salon where Jennifer Hubbell was laid out. Dark clothes and black veils abounded in the mint-colored room with its statuary niches, and boxes of Kleenex were placed on every end table. Every seat was taken, and people stood, lining the walls, speaking in low voices and staring in fascinated horror at the sight of a dazed, exhausted-looking Ron Hubbell, seated beside a closed casket banked by an unruly riot of floral arrangements. A heart-breaking wedding picture of Jennifer, her hair sprinkled with white flowers, her smile a blaze of happiness, was propped atop the coffin.

At the front of the room, Ron's parents huddled together on a damask-covered settee, sniffling into handkerchiefs. Ron sat alone, seemingly oblivious to the other mourners, and stared at the coffin which held the body of his wife. When someone bent over to speak to him, or squeeze his arm, he would whisper a reply, but his gaze never wavered from the bier. Occasionally, he would reach up and touch the shining, wooden casket. The terrible look in his eyes made Lou feel like a voyeur for just glancing at him. As he looked around the room, studying the faces, Jake Smith came up to him and began to pump his hand.

'Lou,' he said urgently, 'do you have news for us?'

'Well, we still have a lot of questions,' he said, being deliberately vague. 'I hoped I might be able to talk to some people here. If you could introduce me. I know it's a terrible time . . .'

'No problem,' said Jake. 'I need something to do. I can't just sit and look at her.'

Lou knew Jake was referring to his daughter's coffin. Years of running the hotel made introductions and social patter as natural as breathing to Jake Smith. He began to introduce Lou to people in a low voice.

'This is Susan . . . what is your name now, dear? Hammersmith. She was a friend of Jennifer's in high school.

'I hadn't seen her since she got back,' Susan explained, dabbing at her eyes. 'I've been away. But we often got together over the years, when she'd come home in the summer, or at the holidays.'

Lou asked a few questions, and Jake moved on resolutely through the crowd, making introductions and remembering names as if this weren't the worst day of his life.

'Over there,' said Jake, pointing across a row of heads, 'is Mayor Elwell. You know him, obviously. And beside him, sitting by herself there, is Dena Russell. You remember, Jennifer's friend that was staying at their house.'

As if she had heard her name, Dena looked up and met the chief's critical gaze. Lou noted that her eyes were red-rimmed, and she had a wad of Kleenex crushed in her hand which she used to dab at her tears. Although the chief disliked Dena, without even knowing her, for having driven Brian to such despair, he could, at least, see that she was genuinely stricken.

'And this is Laura Mallory. And her fiancé, Skip Lanman,' Jake continued. 'Laura and Jennifer were best friends in Boston. They flew in last night.'

Lou looked into the puffy, reddened eyes of a pretty woman with long, ringleted dark hair and a splotchy complexion. The fiancé stood stoically by, clutching a handful of Kleenex. 'I'm so sorry,' Lou was moved to say by the sight of the woman's misery.

'Thank you,' she said politely.

'Cold up there in Boston?' Lou asked, trying to make small talk.

'Laura came in from Chicago, actually,' said the fiancé, trying to spare her the need to reply. 'She was out there on . . . uh . . . business. I came down from Boston. It is a little chillier there than here actually.'

'Who would do this?' Laura wailed, oblivious to their stilted conversation. 'Jennifer was . . . the best . . .' Her words ended in a squeak as fresh tears overflowed.

'Miss Mallory, maybe you can help us with our inquiries. Did Jennifer have any enemies that you knew of?'

'Oh, Chief, you don't know how crazy that sounds when you talk about Jennifer.'

'Were there any problems in the marriage, anything she might have only told a best friend?' he asked Jennifer's distraught friend. 'Any indication that either one of them might have been . . . well, you know, seeing someone else?'

Laura Mallory seemed to understand the seriousness of the question, and she gave the chief as level a gaze as she could muster. 'I swear to you, Chief Potter. There was nothing. Ron adores her. They are the happiest couple . . . Were,' she added in a whisper.

'What about Ron, Mr Lanman? Was he in the habit of confiding in you? Did he ever mention any . . . suspicions he had about Jennifer? Any . . . evidence of infidelity?'

Skip Lanman was a frail-looking man, but his answer was authoritative. 'Infidelity, absolutely not. That's outrageous. It's not even . . . it's unthinkable.'

'Don't be angry, sir,' Lou said. 'We have to consider every possibility.'

Laura looked over at Ron Hubbell, paralyzed beside his wife's casket. 'Can you honestly look at that man and think he could be responsible . . .?'

Skip put his arm around her as she began to sob.

'It's awful,' Lou agreed. 'But we need to find out who *was* responsible. If either of you thinks of anything . . .'

Laura rubbed her forehead as if she had a headache. 'You'll have to excuse us, Chief. I took a Valium before I came and it's hard to think . . .'

'I understand,' Lou said. 'But if you could *try* to remember. Anything Jennifer might have told you that could be important . . .'

'We will. I promise you. But right now . . .' She shook her head, unable to say more, pressing the soggy hanky to her streaming eyes.

Lou patted her gently on the arm. 'You can call me at this number any time,' he said, handing her a card. He left her, and continued to move through the crowd. Most of the people there were friends of Jake Smith, here to console the grieving father in his darkest hour. But there were a lot of young people too. He recognized employees from the hotel, and Jake introduced him to three young people who had been in Jennifer's Sunday School class some fifteen years ago, and felt they had to come. Lou asked Jake about one woman, a bohemian-looking person with gigantic dangly earrings. Jake drew a blank, but she turned out to be Jennifer's Lamaze instructor. It was overwhelming, the number of people touched by the fate of this young woman, who had grown up here, and come home, only to meet this horrible death.

The minister from the Presbyterian Church stepped up to the podium at the front of the overflowing chapel and cleared his throat. The noise died down to a murmur, punctuated by gasps and the groans of those too overcome to respond to the call to order. The minister began to speak, and Lou looked around the room, seeking the eye averted from the gospel readings. Most people were either weeping with their heads bowed, or listening intently. Everyone around him seemed to be crushing in closer for the minister's words of comfort and warning, although this was one of those cases where only the deeply faithful were going to find solace in their prayers. For the rest, there was pity and fear.

Lou waited through the first prayer and then began discreetly elbowing his way to the door. He found himself thinking about his granddaughter's birthday party this afternoon. Those little kids' parties sometimes gave him a headache, and he avoided them, but today he was going to make time to go. It would be like an antidote to the misery of this occasion. Lou felt as if he was being hemmed in by the crowd, squeezed into too small a space. He found it difficult to catch his breath until he found his way to the door, and pushed his way out to the parking lot.

SEVENTEEN

Protected from the drizzle by the canopy above the open grave, the minister addressed the umbrella-wielding mourners. 'The family has requested that you join them back at the Endicott Hotel immediately after the service.'

There were murmurs and more tears as the minister said the final blessing, and people began to drift back to their cars. Dena lingered beside the shining coffin, strewn with single roses, saying a prayer and bidding her friend a silent farewell with her head down.

When she looked up, she saw Ron standing at the foot of the bier, staring at her. She wished she could hide from his tormented gaze, but there was no avoiding it. No avoiding what needed to be said. She walked haltingly to him. 'Ron,' she said. 'I'm sure you must blame me for this. If I hadn't come to stay with you . . .'

'It might have happened anyway. We don't know,' he said.

'I know what you think though,' she said.

Ron did not reply. She understood what his silence meant.

'I'm just praying that it's not true,' she said. 'I'll never stop feeling guilty.'

'Jennifer wanted you there,' he said firmly. 'She was glad you came to us. That was the way she was. She never got over . . . what happened to her sister. Wishing she had done more . . .' He had difficulty continuing.

Dena squeezed his hand. 'You and I don't know each other that well, but I know how much she loved you. How happy she was to be your wife.'

Ron lifted one of the roses from the coffin and cradled the flower in his palm. 'The police seem to think I killed her,' he said.

'It's . . .' Dena shook her head, searching for a word. 'It's unspeakable . . . I've told them what I think about that theory.'

Ron began to weep again, and he squeezed the stem of the rose. 'Why would I kill her? She was my whole life.'

Dena put an awkward arm around him and he seemed to sag against her. 'I know it. This . . . this is just torture. They're going to find out who did this horrible thing, sooner or later.'

'I don't know,' he said, raising a hand to wipe his eyes. A rivulet of blood ran down his palm and into the cuff of his white shirt from where he had impaled his fingers on a thorn. 'They seem to have made up their minds.'

'Well, no one else believes it,' she said. 'Remember that.'

Ron drew himself up and nodded. 'I have to go,' he said. 'Are you coming to the hotel? Do you need a ride?'

'No, thanks. I have my car,' said Dena. She gestured toward the curving road which wound through the graveyard. 'I'll see you over there.'

As she turned to go, he caught at the sleeve of her coat. 'Dena,' he said. 'I'll tell you the truth. Sometimes, when Jennifer would go on about Brian, and . . . and what happened to her sister, I didn't always believe her. I mean, part of me thought she was exaggerating . . . or the police would have done something about it. Right? I mean, they investigate these things. They don't just let people get away with murder. But now . . . Dena, don't ever go back. Promise me.'

'Not a chance,' she said. He reached out for her and they embraced briefly, and then each went on their way.

Due to the huge turnout, she had had to park her car a fair distance from the gravesite. Her dark green Camry, barely visible through the trees, was one of the few cars remaining now. Most of the mourners had hurried to disperse in the rain.

Dena followed the neatly kept path around to her car and unlocked the door of the Camry. She slid in with a sigh, noting that she could hardly fit behind the wheel anymore. She closed her eyes for a moment, to rest them from weeping. Sometimes it was hard to believe in a heaven, she thought. It seemed such a childishly optimistic hope in the face of tragedy and loss. But there had to be a heaven, Dena told herself, for where else would her parents and Jennifer be?

Time to go, Dena thought. But as she lifted her key to place it in the ignition, she noticed the car felt strangely unbalanced. 'What is the matter with this thing?' she said aloud. She got out and walked around to look. She could see that the car was listing, but it was not until she walked back to the curb that she saw the tire on the back passenger side that she realized why. It was completely flat, the hubcap virtually scraping the ground. Oh great, she thought.

It wasn't that she didn't know how to change a tire. But she certainly wasn't going to be physically able to do it. Not in this condition. Through the trees she could see activity near Jennifer's grave where a couple of cemetery workers were lowering the coffin and dismantling the canopy. She thought of going to ask them for help, but it seemed somehow wrong to interrupt them when they were tending to Jennifer's remains. She closed her eyes. 'Goddamit,' she whispered.

Oh well, she thought. She reached in her purse for the phone and called AAA.

'OK, where are you?' the man at the garage asked gruffly.

'I'm in Belleplain Cemetery,' said Dena.

'Well, where in the cemetery?' he asked.

Dena, who was seated in the car, looked around her with a frown. It wasn't as if there were street signs. Or landmarks, for that matter. All the graves looked pretty much the same. 'I don't know. I came here for a funeral. I followed the funeral cortege.'

'OK, OK,' he said. 'I guess we'll find you. Are you far from the entrance? Maybe you could walk up and meet my guy and lead him back to the car.'

'I guess so,' said Dena uncertainly.

'OK, fifteen minutes,' he said, and hung up.

Dena put the phone back in her bag and shook her head. Why did you do that? she thought. Why didn't you just tell him you were pregnant, and you didn't want to walk all that way? The habit of independence was a hard one to break. She considered calling him back, and then decided against it. The walk will do you good, she told herself. At least the drizzle has stopped, for now.

She locked up the car and, using her furled umbrella for a walking stick, began to walk back in the direction of the entrance.

She congratulated herself for wearing flat shoes, not that she had much choice at this stage of things.

Cemeteries aren't that scary, she thought, as she followed the sidewalk path along the rows of graves with their dark, overhanging trees. Just sad. Just so much sadness had occurred here. That moaning people thought they heard when the wind blew through cemeteries was not the sound of ghosts, she thought. It was probably the residue of all the mourners and their cries. Cries that fell on stones. Cries that would never be answered in this life.

A movement among the gravestones caught her eye and she turned to look, but saw nothing. Instantly, she thought, in spite of all reason, that she would see a ghost. Come to prove her wrong. She could not walk fast enough. There are no ghosts, she thought. There are no ghosts. Then, from the corner of her eye, she saw it. A dark shape. Before she could look, an arm surrounded her, a hand was clapped over her mouth. She smelled sweat and alcohol.

'Don't scream,' he said. 'Please, just don't scream.'

She tried to jerk her head away from his hand, but he gripped her tightly. It was difficult to breathe. Something inside her told her to stop, to be still, so he would take the hand away. She wanted to bite him or kick him. Instead, she froze.

Slowly he removed his hand from her mouth, although it hovered, right in front of her face, waiting for her response. She didn't cry out. She knew he would slap it back on her in a minute. He was breathing hard behind her, his strong, muscled body pressed up against her back. She shuddered, thinking how much she had once enjoyed that sensation. The very thought of it made her feel sick. Her mouth was dry. Too dry to speak. He kept his other arm squeezed around her.

'Don't go crazy on me. I'm not trying to hurt you, Dena. I just want to talk to you.'

She licked her lips, but said nothing. Her fingers tightened around the umbrella handle, although her arms were pinned to her sides.

'I knew you'd go to the funeral,' he said. 'I had to talk to you.'

Talk to me, she thought. This is how you talk to me.

'Why don't you say something?' he shouted, and she jumped. He held her tighter.

'I can't breathe,' she whispered.

He loosened his grip slightly. 'There. I'm not trying to hurt you,' he said. Her frantic gaze searched the trees, the graves. There was no one in sight.

His voice was urgent, his breath was ragged in her ear. 'I'm trying to get through to you. And what do you do? You go and move in with your lover.'

'How many times can I tell you? He's not my lover.'

'Liar, liar,' he cried. 'Why are you torturing me? Every time I picture you together. Why couldn't you have just loved me? What is so hard about loving me?'

The words were pleading, but while he spoke them, he was restraining her with his grip, holding her as tightly as ever. This was no time to antagonize him. She thought about what to say, and how to say it. 'Brian, I'm not doing this to make you suffer. I wish you could understand. Can't we talk face to face . . .'

'All right,' he said after a moment's hesitation, 'but if I let you go, will you promise not to run away from me?'

The idea of being treated as his prisoner was loathsome, but she couldn't get away from him unless he agreed to release her. She wasn't strong enough. It was all she could do to nod her head.

He let go of her gently, like a parent freeing a toddler to try and walk. 'There,' he said. 'How's that?'

She drew in her breath and turned to face him. His face was pale, gaunt and darkly stubbled. His hair looked greasy and uncombed. His eyes were haunted.

'Better,' she said. She thought about the tow truck, coming for her car. Would they drive away if they didn't see her at the entrance? Or would they come looking for her?

Brian began to ramble, his voice low. 'If we started over, you would see that you're wrong about me. I can be the man you want me to be. But I can't take it when you treat me like this. Like you don't need me. I believed in you. I believed in our baby. I wanted to have you with me always. Every word you said I thought was true but now I see. All along you were planning to leave me. You were planning to go with him. I can see it in your face. You look at me with those cold eyes, like you have no feelings . . .'

His words were not making any sense. She knew he'd been drinking, but it seemed to have set off a kind of fantasy about her that was almost like a hallucination. A part of her felt sorry for him. 'Brian, I know how bad it's been,' she said, taking a small step back. 'I'm not trying to make it worse for you. I hope you can believe that.'

Despite her noncommittal tone, he seemed encouraged. 'I've done some things I shouldn't have done,' he rushed on. 'I admit it. But, if you'll just talk to me, baby . . .'

'Maybe we could talk,' she said.

'It might lead to something,' he murmured, advancing on her, making up the tiny distance she had put between them. 'Come on. I've got my truck over there. Come with me.'

She shook her head warily. 'I can't right now. I . . . I have to go. Jennifer's funeral. They're having a . . . something at the hotel.'

'You can't go in your car . . .' he said. 'Let me just take you . . .'

'What do you mean?'

'The tire,' he said.

'What do you know about the tire?' she asked.

'Whatever it is,' he said dismissively.

It took a minute for his words to register. And then, she knew. Of course. Why hadn't she known it right away? 'You did it, didn't you?'

Brian shook his head. 'Did what?'

Suddenly, she was overcome with the magnitude of it. He had crippled her car, held her captive. She was dancing around the truth, trying not to set him off. It was unbearable. 'You punctured the tire, didn't you? Brian, you're out of your mind.' She looked around wildly but there was no escape. Nowhere to hide.

Brian lunged forward and grabbed her. 'If I am, it's because you're driving me to it,' he shouted. 'You're just shutting me out.'

Without thinking she lifted her umbrella and cracked him in the side of the head with the wooden handle. She heard the splintering of the shaft, and then Brian let go of her and clutched at his eye where it had struck him.

'You bitch,' he said.

Dena began to run, holding her belly, her breath coming in gasps. She could hear him shouting behind her. She couldn't go much farther. She was going to fall down.

What if she hurt the baby? All of a sudden she heard the rumble of a dump truck. She looked around wildly. Two cemetery workers were driving in her direction. She ran out into the middle of the winding road, flagging them. The truck slowed, and then stopped in front of her. She ran up to the cab. 'Please . . .! Need help,' she said.

The driver looked impassively from the pregnant woman to the man stumbling up the road, holding his eye. Then he turned to his co-worker beside him. 'Help the lady in,' he said.
Dena sagged against the grimy door in relief.

With Ken McCarthy jiggling nervously at his elbow, Tyrell rang the bell at the front door of the run-down one-story bungalow on Cherry Street. He could hear the TV blaring inside the house, but no one came immediately to the door. Instead, there was much scuffling and the sound of muffled voices inside the house. Tyrell rang the bell again. 'Police,' he said. 'Open up.'
Tyrell noted that the pane in the lower-left quadrant was gone, and several layers of plastic were taped in its place. Someone had broken the window, no doubt, in an effort to reach in and open the lock so they could rob the place. Tyrell thought of Dena Russell's window, knocked out for an entirely different reason. A frustrated lover had tried to get to her, and another man – her new man, perhaps? – had hurried to fix it. It hadn't taken her long, Tyrell thought irritably, to find herself a replacement.
Tyrell rapped on the door again, thinking, no one would rush to fix this window. What was the point? It was a sad truth that the poorer you were, the more likely you were to get burgled. The crackheads preyed on their neighbors, breaking in to a house where no one would think it was odd to see them standing on the porch, trying the doorknob.
They grabbed something they could turn over quick, for a couple of dollars. Half the time, the burgled neighbors wouldn't even call the cops. They accepted it, hopelessly, as the price they paid for being poor.
After a lengthy pause, the curtain was pulled back an inch from the window and then it dropped again. There was a sound of locks being turned, and then the door opened a few inches. 'What?' said a girl's voice sullenly.
'Open the door, Keisha. We're looking for Warrick.'
The door opened and a heavy-set teenage girl in a red, zipper-front Tommy Hilfiger sweatshirt, and huge gold hoop earrings looked ruefully out at Tyrell. 'He's not here,' she said.
'May we come in?' Tyrell asked politely.
The girl bit her lip and looked behind her.
'Now,' said Tyrell.

The girl shrugged, and opened the door, admitting the two police officers.

'Mind if we look around?'

'Maybe he's out back,' she said peevishly.

Tyrell turned to Ken. 'Take a look,' he said.

Ken grimaced, but did as he was told, crossing the dimly lit, sparsely furnished living room, with its stained shag carpet and loud, flickering TV, and knocking on the closed doors in the unlit hallway as he went.

Tyrell glanced around the shabby room, and then back at the teenager who was regarding him warily. 'How ya doin' Keisha?' he asked.

'I'm doin' OK. How come you're looking for Warrick? He didn't do nothin'. He's working hard these days.'

Warrick was Keisha's stepbrother. He lived in this house on and off. He'd been busted half a dozen times for various petty crimes, since he was a juvenile. 'Just want to talk to him,' said Tyrell.

The back door of the bungalow opened and a young man in a black Stormzy T-shirt and a backwards baseball cap strutted into the room, looking belligerent. 'Yo Keisha, never mind about this cop. I'll deal with him.'

'Hey, Warrick,' said Tyrell.

'What do you want, man? My boss already called me. He says you're asking questions about me.'

'There was a murder at one of the houses where you helped out on a job.'

'That white bitch? He didn't kill no white bitch,' Keisha cried. 'He never . . .'

Tyrell tried to ignore the girl's shrill cry. 'Your boss said you and Lester had the van out that day.'

Warrick looked at the sergeant with narrowed eyes. 'You kill me, man. You all over my ass when I was hangin' on the corner all the time. Now I got me a good job as a 'lectrician's assistant and you're still all over my ass.'

'Just tell me where you had the van that afternoon.'

'Ask Lester.'

'Can't find Lester. I'm asking you.'

'We did the work we were s'posed to . . .'

Tyrell looked down at his notes. 'I got two hours unaccounted for.'

Warrick crossed his arms over his chest and shook his head.
'Shit.'

'Where were you?'

'We went over to Lester's and smoked some weed, all right?'

'And . . .?'

'And we fixed Lester's water heater on the company time,
with the company parts. Now I'm gonna lose my job – you
satisfied?'

'Excuse me, ma' am . . .' Ken pleaded from the hallway. 'Very
sorry to disturb you.'

Keisha looked at Tyrell, wide-eyed. 'Now you done it,' she said.
'You woke up Mama. I told you he wasn't down there.'

Ken scurried out into the living room, followed by a large, black
woman in a magenta-pink bathrobe and scuffs. She was securing
the robe around her with a belt, and she was muttering and glowering as she did it. When she reached the area of the coffee table,
she planted her feet and put her hands on her ample hips, glaring
at Tyrell.

'Tyrell Watkins, what the hell is goin' on here?' she demanded.
'I worked all night, and then I came home and picked this place
up and put somethin' on the stove and now I'm tryin' to get a
little rest before I have to go back and start all over again.'

'I'm sorry, Miz Allen. I was talkin' to Warrick.'

The woman was immediately wary. 'What's he done, now?'
she said.

Warrick snorted. 'He wanted to know if I killed that white chick,
Mama.'

'Are you crazy?' said Lucinda Allen, throwing her large, handsome head back. 'Is that what this is all about?'

Tyrell looked calmly back at the woman in the bathrobe, and
silently cursed Heath Van Brunt, who had insisted on this waste-
of-time call. 'Just wanted to ask Warrick a few questions. We got
everything straightened out now.'

'Tyrell Watkins, you should be ashamed of yourself. This is all
about that white girl that got beat to death?'

Tyrell's expression was impassive. 'I'm sorry we disturbed you,
ma'am.'

Lucinda Allen removed one hand from her hip and shook a
finger at Tyrell. 'You know they got you doin' their dirty work,
don't you? Right away, they're saying it's a black man that did it.

Of course, it has to be a black man. And they trot you over here like some obedient little mutt and you go barkin' and snarlin' at all your friends and neighbors. You should be ashamed of yourself.' She shook her head in disgust. 'Don't you have any pride, Tyrell? I've got a good mind to march over to your grandmother's house and tell her what I think of you.'

A muscle worked in Tyrell's jaw but otherwise his face did not betray any emotion. 'We're trying to find a killer. We're talking to a lot of people.'

The woman did an exaggerated double-take, as if she could not believe her ears. 'A killer. Warrick ain't no killer and you know it. Boy's finally got himself an honest job. He's trying to learn a trade so he can make a living. Once they hear about this over at Ranger, they'll fire his ass.'

Tyrell turned to Warrick. 'They won't hear about any of this from me. You and Lester have still got time to get a story together and get it straight.'

Warrick snorted again, but there was relief in his face.

'Sorry to trouble you, Miz Allen,' Tyrell said.

The woman followed them to the door and yelled after them as they went down the steps. 'You troubled me, all right. I'm troubled to see the kind of man you've become,' she cried out after him.

Ken and Tyrell returned to their patrol car without speaking. As they slid back into their seats, Ken said, 'Whew.'

Tyrell glared at him. 'What's that for?' he demanded.

Ken looked at him, wide-eyed. 'Nothing,' he said. 'Just that she was kinda tough.'

Tyrell turned the key impatiently and the engine roared. 'She's worried about her child,' he said shortly.

Ken did not reply. Sergeant Watkins was just too touchy right now.

They started to pull away from the curb and the radio squawked. Ken reached for it in relief. He listened to the garbled message. 'Some trouble out at the cemetery,' he said to Tyrell. Tyrell had already understood.

EIGHTEEN

Dena sat shivering, her feet flat on the greasy cement floor, staring at a sun-kissed calendar girl in a mesh bikini over the littered, gray metal desk in front of her. An ashtray piled high with cigarette butts was balanced precariously on a pile of automotive catalogues. A grimy mechanic in coveralls came into the cluttered office, wiping his hands on a gray hand towel. 'Somebody punctured it, all right,' he said. 'You want to take a look?'

Dena said, 'Sure,' although she knew she would have no idea what she was looking at. The mechanic led her back into the garage and hefted the tire, which was leaning up against her car. He rotated it in his filthy hands as if it were a balloon.

'What am I looking at?' she asked.

'Well, look here,' he said. 'You got a hole right there. A nice neat hole. And no nail. Somebody stabbed with something. An awl, maybe. Anyway, the tire's shot. It couldn't be repaired. I had to give you a new one.'

Dena had only one concern at the moment. 'Is it ready?' she asked.

The mechanic shrugged. 'Sure. Take it away. You can pay in the office.'

'There's nobody there,' Dena said.

'She's just takin' a leak. She'll be back in a minute.'

Sure enough, when Dena returned to the office, a dark-haired woman dressed in layers of flannel was at the desk. Dena settled her bill and thanked the woman for her keys. Then she went back to get her car. As she was backing out into the gas-pumping area, a police patrol car pulled in. She recognized the dark, solemn face of the driver.

She stopped the car and stared at him, unsmiling.

Tyrell Watkins got out and straightened up. Ken McCarthy got out on his side and the two conferred for a moment. Then Ken went inside the garage and began to talk to the mechanic. Tyrell walked slowly over to the window beside Dena and tapped on it.

She thought angrily about just driving away but then she pressed the button and lowered the window.

'You took your time,' she said coldly. 'How surprising.'

Tyrell leaned down, his large hands resting on the side of the Camry. 'We've been out talking to the fellows who picked you up. They said you rode back here with the tow-truck driver.'

'I suppose you're going to tell me I should have waited there for you.'

Tyrell grimaced and looked into the distance. 'Not necessary,' he said. 'They told me what happened.'

Dena stared straight ahead through her windshield. 'Now I suppose you're going to tell me that boys will be boys, right, Sergeant?' Her tone was sarcastic, but her voice was shaking.

Tyrell shook his head. She thought she glimpsed a slightly apologetic look in his eye. It did little to assuage her outrage. 'You may not believe this, Miss Russell, but I went out and talked to him just this morning,' he said.

Dena scarcely trusted her voice. 'I guess you really scared him.'

'He promised me up and down that he'd leave you alone.'

'Well, he didn't,' she said curtly.

'Are you hurt?' he asked.

'No, I'm furious,' she said.

Tyrell nodded. 'Well, I guess so,' he said slowly. 'I don't blame you.'

At that moment Ken emerged from the depths of the garage and joined Tyrell beside the Camry. 'I talked to Mack,' he said. 'He said it was no case of road wear. The tire's been punctured.'

Tyrell nodded. 'Ask him to sign a statement to that effect.'

'Will do,' said Ken, returning to the bay where a Subaru Outback was being raised on a lift.

'Are you going to arrest him now?' Dena asked.

'I'll pick him up.'

'Good.'

Tyrell grimaced. 'We probably won't be able to keep him for very long.'

'What's very long?'

'A couple of hours. Maybe overnight.'

'Jesus Christ,' said Dena. She rested her forehead against the steering wheel in frustration. Then she straightened up. 'Do you realize that we're talking about a man who may have killed a woman? Does he have to kill me too, before you do something about it?'

Tyrell sighed. 'There is something we can do.'

'Then do it,' she said.

The Evermay Room, one of the two dining rooms in the Endicott Hotel, was nearly empty now, save for a bartender wiping out glasses at the linen-covered table which had served as a bar, a few waitresses, carrying trays of small, dirty plates back to the kitchen, and a few people still seated around small tables in the room. An hour ago the room had looked like the scene of one of the many celebrations that had been held here over the years, except that all the guests were dressed in shades of gray and black. People greeted each other lovingly, and conversation rose to a party level as the mourners for Jennifer Hubbell devoured drinks and hors d'oeuvres after the funeral. Jake Smith supervised the gathering. He understood well, in his middle age, that people responded to death first with tears, and then with a heightened appetite for life. He had provided well for these friends who mourned with him. It was the last party he would ever give for his beloved daughter, and he had insisted that it be lavish.

In one corner of the room, Ron Hubbell sat, knee to knee, with his old friends.

Laura rubbed his back as Skip spoke earnestly to him.

'Look,' said Skip, 'we think you should come back home with us. There's nothing left for you here.'

Ron looked vaguely around the room. 'I . . . I can't leave,' he said.

'Listen to me,' said Skip. 'I've known you most of my life. Thanks to you, I've found my soulmate.' He and Laura exchanged a tremulous glance. 'We want you to come back to Boston where we can take care of you. You have lots of friends who want to see you. You can stay in our house. We have plenty of room.'

Ron's heart felt like a stone in his chest. He looked at his friends as if from a great distance. 'That's nice of you,' he said lifelessly. 'But the police won't let me leave. Besides, I'd only be in the way.'

'Never,' said Laura fiercely. Skip put a hand on her shoulder. She took a deep breath, and addressed Ron again. 'This can't last much longer. And then, we will come and get you. We're not saying this to be nice. We need to do this. I need to do it. For Jen. She would never forgive me if I didn't look after you . . .' Her voice was urgent and thick with tears. 'She got me through the darkest days of my life. I often think I would never have survived without her. I could never thank her enough, but by God, I can do what she would want me to do. She would want me to help you get through this, any way I can.'

The determination of her words seemed to penetrate Ron's shroud of numbness and grief. For a moment he looked her in the eye and Laura saw a glimmer of life, even if it was only based on his memories.

'OK,' he said. 'OK. When they say I can go . . .'

'Skip's been on the phone to the president of the company. He said you can work up in the Boston office. And you can come back to work when you're ready. Really, Ron, people are so upset. They just want to help . . .'

Ron nodded. 'I know,' he whispered. 'It does help.'

Ron's mother came over to where they sat, her face puffy from weeping. She put a hand on Ron's shoulder. 'I need to talk to you, dear,' she said. 'There are still some things . . .'

Ron looked at his friends. 'Will you excuse me?' he said.

Skip and Laura stood up. 'Buzz our room if you want to talk,' said Skip. 'Or just sit. Whatever you need.'

They all three hugged again, and then Laura and Skip left the dining room and walked out to the ancient elevator. As they pressed the button and waited for it to descend, Laura said, 'We'll have to come back and get him. I can't imagine him making the trip by himself.'

'No, of course not. We'll drive down the minute he's ready. Pick up his stuff. Bring him back with us.'

'Will Dr Hackler cover for you?' Sara Hackler was new to their practice.

'I'm sure she will. If not, somebody else will have to do it. They'll have to carry on without me,' he said grimly, letting Laura step into the elevator as the door opened. Skip followed her in and pressed the number for their floor. 'Ron is my dearest friend. You have to help somebody out when they need you. Not when it's convenient.'

Laura squeezed his hand. 'I knew I loved you for a reason,' she said.

They sighed and rode quietly to their floor, walking down the empty hallway to the door of their room. Skip put the key in the lock.

'We have to pay them for this room, Skip,' Laura fretted.

'Believe me, I have tried to settle this at the desk, but Jake Smith has been adamant about it. He refuses to let us pay.'

Laura walked into the room and kicked her shoes off on the rose-colored carpet.

She flopped down on the bed and stared up at the ceiling. Skip lay down beside her. 'These rooms are very comfortable,' she said. 'Jennifer was always so proud of her parents' hotel. She used to enjoy working here when she came home on vacations.'

'I can see why she liked it,' he said. 'There's something very homey about it. Elegant but homey. It's like a big old English country house or something.'

'Yes,' she murmured. 'Very comfortable.' Then she yawned. 'I'm exhausted,' she said.

'Me too,' he said. 'I feel like we've been apart for a month rather than a couple of days.' For a while, he wrapped his arms around her and they clung together, thinking about the terrible events of the day, the week.

'How was the trip to Chicago?' he asked.

'The usual,' she said. 'Lots of interest. No results. I called Jennifer from the hotel there. I wanted to tell her our news. She was so excited. I still can't believe it.'

'I know,' he said.

'God, how the Smiths must be suffering,' she said, staring past his shoulder. 'There's nothing more futile than wishing you could turn back the clock.'

'No, there isn't,' he said.

'I do it anyway,' she said. 'I can't help it.'

Skip nuzzled her hair. 'We have to look ahead.'

'There is no pain that can compare to the loss of a child,' she said.

'Don't think about it,' he whispered. 'Try and rest. Take a nap.'

She lay silent for a moment. 'Are you going to sleep?' she asked.

Skip leaned across her and picked up some medical journals from the night table. 'I'm going to read for a while,' he said.

She smiled at him. 'Something light, no doubt.'

Skip grinned sheepishly. 'Bone and Joint Surgery.'

Laura yawned. 'Can I stay right here beside you?'

'You'd better,' he said.

Laura closed her eyes, thinking she would fall asleep immediately, but the minute her eyes closed, her brain seemed to start buzzing. 'I can't sleep,' she said.

He glanced down at her, pressed beside him. 'Sure you can,' he said. 'I'll read to you.'

She smiled in spite of her pain. 'You'll bore me to sleep.'

'Hopefully,' he said.

She was quiet for a minute while he searched for his page. Then she said, 'That police chief asked me if Jennifer had enemies . . .'

'I think they're clutching at straws,' said Skip.

'Mmmm, maybe,' she murmured. 'Enemies . . .'

'Maybe you'll think of something,' he said.

She did not reply. Her eyes were closed. Good, he thought. She's so tired.

Laura slept uneasily, as Skip began to read, her dreams a jumbled puzzle of everything she was trying to remember.

The courtroom was quiet and virtually empty when Dena and Tyrell arrived.

There was a clerk, seated a step down from the bench, and a court officer in the corner, standing guard by the door, his mind obviously wandering as he performed this obligatory function.

Tyrell indicated a seat a few rows back from the empty tables where the defense and prosecution sat during a trial. Dena sat down, and the officer took a seat beside her, leather creaking as he leaned back and extended his legs.

'Are you going to arrest Brian?' she asked.

'I told Ken to pick him up.'

'What happens now?' Dena asked nervously.

Tyrell's eyes scanned the room automatically, as he answered. 'The cemetery workers should be here any minute. They had no problem about showing up. I called the municipal court judge on duty. She's on her way. The judge will come in and I'll be sworn to testify. I'll give her the facts so far, and then, you'll tell her what happened. If she wants to hear from the guys who picked you up, she'll have them sworn.'

'And then . . .?'

'And then, if all goes as I expect it to, she'll issue a temporary restraining order.'

'Which means . . .'

'Which means he can't come within a hundred yards of you again or he'll be arrested,' Tyrell explained.

Dena nodded. 'Do you think she'll . . . you know . . . give it to . . . me?'

'Grant the order?' he asked. He nodded. 'She's tough on domestic violence. You were lucky to get her.'

'Lucky,' Dena said, shaking her head.

Tyrell looked over at her and smiled. She had never actually seen him smile before. It changed his face so dramatically that she found herself staring at him. 'I know,' he said. 'You don't feel lucky.'

'No, I don't,' she said adamantly. And then, she put a hand gently on her stomach. 'Well, that's not true. In some ways, I do. Do you have any children, Sergeant?'

Tyrell frowned and shook his head. 'Me? No. No, I'm not even married.'

Dena sighed. 'Well, that's not a prerequisite these days.'

'It is for me,' he said.

Dena did not look at him. 'That's what I always thought,' she said. 'But, what is it they say? Life is what happens to you while you're busy making other plans.'

'Not if you're careful,' he said.

Dena was stung by the implied rebuke in his words. She turned away, looking toward the door beside the judge's bench, wishing the judge would appear. Wishing this was over.

'Sorry,' Tyrell murmured. 'I shouldn't have said that.' Dena looked at him in surprise.

He met her glance, and wondered about Brian's accusations. Was she having an affair with that other guy? She seemed awfully straight, but . . . 'You don't always know about people,' he conceded.

Dena sighed. 'No, you're probably right. Things *don't* just happen. When I met Brian, I was almost thirty, single, afraid I would never have a family. Let's face it. A little . . . desperate. So, I got in over my head with someone I hardly knew. I let it happen. I wasn't cautious. I jumped in, not knowing . . . I had no idea . . .' She shook her head.

'I think he'll pull back, now.'

'I hope you're right. Sometimes they just ignore these orders.

You read about it all the time. Oh, I just want to get away from here.'

'Something's bound to break on this murder pretty soon,' he said.

'Not as long as you people keep trying to blame it on Ron,' she said.

'We're not trying to blame it on anybody. We're just trying to figure out what happened,' he replied impatiently.

'It could not have been Ron.'

'How well do you know him?' Tyrell asked.

'Not that well. But I was with them. I saw them together. I could just tell.

'No offense, ma'am, but if you were that good a judge of character, we wouldn't be here right now,' he said wryly.

Dena thought about taking offense, but decided there was truth in what he said.

'What I want to know is, have you people even questioned Brian about . . . Jennifer's death. You know about her sister, don't you?'

Tyrell frowned. 'I've heard about it. But he was not implicated . . .'

'Officially, I know,' she said. 'But it seems to me that everything he does is OK with the police. Everything he says is taken for truth, while the rest of us are treated like liars. I mean, why is that, Sergeant? Why is he immune?'

'He's not,' said Tyrell. 'We're here, aren't we?' But, even as he said it, he knew there was something justified in her complaint. Something he didn't understand himself.

Before Dena could reply, the door at the front of the courtroom beside the bench opened and a small-boned woman with coffee-colored skin and a short gray afro entered the courtroom wearing a black robe. The court attendant beside the door called out, 'All rise.'

Automatically, Tyrell reached for Dena's elbow to help her to her feet. She shook off his hand and stood up to face the judge.

NINETEEN

Tyrell opened the back door to his grandmother's house and inhaled the aroma of country ribs and black-eyed peas cooking on her stovetop. He still had to serve that restraining order on Boots Riley, but there was no hurry. He'd be locked up for a few more hours at least, even if the duty judge heard his case tonight. Tyrell wanted to have a bite of dinner before he faced the next phase. And there was no cooking in town that could compare to the cooking of Ella Brown. She was standing at the stove when he opened the door, her old figure still tall and lean. Tyrell figured he'd gotten his height from her. He walked over and gave her a kiss on her soft, lined cheek.

'Hi honey,' she said. 'You're just in time. Grab a plate and join 'em.'

The kitchen had been noisy when he walked in, with the sounds of teasing and the whoop of laughter. Out of the corner of his eye he saw Cletus and two of his friends seated at the table, their heads bent over steaming plates. But when Tyrell entered the kitchen, they fell silent. He was too tired to wonder why.

'Let me wash up,' he said. 'I'll be right back.' He went down the hall to the bathroom with its cheerful orange tiles and ruffled curtains that matched the shower curtain. He turned on the tap, rolled up his sleeves, and leaned over the basin, thinking about the scene in the courtroom. It had not taken long for Judge Hobart to decide. She had taken testimony from Tyrell, who also read the statement from the garage mechanic into the record. She questioned the two workers from the cemetery, who showed up looking anxious and out of place. Dena Russell had been sworn in and explained about the fact that Brian had hit her, and that she had called 911. This had given Tyrell some anxious moments as the judge peered down at him over the top of her reading glasses and wanted to know why this complaint hadn't been pursued by the police.

Tyrell had kicked the problem upstairs, explaining that the chief had promised to see to it personally. 'Well, I shall have to speak to Chief Potter about that,' Judge Hobart had threatened.

Tyrell wasn't worried about his testimony. After all, it wasn't a lie, but nevertheless he knew he would catch hell from Chief Potter once the judge was through with him. But Riley had pushed it too far. Left them no choice.

Tyrell washed his face, mopped it dry and rolled his sleeves back down, buttoning them as he came back into the kitchen. Ella had put his plate on the table next to Cletus but, before Tyrell could pull out his chair, Cletus and his friends stood up.

'We're leavin',' Cletus announced. 'We don't want to sit with no company nigger,' he said.

'Cletus, you apologize right now to your brother,' Ella demanded. 'You should be ashamed of yourself.'

'I apologize to you, Grandma. Not to him.'

Tyrell refused to take the bait. He looked at his brother through narrowed eyes. 'What's up with you?'

Cletus's buddies were sullen-faced, but avoided Tyrell's gaze. He was, after all, a cop. Cletus, however, was not intimidated by his brother's authority.

'We heard how you was lookin' for Warrick Allen. Saying he was the one coming around, calling on that white bitch that got herself killed. It has to be a brother, doesn't it?'

Tyrell sighed wearily, and picked up his fork. 'You don't know what you're talking about,' he said.

'Yeah, not much,' said Cletus disdainfully.

Cletus indicated to his friends that they should exit the kitchen. He muttered something under his breath which Tyrell knew was unprintable. Part of him felt like he ought to get up and get into it with him. But his heart wasn't in it.

'I'll sit with you,' said Ella, in her sweet voice. 'I don't know what is with that boy. Talkin' to you that way.'

Tyrell smiled sadly at his grandmother and began to eat. Suddenly his phone rang. He glanced at the screen. 'Work,' he said.

'Can't they leave you alone long enough to have a square meal?' Ella protested.

Tyrell swallowed what he was chewing, and answered the phone.

Ken McCarthy sounded nervous on the other end. 'Sergeant, I better tell you.'

'Tell me what?' Tyrell asked, frowning. 'The chief let him go,' said Ken. 'I brought in Riley, and before I could process him, the chief came out and told me he'd take care of it. Ten minutes later I saw him walking out of here.'

'Jesus Christ,' said Tyrell, and then looked at Ella. 'Sorry, Grandma.' He threw down his napkin beside his plate. 'All right. I'm on my way.'

'Scrub a dub-dub, there's a bear in my tub,' said Dena, quoting the children's book she had read to Megan twice before she could be nudged to her bath.

Wearing a serious expression, Megan slapped her pudgy arms down into the bubbles, causing a bubble explosion in the tiny bathroom. Dena sat back on her heels, her face flushed from the heat of the bathroom and the effort of bending over the tub in her condition. She brushed her hair back with her forearm and smiled at the child's experiments. Peter had come knocking on her door because his teenaged baby-sitter had canceled at the last minute. Dena had assured the frantic father that she was glad to help with the girls. 'Are you ready to get out of there now?' she asked Megan.

Megan shook her head and slapped the bubbles again.

Dena hesitated, not knowing exactly how to deal with this silent refusal. 'Well, I think that's enough bath for now,' said Dena, hoisting herself awkwardly to her feet.

She picked up a pink bath towel and held it out to Megan. Megan continued to play in the water as if she hadn't heard her. Dena felt a certain helplessness at the sight of her closed, remote little face. What does she want? Dena wondered. And then, she had a bright idea. 'I know two songs I could sing to a girl who was dried off and in her pajamas.'

Megan held her forearms frozen above the bubbles.

'Two really good songs,' Dena announced.

Slowly, as if it were her own idea, the child began to climb out of the tub.

'Wait a minute,' said Dena. 'We missed a spot.' She turned Megan around, ready to wipe off the smudge on the child's lower back and then saw, as soon as she reached for it, that the smudge was actually a star-shaped birthmark. Not wanting to draw attention to her mistake, she wiped the child's back anyway, and then wrapped her up in the towel. The little girl's warmth, her fragrant wet hair and glowing skin were so appealing that Dena wanted to reach out and hug her. The child, as if sensing her intention, froze and shook her head.

Just then, the bathroom door flew open and Tory stood there, dressed in her flowered nightgown, her small face looking pinched and white.

'What is it?' Dena asked, instantly alarmed.

'I heard something. Outside,' she whispered. 'I think somebody's there. I think I saw a shadow, around the side of the house.'

Dena felt her heart start to hammer. She didn't want the children to know what she was thinking. 'There aren't any shadows. It's nighttime, silly,' she said gently.

'I saw one. I did.'

'Did you look out the window?'

'I was too afraid,' Tory said, wide-eyed. Immediately, Megan began to whimper.

'Now stop,' said Dena. 'Both of you. Take it easy. I'll just go and look. Tory, can you help Megan put on her pjs?'

'Don't leave us alone in here,' Tory pleaded.

Dena sighed and let the water out of the tub. Hurriedly, she pulled on Megan's pajamas. 'Come on. I'll walk you both to your room.'

Both children clung to Dena as they left the bathroom, and headed down the hall.

Suddenly, the doorbell buzzed, and all three jumped. Megan started to wail.

'Megan, stop,' Dena pleaded.

'What if it's a monster?' Tory asked.

'Tory, you stop egging her on.'

'But I'm afraid,' the child insisted. 'That woman got killed around the corner. The one you knew. What if that's the killer?'

'What an imagination,' Dena exclaimed. But her voice wobbled. No, she told herself. It couldn't be Brian. Sergeant Watkins had promised her he would be locked up. At least for tonight. 'I'll go and see right now.'

'Don't leave us,' Tory pleaded.

'Then come with me,' said Dena. The buzzer sounded again, more insistently.

Tory stared at Dena in an agony of indecision. Finally, she agreed, being as curious as she was afraid. 'OK,' she said.

Dena and the children shuffled out into the vestibule toward the front door, the children dragging their feet. When they reached the door, both children huddled behind Dena, peeping out from in back of her.

Dena put the chain on, and opened the door a crack.

In the overhead porch light, Dena could see that a man she knew was standing there, but not the man she was worried about.

'Ron,' she said.

'Who is it?' Tory demanded.

'It's all right. It's someone I know,' said Dena, stroking Megan's damp hair.

The child clung to her leg. Dena unhooked the chain and pulled the door back. 'Come in,' she said.

Ron's complexion was the color of dust, and his hair seemed to have gone from salt and pepper to gray overnight. His coat was rumpled and stained, his tie askew.

'I wanted to talk to you,' he said.

'Of course,' she said kindly, relieved – but a little surprised – to see him there. 'Girls, go in your room and get a storybook. I'll be right in to read to you. It's all right. It's . . . it's a friend.'

Ron frowned at the wide-eyed children behind her. 'Who are they?' he asked.

'I'm baby-sitting them tonight. Tory, do as I say. Take Megan.'

Reluctantly, the child complied, glancing back behind her to stare at the man who was entering their living room, sitting down on their sofa, clutching his head in his hands as if to quell some throbbing pain.

Dena looked at him helplessly. 'Can I get you anything?'

'No,' he said. 'No.'

Dena sat down gingerly beside him and put a hand on his arm. 'Ron, you should be resting. You've been through so much.'

'I'll rest when I'm dead,' he said flatly.

Those words, which usually indicated that a person was having too much fun to rest, took on an ominous meaning coming from him. His despair was palpable. 'Didn't the doctor give you some-thing . . . a prescription to help your nerves?' she asked.

'Nothing wrong with my nerves,' he insisted. Ron shook his head. 'No.' Then, he said more briskly. 'No, the reason I came over is . . . I was thinking about the baby's things.'

Dena grimaced at the thought of the lost baby. Dead in his

mother's womb. It was too awful to contemplate. 'What about them?' she asked.

'I'm . . . cleaning out the house, you know. To sell it. Is this where you live?' he asked.

Dena shook her head. 'I live upstairs. I'm just watching the children for my neighbor.'

Ron nodded, as if he had difficulty understanding, and looked sadly around the partially dismantled apartment.

'You were saying about the house?'

'Right. I'm gonna clean it out.'

'It's so soon,' said Dena. 'Maybe you should wait.'

'What for?' he demanded. 'In case she might come back, and start looking for things?' His voice was loud and high.

Dena shook her head. 'No. I didn't mean that.'

'Sorry,' Ron mumbled. 'Sorry.'

'You're just so . . . you're suffering so right now. I thought it might be better to wait.'

'No.' Ron stood up and began to pace around the small living room. 'No. I want to take care of everything.'

'Well, what can I do to help you?' Dena asked, spreading her hands wide.

'She had so many things ready . . . for the baby. In the nursery,' he said. It was as if he was stabbing himself with the words. They seemed to emerge in a groan of pain.

'I know,' said Dena. She felt tears spring to her eyes.

'She'd want you to have them,' he said. 'You take them. Use them for your baby.'

The thought that came to her mind, but not to her lips, was that she was leaving town, and wouldn't be able to take them. She knew Jennifer had everything – furniture, blankets, a rug. She couldn't carry all that. But she also knew, looking at him, that she couldn't say it. Not even hint it. It would be cruel – heartless – to refuse.

'That's so kind of you,' she said.

'She would have wanted it that way,' he insisted. 'I know she would. I know my Jenn . . .'

Protests and logistics rose to her mind, but she stifled them. She would take whatever things he wanted to give her, and she would find a way to transport them. She was not about to make it his problem – asking how she could move the baby's things, and where she could store them. She would figure all that out. All that was important right now was that she say yes, and be grateful. He needed her to do that. It was little enough to ask.

'That would be so wonderful,' Dena said, clasping his hand in hers. 'I have hardly anything for my baby. I'd be so pleased to have them'

He didn't exactly smile, but the thundercloud on his face seemed to clear slightly, and a dazed kind of satisfaction peeked through, for a second, like a ray of sun on a stormy day. 'Really?'

'It was so kind of you to think of me,' she said. 'When would you like me to come and get the baby's things?'

'Tomorrow,' he said.

So soon, she wanted to cry. Give yourself a chance to grieve. But she could see he was in a hurry, though she wasn't certain why, and she didn't have a good feeling about it. 'That will be fine, Ron,' she said. 'Whatever is convenient for you.'

'All right,' he said. Abruptly he stood up. 'I've got to go.'

'But you just got here,' she said, following him to the door.

'I can't stay. I can't talk. It's not you. I can't talk to anyone. I'll see you over at the house,' he said.

'You don't have to talk. Just let me keep you company,' she said. She hardly knew him, but he seemed like such a decent man. And his suffering was so vivid to her.

'No. No, I can't,' he said, his voice breaking. He got up and stalked to the door before she could delay him.

Where are you going in such a hurry, she wondered. It was as if he was trying to settle everything quickly. Get it out of the way. There was a recklessness about his grief that scared her. He rushed off into the darkness, with Dena calling after him to take care.

TWENTY

The sound of a car door slamming jolted Dena awake, and for a moment she felt frightened. She looked around at her unfamiliar surroundings, and then she remembered. She was at Peter's, staying with the girls. Then, she looked at her watch. It was Peter. It had to be. It was time for him to come home. As she glanced at the door she heard the sound of his key turning in the lock. She sighed with relief.

She didn't remember drifting off. She had been trying to read, but was unable to concentrate. She recalled wishing that Peter had a TV so she could flip on one of those old movies from the 1940s with women in satin gowns and white furs throwing their marcelled heads back and emitting tinkly laughs at the witticisms of sleek men in tails. A little escapism from real life. The comfortable living room looked a little forlorn. All around her were boxes packed and sealed in the corners, and many of the pictures were off the walls. Peter and his daughters were preparing to leave. Leaving her alone.

Dena rubbed her eyes, and struggled to her feet as Peter opened the door and came inside, letting in a cold breeze.

'Hi,' she said.

Peter smiled. 'Cold out there.'

'Winter's coming,' she said.

Peter nodded and went to the closet to hang up his coat. 'Everything all right?'

'Just fine,' she said.

'The girls went right to sleep?'

'No problem. Well, actually, we had a visitor tonight and they got a little scared, but then they were OK.'

Peter stopped, gripping the hanger one hand. 'A visitor? It wasn't—'

Dena shook her head. 'It was Ron. The husband of my friend who was killed.'

'Oh?' he asked, adjusting his coat neatly on the hanger and replacing it in the closet. 'What did he want?'

Dena sighed. 'He wanted me to have the things that Jennifer bought for the baby.'

Peter shut the closet door and walked over to the refrigerator. He opened it and looked inside, pulling out a bottle of juice. 'How morbid,' he said.

'He didn't mean it that way. It's very difficult for him,' Dena said loyally. 'I'm sure you of all people could understand.'

'Me?' Peter said, surprised. 'What would I know about it?'

'You had to dispose of your wife's things after she died. I'm sure it wasn't easy.'

Peter poured his juice and put the bottle away. 'Just something that had to be done,' he said shortly.

'I'm sorry, Peter,' she said. 'I didn't mean to remind you . . .'

'Not at all,' he said. He smiled brightly. A little falsely, Dena thought. 'It was long ago. Time heals all wounds.'

Dena wondered about that. 'Well, I'd better be getting upstairs,' she said.

'I was concerned when you said you had a visitor,' he ventured. 'I thought maybe it was Brian.'

Dena shook her head. 'I didn't get a chance to tell you earlier. I had a restraining order served on Brian. He's not allowed to come near me.'

'Right,' Peter snorted. 'Like that will stop him.'

'I had to do something,' Dena said defensively.

'Don't you know you can't rely on the legal system?' he said. 'That's a piece of paper. It's meaningless if he decides to come after you.'

'Well, what do you suggest I do?' she demanded irritably.

'Get a weapon,' he said. 'The next time he comes after you, use it.'

'Oh, for heaven's sake, Peter. I can't do that. I'd be more dangerous to myself than to him.' A weapon. The very idea made her feel shaky.

'Then get out of here. Get away from him. As far away as you can get.'

'Believe me, I'd like to. I can't leave,' she protested. 'The chief of police forbid me to leave town until Jennifer's killer is apprehended.'

Peter shook his head. 'Catch-22. The police won't let you leave, and they can't protect you as long as you stay here. Perfect.'

'Don't say that,' she insisted. 'You're scaring me.'

'I'm just stating the facts. You're relying on the legal system for justice. It isn't about justice. It's about lawyers' fees and corrupt officials and bureaucracy. They want you to think that your rights are protected. That the law is on your side. That's simply not true. You have to protect yourself. And your child.'

'I'm doing what I can to protect myself,' she said angrily.

Peter shrugged. 'It's foolhardy to assume that because the legal system has issued you a piece of paper, everything is going to be fine.'

'You're awfully cynical,' she countered.

Peter hesitated. 'You'll have to forgive me. My mother was an attorney. If I'm cynical, it's because I watched the way she operated. She was an . . . unscrupulous person.'

'Well, I'm sorry you felt that way. But, I feel safer now that it's done.'

He looked as if he was about to reply, and then thought better of it. 'Well, it's late,' he said. 'Let me walk you upstairs.'

'I don't need anyone to walk me upstairs,' she said. 'I'm perfectly capable of getting upstairs on my own.'

Peter looked at her with one eyebrow raised. 'Don't take it out on me,' he said.

'What do you mean?' she asked.

'The fact that the system doesn't work.' He came out from behind the kitchen counter. He was still dressed in his European-cut suit from work, his hair and beard trimmed to a stylish length so that he looked like an ad from *Gentleman's Quarterly*. 'Now, like it or not, I'm walking you upstairs,' he said. 'I'm old fashioned.'

'An old-fashioned anarchist,' she said wryly.

'A realist,' he said. 'But don't take my word for it. Wait and see how long that legal paper keeps him at bay.'

'Are you hoping you're right?' she asked coolly.

'I am right,' he said.

Paper streamers still hung from the overhead fixture in the dining room, and confetti littered the table. Half of a devil's food cake stood under a glass dome on the sideboard. Lou Potter's daughter, Kim, a compact, freckle-faced blonde woman, was folding up wrapping paper and stuffing it into a paper bag for recycling. Kim's thirteen-year-old son, Jeff, led Tyrell into the dining room where his mother was trying to pick up after his little sister's birthday party.

'Hey, Ma, look who I found prowling around outside,' said Jeff.

Tyrell punched the kid lightly on the arm. 'Hey Kim,' said Tyrell. 'Where's the birthday girl?'

Kim laughed and pushed her hair back off her forehead. 'Doin' her homework,' she said. 'Birthday or no birthday. Second grade is tough. What brings you here?'

'I was just down at the station,' Tyrell said. 'They told me Lou came home.'

Kim frowned. 'Can it wait?' she asked. 'He is awful tired. Between the funeral, and the party this afternoon, and then he had to go back down to work. Something about Brian. I am really worried about his health.'

Tyrell regarded Kim curiously. She was as good a person as he knew, and always had been. He wondered if she might be able to explain this to him. 'Kim,' he said, 'Lou . . . your dad and Brian Riley's dad were great friends, right?'

Kim smiled, and wound a fat pink ribbon around her hand. 'Still are. The best of friends,' she said. 'Known each other all their lives. Our mothers were friends too. We were like one big happy family for a long time. Until Janine . . . Brian's mother . . .'

'They're divorced, aren't they?' Tyrell asked.

'Well, yes,' Kim said. 'She left them when Brian was about nine or ten. She moved away. She moved to California. Brian went back and forth between them. I guess none of the grown-ups were that surprised. Apparently, Matt Riley was always kind of a hard man to get along with. Very demanding. It was sad, really. Tough on Brian.'

'Your father seems to be very fond of Brian.'

'I think he always felt sorry for him,' said Kim. 'He's a softie. You know him.'

'Yeah, I know,' said Tyrell. 'Is he out back?' After Kim's mother died, her husband built a little apartment for his father-in-law above their two-car garage. The arrangement seemed to work out for everyone.

Kim nodded. 'But please, Tyrell, let him rest. Ever since Mom died I can't get him to take care of himself. If it can wait until tomorrow . . .'

'I don't think it can,' said Tyrell.

'Well, go on then,' she said. 'You know the way.'

Tyrell left the house by the kitchen door and went out to the garage. He walked up the steps and knocked on the outside door. Lou hailed him from inside and Tyrell opened the door.

Lou's apartment was cozy but plenty spacious for one person. It had a bedroom, bathroom, a galley kitchen and a little living room. In front of the television was a roomy recliner in a nubby oatmeal-colored fabric. It was well worn, in contrast to a similarly upholstered loveseat, which looked like no one ever sat in it.

Lou was already in his bathrobe, pajamas and slippers, carrying a cocktail glass of whiskey over to his single end table when Tyrell came in. The bookshelves in the room had very few books on them, but many photographs of all sizes clustered in the empty spaces.

'Hey Tyrell,' said Lou, holding his cocktail glass aloft. 'Caught me cheating. Can I fix you one?'

Tyrell shook his head.

'Sit down,' said Lou, indicating the pristine loveseat. Tyrell hesitated, and then perched on the edge of one cushion while Lou settled himself in the recliner. As Kim had said, Lou looked tired. The circles under his eyes were darker than usual, and his skin was almost the same color as the upholstery on his recliner. 'What's up?'

'Lou,' said Tyrell. 'I'm here about the Riley kid.'

Lou placed his cocktail on a folded paper towel. 'What about him?'

'I told Ken to pick him up and charge him, and Kenny told me that you let him go tonight.'

Lou waved a meaty hand dismissively. 'It's more of the same baloney. That woman is a hysteric, Tyrell.'

Tyrell leaned forward and tried to catch the chief's eye, but Lou avoided his gaze.

'Lou; he followed her out to the cemetery. He punctured a hole in her tire. He was chasing her when she was spotted by some workers out there.'

'Lovers' quarrels,' Lou said stubbornly. 'Whoever decided we should start interfering in the private squabbles between a man and a woman?'

'Judge Hobart issued a restraining order this afternoon.'

'Well, what can I tell you? You know she's one of those women's lib nutcases. Tyrell, why are you wasting so much time on this? We got a murderer out there to catch.'

'Yes, and it could be that Brian Riley is the man we're looking for,' Tyrell snapped.

Lou turned a glowering gaze on him. 'That is not true,' he said.

Tyrell, who was holding his hat in his hands, kneaded the brim between his long fingers. 'Lou,' he said, 'I'm trying to understand this. I've never known you ignore the law. You always try to treat people equally. That's one reason I wanted to work for you.'

'Thank you,' said Lou gravely. 'I try.'

'But you've got a blind spot when it comes to Riley. This is twice you've let him off with a slap on the wrist.'

Lou sighed. 'I know I may favor him a little bit. You've got to understand, Tyrell. Not only is he . . . my best friend's boy, Brian's had it rough in his life. His parents . . . There were a lot of terrible things that happened to him, through no fault of his own. His parents ended up very bitter towards one another. I'm afraid his dad sometimes took it out on Brian. His mother was a . . . strong-willed woman. Very beautiful but not always . . . she could be cruel. I mean, she wanted what she wanted and she didn't care who got hurt. So, Brian was the one who suffered . . .'

'Chief, my mother's a drug addict who left me and my brother almost as soon as she had us. That doesn't give me the right to break the law.'

'Yes, but you had Reggie and Ella to love you and set you a good example. Brian didn't have that. He has a little trouble sometimes knowing how to treat women . . .'

'A little trouble? Are we talking about letting a man get away with murder? You said you questioned him. Does he really have an alibi for the time when Jennifer Hubbell was murdered?'

Lou glared at him, wounded. 'You disappoint me, Tyrell. I believed in you. I gave you opportunities when some other people might not have. You've never had any reason to doubt me.' Lou's phone rang and Lou picked it up. 'Excuse me,' he said with exaggerated politeness.

Tyrell looked away from the chief's rueful gaze. It was true that Lou had been his mentor. He hated that it had come to this. His gaze fell on the many photos on the bookshelves. He recognized many of the people pictured there. Kim, her husband in wedding gear. Hattie and Lou, heads tilted together, smiling. Some sepia-toned pictures of people in Victorian outfits. School photos of the kids, gap-toothed against a sea-blue background. And there, a man with his handsome face nearly obscured by a cowboy hat. At first, Tyrell thought it was Brian Riley. Then, on second glance, he realized it had to be Matthew Riley. He was standing beside a beautiful woman with long black hair, holding a baby. Brian and his mother. In the picture, Matthew stood next to them, but apart from them. The woman seemed to be holding the baby away from him, while Matthew stared, unsmiling, into the camera. It was a good friend, indeed, Tyrell thought, whose picture you kept among the photos of your own family.

Lou hung up the phone and sighed. 'Some friends of the dead girl,' he said. 'Something they want to talk about before they leave tomorrow.'

Tyrell stood up. 'Lou,' he said, 'I'm going to go serve this restraining order on the Riley kid. After this, it's everything by the books. The judge explained her rights to Miss Russell. Now you know he can't come near her or harass her in any way or we have to pick him up. We can't fuck around with this now, Lou, or the judge is going to be all over our butts.'

'Don't tell me how to do my job,' Lou grumbled.

Tyrell felt like saying that somebody had to, but he held his tongue.

Vibes was the name of the bar downtown where Tyrell had been directed by an aide out at the nursing home. He had been looking in vain for Brian, first at the Riley farm, and then at the nursing home, but his queries finally led him to a girl in a turquoise smock with an underwater print on it of fishes and coral. The aide was young, early twenties maybe, and she had explained that it was her favorite place to stop after work. She had often seen Brian Riley there when she stopped in. Tyrell thanked her, and made his way there.

As he opened the door, the smoke inside changed the air quality from crisp to heavy. The noise coming from the bandstand in the back was the music of a group of skinny tattooed white boys, all dressed in black. The bar was three deep in patrons, all laughing, talking in loud voices and drinking steadily.

Tyrell felt a number of gazes swivel his way when he walked in. He could hear the din of chatter subside somewhat as the people in the bar realized he was there. He wasn't sure if that was because he was black or a cop or both. He had a feeling that his presence would have quieted the patrons either way. There weren't any other black faces in the crowd and he didn't need any of these liquored-up rednecks to start thinking he had come in here to hit on their women.

Tyrell coughed, choked by the blanket of smoke. He edged his way down the bar, meeting every glance that came in his direction with an inscrutable, slightly challenging stare. So far there was no sign of Boots. He found a break in the jostling of bodies and leaned into the bartender. He had to yell to make himself heard over the evening commotion.

The bartender, as befitted a man who sold liquor to people without benefit of identification, leaned toward him with a solemn, helpful expression on his face.

'Brian Riley?' Tyrell shouted.

There was no need to repeat himself. The bartender peered down the bar through the crowd and then pointed out the space in the back, in front of the bandstand. Tyrell thanked him and the bartender nodded. Tyrell resumed pushing his way through the cheerful mob, trying to avoid being burned by the ends of cigarettes which were waved about for conversational emphasis. The noise level in the room had resumed at high decibels.

Once he got past the bar itself, and gazed into the small, tightly packed area of tables, it was easy to spot his man. Brian was seated at a table with four other people, two of them young women in tank tops and multiple earrings. The tabletop was covered with glasses and beer bottles in varying degrees of emptiness. Tyrell stood there, waiting, and Brian looked up, as if he sensed the policeman staring at him.

His immediate, unguarded reaction was alarm, but he quickly covered it with his wide, winning smile. 'Tyrell,' he cried. 'My man.' He rose partway to his feet, and pointed out the cop to the other people at the table. They turned and gazed at Tyrell with suspicion and mistrust in their eyes, making no effort at sociability. Underage, Tyrell suspected. But right now, he had other concerns.

He waded toward the table and ignored the friendly hand which Brian extended to him in greeting. Instead, he slapped the paper into Brian's palm.

Brian, who was having trouble focusing his gaze, wrinkled up his nose and looked up innocently at the policeman. 'What the hell is this?'

'Restraining order,' said Tyrell.

Brian shook his head helplessly, to indicate that he had not heard.

Tyrell cocked his head back toward the door. Brian crushed the paper in his hands and followed the policeman out. When they reached the sidewalk, the night seemed suddenly silent and clear. Stars winked above Main Street, and the noise from inside the bar was dim and faraway.

Brian shivered. 'Shit, it's freezing out here, man.'

Tyrell could feel the other man trying to be familiar, friendly. He wasn't about to return the friendliness. Not this time. 'That's a temporary restraining order on you, Boots,' he said, the nickname his only concession to familiarity. 'It was handed down by Judge Hobart late today.'

Brian frowned at the paper in his hand. Then he shoved it back at Tyrell. 'I don't want this,' he said.

Tyrell roughly pushed his hand away. 'This means you are not to get anywhere near Miss Russell, or harass her in any way, or I'm going to throw your ass in jail.'

Brian peered at him, the affable expression gone from his face. His eyes glinted at Tyrell in the darkness. He said nothing.

'Now I know the chief saved your butt again tonight, but that's the end of it. Do you understand what I'm telling you?' Tyrell asked. 'Nowhere near. Not within a hundred yards of her. Clear?'

Riley shook his head. 'That bitch,' he muttered.

'Come again?' Tyrell demanded.

Brian did not reply.

'Your troubles are just beginning, man. You stay away from her.'

Brian looked at the paper, and then, coldly, up at the cop. 'You mind if I go back in there with my friends?' he said bitterly. 'I don't like the weather out here.'

Tyrell shrugged, as if to indicate that he didn't care. 'That's a court order,' he said. 'Mind how you go.'

'I should have let those guys have you,' Brian said bitterly.

Tyrell didn't take the bait, though he knew what Brian meant. 'I'm watching you,' he said.

TWENTY-ONE

Lou Potter pulled his police cruiser into one of the metered parking spots in front of the Endicott Hotel, thankful that he wouldn't have to walk too far on this windy, rainy morning. In its day, the Endicott had been a grand hostelry, the centerpiece of Monroe, located smack in the middle of Main Street. Thanks to the care of Jake Smith, it remained a fine establishment, although there was nothing trendy about it. The dining room still served pork chops, fried chicken and prime rib, as it always had. And, for breakfast, they served a feast worthy of a farmhand. Sausage and scrapple, eggs, pancakes and fried apples. Lou knew he wasn't supposed to eat like that – his doctor was always lecturing him about his angina and his test results. But this morning he thought maybe he might stop in the dining room and treat himself, once he finished talking to Miss Mallory. She and her boyfriend were flying out early, and she wanted to speak to him before the airport limo came to pick them up. He'd been forced to skip breakfast at home in order to get here early enough.

Lou climbed the marble steps and opened the large, carved mahogany door to the lobby. The lobby of the Endicott was the kind of place that made you want to sit down and put your feet up. There were several groupings of comfortable armchairs and loveseats in faded velvets, illuminated by old standing lamps with silk shades. The flower arrangements on the many occasional tables were elaborate, and made of silk.

There was a large hearth but the fire was not lit as it customarily was. This struck Lou as kind of sad. Evidence that Jake Smith was distracted and had lost heart for the job after the death of his child. Lou was thinking about where to sit down when the elevator door opened and Laura Mallory came into the lobby, followed by her boyfriend with the glasses and thinning hair. She gave Lou a wave and then looked around anxiously.

'Your bags are behind the desk,' said the clerk, emerging from the back. 'All ready for you.'

'Oh good,' said Laura. Even though it was warm in the lobby, she pulled her coat tightly around her, and indicated a gold sofa nearby. Lou, who disliked sitting in sofas, sat down opposite it in a brocaded armchair. The couple sat on the sofa, side by side, holding hands. They both looked extremely tired.

'So, you two are leaving today,' said Lou, his hands resting on his thighs.

Skip nodded. 'Temporarily. We're going to come back and get Ron when you say it's all right for him to leave.'

Lou heard the criticism and the disbelief implied. Naturally, these people would find it hard to believe their friend was a killer. It spoke well for them as friends, and for Ron's ability to command loyalty, but lots of the people filling up penitentiaries had loyal friends and families.

'Will he be staying with you?' Lou asked, as if agreeing that it soon would be all right for Ron to leave. He had no wish to pain or antagonize them.

Laura nodded. 'For a while. Our house is big enough so we won't be tripping all over each other. It'll give him a chance to decide what to do. His old boss is eager to have him back.'

'Well, that's good,' said Lou. 'He seems to have a lot of friends.'

'He's a wonderful man,' said Laura.

Lou sighed. In these domestic things it usually wasn't a case of one person being bad and the other being good. It was usually about people knowing how to push one another's buttons. Then, one of them snaps out in rage and you've got violence. Hardly ever violence this extreme, but it happened.

'He didn't deserve this,' Laura went on. 'Well, nobody does. I mean, you always think, "why me?" But that's one of those questions without an answer. You have to find a way to go on.'

'That's true,' said Lou. For a minute there was an awkward silence. 'What time's your flight?' Lou asked.

Laura and Skip glanced at one another. 'We're on different flights,' Laura explained. 'I have some . . . I'm headed to Chicago. Skip is going back to Boston.'

'Well, I won't hold you up,' said Lou. 'You said on the phone you might have remembered something.'

Laura leaned forward and kneaded her hands together. 'I'm not saying that I know what happened,' she said.

'I understand that,' said Lou.

'OK. I was thinking about what you'd asked me. If Jennifer ever confided anything in me . . .'

'And . . .' he prodded.

'Well, you know Jenn and I were friends for about five years. Very close friends, but I didn't know her when . . . when her sister died.' She bit her lip and squinted into the dark fireplace.

Uh oh, Lou thought. What's this all about?

Laura sat up and intertwined her fingers with Skip's once again. 'After the funeral, I fell asleep while Skip was reading to me . . .'

A dream. Dandy. Just what I need. He was not one to rely on dreams, premonitions, or portents. He had been hoping for some real information.

'And when I woke up, I remembered something that happened.'

Lou felt guardedly interested again. 'Something that actually happened,' he said, making sure.

Laura nodded. 'I never saw these letters, you understand. That's why I didn't think of them right away.'

'What letters?' Lou said warily.

'Well, after her sister was . . . after she died, the family was convinced that the Riley fellow was responsible.'

'There was no evidence of that,' Lou said stubbornly. 'I don't
know how many times we have to tell you people that . . .'

'I'm not saying . . .' Laura collected herself and began again.
'You asked me about any enemies that Jennifer might have
had. You can have an enemy and not know who it is.'

'I suppose,' said Lou, frowning.

'Jennifer was trying to find some kind of proof that Brian Riley
had killed her sister. She talked to the doctor who examined her
body, and to people that knew Brian . . .'

'She talked to me,' said Lou irritably. 'And I told her what I'm
telling you now . . .'

'I know, I know,' said Laura. 'I'm talking about the letters.
Sometime after she came home here, trying to dig up some information, she received a couple of letters. Anonymous letters.'

'Oh?' said Lou.

'As I said, we met after this happened, so I never saw the letters.
But I remember her telling me about them. Basically, the letters were
threatening. They told her to stop involving herself, stay out of it or
else. That kind of thing. I don't remember the wording.'

'Did she . . . have any idea who sent them?' Lou asked.

'Well, naturally she thought it was Brian.'

'Naturally.'

'But it wasn't. I forget how they determined that. Wait, I
remember. They were postmarked from here, but he had gone
away after Tanya's death. I think he went to California. Anyway,
she was satisfied that he hadn't sent them. But she wondered who
had. After a while, I guess she stopped caring who sent them.
There was nothing she could do.'

'Well, it's interesting,' said Lou. 'But I don't see how it could
matter now . . .'

'Well, you wondered if she had enemies. I'd say she had at
least one enemy in this town. Wouldn't you?'

Lou nodded. 'That could be.'

A horn sounded outside and Laura and Skip exchanged a look.
'I'll go see,' he said. He got up and walked over to the front door and
looked out. Then he nodded and walked over to the front desk.

'The airport bus,' she said apologetically. Lou shook his head.
'You were saying?'

'Well, I got to thinking. If she still had the letters, maybe
your department could determine who sent them. Fingerprints or

whatever. I think now you can identify the sender by DNA from saliva on the envelope. They might still be among her belongings. I didn't want to upset Ron with this until I mentioned it to you.'

Lou nodded slowly, avoiding her gaze.

'Honey,' Skip called from the door of the hotel.

Laura stood up. 'I don't know if that helps, but it seems to me it might be important. I'm sorry to have to run . . .'

Standing up, Lou said, 'It's all right. Thanks for telling me. And I will see to it that the matter is looked into.'

He watched the two of them pick up their bags, hurry down the steps and bundle into the van. He waved to them, and he could see their hands, like white moths against the tinted windows, waving back. Then he turned slowly and headed toward the dining room.

'Sit anywhere,' said the hostess, indicating the half-empty pink room with its snowy linen and mirrors. Lou walked to a nearby table and sat down.

A young girl in a white shirt, gray skirt and a ponytail came up to him and smiled brightly into his ashen face. 'Coffee?' she chirped.

Lou nodded, and she filled the cup. 'I'll be right back,' she said.

Lou put his forearms against the tabletop and lifted the cup toward his mouth.

The cup shook in his hands. Brian, he thought.

He took a sip and the coffee hit his stomach like a rabbit punch, backing up and burning his esophagus. Lou tried to burp, to get rid of the burning sensation, but he couldn't. He fumbled in his pocket for an antacid tablet and popped it in his mouth. His mind was churning along with his stomach.

It had been such a long time since Tanya Smith had died. One of those things that people got all upset about at the time, and then it blew over. Sweat broke out on his forehead, and he mopped it with the large linen napkin.

Lou never could understand, not for the life of him, why Jennifer refused to let it go. People slipped in the shower every day. She seemed unable to grasp that fact, no matter how many times she heard it. She was determined to try and ruin Brian's life with her suspicions. She didn't realize the anguish she was causing, going on about it like she did. And now Jennifer was dead, and once again there were people trying to implicate Brian. It never seemed to end.

If only Brian had not been acting so recklessly lately. Disregarding

Lou's warnings. Still trying to get to Dena Russell. He didn't seem to understand that there was only so much you could do. Only so many times you could keep something quiet. Cover it up. Even when you knew you were doing what you had to. Doing what was best for everyone. But, even as he thought it, he recalled his conversation with Laura and Skip just minutes ago. She had been saying what a wonderful man Ron was, and Lou had been thinking that it was difficult to believe the worst of the people you cared for. Like Brian . . .

No, Lou thought again, absently rubbing his gut, waiting for the antacid to kick in.

It was impossible. Brian's behavior had been – annoying, not dangerous. Men who harassed their wives or girlfriends weren't killers. Not usually. It was something men understood about other men. You didn't have to explain it to everybody. The occasional flare-up with a woman didn't mean a man was bent on murder.

No, it couldn't be, he tried to tell himself.

But, of course, it could. Lou was not a fool. He knew that such things did happen. It was just that he'd gone so far in protecting him, he thought. People were beginning to question his motives, and he couldn't let them find out. Even Tyrell, whom he had trusted, and taken under his wing, was questioning him now. And what would happen if these meddling friends of Jennifer's got their way? Dredged up these old letters. What if everything started to come out into the open?

A pain scalded the inside of Lou's chest like a branding iron. The girl in the ponytail came up to Lou's table, pencil and pad in hand. She looked down at the gray-complexioned man clutching his chest and her smile faded. 'Is something wrong, sir?' she asked, a faint sound of worry in her voice.

Lou looked up at her, his eyes dull. 'I think I need a doctor,' he whispered.

'Right,' she said. Then she turned, calling out the name of the hostess in a high, urgent voice.

Lou stared at the coffee cup without seeing it. He was seeing Brian, all innocence, smiling up at him. It felt as if an iron claw was reaching into his chest and squeezing on his heart. Around him, he could hear murmurs of concern, people pushing their chairs back and standing up to stare. He wanted to tell them to sit down and stop gaping at him, but all his energy was focused

now on that burning hole in his chest, the shooting rays of pain
that were in his shoulder, his arm. He reached for the glass of
water at his place and missed, knocking it over. Water ran everywhere as Lou's weakened hand groped and then grasped the white
linen of the tablecloth. He held onto it, trying to stay upright, but
it was no use. There was a crash of silverware and glass breaking
as Lou toppled from his seat, and hit the floor.

TWENTY-TWO

The smell of coffee, banana and something rich and eggy
wafted into the hallway as Dena descended the stairs from
her apartment. She felt a pang of hunger but, at the same
time, couldn't imagine actually eating anything. Still, as she looked
at the closed door of Peter's apartment, she felt a kind of yearning,
an envy of Peter and his daughters, in there together, having their
breakfast, while she was about to embark on this painful visit to
Jennifer's now-forlorn nursery.

As if she had read Dena's thoughts, Tory threw open the apartment door just as Dena reached the bottom step. She was wearing
an apron and had a spatula in her hand. 'We made banana pancakes,'
she said. 'Do you want some?'

Dena smiled at the child, looking so grown-up and . . . motherly.
'Oh, what a lovely offer,' Dena said.

'We made extra,' said Tory.

Dena hesitated and then thought that it wouldn't hurt to step
in for a minute. She was dreading going out into the gray morning.
It was dark and rainy once again. And she was dreading the sight
of Ron, and having to look at all those baby things with him,
reminding him of his loss. 'All right, I'll have one bite,' Dena
said.

The child's face lit up with joy and Dena was glad she had
agreed. But when she walked into the apartment, her spirits sank
once again. 'My, you got a lot done,' she said, looking around at
the bare shelves, everything emptied and packed, as she laid her
coat on a chair by the door.

'We've been up for hours,' Tory confided as she led the way to the kitchen, where Peter was dividing pancakes onto plates and pouring milk.

'Guess what. Make a plate for Dena!'

Peter looked up in surprise. 'Good morning,' he said.

'I was waylaid by the chef,' Dena said, blushing.

'Here, sit,' he said, indicating a chair.

'Just one for me,' said Dena, shaking out a napkin and tucking it into her jumper, since she no longer had a lap in which to set it. Carrying the plate with both hands, Tory set it down in front of her.

'These look delicious,' Dena said.

'Dad's recipe,' Tory said proudly, beaming at her father.

Dena nodded, and waited until they were all seated. Megan came in at the last minute, still wearing pajamas. They began to pass butter and syrup. Then the children bent their fair heads over their plates and began to eat. A recording of *The Four Seasons* played softly in the background. The scene was so idyllic that Dena sighed, in spite of herself. How did Peter do it, she wondered? He was mother and father both to these girls. Dena had doubts about her own ability to even be an adequate mother.

The landline rang and Tory dropped her fork and lunged to answer it, turning her back on the table.

'Who is it?' Peter demanded.

Tory turned around with her hand over the mouthpiece. 'A girl in my class,' she said.

Peter watched his daughter intently as she talked to her schoolmate.

Tory said, 'I don't know. I'll ask.' She looked at her father. 'Can I go over to Jacqueline's and play tomorrow?'

Peter looked at her incredulously. 'Tory, we're leaving tomorrow.'

Tory did not miss a beat. She said calmly, 'No, I can't. I'm moving tomorrow. But thank you for asking.' She hung up the phone and sat back down at the table.

Megan, who was watching this exchange with wide eyes, suddenly began to wail. 'No, I don't wanna go.'

'You have to,' said Tory. 'Dad, tell her she has to.'

'That's enough now,' said Peter, clapping his hands. 'You girls still have work to do on your room. Tory, help your sister.'

Tory obediently bent down, wiped Megan's face with a napkin and took her hand. 'Come on,' she said. 'I'll let you pack my Barbie trunk.'

Reluctantly, tears still streaking her cheeks, Megan gave in to the alluring offer, and allowed herself to be dragged down the hallway.

Dena watched them go, and then wiped her own mouth and stood up. 'I'd better be going too. I'm going to meet Ron over at his house. To go through the baby stuff. Thank you for the pancakes.'

'Glad you could join us,' he said.

She shook her head and looked toward the doorway where the children had disappeared. 'You know, I watch you with your children and I'm just amazed. I didn't know men existed who were so committed to their kids. It makes me . . . jealous for my own baby. Every child should have a father like you.'

'Ideally,' he agreed with a smile.

'I hardly remember my dad. He died when I was six. But I believe that he loved me like that. My mother always said he did.'

Peter stood up and began to collect the plates. 'My dad played piano on a cruise ship, or so my mother told me. I was the result of a one-night stand,' he said. 'I guess that's where I got my musical gift,' he said wryly.

Dena shook her head. 'Oh, Peter, that's a terrible thing to tell a child.'

'She was nothing if not blunt,' he said, smiling thinly.

'So you had no . . . model for fatherhood, so to speak.'

'Or motherhood. I'm a self-made parent,' he said.

She sighed. 'Well, you're a good one. I wish you weren't leaving tomorrow. I'll miss you . . . all so much.'

Peter put the dishes in the sink and turned on the tap. 'I think you should come with us,' he said.

'I wish I could,' she said.

He turned, wiping his hands. 'It's on the way. We could take you as far as your sister's.'

'That's very nice,' she said. 'But I'm sure I'll be leaving soon.'

Peter walked her to the door. 'It's up to you . . .' he said curtly.

Dena turned at the door and impulsively put her arms around his neck, hugging him. He stiffened against her embrace as if it were unwelcome. She pulled away from him in confusion. Avoiding her questioning gaze, he patted her swollen belly.

'A baby is the greatest gift there is,' he said. 'You should treat it like a treasure.'

Dena wondered if he was annoyed about the ride. 'I really appreciate the offer,' she said. 'But I think I'm doing the right thing.'

'Let's hope you don't live to regret it.'

'I should hope not,' she said. She picked up her coat and purse and left the house.

The yellow tape still encircled the Hubbells' cottage, but there was no patrolman at the door as there had been before. Dena climbed the steps reluctantly, and peered into the porch windows. The house was completely dark, and she wondered if she had gotten the time mixed up when Ron had asked her to come. She knocked once, and then tried the bell. The house was silent and Dena felt a distinct desire to turn away. At that moment, she saw an unsmiling face materialize in the gloomy interior.

'Ron?' she asked.

Ron came out onto the porch and opened the door for her. He was wearing the same clothes he'd had on the day before, and he looked exhausted. 'Come in,' he said.

'Where's your friend?' Dena asked.

Ron looked at her in confusion. 'Who?'

'Your friendly policeman seems to be missing.'

'Oh, yeah,' he said. 'They called him in. I heard him talking on his radio. It sounded as if something happened to the chief. They were taking him to the hospital.'

'Oh,' said Dena. 'I wonder what.'

'This way,' said Ron, pointing to the stairs. It was clear that he did not wonder at all about the chief.

He indicated that she should walk in front of him and she hesitated and then said, 'Could you put the light on?' She put a hand on her belly. 'I'm so clumsy these days.'

'Oh, sure,' he said.

Dena began to climb up the stairwell, now illuminated, toward the second floor. She knew what she was going to find. She had looked longingly into the nursery when she was staying here. Still, when she reached the doorway in the hall, she was reluctant to push it open.

'Go ahead,' he said. Ron came up behind her, and she could smell his clothes, the mixture of aftershave and perspiration on them settling into a stale, suffocating funk around him. Partly to get a little distance from him, she steeled herself and opened the door.

The nursery was exactly as Jennifer had left it. The crib was set up with bolsters, bedding and a mobile hanging over it. The changing table was equipped with lotions and powder and an unopened bag of newborn Pampers. The cheerful hooked rug, the painted cushioned rocker and the framed nursery rhymes combined to make a heartbreaking tableau. For a minute, Dena was overwhelmed by the sheer hopefulness of the room, and had to turn away. Ron waded in, however, like a man used to swimming below the surface of murky waters. He walked over to the wall and rubbed his fingertips onto an invisible pattern that only he could see, waist-high.

'She was going to stencil this part,' he said. 'She showed me a couple of different colors and designs. She was good that way. She really was. She had the ability to take something plain and make it beautiful. That's the way she was,' he murmured.

'Yes, she was,' Dena agreed, not knowing what else to say.

'Go ahead and look,' he urged her. He pulled open the dresser drawers. 'Full of clothes. All of them are unisex. We didn't want to know the secret, so she bought all colors that either a boy or a girl could wear. Take them all.'

In what? Dena thought. She hadn't planned to carry stuff away today. 'These clothes are beautiful,' she said, gently patting the pastel coveralls, pajamas and sweaters. 'My baby will be lucky to have such wonderful clothes.'

Ron opened the doors on the changing table and pulled out a diaper bag. 'Here, put them in this. Top of the line. She pored over the catalogues until she found a diaper bag that did everything but change the baby itself. Here, take it,' he said, pushing it at her. 'Fill it up with anything you want,' he cried. 'The stuff cost a fortune.'

He was roaming around the nursery, pulling toys down off the shelves and tiny outfits on hangers from the closet, and tossing them behind him so they fell on the floor.

'Ron,' Dena said anxiously. 'I don't think this is the right day for this. It's too close. It hurts too much.'

Ron turned and looked at the heap he had made on the yellow hooked rug. 'I thought she was spending too much money,' he said. 'I had heard rumors I was going to lose my job. And the house was costing more than we anticipated. Meanwhile, she kept buying things for the baby. She tore off all the tags so that nothing would go back. She wasn't taking anything back.'

'Well, she was excited about the baby . . .' Dena said, not sure what he expected her to say.

'Yes, the baby. She wanted that baby more than anything. She thought that's what I wanted too. She assumed it. She assumed every man wanted to have a child . . .'

'You didn't?' she asked softly.

Ron stared into the dark closet, one hand resting on the edges of an empty drawer. 'No. Not really. Not at first. What was the big rush? I wanted it to be the two of us for a while. But, I'm a "yes" man. I tell people what they want to hear.'

Dena frowned. Every marriage was a mystery, she thought. The secret fears and disappointments partners kept from one another and the world. It was sad to hear him saying these things now, in the wake of Jennifer's death. There was no need to admit to any faults in their marriage anymore. She wondered why he was telling her this.

'Are you surprised?' he asked coldly.

'Surprised at what?' she asked.

'The truth,' he said.

Dena searched for the right words. 'I think you're being a little hard on yourself,' she said. 'I saw you at those Lamaze classes. You can't tell me you weren't happy about that baby. I mean, everybody has reservations at first, I think.'

'No, not everybody,' he insisted.

'Sure,' she said gently. 'Such a big change in your life. Jennifer understood that. I'm sure she did. I think women just have some kind of . . . I don't know what . . . some chemical in their body that makes them look forward to babies. Tides the men over until they can get used to the idea.' The good men, anyway, she thought.

'I was worried about the money,' he protested, as if he wanted to convince her of how loathsome a person he was. 'I thought about it all the time.'

Dena walked over and put a hand gently on his shoulder. 'It's only natural. Babies are expensive. You can spend a small fortune on getting them outfitted.'

'She was determined to have everything ready when the baby came. Everything in its place and it didn't matter to her what it cost. I wanted her to stop, but I didn't know how to tell her that,' he said.

Dena could see that he was determined to prove that he was

stingy and mean-spirited. In spite of what she knew to be true, he wanted her to agree that he was a terrible person. 'All right now. Come on,' Dena said firmly. 'Come downstairs. I don't want to do this today. I'll be happy to have these things and I'll come back and get them. But you need to get out of here. You're torturing yourself over this and you shouldn't be. You were only concerned about them. Jennifer and your baby. Worried about their security, like any good dad would be.

'Besides,' she said, trying to lighten the gloom a little, 'many a husband has wished his wife liked shopping a little less. It doesn't mean anything. It's just one of those things between men and women.'

'So innocent,' he said, his shoulders sagging. 'Just buying things for her baby.'

'Ron,' Dena said. 'Look. If she were here today she'd be proposing a trip to Babies "R" Us and you'd be cheerfully fuming. Right?'

Ron stared bleakly at the empty crib.

'And, oh, how we wish that could happen,' Dena said, with a catch in her voice. 'That she could walk in that door, credit card at the ready, and say, "Let's go shopping." Right?'

She saw a tear slide down his sallow face.

'Now, you get out of this room right now. Get out of the house. You shouldn't be here.'

He started to gather up the clothes and toys on the floor. Dena intervened. 'Go on now. I'll do that.' She waited until he had shuffled out of the room and then she quickly gathered up and folded the tiny clothes and put the toys back on the shelves. It was strange to realize that she would soon be using these things for her own baby. And she could not suppress a secret feeling of joy that she had her baby to look forward to. She didn't begrudge herself the feeling. She knew Jennifer would understand.

When she had finished, she closed the door to the nursery and went back downstairs. 'Ron,' she called, but there was no reply in the dark house. She walked through the living room and the dining room, avoiding looking at the place where Jennifer's body had been found. She went out into the kitchen, which was much brighter thanks to its many windows. Looking out, she saw Ron standing, coatless, in the drizzly backyard. He was ankle deep in brightly colored leaves, his hands in his pockets, looking around, as if for the last time.

Give him a minute, Dena thought. You couldn't hurry someone through their grieving. She had grieved enough to know. She sat down at the breakfast table, in the very seat where she had last sat when Jennifer was alive. She looked around the neat kitchen, remembering that morning. She and Jenn had talked about their day, their plans, the fact that it was Jennifer's anniversary. And then, she remembered something else.

There had been that phone call, about the flowers. They were going to deliver flowers to her that afternoon. She thought of Sergeant Watkins, asking her to call him if she remembered anything. Did it matter about the flowers? she wondered.

She heard footsteps coming up the back, and then the kitchen door opened, and Ron came in, shivering.

'Ron,' she asked.

He looked at her dully.

'The day that Jennifer was killed. It was your anniversary.' He nodded. 'Someone called about delivering her some flowers that afternoon. Did they ever deliver them?'

Ron peered around, as if trying to visualize the room in the past. 'I don't . . . recall seeing them. I mean, I wasn't thinking about flowers.'

'But you did order them?'

'Yeah, I ordered them.'

'Where?' she said.

'A place near the station. Quilty's, I think it's called. Why?'

Dena shook her head. 'Just a thought, she said, reaching into her pocketbook on the table. I'm going to make a call.'

TWENTY-THREE

The intensive-care ward of Monroe General Hospital was in the newest wing of the building. It was at the end of a short corridor, lined with chairs for those who were waiting to see a relative beyond the swinging doors. A nurses' desk blocked access to any who had no business inside, which meant anyone not in the patient's immediate family.

Tyrell rushed down the corridor, clutching his hat. Just as he reached the bank of seats he saw Lou's daughter, Kim, coming out of the doors followed by her son, Jeff, who was wearing high-tops and a baggy flannel shirt. Kim was normally the soul of good cheer. At this moment, her face was haggard and her blue eyes looked gray and faded.

Her face brightened at the sight of Tyrell, and he scooped her up in a hug. She patted his back as he squeezed her. Then he turned and shook Jeff's hand and the two exchanged a sympathetic, if laconic greeting.

'How is he doing?' Tyrell asked, turning back to Kim. 'I got here as fast as I could.'

Kim dabbed at her eyes with a wadded Kleenex. 'They didn't think he was going to make it, at first.'

'What happened?'

'A heart attack. He was having breakfast at the Endicott Hotel and he just keeled over.'

Tyrell squeezed her hand. 'He's tough,' he said. 'He'll pull through.'

'I hope so,' Kim said in a teary voice.

'Can I go in and see him?' Tyrell asked.

'You go on in,' Kim said, squeezing his hand back. 'It would do him good to see you. But you can only stay a minute.'

'No more, I promise,' said Tyrell.

He walked over to the swinging door and began to push it.

'Excuse me,' cried an imperious voice from the nurses' desk. Tyrell turned and looked at the imposing, white-haired woman with steel-rimmed glasses who was manning it. 'Who were you wanting to see?'

Tyrell glanced over at Kim. 'Chief . . . Lou Potter,' he said.

'I'm sorry,' said the nurse, not sounding the least bit sorry. 'Family only.'

Kim sniffed at her handkerchief and walked up to the desk. 'This is my brother,' she said with a perfectly straight face. Jeff, seated near the door, with his long legs extended, put a hand over his face and laughed into it.

Tyrell stifled the smile that threatened to spread over his broad features. The nurse glared at Kim. 'This is not a joke, ma'am. This rule is for the good of the patients.'

Kim stood her ground without flinching. 'I'm not joking,' she said. 'This is my brother, Tyrell. He wants to see Dad.'

The nurse shook her head, unsmiling, but finally flicked a hand toward the door without looking at Tyrell. 'Bed three. Two minutes,' she said.

Tyrell opened the door and walked slowly through the small, noisy, brightly lit ward. The patients were in glass-enclosed cubicles, attached to every kind of machine and monitor imaginable. Most of them had faces whiter than the sheets they lay on.

Every step made Tyrell feel more queasy. He had to do a double-take to reassure himself that the man on bed three was really the chief.

A young nurse was holding her fingers against the old man's wrist, and looking at the monitors with a serious expression. Lou had his head back, and a clear, accordion-pleated tube was taped into his mouth. There were narrow tubes in his nose, and an IV in each arm. The smell in the ward was at once medicinal and necrotic. Tyrell found it difficult not to gag. At first, he thought Lou's eyes were closed, but then he saw a slit, moist and bright, below his eyelids. Tyrell walked over to the bars at the side of Lou's bed, reached over and took the man's icy-white fingers into his own brown hand. The nurse looked away from the monitors and smiled briefly at him. 'Make it quick,' she said.

'I will.' He looked down at the chief's familiar face, now slackened by pain and medication. 'Hey. Lou. You got to get out of here,' he whispered.

The only response was the gurgling noises of the respirator.

'I'm not supposed to stay. I just wanted you to know I was here, and I'm pulling for you, my man.' It was hard to know what to say to a person in Lou's condition. Hard to know if they understood you, or even heard you. Hard, because they couldn't reply, no matter what you said.

Lou opened his eyes to half-mast, and Tyrell saw a look of urgency in the haze of his gaze. There was a tiny motion of the cold, white fingers against Tyrell's palm.

'No, no,' said Tyrell. 'Don't. Take it easy. Don't worry. Everything will be all right. You just get well. We'll get by, until you're better. Just make it quick, OK? I'd better get out of here. I wasn't supposed to be in here but Kim told the nurse I was her brother. For some reason, I don't think the nurse bought it.'

There was the faintest hint of a glint in Lou's eyes, as if he got the joke.

Tyrell reached up and smoothed back the thinning gray hair on the chief's head. Then he placed Lou's hand back on the scratchy sheet and smiled at him, before he left the cubicle, holding his breath against the smell of the ward.

As he pushed the door open, he saw the trim, uniformed figure of Heath Van Brunt, standing in the corridor talking to Kim. He walked over to them. 'Captain,' he said solemnly.

'How's he doing?' Van Brunt asked.

Mindful of Kim's anxious presence, Tyrell expressed an optimism he didn't exactly feel. 'He's a tough guy. He'll come through this.'

Van Brunt nodded thoughtfully. 'Well, I just wanted to come over and express the good wishes of the department to you,' he said to Kim. 'I'll be acting chief until your dad is ready to come back and take over the helm. Anything you need, you let me know.'

'Thank you, Captain.'

She turned and smiled at Tyrell. 'Thank you for coming, Tyrell,' said Kim.

'I'll be back,' Tyrell promised. 'You take it easy. Jeff, my man, look after your mama here.'

Jeff nodded and smiled. 'I will.'

'Sergeant,' said Van Brunt, summoning him. He began to walk down the hall and Tyrell fell into step beside him. Tyrell put his hat back on as they reached the hospital exit. Once outside, under the portico, Van Brunt said, 'I've been going over the information we've accumulated. I think it's time we brought the husband in in the Hubbell case and put the screws to him a little bit.'

'If you think so, sir,' said Tyrell.

'You don't agree?'

Tyrell knew full well that his opinion carried no weight with the captain. Still, he had to try. 'I'm beginning to think we may have been too hasty in overlooking Mr Riley.'

'Sergeant, I have the chief's notes here and they clearly state that Mr Riley had an alibi for that time, and should not be considered a suspect.'

Tyrell wished he could see those notes. But he knew better than to ask. 'Sergeant?' Van Brunt said impatiently.

Tyrell sighed. 'Well, we haven't got anybody else. We know it wasn't the Ranger Electric van at the house that day. I have confirmation on that . . .'

Van Brunt drew himself up to his full height, which still made him several inches shorter than Tyrell. 'As I say, let's bring Ron Hubbell in and work him over a little bit. Figuratively speaking, of course.'

The two men parted and Tyrell loped toward his car, avoiding the rain. He got in, turned on the engine, and then felt his cell phone buzzing in his jacket pocket. He pulled it out and replied.

'Sergeant Watkins?'

'Speaking.'

'This is Dena Russell.' For a moment he was irritated. Irritated that Riley was at it again and would not get the message. Irritated because sometimes he found himself thinking about her, and he didn't want to think about her. He wanted her to get out of his head.

'Yeah,' he snapped.

At her end, Dena could hear the impatience in his voice. And, she understood it. He had done what he could to help her. He probably thought this was more trouble with Brian. She felt kind of pleased that she had something to offer, instead of something to ask this time.

Skip Lanman slipped down in the molded-plastic seat at the airport gate and shook his head in disgust. Laura, who had just visited the ladies' room, came walking back toward him and looked at him quizzically. He nodded toward the desk, manned by two pretty young women wearing navy blue jackets with red kerchiefs at the neck, where a knot of anxious passengers were insisting that they had to leave, despite the fact that another hour's delay had just been posted.

'Another delay?' Laura fretted. 'You'll be so tired by the time you get home.'

'It's all right,' Skip said. 'This way I can keep you company a little longer. Is your flight still on time?'

'So far,' Laura nodded. She sighed and looked around at the options for distraction, which were few, surrounding the departure gates. There were monitors overhead which ran CNN incessantly, and a few unappealing snack bars. 'I think I'll go buy a magazine,' she said. It'll give me something to do. I can browse through everything – wrestling to home improvement. Do you want anything?'

Skip frowned. 'Get me a pack of gum,' he said. 'Keep my ears from popping on the plane.'

'Will do,' she said. She took off across the blue-carpeted waiting
area to go in search of a newsstand. He watched her go, thinking
how good she looked in her oversized trench coat, her long curls
soft and shining against the turned-up collar. He knew she would
stop at every kiosk from here to the security checkpoint, roaming
restlessly in and out of the little shops, looking at her watch every
few minutes, hating the wait.

They were very different that way. Years of illness as a child
had taught him to be stoic in the face of a long wait. Enduring
the tests and the needles had taught him that there was no use
in wishing it would be over. He had learned to accept his fate.
Laura was different. She would never accept her fate. Different
responses to different situations, he thought. You handle it as
best you can.

He turned his attention to his fellow passengers, who were also
waiting. Two rows up, a red-faced man who was, unaccountably,
wearing a pair of Bermuda shorts, was snoozing. At the end of
Skip's row, a grandmother was trying to keep a cranky toddler
entertained, and clearly wearying of the task. Across the aisle, a
man in a black raincoat had his arm around his pregnant wife.

The sight of the couple turned Skip's thoughts back to Ron.
Ron had suffered so much in the years they had been friends. It
was one of the things that solidified their friendship. They were
two people who understood about suffering. Most of Skip's
suffering had been physical. For Ron, it was losses that were
emotional. The end of his marriage to Anita had been tough – and
humiliating. But this. This was the worst of blows – the murder
of Jennifer.

Skip wondered what Ron would make of the news about the
anonymous letters. Skip had agreed with Laura that it was important to tell the police about the letters, once she remembered them,
but they hadn't had a chance to mention them to Ron. They had
to leave before they had a chance to tell him. Skip wondered if
Jennifer had ever told Ron about the letters. He wondered if she'd
kept them. And then, he thought of something else. Ron was
cleaning out the house. No matter how much anyone told him to
leave it, to come back and do it another time, Ron was determined
to get on with it. It was a kind of self-flagellation, Skip figured,
forcing himself to go through her things, to face, with every item
he had to discard, the loss of her all over again.

The problem was, if those letters were among her things, they might get tossed out with piles of old receipts or bills.

Perhaps the sheriff had contacted Ron by now. But what if he hadn't? What if, at this very minute, Ron was tossing away evidence that might be crucial? Skip looked up, but there was no sign of Laura. In his mind's eye, he could see her, puttering through those kiosks, searching, always searching, under the guise of browsing through the airport. She could be gone for quite a while.

One of the women behind the desk amended the flight information board to read 'two-hour delay'. All right, thought Skip. That does it. He reached into his pocket for his phone.

TWENTY-FOUR

The smell of gardenias filled Tyrell's nostrils as he opened the door to Quilty's flower shop and found himself surrounded by banks of the glossy-leafed plants. There weren't many flowers he could have identified by name, but he knew gardenias because they were his grandmother's favorites. He had bought her many a gardenia plant over the years, and she always exclaimed with pleasure and remarked that they reminded her of Billie Holiday, Lady Day, who famously liked to wear a gardenia tucked behind her ear.

A young, but completely bald man behind the counter was twisting wires onto yellow mums and sticking them into the green Styrofoam which anchored an arrangement on his counter. A petite, middle-aged woman approached Tyrell and asked if she could help.

'I need to speak to the manager,' said Tyrell.

The woman looked over her shoulder. 'Keith,' she called out. 'This policeman wants to talk to you.'

Keith, the man behind the counter, waggled his beringed fingers at Tyrell. 'Hello,' he said, gazing at Tyrell appreciatively. Keith was a muscular fellow, wearing a sky-blue T-shirt with clouds printed on it that was stretched tight across his chest, and two gold earrings in one ear.

'What can I do you for?'

Tyrell ignored his admiring glance. 'You're the manager?'

Keith stood up and extended a hand, angled slightly downward. 'Keith Quilty. It's my shop.'

Tyrell shook his hand politely. 'I'm Sergeant Watkins. I'm investigating the murder of Mrs Jennifer Hubbell.'

Keith looked genuinely stricken. 'Oh. Wasn't that horrible?'

'Did you have an order from Mr Hubbell to deliver his wife flowers that day?'

Keith nodded. 'Unbelievable. Yes. He was in here that very morning.'

'Did you ever actually make the delivery?'

'Well, we tried to.'

'You don't happen to . . . What does your delivery truck look like?'

'That's it right now,' said Keith, pointing out the window at a dark green van that was pulling into the nearest parking space. 'The Windstar.'

Tyrell felt the little surge of adrenaline that came with putting a significant piece of the investigative puzzle into place. He silently blessed Dena Russell for her alertness. He looked from the van to the store owner. 'Is this the same delivery person who was delivering for you on the day of Mrs Hubbell's death?'

'Oh yes,' said Keith. 'He's worked for me for over a year now. A good kid. Very reliable.'

A slightly built, good-looking young man wearing a thermal undershirt and blue jeans came in through the front door.

'Dante,' said Keith, 'This is Officer . . .'

'Watkins.'

'Officer Watkins. He wanted to ask you about that order for roses the other day. This is Dante DiBruno.'

Tyrell turned to the young man. 'You had a delivery order for Mrs Jennifer Hubbell.'

'Yeah. The woman that got killed. But I never delivered them.'

'Are you saying you were never at Mrs Hubbell's home two days ago?'

'No. I was there. She said don't come in the morning. So, I went over there about, I don't know. Three, three thirty. Knocked on the door. No answer.'

'Did you see or talk to anyone while you were there?'

'No, I figured she wasn't home yet.'

'You're saying you never saw Mrs Hubbell.'

The young man shook his head. 'Nobody answered.'

'Did you open the door and call out to her?'

'I wouldn't open the door,' Dante said, offended.

'So when nobody answered the door, you just left.'

'That's right.'

'Why didn't you just leave the flowers there?' Tyrell asked suspiciously.

'Officer Watkins,' the shop owner protested. 'They're *roses*. Roses require refrigeration. You don't just set a vase of roses on somebody's doorstep and walk away. Dante knows that.'

Dante nodded agreement. 'So, I was driving away, and I seen Mr Hubbell walking up the street, coming home from work. I remember thinking it was early to be coming home.'

'Mr Hubbell? Do you know Mr Hubbell?'

'I didn't know him but I saw him when he came in that morning and ordered the flowers. He looks exactly like my cousin, Rocky. Only dressed nice.'

'So, you recognized him when you saw him again.'

'Yeah. He could be Rocky's twin. I remember thinking that. I mean I just had a quick look at him while I was waiting at the light, but it was him.'

'How do you know he was coming home from work?' Tyrell asked.

'Well, he was wearing the suit and all, carrying his briefcase.'

'And then?'

'Well, then I thought, hey, now somebody's home, I can bring the flowers back. I mean, I knew he wanted the wife to receive them herself, but I can't make people be home if they're not . . .'

'Nobody said you could, Dante,' Keith reassured him.

'So, I figured, I had two other deliveries. I'd run them over where they were going, and head back to the Hubbells'. It took me maybe half an hour to make the other deliveries, and back I went.'

'And . . .?' Tyrell asked.

'And when I got back there, there was cop cars and ambulance and the whole nine yards. I slowed down with the rest of the traffic, and I asked a cop who was out there keeping things moving what was going on. He said there was somebody killed in the house. Well, I didn't think that was the time to be delivering flowers, you know . . .'

Tyrell nodded. Unexpectedly, this young man was giving their prime suspect an alibi. He found that he didn't mind. He'd never liked the idea that someone could simulate the kind of grief that Ron Hubbell had exhibited. 'Mr . . . DiBruno. It's very important about the time. Can you pin the exact time down for me that you saw Mr Hubbell and then the time when you came back to the house.'

The young man, somewhat flattered by the apparent importance of his information, screwed up his forehead and concentrated. Then his face cleared and he smiled. 'Three thirty. It was three thirty when I saw Mr Hubbell walking up from the station. The reason I know that is because my girlfriend gets out of school at St Catherine's at three forty and I had a delivery out that way. I figured if I could time it just right, I could run into her.'

'You'll swear to that?'

'Yeah. She'll swear to it. I found her all right. We had a couple of minutes together, you know what I mean, before I had to get going . . .'

Keith Quilty rolled his eyes, but Tyrell made a note on his pad and nodded. The 911 call had come in at 3.40. It had happened exactly as Ron Hubbell said. He had walked in, found his wife already dead, and called the police. 'Thank you, Mr DiBruno. Mr Quilty. Thank you very much.'

From her position at the switchboard, Peg gave Tyrell a warning look as he entered the station house.

'Van Brunt wants you,' she said. 'On the double.'

Tyrell was not concerned. It was true that he hadn't picked up Ron Hubbell, but this statement from Dante DiBruno would make that unnecessary. While it wasn't exactly putting them closer to a solution, it didn't hurt to eliminate such a significant suspect from the mix.

Tyrell walked back, and peeked into the chief's office, half expecting Van Brunt to have taken up residence there already. He continued down to the captain's office and tapped on the open door as he entered. A man was sitting in front of Van Brunt's desk, and he turned as Tyrell entered. It was Ron Hubbell. Tyrell couldn't help smiling at him.

'Sergeant,' said Van Brunt grimly. He was standing behind the desk resting his fingertips on his spotless blotter.

Tyrell raised one finger. 'Can I talk to you a moment, sir? Very important. It regards Mr Hubbell.'

'Excuse me,' said Van Brunt. He came around the desk and joined Tyrell just outside the door. Tyrell handed him the statement signed by DiBruno. 'He's off the hook,' Tyrell said, inclining his head toward the man sitting in the office.

Van Brunt snatched the paper from him. 'What is that?'

'Alibi. Witness who saw him coming home at the time he said. Just minutes before the 911 call. The time's been confirmed.'

Van Brunt scanned the paper angrily.

'I'm sorry I didn't pick him up when you told me to,' said Tyrell. 'But I got a tip on this and I thought I'd better follow it up first.'

Van Brunt turned without a word to Tyrell and re-entered his office. 'Good news, Mr Hubbell,' he said smoothly.

'You're welcome,' Tyrell whispered under his breath. He sighed and went in.

Ron Hubbell was listening to Van Brunt's explanation of why he had been eliminated as a suspect with something less than jubilation. He did, however, look to Tyrell and thank him for tracking down the information.

'No problem,' said Tyrell kindly. 'You're free to go,' he said, and then he looked to the captain, realizing he had exceeded his authority, 'if the captain agrees,' he added, wondering why Van Brunt was wearing such a sour expression.

'Mr Hubbell is not here because he is under suspicion,' said the captain.

'Oh,' said Tyrell.

'You see, a friend urged Mr Hubbell to go through Jennifer's belongings and see if he could find several threatening letters she received some years ago. Mr Hubbell found those letters and brought them to us.'

'I see,' said Tyrell, not sure where this was leading.

Van Brunt turned to Ron Hubbell. 'I want to thank you for finding these. We appreciate your cooperation at this difficult time.'

Ron looked slightly confused. 'Is that . . . it?'

'We'll be in touch,' said Van Brunt.

Ron nodded and made his way slowly toward the door and out of the station.

Once Ron was out of sight, Tyrell frowned and gazed at the plastic bag of papers. 'I don't get it. What's this all about?'

'The letters were anonymous, of course, and related to some questions Mrs Hubbell had about the death of her sister when she lived with Mr Brian Riley,' said Van Brunt.

'Oh, yes. I heard about that,' said Tyrell.

'You knew about this!' Van Brunt exclaimed.

'Well, I knew she had some questions. The chief told me there was no substance to her allegations.'

'Yes, I'm sure,' said Van Brunt. 'Well, it seems that Mrs Hubbell inadvertently stored her letters in a manner ideal for document preservation.'

'A sealed baggie,' said Ron.

'Exactly. I brought a document examiner in to look them over and see what he could determine about their authorship. He quickly determined something extremely interesting.'

'What's that?' Tyrell asked, genuinely curious.

'The paper and envelopes used by the author of these letters appear to have come from this very office.'

'What?'

'After that it was a simple process of elimination and the lifting of two intact latent fingerprints to determine the authorship of the letters. Just to be a hundred per cent sure, I've sent the envelopes for a DNA analysis, but it's a formality.'

'Someone in this office sent them?'

'I regret to have to tell you that the author of these letters warning Mrs Hubbell not to pursue her suspicions of Brian Riley was our very own Chief Potter.'

'No,' said Tyrell. 'Not the chief.'

'Oh yes, Sergeant.'

'But . . . You're not saying you think he killed her?'

'You're not very quick, Sergeant. No, I don't think he killed her. I think he's covering up for the killer.'

Tyrell felt stunned by this news. It took him a moment to realize what the captain was saying. 'Brian,' he breathed.

'Imagine my surprise,' said Van Brunt sarcastically, 'when I did some quick checking and found that there was no report filed on Mr Riley's first assault on Miss Russell. You took that call, didn't you, Sergeant?'

Tyrell said, 'Yes . . . well . . .'

'Yes, well, we'll discuss this later,' Van Brunt warned. 'Right now, in light of all this information, I think it's time we brought Mr Riley in here to talk to him. Go pick him up, Sergeant, and don't make any detours on the way.'

Brian looked out the window of his father's room toward the parking lot and the treeless, well-tended grounds of the Roosevelt Long-Term Care Center. All this needs is a barbed-wire fence, he thought, and you'd feel like you were in prison. Behind him the television droned, and Matt Riley sat up in his wheelchair, staring at it. Brian turned around and looked at his father who was watching the screen blankly, his mouth hanging open, slack on one side. There was no improvement from one day to the next, he thought. No real change, he thought. What was the use?

Lucy, Matt's favorite nurse, came bustling in, and Matt seemed to perk up at the sight of her. 'How's my pal?' Lucy asked in a loud, jovial voice.

Matt tried to answer, and she seemed to understand. 'All right, honey,' she said. 'I need your menu. Did you mark it yet?' She hunted around in his bedside table and found the blue sheet of paper she was looking for.

'You didn't mark it yet!' she cried, as if she were talking to a four-year-old.

Matt's expression looked slightly sheepish. Lucy expertly swiveled a rolling tray table across Matt Riley's lap. 'Here,' said Lucy, handing him a little pencil and the blue sheet of paper. 'You do it now.'

Brian wanted to protest that his father couldn't possibly fill out that menu form, but Lucy settled herself contentedly to wait, and Matt bent over the paper and gripped the pencil tightly in his better hand around the point.

Brian glanced at the TV. Oprah Winfrey was on, with her daily talk show and her usual assortment of whining housewives for guests, Brian thought. It always annoyed him when Dena bragged about making a cake once for the TV host. 'Why does he watch this stuff?' Brian asked aloud. 'Isn't there a ball game on or something?'

Lucy was unruffled. 'It's good for him to follow the conversations,' she said.

'If you can call these conversations,' said Brian.

'This is interesting,' said Lucy brightly. 'It's all about father's rights. You should be interested in this. You're going to be a dad soon, right?'

Brian shrugged.

'Where is that little gal of yours?' Lucy asked. 'I haven't seen her around here lately.' Before Brian could answer, she got up and bent over the tray table where Matt was laboring. 'No, hon. You picked two desserts and no supper here. Do that one again.'

Maybe he wants two desserts, Brian thought.

'She must be getting pretty close to due,' said Lucy amiably.

Brian shook his head and looked at the TV to avoid her gaze. 'I don't know. She's . . . mad at me. She moved out.'

'Well, hey, then you really should watch this show. You can get a lot of useful information from watching these shows. You know she can't keep you from seeing that child if it's your child. Not if you want to see it. Of course,' she said, casting a critical eye at the screen, 'they're talking about people who acted kind of extreme when they didn't get custody. But you should look into it.' Lucy hauled herself to her feet and went over to Matt. She examined the menu and then rewarded him with a big smile. 'Good job,' she said. 'You did excellent.'

Brian hated the way these people talked to his father. They hadn't known him as Brian had. A domineering man with an iron will. Impossible to please. Did he still exist? Brian wondered. Or was this shell of a human being all that remained of Matthew Riley? All that would ever remain.

Lucy collected her menu and bid them both farewell. The minute she was out of the room, Brian picked up the remote and started to surf the channels. He heard a noise of protest from his father and looked up to see that he was very indignant, very red in the face, staring at the remote.

Brian looked at him in disbelief. 'You want to watch that stuff?' he asked. Matt settled back in his chair, and Brian switched the channel back to Oprah.

'OK,' Brian said. 'Whatever you want. I'm outta here. I've still got work to do.' He did have work to do but, the truth was, he was thinking hard about a drink, wondering if it would be too soon to stop by Vibes and have a couple of pops on the way home.

'I'll see you later, Dad,' said Brian to his father, who was already reabsorbed in the talk-show quandary of the day. Brian pulled on his blue jean jacket, but was met by Lucy, looking anxious, at the door.

'Brian,' she said.

Before she could get any farther, Brian saw Tyrell Watkins and two uniformed officers whom Brian did not recognize outside the door of his father's room.

'Mr Brian Riley,' said Tyrell in a formal tone, 'we need you to come along to the station with us to answer a few questions regarding the murder of Mrs Jennifer Hubbell.

Brian looked shocked. He glanced back at his father, but the other man was glued to the TV. Lucy avoided his gaze. 'What is this?' Brian demanded. 'Does Chief Potter know about this?'

Now that he knew about the letters, Tyrell was sickened by these words. What did this guy have on the chief that Lou would jeopardize everything to protect him?

Tyrell glanced inside the room at the man in the wheelchair. Knowing about his long friendship with the chief, he didn't want to upset the disabled man. 'Chief Potter suffered a heart attack today,' he said quietly.

'What do you want with me? I don't know anything about Jennifer's murder.'

'We'll decide that. Come along, Mr Riley.'

'I'll sue your whole department for false arrest,' Brian threatened.

'You're not under arrest, yet,' said Tyrell.

'Then I don't really have to come with you.'

'It's in your best interests to do so,' said Tyrell impassively.

'I want to talk to a lawyer,' said Brian.

Tyrell felt a contempt bordering on hatred for this unrepentant bully. Lou Potter was a good man, and he would be destroyed by this revelation. There would be nowhere for him to hide when the word got out that he had covered up for Brian Riley. Did he really believe Brian was innocent? Or was it blackmail? Tyrell couldn't imagine the chief doing something so foolhardy unless it was under duress.

But he wouldn't give Brian Riley the satisfaction of asking him. 'Come along, Mr Riley,' he said. 'We haven't got all day.'

TWENTY-FIVE

Pam Pittinger, wearing an apron over the gray crepe skirt of her Ellen Tracy suit, padded around her huge, ultra-modern white kitchen with bedroom slippers on her stocking feet. Vanessa was sitting at the breakfast bar, slumped over her homework, her face supported by the heel of her hand. The local news droned on the TV on the counter.

'Daddy's having dinner with a client,' said Pam, 'so it's just you and me tonight.'

'Let's go to Pizza Hut,' said Vanessa.

'I'm too tired to go out,' said Pam. 'And you're still getting over that cold. I'll make you some soup.'

'I hate soup,' said Vanessa.

'It's good for you,' Pam insisted. She knew she had a box of that Lipton chicken noodle soup in her pantry. And she could make up some tuna-fish sandwiches. That would be nutritious, she thought. And not too difficult. 'How's the homework coming?' she asked. 'You need any help?'

Vanessa shook her head. 'It's easy,' she said.

Pam smiled at her only child and thanked her lucky stars that Vanessa hadn't yet started acting like a teenager, despite her chronological age. She still did her schoolwork faithfully, showed no interest in boys, and only loved animals. Pam knew it couldn't last much longer before she and Dick would be waiting up nights, worrying about her being out on dates. She shuffled into the pantry and opened the closet doors to see what she had. There was some canned pineapple. She could make the pineapple smoothies that Vanessa loved for dessert. And get a little calcium and vitamins poured into her child at the same time. Her hand hovered over the shelves until she located the red box of soup mix. One of these days I'm going to organize this mess, she thought.

'Mom!'

Vanessa's shriek made Pam jump. Still clutching the pineapple can, Pam rushed into the kitchen to find her daughter standing in the middle of the room, grabbing her head with her hands and staring open-mouthed at the TV.

'Vanessa, what is it?' Pam cried. 'What's the matter?'

'Oh my God, oh my God,' Vanessa cried, turning around to beat her fists on the counter.

Pam looked at the TV. A female reporter, holding an umbrella, out in front of the Monroe Police Station, was saying, 'Our sources tell us that an arrest is imminent. Mr Riley reportedly had a long-standing feud with the victim over the death of her younger sister. We'll be here, for up-to-the-minute reports on this case. Now back to you, Brad.'

The perfectly coiffed anchorman said, 'Thank you, Jean. Jean will be standing by, and we'll bring you any late-breaking developments in this case as they occur.'

'What in the world?'

'It's not true,' Vanessa cried, hurling herself into a chair and burying her face in her arms. 'It's not true. I know it's not true.'

'Vanessa. Stop being a drama queen. What are they saying? They think Brian Riley killed that woman?'

'Oh, he didn't, Mom. He never would . . .'

'Well, they must have something on him or they wouldn't be saying this. I can't believe it. And I let you go over there, by yourself . . . all alone with a murderer.'

'No,' said Vanessa, leaping up. 'No. That's not true. Take that back!'

'You're right. That's unfair. They haven't even charged him yet. I shouldn't have said that.'

'It doesn't matter what they say . . .'

'Well, honey, I know all about innocent until proven guilty and all, but believe me, they wouldn't arrest him if they weren't pretty sure.'

'That's a lie. I hate you for saying that.'

'Vanessa!'

Vanessa lowered her head to her arms again. 'I didn't mean it, Mom. I don't hate you.'

'You'd better get used to it, honey. A lot of people are going to be saying that.'

'But they don't know him. He wouldn't do that.'

'Darling, listen. You don't know him all that well yourself. I mean, I think the fact that he has horses kind of . . . colors your opinion. It automatically makes him a good guy in your book. But believe me, sweetie, sometimes people do terrible things, even people you think you know . . .'

'I have to do something,' Vanessa whispered.

'Vanessa, honey,' said Pam patiently. 'There's nothing you can do. You're only a child.'

'I can, too,' Vanessa said quietly.

'Oh, sweetie,' Pam said, patting her on the shoulder. 'I know how much that barn means to you. And the Rileys. They've been very patient about you hanging around there. I'm sure Brian will appreciate your loyalty. It's a good quality. But we'll find another barn.'

'I don't want another barn.'

'I know you're upset. But, you have to realize that if Brian goes to jail for this, that's the end of the barn. I'm sure that's the least of his worries, right now.'

'Mom, what if . . . what if I can clear his name?'

The words sounded comical coming out of Vanessa's mouth, but Pam didn't feel like laughing.

'Don't be ridiculous, Vanessa.'

'It's true, Mom. It happened that day I was home sick. Right?'

'Right.'

'Well, I didn't tell you this, but I was over at the barn.'

'Vanessa!'

'Remember, there was nobody here when you called?'

'You said you were listening to your music.'

'I didn't tell you the exact truth. I was afraid you'd get mad. I mean, I was listening to the tapes, part of the time. But the rest of the time, I was over there.'

'Well, why didn't Brian just tell the police that?'

'He didn't see me,' she cried.

Pam set the pineapple can down on the counter with a thud. 'Now look, honey, I know it might seem . . . exciting to be involved in a big news story like this. But this is not some party game. We're talking about a murder here. A woman was killed . . .'

'I was there, Mom. He didn't see me. I was hiding. I . . .' Vanessa avoided her mother's skeptical gaze. 'I just wanted to go over and see the horses and . . . I thought he might get mad if he knew I was in the barn . . .'

'That much I can believe,' said Pam. 'You and those horses . . .

You know you're not allowed to leave the house when you're sick. You're trying to get over a cold and instead of being in bed, you're mucking around in the barn . . .'

'And then I was trapped there in the barn,' Vanessa explained eagerly, 'while he was working. I was afraid he would throw me out if he knew I sneaked in there without his permission.'

Pam shook her head. 'Are you sure about this?'

'Yes, don't you see? He has an alibi and he doesn't even know it.'

'An alibi?' Pam said.

'Well, that's what it's called. It's on every show.'

Pam nodded, and folded her arms across her chest.

'And this could save him. I could save him with this. Mom, we have go down to the police station. Right now.'

Pam looked at her daughter with narrowed eyes. 'This is serious business. A life-and-death matter. You'd better be telling the truth, young lady.'

'I am,' Vanessa insisted. 'Why would I lie?'

The questioning had been going on for several hours and finally Morton Cheswick, Brian Riley's attorney, had demanded a break for his client. Captain Van Brunt had immediately sequestered himself in his office, alone, while the other officers still at the station had gathered in groups to discuss it.

Tyrell felt as if he needed some fresh air, and a few minutes alone. But once he had pushed past the reporters and was out in his car, cruising, he found himself heading in the direction of the restaurant where Dena Russell worked. If there was anyone who needed to hear about this, it was she. He pulled up in front of the restaurant but a slender man in a gray suit came hurrying out saying, 'No, no, no, please don't park here. You can park it in back. It's so bad for business to have a police car parked out here.'

'I'm looking for Dena Russell,' he said.

'Well, I'll call the kitchen and have them send her out the back way. There's a little office back there where you can talk.'

Tyrell didn't feel offended. He knew this guy was the owner. Only a business owner would have the nerve to ask the police to move because it didn't look good. You had to admire the guy's single-mindedness, even if it was a little over the top.

Tyrell drove around to the back of the restaurant, which was almost as attractive as the front. A narrow part of the canal flowed over the rocks in the deep bed behind the restaurant and the stucco farmhouse was covered with trellised vines that traveled up to the slate roof.

Outside the back door of the restaurant was a little wrought-iron table and chairs on a patio that would have been pleasant to sit at if it weren't raining. An old gaslight-type lantern illuminated the oak door. As he walked up to knock, the door opened, and Dena stood there, in her white smock with the sleeves rolled up, a dusting of flour on her face.

'Sergeant,' she said. 'Come on in. Get out of the rain.'

She ushered him through the door and past the kitchen, where a bunch of people were working busily and noisily, into a quiet little corner office. The graceful desk was covered with paper-work, but the curtains were a lovely, deep blue with a tiny print, and there were two comfortable-looking armchairs with rush seats and cushions decorated with roosters. Dena indicated that he should sit, and he did. 'I haven't got long,' he said. 'We're taking a short break.'

'Dinner break?' she asked.

He nodded.

'Wait a second.' She disappeared into the kitchen and came back in a moment with a pastry on a plate and a fork.

'Here,' she said. 'Do you like seafood? It's a mille-feuille pastry with shrimp and crab in a champagne sauce. We serve it as an appetizer.'

Tyrell took a bite and the pastry dissolved on his tongue. 'This is good. Did you make this?'

Dena smiled and nodded.

'You can cook a little bit.'

Dena thanked him. For a moment there was an awkward silence between them.

Then Tyrell said, 'You don't know, do you?'

'Know what?'

'Well, before I get into it, I wanted to thank you. Your tip about the florist ended up clearing Mr Hubbell.'

'Really?' she cried. 'That's wonderful. Oh, Sergeant. That is really wonderful news. How?'

'It's a long story,' he said. 'I'll tell you another time.'

'There's something else,' she said warily.

Tyrell reluctantly put the plate to one side. 'I thought you'd want to know,' he said. 'We've got Brian down at the station. If I'm not mistaken, he's gonna be arrested tonight.'

'For what?' she cried.

'The murder of Jennifer Hubbell.'

Dena stared at him. 'Brian?'

Tyrell sighed. 'Did you know the chief was protecting him?'

'Chief Potter? Why?'

'We don't know why. Do you have any idea?'

'I know he was friends with Brian's father.'

'This goes way beyond friendship. Our whole investigation of Jennifer's murder is tainted because of the . . . extreme measures he took on Brian's behalf.'

Dena frowned. 'I don't know. Maybe I was being dense, but I never noticed any particular . . . what, interactions between them. It wasn't like we had him over for dinner or anything. I mean, they said hello when they met on the street. That kind of thing. I never even actually met him. I knew who the chief was, but that was it . . .'

'Well, we can't ask him right now because he's hooked to a respirator. But suffice it to say, he went way out on a limb . . .'

'So now you're saying that Brian killed Jennifer, and the chief covered it up?'

'Well, we don't know for sure. We're hoping Brian can illuminate this for us. We're also hoping for a confession, though he's got a lawyer with him. But I have a feeling he's gonna be looking at an arrest tonight.'

Dena sat very still, her hands limp in her lap.

'I know it's not . . . exactly good news,' said Tyrell. 'But, maybe you can breathe a little easier. I don't think he'll be bothering you any more. He's got bigger problems, right now . . .'

'Yes,' she said, still stunned by the news. 'Well, yes . . . it is a relief. In a way.'

Now, seeing the look on her face, Tyrell wondered if he should have come. He had been thinking she would be glad to have Riley off her back, but he really hadn't given any thought to the fact that she might be upset to learn that the father of her child . . . That one day she would have to explain to that child that its father was in jail for killing a woman. No. It was not exactly good news. He wished now that he had not been so impulsive. Tyrell stood up, realizing that she needed to be alone to digest the information. 'I'm going to head back. We'll be starting again. Thanks for the pastry.'

Dena got up, distracted, and followed him to the door. 'Yes, well, thank you Sergeant, for letting me know.'

'No problem, Miss Russell. You'll be around if we need to question you any further?' he asked apologetically. 'I have a feeling there's going to be a lot more questions.'

'Sure. Yeah,' she said. She felt as if her head was spinning. 'I . . . I'll be around.'

'Well, you take it easy, Miss Russell.'

'You too, Sergeant. Thanks,' she said dully.

She closed the door behind him and stood rooted to the spot. Despite her own suspicions, despite her fears, despite everything, it was difficult to grasp the fact that the man she had lived with, planned to marry, the father of her baby, was about to be arrested for murder.

TWENTY-SIX

Morton Cheswick washed his hands in the men's room, and then re-entered the interrogation room where Brian Riley sat staring, with a queasy look on his face, at the hamburger that had been delivered to him by a uniformed officer.

Morton sat down beside his client, carefully shifting his open briefcase away from the food, so that the greasy onions which had dripped on the waxed paper holding Brian's meal did not stain the calfskin.

'Aren't you hungry?' Morton asked.

'Not really,' said Brian. He wrapped up the sandwich and stuffed the waxed paper bundle back into the brown delivery bag.

Morton nodded. 'I think we're almost through here.'

'I hope so,' said Brian dully.

Morton closed his briefcase and folded his arms over it protectively. 'Well, the fact is that any steps the chief might have taken to shield you were the results of a unilateral decision. There's no evidence to suggest that you needed protecting.'

'I still don't know why he did that,' Brian said. 'I mean, I did call him after that business with Dena, but they seemed to think there was a lot more to it than that.'

'They're not telling us everything,' said Morton Cheswick. 'That much is obvious. At any rate, you are not responsible for the chief's actions. They know we're unshakable on that score. Of course, we're hurt by this longstanding animosity between you and Mrs Hubbell. But, the rest of their case is flimsy. Not much in the way of hard evidence. Circumstantial.'

'So, you don't think they're going to arrest me?' Brian asked hopefully.

'Well, if they do, I doubt they're going to be able to convict you.'

'I didn't do it,' said Brian.

Morton, who had defended many a client in the criminal justice system, did not place a lot of weight on the profession of innocence, since he'd never had a client who professed anything else, at first. Still, he knew a weak case when he saw one. 'It would be helpful if you could account for where you were at the time.'

'I told you, I was at the barn, working. Alone.'

'As I say, I don't know that they have enough to hold you, right now.' Brian rubbed his palms together nervously. Then he turned back to Morton.

'You're a lawyer. Let me ask you something,'

'Of course,' said Morton calmly.

'What kind of rights do I have to a child if I'm not married to its mother?'

Morton frowned. 'Excuse me?'

'I saw this show on TV and it got me thinking. Doesn't she have to let me be with the kid? I mean, she just can't take the kid and go . . .'

Morton felt a little jarred by this non sequitur, from a man who was trying to face down a murder charge. 'No, she can't,' said Morton, 'although this might be something you want to think about when your *other* problems are resolved . . .'

'I need to know this right now,' he insisted. 'What are my rights here? What does she have to give me?'

Morton shook his head, and drummed on the briefcase with the fingers of one hand. 'I assume you're referring to the woman you . . . allegedly battered,' he said.

Brian flexed his fists and then gripped the back of a chair. 'It was . . . accidental,' he said. 'I never meant to hurt her.'

Morton nodded. He'd heard that one before. 'Well, this is an area of the law that's in transition right now. The law hasn't been able to keep up with the changes in our society, and thus is constantly being challenged. You do have rights. But I think we can assume, given the hostility of your current relationship with this woman, that you will be facing a court battle for every inch of ground. Your history here is not going to help.'

'But she can't shut me out of her life.'

'Of her life? Yes, she can. Of the child's life, no, within limits.'

Brian nodded. 'Good.'

The door to the interrogation room opened and a patrolman stuck his head in. 'Mr Cheswick. Somebody here to see you.'

'Excuse me,' said Morton. Brian sat back down and cupped his hands together, tapping them thoughtfully against his upper lip. He did not seem to notice that the lawyer was leaving. Morton Cheswick stood up, shooting his cuffs, and shaking out the creases in his pants. Then he stepped out into the hall. A good-looking businesswoman in a gray suit and pumps was standing there, nervously fiddling with her purse straps. Beside her stood a teen-aged girl, tall and thin, with shiny hair pulled back, and braces on her teeth. Her face was pale and she looked terrified to be in the police station.

'This is Mr Cheswick,' the patrolman said to the older woman.

She stuck out her hand. 'Mr Cheswick. My name is Pamela Pittinger, and this is my daughter, Vanessa.'

'How do you do?' said Morton gravely.

'You're representing Mr Riley?'

'Yes.'

The woman put her manicured hands on the girl's narrow shoulders. 'Vanessa has something to tell you which may be important for your client.'

Morton raised his eyebrows. 'Really? Well, let's find a quiet place where we can sit and talk.'

Dena got out of her car and watched as Peter loaded a couple of boxes into his trunk and slammed the lid. She sighed and walked over to him.

'All ready to go?' she asked.

'Well, not quite. The girls still have a few things to load up.'

'Tomorrow?' she asked.

'Tomorrow,' he said. 'Tory's insisting on going to school cause they're having some kind of party. So, we'll leave after school.'

Dena nodded. Then she looked toward the house. 'Is Hilary here?'

'No, actually. They're at Hilary's house tonight. Since their toys are packed and all, I told them they could go to Hilary's. They watch TV there,' he said.

'Ahh,' said Dena, bemused.

'Well, sometimes you can't avoid it.'

'I suppose not.'

'What about you?'

'I'm going to go up and take a bath.' She hesitated, then decided to tell him. 'Sergeant Watkins came by the restaurant tonight.'

'Oh?'

'Since you don't have a TV, you probably don't know this. Brian's being questioned about my friend Jennifer's murder.'

'Brian,' he said.

'Yeah. Sergeant Watkins thinks they're going to arrest him.'

'Hmmm,' said Peter. 'Well, great news.'

She reddened, a little put off by his reaction. 'It's not what I would have wished for,' she said.

'Why not? I'm relieved. He can't bother you if he's in jail.'

'I suppose,' she said ruefully. 'Where are you off to?'

'I've still got twenty errands to do before we go.'

'Well, maybe we can have a . . . glass of juice together, or something. Toast your departure.'

'Maybe later,' he agreed.

'I think I'll go take that bath,' said Dena. 'I've finally gotten that bathtub clean enough to soak in it.'

Peter got into his car with a wave. 'Light some candles,' he said. 'Think pleasant thoughts for the baby's sake.'

Dena nodded and trudged up to the house. She still could hardly believe that Brian was now the prime suspect in Jennifer's murder. Every time she thought about all the things she hadn't known about him, she felt dazed. Wearily, she unlocked the door and entered the little foyer. She stopped to look at the mail on the table. It was the usual couple of circulars. She didn't know why she looked. So few people even knew she was here.

She started up the stairs, rummaging in her purse for her keys. Just as she reached her door and inserted the key in the lock, the doorbell rang and made her jump. It probably isn't for me, she thought. She was tempted to ignore it. But, after a moment's hesitation, she walked back down the stairs, and went over to the door, first putting on the chain.

A plump, middle-aged woman with graying curly hair stood on the doorstep, holding a black-and-white checkered wool coat together at the neck with her left hand. She gave Dena a nervous smile. 'Is Peter here?' she asked.

Dena undid the chain and opened the door. She shook her head. 'No, he's out.'

'He wasn't at the restaurant,' the woman in the checkered coat said.

'No,' said Dena, realizing this had to be a friend, someone who knew about his job. 'He had a lot of errands to do. I don't know when he'll be back.'

'Well, um, OK. Are the girls asleep?'

'Oh, no. They're at the baby-sitter's.'

'Oh, I thought you might be . . . no, never mind. OK,' said the woman. She was squinting into the distance, obviously thinking about what to do next.

'Shall I tell him you were here, or to call you?' Dena asked politely.

'No,' said the woman slowly. 'No, that's all right.'

'Who shall I say was here?'

The woman shook her head. 'Don't say anything. I want to . . . surprise him.'

'OK,' said Dena. 'No phone number or anything?'

The woman smiled briefly. 'No. I'll come by tomorrow.'

'Better make it early,' said Dena.

The smile faded from the woman's face. 'Why?'

All of a sudden, Dena thought she shouldn't be telling Peter's plans to anyone who knocked at the door. It wasn't her place. 'It's just easiest to catch him then.'

The woman looked at her quizzically. 'OK, well, thank you. Good night.' She turned and headed for her car, a little purple Geo that was parked in front of Dena's Camry. Wielding her keys, she went around and let herself in to the driver's side.

Dena gave a half-hearted wave and looked back up the stairs, as if it were a mountain to climb. Time for that bath, she thought.

Brian reached out and hugged Vanessa as hard as he could and Vanessa wrapped her arms around his neck, savoring the moment she had dreamed of for so long. The stubble on his face, the rough cloth of his jacket collar against her soft skin made her want to rub against him until her own cheeks were raw. His shoulders were trembling and she thought he might be weeping. Blood pounded in her ears, like the sound of the ocean, and she was transported. She closed her eyes and, for that brief moment, she floated in some paradise better than any she had ever imagined. It was over in an instant, but it made everything worthwhile, and, at the same moment, filled her with despair.

'Thank you, Vanessa,' he whispered.

She smiled, keeping her lips closed so that he couldn't see her braces, and nodded, her eyes searching his for a sign. All she could see was weariness and distraction.

Morton Cheswick shook Pam's hand and then reached for Vanessa's. She shook it, scarcely able to take her gaze from Brian's face. 'That was a very commendable thing you did, Vanessa. Coming forward with that information.'

'I was glad I could help,' she said, looking down.

'Indeed,' said Morton, pulling on his topcoat.

Tyrell watched their parting in the hallway in amazement.

'Sergeant Watkins,' Van Brunt commanded. 'In here.'

Shaking his head, Tyrell followed the captain into his office.

'Close the door,' Van Brunt barked.

Tyrell shoved the door and it slammed.

Van Brunt's eyes were white around the pupils. 'Sergeant,' he barked.

'Sorry, Captain. I'm just frustrated to see him walk out of here.'

'You're frustrated? You're the one who made it possible.'

'Me? How is this my fault?' Tyrell demanded. 'He has an alibi.'

'She's lying,' said captain disgustedly. 'Any fool can see she's lying.'

'Hey, I don't like it any more than you do. But the kid said she saw him there. She'll swear to it.'

'She'll swear to anything for that dirtbag's sake. The lawyer knew it. I could see it in his face. She has the hots for Riley and she was just making it up as she went along, hoping he might give her a roll in the hayloft in gratitude.'

'She's a child, Captain. Just a kid trying to do the right thing . . .'

'Your judgment, Sergeant, as we already know, cannot be relied on.'

'Captain, I know you hate to lose your prime suspect, but I don't see how you can blame me because the kid came forward and gave him an alibi.'

'I'll tell you how it's your fault, shall I? You and that old man in the hospital. You two bungled this investigation from the very beginning. Now, I'm in charge and have to deal with your mess. Lou Potter thinks you can run the police department like a clubhouse, and you, you don't even have the qualifications for your job. The chief completely ignored the code requirements when he gave you your rank. In the old days, you would have been called his fair-haired boy, although in this case it doesn't really apply, does it?'

'He's had no reason to regret his decision, Captain,' Tyrell said stiffly.

'Well, fortunately, it's no longer up to him.'

'What are you talking about? You're just fillin' in,' Tyrell blurted out.

Van Brunt could hardly keep the satisfaction out of his voice. 'Oh, come now, Sergeant. You can't seriously believe he'll be back. Not after the way he abused the power of his office. Apparently the city council had a vote on it today. As soon as he's off the respirator, he will be offered either prosecution or an early retirement. Effective immediately. Which do you think he will choose?'

Tyrell did not reply. For a moment Tyrell felt betrayed by Lou. How could he just give up like that? Not try to fight. It was like admitting to whatever they wanted to say about him. But what did he expect? Lou would be lucky to recover from this heart attack. The stress of defending himself would probably kill him. 'Retirement, I imagine,' said Tyrell grimly.

'Yeah, well, you better believe it, Sergeant. And your free ride is about to end.'

Free ride, Tyrell thought, outraged. My free ride. He had worked as hard as he could these last two years to prove himself worthy of Lou's confidence in him. Years of military discipline warred, inside Tyrell, with the urge to say what he wanted to say. He knew he had to keep a lid on it, before he threw everything away. But what was the use of buckling under? It was one thing to try and win a man's respect. This man didn't know the meaning of the word. He told himself that if he spoke out now, that would be the end of it. He thought of his grandmother, and how disappointed she would be. And Cletus, who would smirk.

Van Brunt tugged at the hem of his coat and then adjusted the university ring on his finger. 'In fact, Sergeant, in light of your part in all this, I have decided to suspend you . . .'

'Suspend me! For what?' Tyrell blurted out.

'Read the manual, Sergeant. Failure to comply with General Order 43 of the Monroe Township Code – Domestic Violence Policy and Procedure. If you and the chief hadn't covered up for that Riley boy in the first place, this whole situation wouldn't have gotten so screwed up. Do you think these domestic violence complaints are a joke, Sergeant? Something for you boys to laugh about in the locker room?'

Tyrell despised being lectured by Heath Van Brunt, a man who had just implied that a skinny teenage girl with braces was a slut. A man who had baldly stated that any husband had more than enough reason to want to kill his wife. Hypocrite, Tyrell thought. Bigot. But, at the same time, a part of him could not react with too much righteous indignation. He had gone along with the chief, and let Riley walk out after he hit Dena Russell. He hadn't liked seeing a pregnant woman with a bloody face, but he hadn't insisted that Riley be held accountable either. In fact, when the chief made apologies for him, Tyrell had agreed. Not just gone along with the decision. Endorsed it. Maybe he'd seen too much of the underbelly of human nature in this job. Admit it, he thought. At least to yourself. It was a crime, and you let it slide. Tyrell wanted to call Van Brunt an asshole and storm out, but a sliver of self-doubt wouldn't let him do it.

Van Brunt was droning on. 'I'm going to run this place, and I'm going to run it by the books. And I'm going to start by making an example of you. You are hereby suspended without pay for thirty days.'

Tyrell hesitated. Then, he unhooked his badge and threw it on the desk. He walked out without a word and shut the door quietly behind him.

TWENTY-SEVEN

n the medicine cabinet above the bathroom sink, Dena found a small bottle of bubble bath, the size they give out in hotels or sell in bins by the door of discount drugstores. It looked like it had been there for a while. She unscrewed the lid and sniffed. It smelled kind of faint but pleasantly floral. Hey, beggars can't be choosers, she reminded herself. She pulled up the stopper on the bathtub, turned on the taps, and dumped the contents of the bottle into the water. Immediately, bubbles began to form, giving the bath a cheerful, rainbow luster. Good idea, she thought.

She left the tub filling, and went into the bedroom, taking off her clothes and tying a flimsy, plus-size bathrobe she had bought in the Kmart around her girth. Then she padded into the kitchen in her bare feet. Candles, she thought. She kind of liked that idea, too. She had come across a pair of squatty white candles set in glass ashtrays on a shelf in the kitchen, probably for emergency use during power failures. They'll do, she thought. She carried them into the bathroom and set one on each of the squared edges of the foot of the ceramic tub. The water was getting pretty high by now, with a frothy, steamy surface that looked inviting. She lit the candles with a match, turned off the taps and the lights, and removed her bargain bathrobe, hanging it on a hook behind the door.

She pulled up her hair in a fabric scrunchie, and stepped into the tub. Just like Canyon Ranch, she thought, smiling to herself. If you close your eyes.

Carefully, she lowered herself into the water. It was very warm, but not too hot. She'd read somewhere that was bad for the baby. As she eased herself down, her belly nearly touched the sides of the tub. She remembered a girl at work once saying that she got stuck in her bathtub when she was pregnant and had to wait until her husband got home to help her get out. That had better not happen to me, Dena thought. I've got nobody to help me. I could be in here until morning. She pulled a hand towel off the rod above the tub, and settled it behind her neck, like a pillow. The candles flickered in the dark room, and she thought, as she closed her eyes, how utterly luxurious it felt. She put her arms around her baby and thought, life has so many small pleasures. And I'm going to make sure that your life is full of those pleasures. Your happiness is going to be my main business. The thought filled her with peace and, for a moment, she drifted, close to sleep.

The buzz of the downstairs doorbell cut through her reverie and clawed at her nerves. It's probably that same lady, she thought. I'm not going down there again. I told her to come back in the morning. It's not up to me to go trudging down there every time she comes back. The bell buzzed again and she thought, for a moment, of Sergeant Watkins. She pictured him out there, as she had seen him tonight, under the gaslight at the restaurant. He had the most penetrating gaze. His dark eyes seemed to look right into her. The thought of it was vaguely disturbing. But then, she shook her head. It wasn't him. He wouldn't be stopping by here unsummoned. It would seem . . . undignified, and she could tell somehow, though she hardly knew him, that propriety was important to him. He had come to the restaurant to tell her about Brian, and he would leave it at that.

The thought of Brian made the bathwater seem colder. She put the hot water tap on and let a little more run into the tub. She should turn on the TV and find out what had happened about Brian. But she knew it would only bring all her problems back in a rush. Just a little while longer in this ignorant bliss, she thought.

Go away, whoever you are, she thought. As if in response to her wish, the ringing stopped. She sank down to her neck, and closed her eyes again. Suddenly, she sat up. She distinctly heard the sound of someone climbing the stairs. Gooseflesh broke out on her arms, now gripping the sides of the tub. Impossible. How could they get in?

Before she had a chance to think, she heard the pounding on her door. 'Dena, let me in.'

Brian. Her heart began to pound and she tried to get up from where she lay. It was impossible to pull herself up. No, she thought, remembering the woman who got stuck in the tub. No. She swiveled her hips around and hoisted herself up onto her knees. The pounding was louder now. 'I know you're in there,' he yelled.

The sloshing of the water as she clambered to her feet extinguished the candles, and little plumes of smoke rose in the dark bathroom as she managed to climb out of the tub, dripping wet.

She grabbed a towel, ran it over herself for a second, and then reached for her flimsy robe as he banged on her door. Her heart was hammering also, although more fearful than defiant this time. There was something about being caught in the bath that was so . . . demeaning.

'Dena, open this door or I'll break it. I swear I will.'

Her hands trembled as she tried to tie the robe. Damn, damn, she thought as the fabric stuck to her, made it hard to close.

She thought of her cell phone, and Sergeant Watkins. Be calm, she told herself. Get to your phone. She knew where it was. In her purse, by the door. She ran from the bathroom, nearly slipping on the tile, and rushed to her pocketbook. She was freezing, after her hasty exit from the bath, shivering all over. She reached into her bag.

At that moment, she heard the splintering of wood. She looked up in shock and saw the door burst open. Brian stepped across her threshold.

'Jesus, Brian,' she wailed, running behind a chair. 'What are you doing?'

He stared at her, and his arms fell to his sides, limply holding the wrench that was in his hand. 'Why didn't you answer me?' he asked.

She pressed her hands to her eyes, as if, by blocking the sight of him, she could make him disappear. 'Get out of here, Brian. I have a court order.'

He started to walk toward her. 'Mmmm, you smell good,' he said. 'Getting ready for your lover?'

'Oh Brian,' she said. 'For God's sake. Please. Get real. Look at me, Brian. I'm the size of a whale. I'm wearing a housecoat from the Kmart.' There was a time, way back in the beginning, when he might have smiled. Seen the humor of it. But she realized, looking into his angry eyes, that he was controlled by his jealousy now, in the grip of his obsession.

'You know what I found out today?' he said, coming closer, the wrench still dangling at his side. 'As long as you keep saying that baby is mine, it legally belongs to me. Even if we're not married. Did you know that, Dena? You have to let me see it. You can't keep it away from me.'

'Oh, it is yours,' she said. 'But I will keep it away from you. I promise you that. Is this the kind of behavior a child is supposed to see?'

'Why not?' he said bitterly. 'Why shouldn't the child know the truth about its mother? That she's a slut, who sleeps around . . .'

'Brian, I'm warning you, if the police come . . .'

'Why is everything about the police with you? What makes you think they can stop me? They can't stop me.'

His handsome face was twisted by rage, just as limbs could be twisted by disease. Suddenly, looking at him, she saw the pain that it caused him. He was as helpless as she felt. 'Brian, you're making yourself sick,' she cried. 'This isn't real. It's something you imagined. I never cheated on you.'

Unexpectedly, he dropped the wrench, and sank down into a wooden chair. 'Yes, you did. Or you would still love me.' Tears filled his eyes.

Dena was trembling all over, holding her robe closed at the neck. She felt an intense pity for him, but she didn't trust him for a moment. He was like some kind of wounded mountain lion, stopping to lick his wounds before he resumed his attack.

'I tried to love you,' she said. 'But I felt like a prisoner. You were always accusing me of something. Right from the start.'

'You deserved it,' he said. She could see him starting to build up another angry head of steam. 'You were unfaithful.'

'I wasn't,' she said wearily. 'What's the use?'

Brian stood up. 'I give you everything and you say "what's the use"?' he demanded.

'Is this how you loved Tanya?' she asked.

Brian's eyes widened. 'Don't say that.'

'Did you think she was unfaithful too? I know you used to hurt her. She'd call her sister, crying.'

'She fell in the shower. It was an accident,' he snarled.

'I don't know what you're capable of, Brian. I don't know you. The man I came to live with seemed kind and decent. I don't know this man who breaks down doors and threatens me. I don't know what happened to that other man. I guess he was just . . . what I wanted him to be.' She suddenly felt faint, as if she couldn't stand there shivering for another minute.

Brian shook his head. 'I'm still the same. You've made me do these things by being so hardhearted. By cheating and lying and deceiving me. I have been deceived my whole life,' he shouted. He lifted the wrench and shook it at her.

It's coming, she thought. If you stand here and do nothing,

you're going to end up with that wrench in the middle of your forehead. Dena looked from where Brian was sitting toward the open door. It wasn't that far. He was blocking her way to the phone, but she was closer to the door than he was. She thought about it for a second, and then, she made up her mind. She bolted for the door.

In an instant, he was after her. She was on the landing when he grabbed her by the wrist, trying to draw her back inside. She saw the wrench in his other hand. Then, out of the corner of the eye, she thought she saw movement on the staircase. And, in the next instant, she heard a roar of protest as Peter, who had been climbing quietly, lunged up the steps and grabbed Brian around the neck. Shocked, Brian dropped her wrist, and tried to fight back. But Peter had overpowered him by surprise. They struggled briefly, and the wrench came loose, and clattered down the stairs. Dena cowered back against the smashed-up door. It only lasted a moment as Peter landed a punch on him, and Brian staggered backward. Dena screamed as he started to fall. The sound of his body thudding down the steps was sickening. Peter looked on impassively.

Brian landed near the bottom step and lay still, the wrench beneath his head. 'Oh God,' Dena whispered. Without thinking, she started down the steps to him, but Peter held her back.

'Leave him there,' he said.

'I can't. Peter, he might need help . . .'

Then, suddenly, Brian groaned, and picked up his head. Dena began to breathe again. He struggled up to his feet, and looked up at Dena and Peter on the landing. 'I knew it. I told you. Fuck you,' he said. 'Fuck you both.'

'He's all right,' said Peter disgustedly. 'Get out of here. Don't come back.' Dena shook her head, and closed her eyes.

Brian staggered to the front door, where he had smashed the lock, opened it, and looked out at the night. Then he looked back up at them. His eyes narrowed, and he opened his mouth as if he was going to say something, but then he just sighed. He stumbled out into the night.

Dena exhaled with relief, and then went inside and collapsed on a chair. She was shivering from head to toe. Peter came in after her, examining his fist, which was scraped. 'Are you OK?' she asked.

He nodded. 'I'm OK. How about you?'

'I'm freezing,' she said. She got up and walked to the bedroom, taking a blanket from the foot of the bed. She wrapped it around her, slipped her bare feet into shoes and came back to the little table. She sat back down and looked at Peter.

'I can't thank you enough,' she said. 'If you hadn't come along . . .'

'I was going to get the girls when I noticed the door standing open.'

'This is unbearable,' she said.

'I thought they'd arrested him.'

Dena shook her head. 'They did. But for some reason they let him go. I don't know what to do,' she said.

'About what?' he asked.

Dena threw up her hands. 'I have a protection order. He doesn't care. What good is it if he just comes after me anyway?'

'I told you that,' said Peter, flexing his fist. 'I told you it wouldn't make a bit of difference.'

Dena sighed. 'I'd better call them.' She went to her pocketbook and fished out the phone. She began to punch in the number. She had it on speed-dial. 'They said not to wait.'

'Who?' he asked.

'The police. Maybe they'll arrest him this time.' The phone was ringing. 'Monroe police station,' said a voice.

Peter stared at her. 'He'll be out by tomorrow.'

'Sergeant Watkins, please.'

'I'm sorry. Sergeant Watkins is . . . temporarily off the force. Can someone else help you?'

'Off the force? Since when? I saw him tonight.'

'I'm sorry, ma'am. I can't give out that information. Would you like to speak to someone else?'

'No.' Dena pressed the off button and sat back down in the chair. She was stunned, and somehow betrayed. 'They said the sergeant is no longer on the force. Is that possible? I saw him just this evening. What could have happened?'

Peter raised his shoulders indifferently. 'He wouldn't have been much help anyway.'

'You know something,' she said slowly, 'you're right.'

'I know I'm right,' he said.

'They want to keep me here but they don't care what

happens to me. I won't have a moment's peace if I stay here. I'm not going to sit here and wait for him to come after me again.'

Peter stood up. 'What are you going to do?'

Dena looked up at him. She pulled her blanket more tightly around her. 'You're leaving tomorrow?' she said.

Peter nodded.

'Is that offer for a ride still good?'

TWENTY-EIGHT

Albert Gelman tugged free a faded sprig of scarlet Alstroemeria from the huge arrangement on the piano. Then, he stepped back and critically surveyed the remaining blossoms, eyeing them for any signs of incipient lifelessness that would mean they needed culling.

From the doorway, Dena watched him tending the piano's bouquet and tried to work up the nerve to speak. He was a perfectionist, and thus was demanding to work for, but he had been fair and kind to her, and what she was about to do was unfair – to leave him with no notice, no warning. She dreaded telling him.

Before she could figure out how to begin, he seemed to sense her presence and looked around. 'Good morning,' he said. 'Where are your whites?'

'Albert,' she said. 'I need to talk to you.'

'Uh-oh,' he said. 'What?'

'Can we sit?'

Albert looked around the room for the most convenient spot and then sat down on the piano bench, patting the chair beside it for her. Dena settled herself awkwardly on the edge of the seat, her feet flat on the floor. She knitted her fingers together and sighed.

Albert glanced at his watch, and then back at Dena. 'Well?'

Dena took a deep breath. 'You know that Peter's leaving town today.'

Albert made a face. 'Yes, I certainly do. And, I have to say, he has a strange way of showing his gratitude. Did he ever tell you about how Eric and I found him in that garish old people's palace in Miami? We rescued him. I mean, literally. They were living like gypsies in two little rooms over a Cuban restaurant. We offered him good money. I made a deal with my friend for that house . . .' He interrupted his own tirade. 'Is this about the house? I know it's nothing grand, but until you get yourself sorted out . . .'

Dena realized how difficult this was going to be. 'No, the house has been fine. You really rescued me, too, Albert.'

'I don't think he's going to find it so easy out there in East Jibib, or wherever it is he's going. He claims to be such a devoted father, and then he uproots these children, turns their lives upside down, drags them across the county. Oh, don't get me started. Now what is it, sweetie. More trouble with the boyfriend? I know you don't want to be alone there, and my friend assures me that he's got somebody else for the other half of the duplex, but if you want to switch apartments—'

'Albert . . . Albert, I'm going with him. I'm leaving town with Peter . . . today.'

Albert shifted around on the piano bench, crossed his legs, and folded his hands over his bony knees and the perfect crease of his trousers. 'You're kidding, right?'

Dena shook her head. 'Brian broke the door down to my apartment last night.'

Albert's eyes widened. 'Did you call the cops?'

Dena sighed. 'Albert, I have a restraining order against him. It doesn't matter. He doesn't care. He's not going to stop.'

Albert pursed his lips and picked some imaginary lint off his trousers.

'I'm afraid that if I don't get away from him, something terrible is going to happen. I can't just sit around here and wait for it to happen . . .'

Albert raised a hand to silence her. 'I understand. I understand that. I'm not going to tell you that you shouldn't be worried. Only a fool would say that. But why go off with Peter?'

'I'm not going off with Peter,' said Dena. 'I'm going to my sister's. I'm just going to hitch a ride to Chicago. They're heading that way.'

'I don't understand this. You have a car, a place to live, a job. How can you just get up and walk away? Your baby will be here before you know it. Did he talk you into this?'

'No. Not at all. I'd already decided to leave here. I called my sister even before Jennifer . . . I called her when things went bad with Brian to tell her I was coming. I thought I could take my time and work everything out. But now I know I can't. I can't stay here. Brian has made it impossible. I have to go now, and worry about the details later. I mean, I can pay somebody to drive my car out. I won't embarrass you with your friend. I'll send an extra month's rent to the landlord. As for you, my job, I don't know what else I can do. I need to have my baby somewhere where I feel safe. Peter has offered me an escape and I'm going to take it.'

Albert sat tensely, and stared at his hands, folded around his knee. Then, he abruptly unfolded hands and knees and stood up. 'Well, you do whatever you feel you have to,' he said. 'Although it's extremely unprofessional of you to walk out like this with no notice . . .'

'I know it is. And I am sorry. I'm truly sorry.'

'Have you told René?'

'Not yet,' she said miserably. 'I thought I ought to speak to you first.'

'Well, you've spoken. You seem to have made up your mind. There really isn't any more to say.'

He was acting angry, but she could see that he was hurt. He had been a friend to her when she needed one. He didn't deserve to be treated inconsiderately. She could understand how he felt, but it didn't change anything. She had to go. Still, she wished he could understand. 'After last night, I don't feel like I have a choice. I can't spend another night like that. I had to sleep on Peter's couch because Brian broke my door in. You've been very kind to me, ever since I came here. It's been a wonderful place to work, and I hate to leave like this.'

Albert was no stranger to partings – friends, lovers, employees. As a child he'd been a weeper, his easily broken heart the object of derision by other children. Over his lifetime, he'd developed a crust – he could raise that shield when he needed it. He smiled thinly at Dena. 'No one's indispensable,' he said. 'You'd better go and speak to René, and it would be polite to tell Eric as well.'

Dena stood up, looking pale and shaky. 'I will,' she said. 'I'm sorry, really.'

Part of him actually felt sorry for her. A small part. But, for the most part, he just felt betrayed. He had tried to help her and this was what he got. He knew he should wish her good luck, but he couldn't bring himself to do it.

Peter rummaged in the Little Mermaid suitcase on the floor of Megan and Tory's room. 'Here,' he said cheerfully, over the sound of water filling the bathtub in the next room. He held up a faded sweatshirt and matching sweatpants. 'After your bath, you can put these on. But first I want you to have a good bath, and get all clean while I finish up around here. That way we'll be all set to leave when Dena gets back, and Tory gets out of school.'

Megan, still in her pjs, sat on the edge of her bed, staring at him, her thumb in her mouth.

'Megan, take that out,' he said, prying it firmly away from her face. Megan's eyes filled with tears, but she did not protest aloud.

'Listen,' said Peter. 'You help me by having that bath so we can go away from here and never come back anymore. Won't that be good?'

The child gazed at him, her rosy lip pushed out, the tears sliding down her face.

'Of course it will,' he said. 'We'll start fresh, with a new house and maybe even a new baby.' As he talked, he began to remove the remaining clothes from the dresser drawers and pile them up on the bed. He made sure that each sock had a match before he put it into a box. 'I know you don't like it here anymore,' he went on in a soothing voice. 'And I don't blame you. The place where we're going – out west – they have mountains and cowboys and—'

'Indians?' she cried.

'No,' he scoffed. 'No Indians. We'll be perfectly safe there. No sneak attacks. Maybe we'll get a house out in the country. Far away from other people. Would you like that?'

Suddenly, from the living room, a voice called out, 'Peter, Peter are you home?'

Peter and Megan looked at one another. Megan was wide-eyed, her whole body stiff, but not with fear. With excitement. She was trembling. 'Miss Kay,' she cried. 'Miss Kay!'

Peter, who had not recognized the voice as quickly as the child, frowned and nodded. 'I think you're right,' he said. 'I think it is Miss Kay!'

Megan shrieked and slid down off the bed. She went running out the door, toward the living room, her father following behind her. He stopped to turn off the water in the bathtub, which was already deep enough. There were shouts of 'Miss Kay' and 'Meggie', and when Peter entered the living room, he saw Megan, enveloped in the black-and-white checkered coat of a middle-aged woman, who was kneeling on the floor, rocking the child and murmuring to her with an expression of delight on her face.

'Brenda,' he said, staring at their former baby-sitter, whom they had not seen since she left to live with her daughter. 'What a surprise.'

Brenda Kelly squeezed Megan gently and then released her. She got to her feet and extended a hand to Peter, who shook it briefly. 'Hello Peter,' she said gravely. 'How are you?'

'I'm fine,' he said. 'I didn't expect to see you here.'

Brenda clasped Megan's hand and swung it in her own, looking down fondly at the beaming child. 'Well, you didn't think I'd just forget all about you folks. I told you I'd come and visit.'

Peter smiled thinly. 'I . . . just thought you'd give us some warning.'

'Warning?' she said. She was looking at him intently, as if she had never really seen him before.

'You know, let us know you were coming,' he said uneasily.

'It was a spur-of-the-moment thing,' she said.

'Well, it's good to see you, in any case,' said Peter. 'It's been tough managing without you.'

Brenda looked around the disassembled rooms. 'I see you're moving,' she said.

'Yes, leaving today, as a matter of fact. You should have told me you were planning to visit,' he said, a faintly disapproving note in his voice.

'Kind of sudden?' Brenda observed.

'Job offer out West,' he said. 'I had to grab it.'

Megan clung to the older woman's hand and stared up at her with shining eyes. 'Miss Kay, Miss Kay,' she cried. 'Come with us.'

Brenda smiled. 'I can't, honey. I have to get back to my grand-children. They'd be awful mad if I just up and left them.'

'How's it going with Regina and the kids?' Peter asked politely.

Brenda shook her head. 'The kids are great. Regina . . . that's another matter. This divorce seems to have thrown her for a loop. She's out drinking in bars after work, when she should be home with the children. They notice it. It's tough on them. Tough on me, too, but no matter what I say—'

'Well, I'm sure it's an adjustment for everyone,' said Peter with a decided lack of interest.

Brenda Kelly recognized the hint, but didn't take it. 'I need to talk to you, Peter,' she said stubbornly. 'Can I sit down?'

'Well, it's a busy time . . .'

She gazed at him implacably.

'Of course,' he said, clearing some boxes off the sofa. 'Sit down.'

Brenda sat down heavily and Megan instantly climbed up on her lap. Brenda smiled sadly at the child, smoothing her hair away from her eyes, and caressing her round cheek fondly.

'What can I do for you?' Peter asked.

Brenda continued to gaze at Megan. 'Honey,' she said. 'Listen. I need to talk to your daddy alone. Grown-up talk. Can you go in your room and give your dolls some tea and cookies while Daddy and I talk? You still have that tea set I gave you, don't you?'

Megan nodded gravely. 'Oh yes.'

'And you still give your babies their tea, don't you?'

Megan slipped down off her lap and landed with a thud on the floor. 'I make tea,' she said.

'Never mind tea,' said Peter. 'You get those pajamas off and hop in the bathtub. The water is nice and warm.' He sighed. 'I want to get her bathed right away so I can pack up the bathroom stuff. Dry out the bathmat and all that.'

Brenda nodded, but showed no inclination to depart. Peter turned to Megan. 'Maybe if you're good, Miss Kay will help you wash your hair later,' he offered.

'Oh, I'd like that,' said Brenda, nodding at the child.

'I take my bath,' Megan promised, wide-eyed. Brenda watched the child scamper back toward her room and then turned to Peter who was studying her.

'Brenda, what's the matter? You seem so . . . serious.'

Brenda took a deep breath. 'This is serious,' she said. Then she hesitated. 'Very serious. I wasn't sure I should come.'

'Well, what is it?' he asked.

She did not look at him. She gulped in another deep breath, and then placed a hand flat on her chest, as if it were difficult to inhale enough air. 'OK. OK. I told myself I was going to come here and speak to you about this and I'm going to. But, I'm nervous.'

'What?' he asked. 'You're making me nervous.'

'Peter, I have no argument with you. You know that.'

'No. None that I know of.' He frowned, and waited.

'OK. I was watching my programs yesterday afternoon. Oprah had a show on about . . .'

'Oprah?' he asked in a bemused tone, as if relieved.

Brenda Kelly met his gaze with her own, unsmiling eyes. 'It was a show about fathers and child custody.'

Peter raised his eyebrows, as if feigning interest.

'There was a woman on the show talking about how her husband was denied custody, so he took their two children and ran away. She showed a picture of them. The children looked completely different than they do now, of course. No resemblance, really.'

'Wait a minute, hold it,' said Peter. 'What in the world are you telling me this for? What has this got to do with me?'

'Quite a bit, I'm afraid,' she said.

'Brenda, my wife, died, as you well know.'

'I know that's what you said. I admit, I wasn't thinking about you, although the man's face looked familiar. It was sort of fuzzy, but it rang a bell. He was clean-shaven, but his features were similar. Still, why would I think of you? I believed that your wife was dead. I wasn't even paying that much attention. And then the woman mentioned the birthmark. Star-shaped. On the little one's lower back.'

'That could be anyone,' he muttered. 'Lots of kids have birthmarks.'

'But it wasn't just anyone,' Brenda persisted. 'She showed a picture. I bathed Megan often enough. So I looked more closely at the photos they were showing on the screen. They didn't just show them once. They showed them over and over again, Peter. That little girl with the birthmark. It was Megan. And the other one was Tory. Although they had different names when they were born. It was you.'

Peter looked out the front window with narrowed eyes, his lips white where they were pressed together.

Perspiration had beaded on Brenda's forehead. She was still wearing her coat. She tugged out a Kleenex and blotted the beads of sweat. 'Once I realized it, I felt like somebody had just kicked me in the gut. I didn't know what to do. At first I thought, just forget it. Let it go. You're out of their lives. But I couldn't.'

Peter looked down at his hands, clenched in his lap.

'I didn't know what to do. I decided that I had to talk to you before I did anything. I had to give you the benefit of the doubt. I know how you love those girls. No one knows better than me what a devoted father you are, Peter,' she said gently. 'You've got to believe me. I'm not judging you. I just want to know.'

'I didn't say it was true. You can believe what you want.'

'Oh, it's true,' she said.

'I suppose you've called the police,' he said.

'No,' she said. 'I didn't tell a soul. I wanted to hear your side. I owe you . . . and the girls . . . that much. I love those kids. I want to do what's best for them.'

'So do I,' he whispered.

'I know you do,' she said vehemently. 'But running away. Telling them their mother is dead . . . Wasn't there any other way?'

'No. You don't think I . . . that this happened without considering all the options, do you? Those girls are everything to me. They were trapped. I had to do something.'

'But it was wrong,' said Brenda earnestly.

'God, when I woke up this morning I never thought . . . Getting ready for our trip. We were so happy . . .'

'Tell me what happened,' Brenda insisted.

Peter got up and paced around the room. The expression on his face ricocheted between anger and despair. 'She was unfit. Completely unfit. But I couldn't prove it in court. They didn't see what I saw. She was a monster. Out of control, emotionally.'

'She seemed normal enough on the TV,' said Brenda.

He turned on her with rage in his eyes. 'Oh, she could seem as normal as apple pie. That's why the court wouldn't believe me. But I had to live with her. Sit by and watch, while she destroyed my children. Should I have done that, Brenda? Given up and just let her . . . do her worst. I'm not that kind of man.'

'The courts always favor the mother,' Brenda agreed. 'I swear sometimes I think my own grandchildren would be better off with their father.'

Peter knelt down in front of her and grasped her hands. 'You understand what I'm saying. I tried to do it their way. But every day that went by, those girls were in danger from her. I had to do something to protect them. I know what it is to be raised by a twisted, heartless mother. I couldn't let that happen to them.'

Brenda looked at him sadly. 'No. I understand. I know how much you love them. But living like this.' She extricated her hand from his and waved it around the room. 'Always on the run. This is no way for children to live.'

'Brenda, it's not an easy life. I know that. I don't make much money. It's more important to me to be with the girls. Fortunately, when she died, my mother left me some stocks that I was able to liquidate. So, we're able to manage all right. We have enough money to live simply. You know there's nothing extravagant in the way we live.'

'I know that,' she said, nodding. 'You're very responsible that way.'

'For the most part, we have to keep our distance from people. But at least I know my girls are safe. I would give my life for those girls.'

'I know you would,' she said sadly. 'But they don't know the truth about their own lives. Do they? Does Tory know? She must remember her mother.'

'She accepts what I told her. That her mother died. She doesn't seem to remember too much. Someday, I'll tell her. I'll tell them both. When they're older, and she can't hurt them anymore.'

'What did she do to them? Was she an addict or something?'

'Worse than that,' he said. 'I can't go into it.' He looked up. 'Shhh . . . Megan might hear us. But, Brenda, you know I'm a good father . . .'

'You're a very good father. I mean, you're a little demanding with them sometimes—'

'Demanding,' he cried. 'Because I want them to be their best?'

Brenda shook her head. 'I know you have good intentions. And I'm sure your wife had her problems. Believe me, I know. I look at Regina . . .' Brenda shook her head. 'But children need their mother. They need a mother's love.'

'Miss Kay,' Megan called from the bathroom. 'Come wash my hair.'

'I'm coming, honey,' Brenda called back absently.

'There's no sacrifice too great,' Peter said urgently. 'You must know I meant that.' He looked at her with imploring eyes. 'Tell me I can trust you. Tell me you'll keep my secret,' he said. 'Please, for the girls. If we go back, they'll put me in jail. They'll say I kidnapped my own children. How is that possible, Brenda? How can they call it kidnapping, when it's your own flesh and blood?'

'But their mother must miss them,' she said sadly.

'More than I would miss them, if the law ripped them away

from me? Brenda, think about it. If you don't keep my secret, that's what will happen.'

'You're asking a lot, Peter.'

'Please, Brenda, I know how much you care for them.'

Brenda sighed, and looked doubtfully into his woeful eyes. 'I don't think I could ever be responsible for separating them from you.'

Peter bent his head and kissed her hands. 'Bless you,' he said.

TWENTY-NINE

Dena came home to find Megan, seated on the front step, her hair still wet from her bath, her forehead pressed to the knees of her sweatsuit, her arms wrapped around her head as if to hide herself from sight.

'Hi honey,' Dena said as she came up the walk. The child did not move or look up at her. Dena wondered if maybe she had a problem with her hearing. That might account for her shyness – perhaps she didn't hear what was being said to her. She resolved to mention it to Peter.

She walked up and touched Megan on the shoulder. The child did not flinch or look up. She remained as she was. At that moment, Peter came out of the house, looking distracted and harried.

'Hi,' she said. 'What's the matter with Megan?'

'I just got off the phone from Tory's school. We're ready to leave now. Are you ready?'

That probably explained Megan's apparent misery. Everything was moving too fast. 'Right now?' Dena asked.

'You wanted to get away from here,' he reminded her sharply.

'Well, yes . . .' Dena tried to think. What did she have to do? Very little really. But there were people she might have stopped to say goodbye to. Nanette from work. And Ron. Even Matt Riley out at the nursing home. And, absurdly, she thought of Sergeant Watkins, and wondered why he had been suspended from the police force.

'I told Tory we'd pick her up in ten minutes,' he said.

Dena didn't like being rushed this way. She had half a mind to tell him to forget it, but at the same time she realized that he might be hurrying for her sake. And she didn't want to be the one to hold everything up. 'I was thinking,' she said. 'Maybe we could kind of caravan, you know. I could follow you in my car and then I wouldn't have to worry about how to get my car out there . . .'

'Dena, for heaven's sakes. There's no guarantee that we can stay together on the highway. Look,' he said, exasperated, 'if you don't want to come with us, then don't. Go whenever you're ready.'

She tried to ignore the sharpness in his tone. He's doing you a favor, she reminded herself. He needs a hugely pregnant woman along on this trip like he needs a hole in the head. 'You're right,' she said. It will only take me a few minutes. I promise.'

'I'll tell you what,' he said. 'I'll go get Tory and swing back around here. Don't try to carry your stuff out to the curb. I'll go upstairs and get it when we get back.'

'Well, all right,' said Dena.

She expected him to call to Megan, but instead he reached down and picked her up off the front step, cradling her in his arms like a baby. The child kept her face covered with her hands. Dena watched him take Megan to the car, and strap her into the back seat. He looked back and saw Dena watching him. An impatient expression crossed his face. Dena hurried up the stairs to her apartment. She looked around it with only a sense of relief to be escaping. The door was still broken. She had enclosed an additional amount for fixing it in her check to the landlord. As for the few things she'd bought for the apartment, they could stay here. They would only be in the way at her sister's. Most of her stuff, luckily, was still in storage, out in Chicago. Maybe you always knew it wouldn't last, she thought with a sigh.

It didn't take long to pack up the one suitcase she had, and a shopping bag. I don't need him to help me, she thought, as she carried them down the stairs, holding onto the railing with her other hand. The stairs were steep, and she was not at her most surefooted these days with this huge stomach. For a moment she thought of Brian, crumpled there at the bottom. She had thought for a minute that he might be dead, and tried to remember what she felt at that moment. Horror, mainly. And maybe the tiniest bit of relief. And then he had stood up.

A horn sounded. Peter was back with the girls. She sighed and looked out. He was so jittery today. Peter usually seemed so . . .

in control. The thought of the move, she decided. It was enough to make anyone anxious. She started out the door and he ran up the walk to meet her, snatching the suitcase from her hand. 'I told you I'd get it,' he said.

'Hey,' she said. 'Take it easy.'

'Sorry. Right. I'm just anxious to get going.'

'I know,' she said. 'Do you think my car will be all right there?'

'Sure,' he said. 'People leave their cars parked on the street for weeks at a time.'

'You're right,' she said. He motioned to her to hand him her bags so he could put them in the trunk. She didn't argue. She opened the door to the front seat of Peter's car and slid in on the passenger side, struggling to pull the seat belt around her distended middle. She glanced into the back seat. Tory sat glumly, her forehead pressed against the side window. Megan had her knees pulled up, and she was hugging them to her body, rocking back and forth with a dazed expression on her face.

'Hey, you two. I hope you don't mind me coming along.'

'I missed my party,' said Tory angrily.

'Oh, there will be lots of parties,' said Dena, 'when you get to your new home.'

'How do you know that?' Tory asked.

'Tory,' Peter snapped, climbing into the driver's seat. 'Stop sulking.'

Dena sighed and looked out her window. She could tell that the children were unsettled by the abruptness of their departure. She didn't blame them for being out of sorts. She felt a little that way herself.

Peter turned on the engine, looked both ways, and then pulled out. 'We're off,' he said cheerfully.

Dena nodded but did not reply. She stared out the window at the familiar streets of Monroe. It was a quiet little town, going about its quiet little business. A few people stopped to talk on the sidewalks, but mostly the streets were empty. She thought of the day she had arrived here. Brian had been so nervous about her arrival that he'd already had a few drinks by the time she pulled in at two in the afternoon. That first weekend had been awkward, trying to find a place for her stuff in his little house, and being faced with the permanency of moving in. But it had been hopeful too. Moments of laughter, and desire. Waking up at dawn, looking out the window at the horse farm and thinking, this is my new home. Dena sighed. It seemed like a lifetime ago.

'What are you thinking about?' Peter asked.

Dena shook her head. 'Nothing special,' she said.

'Well, cheer up. We're on our way! Girls, what do you think? We're headed for the highway. Shall we sing?'

A dull murmur of protest came from the back seat. 'You girls are no fun,' he said.

'You certainly were eager to get going,' said Dena, trying not to sound critical.

'I'm excited about it,' he cried. 'It's a new adventure. That's why I want to sing.'

'Let's sing later,' Dena said. 'It's too soon to sing. I need to get away from this town before I can sing.' It was easier than telling him the truth. That she felt as if she would never sing about anything again. And then she amended that thought, cradling her baby. Except to you. I'll sing to you, she promised her baby. Although at the moment she couldn't imagine the song.

After school, Vanessa took special care getting ready for the barn. Normally, she pulled on her old jeans and her boots and didn't bother with much else. After all, she hated to miss a moment with the horses. But today was different. Today would be their first meeting after she had saved him. After the embrace. She combed her hair carefully, and left it loose instead of tying it back as usual. No, that would get in her way too much. She found a barrette and pulled back the top and the front, letting the back hang loose. There, she thought. That would work.

She stared at her face in the mirror. No zits. That was good. Braces were bad, of course. But she could try to keep her mouth closed over them as much as possible. She didn't usually wear any makeup, but this time she decided that a little blusher and mascara couldn't hurt. She applied the makeup to her lovely young face with an uncertain hand. Then she cocked her head, and examined herself from several angles.

Not bad, she thought, imagining him talking to her, while she tilted her head as if in fascination at his words. Then, he would say something funny. She smiled, and saw the braces. She turned away from the mirror in despair at her appearance. Just go, she thought.

Squaring her shoulders, she hurried down the stairs, out the back door, and over the hill to the barn, as she had so many times before. But today was definitely different. She felt little electric shocks all through her as she pictured their eyes meeting. Him knowing what she had done for him. Knowing the chance she had taken for his sake.

He would look at her and it would be as if he was really seeing her for the first time.

She rounded the corner of the barn and saw his truck, parked outside. He was here. Her heart was pounding as she walked toward the open double doors. She imagined him, trying to find the words to thank her. It's all right, she would tell him, soothingly, as he pleaded for her to understand how indebted to her he felt.

She entered the barn and looked around for him. 'Brian,' she called out softly.

Brian stood in a horse's stall, staring at the thing in his hand. He couldn't remember when he had picked it up, or why. And, for the life of him, he couldn't remember what it was called. He heard someone calling his name, as if from far away. 'Who is it?' he tried to say.

Vanessa heard a voice snarl, 'Wizit?' Vanessa frowned and walked down between the stalls. The door to Rajah's stall was open. Brian was standing behind the horse, holding a bridle in his right hand, and staring at it as if he didn't know what it was. He peered up at her, his head cocked to one side.

She looked at him in disbelief. 'You shouldn't stand behind Rajah like that,' she said. 'You know he doesn't like it.'

It took a minute for Brian to recognize her, because he was seeing two of her as she stood there. Then, he realized who it was.

'Nsez,' he mumbled.

Vanessa felt her spirits sink, her excitement fade, but for the moment she didn't care. The only important thing was to get him out from behind Rajah. It was a miracle the horse hadn't kicked his lights out already. She came around and tugged at the arm of his barn jacket. 'Brian, get out of there,' she said.

He squinted, and tried to figure out what she was doing. She wanted him to come somewhere with her and he didn't like being pushed around, especially by a little girl.

Besides, he had a reason for being there in that stall. He just couldn't remember what it was. He struggled to pull his arm away from her.

'Brian,' she said firmly, 'you have to get out of there. Come on.' She knew what the matter with him was, and it shocked her a little. He'd been drinking. It wasn't the only time she'd seen him like this. He'd been sort of like this that day . . . the day she told the police about. The day when he was supposedly working. He'd been swigging from a bottle, and talking out loud about Dena while he dragged her things along the ground outside and tossed them in a heap.

'Come on, come with me.' She tugged at him and finally he came with her, dragging one foot as he walked. She was close to him, and ready to hold her breath against that blast of whisky breath, but he didn't smell that way at all. Actually, he smelled worse. He smelled like throw-up.

He allowed her to pull him out of Rajah's stall, and then he slumped down on a bale of hay in the corridor between the stalls. He rubbed his head, and squinted at her again.

'Here, give me that,' she said, impatiently, pointing to the bridle. 'I'll put it back.' Vanessa sighed. If she had to take care of him, she would. Somebody had to. In a way, it made her feel very grown-up. This was the second time she had come to his aid, although taking care of a guy who was drunk was a lot less thrilling than freeing him from the long arm of the law.

Brian looked down at the object in his hand. It lay across his palm. He tried to close his fingers around it, but they refused to grip. For some reason, Vanessa wanted him to give it to her. It was easier than arguing. 'Huh,' he said, trying to hand it to her. He lifted it up, but when she reached for it, the bridle fell from his hand onto the dusty floor of the barn.

Vanessa wondered if he had dropped it on purpose, just to be mean. She didn't much like the idea of having to get down on her knees and pick up something that a drunk guy had dropped. She felt her hopes for their reunion ebbing away. She picked up the bridle and stood up. 'You are really wasted, aren't you,' she said disapprovingly.

Brian looked up at her angrily. It wasn't true. He hadn't had a drink since last night before he went over to . . . wherever it was. Dena's house. Right. When her boyfriend pushed him down those stairs . . . When he got home he needed a drink, but he couldn't.

Even the smell of it made him sick. He hadn't been able to keep anything in his stomach because of the headache. He'd tried to eat a little something, but just vomited it up. He knew he wasn't feeling right. He was sick. He knew that much. So, he was insulted that Vanessa called him drunk. 'M'not,' he said.

'You're not?' she repeated. 'Is that what you're saying? Not much.'

Brian staggered to his feet. It had come over him kind of gradually, the weakness and the double vision. He could hardly tell which image of Vanessa was the real girl.

But both of them were looking at him disdainfully. He didn't need her here, calling him a drunk and giving him that look. All he needed was some sleep, he thought. He was so tired. He'd never been so tired. 'G'wan. Don' wan you . . . G'wan.'

Vanessa felt something inside her harden against him. 'That's real nice. After what I did for you.' She tugged at the bridle in her hand. 'I should have told them what you were really doing that day. Burning her clothes. Tearing her clothes up and burning them. Very mature. They would have loved to hear that.'

'Bits,' he snarled.

It took her a minute to realize what he was trying to say. And, when she did, she felt completely betrayed. 'Bitch. You're calling me . . . you drunken creep,' she cried. 'What kind of a creep makes a bonfire of his girlfriend's clothes? I lied to the police for you. I told them you were working in the barn that day. I didn't want you to be embarrassed. Most people would be ashamed of doing what you did.'

Her voice was far away, as if she was yelling at him from across the pond. And at first he didn't have one idea of what she was talking about. Burning clothes? What burning clothes? But then, dimly, he remembered. Dena's clothes. He'd made a fire out of her things. He wondered now why he had done that. He didn't like that look on Vanessa's face. It was angry and accusing. They all looked at him that way, sooner or later. He hated that look. It always made him feel so helpless. They all betrayed him.

Every last one of them. For another man. His father said so. 'Fu . . . you,' he said. 'Vess . . .'

'You can't even talk.' Vanessa's eyes filled with tears. After what she had done. After all the dreams she'd had of him. Even if he was drunk, there was no reason to say things like that. 'I hate you Brian Riley,' she said. 'I wish I never saved your sorry butt. If I had to do it all over again, I'd just let you rot.'

Brian saw the tears in her eyes, and he could feel tears coming to his own eyes.

He realized, in that instant, that he needed her to help him. There was something terribly wrong here. He needed her to stay and call someone for him. An ambulance. Some little flicker of rationality told him that he didn't want to go to sleep. He wanted to go to the hospital. He was sick. Even as slowly as his mind was working, he knew that he was in trouble. He didn't know that his fall down the stairs had caused a head injury. That blood was pooling between his brain and his skull. That pressure was gradually building as the blood had nowhere to go, making him sleepy and weak and interfering with his speech and his motor skills. All Brian knew was that his head was pounding, as if someone was hammering on it. 'Ness. Hep muh . . .'

Vanessa saw the tears come to his eyes, but she didn't care. She wasn't going to be fooled this time. It felt good to yell at him. He'd trampled on all her dreams. She hated to leave the horses, but she wasn't about to do his work for him today. Once he'd slept it off, he could do it himself. 'I'm done helping you,' she said. She looked at the bridle in her hand and then she threw it down at his feet. It felt good to do it. Almost as good as something romantic. 'Why don't you go dry out somewhere, you creep.' She turned on her cowboy-booted heel and stormed out of the barn.

Brian watched her go, not exactly comprehending what it was that was happening.

He wondered if she was going for help. If she would be coming back. He'd told her he needed help. That must be what she was doing. He couldn't remember what she had said. All he could think about was this pain in his head. It had started during the night, and gotten worse and worse. Worse than any hangover he had ever had. Worse than the day after Tanya . . . Tanya. He remembered her now. Her coppery hair so soft and pretty. Her sad eyes. He'd heard her fall that night. But he'd had so much to drink. They'd fought for hours. She was crying in the shower. He could hear her sobs above the sound of the water. And then, that sound. A crash. He felt then as he felt now. Something was seriously wrong but he couldn't move from where he was. Couldn't figure out what it was he was supposed to do about it.

Do something, he thought. Brian staggered over toward Rajah's stall to close it, but instead of closing it, he slumped against it. Then, as his vision disappeared altogether, he slid to the ground, landing not far behind the hooves of the spookable horse.

THIRTY

Selma Weiss wiped the perspiration off the bridge of her nose with the forearm of her white sweatshirt, being careful not to clonk herself with the pink plastic barbell-shaped weights that she clutched in her pudgy hands. She managed to do all this without breaking her power-walk stride along the well-worn towpath beside the canal.

She felt righteous striding along in the twilight. She decided that when she got home she would treat herself to a glass of wine while she fixed dinner. The thought of it filled her with a longing to be home, but she put it out of her mind. Dusk. It was a lovely time of day for a walk, she told herself dutifully. And so beautiful around here.

But no matter how often she told herself this, it was no use. She would never get used to it. Norman, her husband, had been in seventh heaven ever since they sold their Philadelphia townhouse and moved to Monroe. As they had gotten older, especially after his bypass surgery, Norman had become more and more leery of city life, more worried about crime.

Whenever they would go to visit friends who had moved to Bucks County, Norman would rave about the place, and she knew exactly what he was thinking. If they lived out here they would be safe. It was peaceful, they would be out in nature, and they could go to those little health-food restaurants and eat couscous and barley soup for lunch. It was what he was dreaming of. And, Selma thought now, as she thought then, he was a good husband, and he'd worked hard all his life. If that's what he wanted for his retirement – a little house by the river up here – he should have it. So, three years ago, they did it. They sold the townhouse and moved up here. They walked, they bird-watched, and they had eaten mountains of couscous and supped gallons of barley soup.

It was a good life; their grandchildren loved visiting here and it was peaceful all right. But face it, Selma, she told herself as she strode along the canal, pumping her weights, you're a city girl through and through. Norman could go on and on about the colors and the beauty of nature. To Selma, it all looked the same. She gazed around her, trying to appreciate the sunset, the falling leaves, the river on one side of her, the canal on the other. It was pretty. Very nice. But the same. Everything the same.

Up ahead, Selma saw the little hill leading up to the bridge that crossed the canal. There were lots of bridges over the canals. She hadn't quite been able to figure out what this canal business was all about. Something left over from the olden days. Look it up, Norman had said. Read about it. You're always curious. You'll find it interesting. Humph, Selma thought. What was interesting about a ten-foot-long bridge in the middle of nowhere? Paul Klee was interesting. De Kooning was interesting. A canal bridge was a bore.

Selma shrugged and then barreled up the hill to the bridge. She stood at the top for a moment, catching her breath before she crossed over and started down the other side. Dutifully, she looked out at the pattern that the falling leaves made on the shallow, green-black water in the canal. Very nice, she thought. Very . . . strange. Selma peered out over the wooden railing to the water below.

Just down the path, near a fallen tree which trailed its upper branches in the canal, she saw something that didn't fit into the soporific autumnal twilight color scheme.

Something black and white, a checkerboard pattern, floating in the water. She strained her eyes to see, and then felt her heart do a flip as she realized it was a garment of some sort – a shirt, or a coat. And there was someone face down in the water, wearing it.

'God help us,' she cried. She dropped her weights on the bridge and began to run down to the edge of the canal, shouting as loud as she could, 'Help, somebody help.' As if anybody in this lonesome, Godforsaken little paradise could ever hear you.

Captain Van Brunt pulled his squad car up beside the Emergency Rescue Van. All the official vehicles were parked as far as possible up on the shoulder, so that the front ends seemed poised to pitch into the canal. The roads beside the canal were winding and twisty.

Even with his headlights on, a driver would hardly have time to avoid hitting you if you left the butt end of your car out in the road. They'd had plenty of accidents like that in the past. Van Brunt leaned across the seat and took his flashlight out of the glove compartment. Then he got out, slamming the door.

He looked around. On the bridge a patrolman was talking to a woman in a white sweatshirt that seemed to glow in the growing darkness. Beside the water, the body was laid out on a plastic ground sheet. The medical examiner, George Taylor, was kneeling down beside the sodden, shoeless figure. Van Brunt decided to head that way first.

'George, what's the story?' he asked.

George Taylor, who was making notes in a book beside the body, squinted up at the captain. 'Looks like a drowning, Captain. That woman up there on the bridge spotted her while she was out power-walking. Victim is a female Caucasian, about fifty-five, no apparent traumatic injury. She's been dead about, oh, five or six hours, I'd say.'

Van Brunt nodded and looked down impassively at the woman in the checkered coat. 'Any ID?'

The ME shook his head. 'Nothing on the body.'

'Captain!' Ken McCarthy slid down the bank in a skateboarding stance and ended up next to him. 'We found her car parked down the road about half a mile. A little purple Geo. Her wallet and license were in the glove compartment.'

'You sure it's hers?' Van Brunt asked.

'Oh yeah,' said the young cop, grimacing as he looked down at the corpse. He handed the open wallet to the captain. Van Brunt aimed his flashlight at it.

'See? Photo ID on the license,' said Ken. 'Her name is Brenda Kelly. She lives in Riverside.' It was a town about half an hour away on the highway.

Van Brunt nodded, examining the mug-shot-quality photo under his flashlight beam, and then he frowned up at the bridge where a few onlookers were clustered. 'You think she jumped?' he asked George Taylor, who was straightening up. He practically had to shout because the news vans were beginning to arrive, reporters and technicians with camcorders piling out.

Taylor shook his head. 'If you wanted to kill yourself, you'd pick something higher than that bridge. Besides, even from that height, she would have had some fractures. I can't find anything like that. I think she was just out taking a walk – might have twisted her ankle or something like that – and she slipped, and fell in.'

'It's not very deep,' Van Brunt observed.

'Well, maybe she couldn't swim. She might have panicked. Or, she might have blacked out for a second. I'll check for a head injury during the PM. But she definitely drowned. That's the cause of death. No question.'

'OK,' said Van Brunt. 'We'll find the next of kin and find out if she could swim or not. First, I want to take a look at that car.' Van Brunt started back up the embankment, passing the EMTs, who were carrying a gurney down the embankment to collect the body.

It did not take long for Dena to realize that she was going to be like an anchor to the expedition west. After sitting in the car for three hours she felt dizzy and slightly sick to her stomach. Her ankles were swollen to twice their size. She told herself that she just wasn't used to sitting still for long periods of time. It was probably something you had to get used to. Perhaps tomorrow, after a rest, she would be better able to travel. 'Peter,' she said, after enduring the discomfort as long as she could, 'I know this is a pain for you, but do you think we could stop before long?'

Without realizing it, she expected him to be sympathetic. He was always sympathetic where the baby was concerned. But, instead of replying, he stared angrily through the windshield. She could see his jaw muscles working like gears, even beneath his beard.

'Never mind,' she said. 'I'm sorry. I know it's a nuisance trying to travel with somebody in my condition. I don't want to hold you guys up. Let's keep going for a little while longer.'

Peter exhaled a noisy sigh, but headed for the next exit on the highway. He mumbled something that Dena could not understand.

'Peter, I mean it. I'm sorry I complained. Keep going.'

'No, no, we'll stop,' he replied. After driving in silence for a while, he pulled into a convenience store and looked around at the children.

'I'll go get a few things we need,' Peter said to the girls in the back seat. 'Then, we'll go find a place to spend the night.' Dena tried to shift herself around to look at the children. Tory seemed oblivious to discomfort. During the ride she had chattered intermittently to the doll and stuffed animals she had in the back seat. Megan had been silent the entire way. When Tory tried to draw her into the fantasy, she merely whimpered. Looking sympathetically at their pale, unhappy faces, Dena thought that they would probably enjoy a break. Their hurried departure had been tough on all of them, but children seemed to be so ritual-oriented. It must have upset them not to be able to carry out their farewell ceremonies. My fault, Dena thought. Peter only did it for me.

She opened the door on the passenger side and swung her legs out. 'I'm going to go in and get some milk,' said Dena. 'How about some ice cream for you girls?'

'No ice cream for them,' he said. 'It'll be supper time before long. If you want milk, I'll get it for you while I'm in there.'

'Well, I really need to get out and stretch my legs,' she admitted.

'Why don't you just wait in the car with the girls? We'll soon be at a motel. You can stretch your legs then. We don't want to leave them alone in the car.'

Dena sat at the edge of the car seat, looking down at her swollen ankles. Not for the first time that day she thought, why didn't you just fly? Why did you listen to your sister's urban legend – pregnant women shouldn't fly. That was it, wasn't it, she asked herself? You pretended you didn't believe her, but you did. She could tell this trip was going to be difficult. Peter was used to telling the children what to do, and was out of the habit of dealing with another adult. He'll just have to get used to it while we're together, she thought.

'I have to pee,' she said stubbornly. 'I'll only be in there a minute.'

Peter sighed. 'All right,' he said in a clipped voice. 'We'll all wait while you go inside. We'll wait for you to get back.'

'Maybe the girls would like to come in, too. They could pick out a treat. Something small that won't spoil their appetites.' She looked back at them, her eyebrows raised, as if encouraging a response.

For a moment Tory brightened, and made an excited bounce on the seat. 'I will buy them an apple,' he said.

Tory sank back down in the seat and resumed staring out the window.

They are better behaved than you are, Dena scolded herself. You're not exactly setting a good example. Try harder. 'Right,' said Dena. 'Well, I'll hurry.' We're tired, she thought. We're all tired and irritable, and Peter has kindly stopped for your sake, when he could have gone on.

She left him drumming his fingertips on the steering wheel, and lumbered into the store. She was tempted to buy something at the candy counter for the girls, but she hesitated with her fingers poised over the M&Ms. Don't do it, she thought. If he doesn't want them eating sweets before dinner, that's his prerogative. They're his children. She made a quick visit to the ladies' room, and then picked up a pint of milk for herself, knowing it was best for the baby, and brought it up to the counter. The uniformed girl behind the counter was talking and joking with a similarly attired young man. While Dena waited, she glanced at magazine cover lines and, at the very last minute, while the girl was already ringing her small order, she scooped two loose, foil-wrapped peanut butter cups from the bin beneath the cash register and put them beside her milk. Peanut butter, she thought. Semi-nutritious. 'These too,' she said.

The girl nodded and totaled up the tab. 'Do you want a bag for this?' she asked.

'Please,' said Dena. She stuffed her change into her purse and headed back to the car, which was parked near the entrance to the store. She opened the door and slid onto the front seat, rearranging her jumper beneath her.

'All set?' asked Peter, pleasant again. Dena nodded.

'I'll be right back,' he said.

As she watched her father enter the store, Tory asked, 'Did you get us anything?'

Dena turned and gave them a conspiratorial smile. She reached into her bag and handed them each a peanut butter cup. 'Here. Do you like these?'

Tory looked at the little candy in its gold wrapper as if it were a nugget of poison. 'Dad said no sweets.'

'But you've been so good. I thought you deserved a treat. You asked me to get you something.'

'A toy or something,' said Tory. She snatched the little candy away from Megan, who was examining it curiously, and handed it back to Dena. 'We'll wait for the apple,' said the child. Megan immediately began to wail.

Dena promptly handed Megan's candy back to her. 'She wants it,' Dena said. 'It won't hurt her.'

Tory watched in horror as the child put the chocolate into her mouth, and then smiled delightedly. 'Quick, swallow it,' Tory cried. 'She's got chocolate on her mouth. Give me something to clean it up.'

Dena fished a hanky from her purse and Tory wiped the chocolate off Megan's mouth while she was still chewing.

Tory handed the hanky back over the seat. 'Hide that,' she said. 'Don't let him see it.'

'Don't worry, honey,' Dena said. 'I'll tell him it was my idea.'

'Please, just hide it,' said Tory anxiously. 'Here he comes.'

Peter got back into the car carrying a plastic bag, which he laid on the seat. He reached into it and handed an apple over the seat to each of the children. Then he turned on the ignition. 'I asked them where it would be good to stay around here. The manager said there were little cabins down by the lake that were still being rented that might be nice.'

'That sounds good,' said Dena.

'Yeah,' he said. 'I might want to stay here for a day or so. Tomorrow I want to take this car over to that lot we passed on the highway and see if I can't trade it for a van.'

'Is there something wrong with your car?' Dena asked, confused.

'It runs pretty ragged,' said Peter.

'Why didn't you trade it in Monroe?' she asked.

'I didn't have a chance,' he said, a slight edge in his voice. 'Besides, it might do you good not to have to get on the road again right away.'

'OK,' said Dena. 'That's fine.' She stared out the window as he carefully backed out of the parking space. When will I get to Chicago, she wondered? Oh well, it was Peter's trip. She had to be a cheerful passenger. And he was right. It would probably do her good to have a day where she wasn't in the car the whole time.

They passed several motels, most of them seedy and deserted-looking on the way to the lake where the manager had directed them. The sign for Hideaway Cabins pointed them down an unpaved road with a dark tunnel of evergreens. Tory looked around excitedly, but Megan whimpered that she didn't like it here.

'Don't be scared,' said Dena. 'It'll be like spending a night in an enchanted forest.'

'Like Ratty and Mole in the Wild Wood,' Tory chimed in.

The bumpy road opened out onto a starkly beautiful vista. There were a series of little cabins which dotted the side of a wide, silvery lake. In the gathering darkness the lights of a few houses were visible through the trees across the lake, as well as a cluster of trailers on the far side.

'This is nice,' said Dena.

'Yes, this should do,' he said. 'The girls can play by the lake while I'm gone tomorrow.'

'I don't see any other cars,' said Dena. 'I hope they are still renting these places.'

'I'll go find out,' said Peter.

She watched him as he got out of the car and walked up to the nearest cabin, which had a 'Register Here' sign hanging over the door.

'This looks great, doesn't it?' she said.

'Can we go swimming?' Tory asked.

Dena looked at the dark trees and the gray, unbroken surface of the water. 'I think it might be a little cold for swimming,' Dena said.

'Oh, please,' Tory begged.

'Well, we'll see tomorrow,' said Dena. 'Maybe it'll be one of those really hot, sunny fall days and you can.'

'Oh, I hope it is,' said the child with longing.

'Me, too,' said Dena. She could see a little dock jutting out into the lake. On the bank, secured to the dock with a rope, was a little blue boat with an outboard motor on it. It looked as if someone had come in from fishing and just left it there. Dena thought how nice it would be to sit in the sunshine, and dangle her feet in the water for a lazy day. Maybe if she had a day to relax, without a lot of pressure, she would be able to sort out some plans for her life.

Peter emerged from the office carrying papers and a set of keys, which he waved to indicate he had succeeded. He climbed into the car and handed the papers and the keys to Dena. 'We're all set,' he said. 'Cabin number five.'

They drove down a short, rutted driveway and pulled up beside a tiny, cedar-sided cottage with leaves piled up to the front step. Peter led the way, unlocking the door, and flipping on the weak overhead light. The three others followed, looking around inside the cabin. It had a central room with two cushioned, wood-frame chairs arranged around a fireplace, a TV on a rolling stand, and a card table with a tablecloth and four folding chairs. There were three doors off the central room, one for a bath, and two bedrooms.

Dena switched on the lights in the other rooms, and was relieved to discover that both bedrooms had twin beds. She didn't mind sharing a room with Peter, but she was not about to share a bed.

'This is our room,' Tory crowed, setting her bag down in a sparsely furnished bedroom with pink spreads on the beds.

Dena looked at Peter. 'Is that OK?' she asked.

'Sure,' said Peter. With his approval, the girls ran out to the car to collect their little duffel bags for their room and get unpacked.

Peter was unloading his bag from the Wawa convenience store onto the card table, as well as a paper shopping bag he had brought in from the car, which contained food he had brought along from the house in Monroe. There were plastic plates and utensils, cold drinks and a bag of sandwiches. Dena had to admire his preparedness. 'You are a very good provider,' she observed.

'I never neglect my children,' he said.

'I've noticed that,' said Dena. She was feeling more relaxed, now that they were settled in for the night. She walked over to the cushioned chairs, lay down on the braided rug on the floor and rested her feet on the seat cushions. Immediately, her legs felt better.

Peter stared at her. 'What are doing lying on the floor?'

'Elevating my feet,' she said.

'That rug is probably filthy,' he said.

'It'll be OK,' said Dena, thinking: you're treating me like one of the children again. 'I'm completely washable.'

'You wouldn't let a baby crawl on that rug,' he said pointedly, putting cans away in the cupboard.

'No, of course not,' said Dena, aware that he was counseling her on childcare.

She looked up at the little peaked ceiling, thinking about her baby. Was she going to be anticipating every hazard, as he seemed to do? Somehow she doubted she would be as careful as Peter. As . . . particular.

'A lot of people are not capable of taking care of their children,' he went on, as he unpacked. 'Like my dear mother.'

Dena turned her head to the side and looked at him. 'You said she was an attorney. Did she leave you with nannies?'

'Sometimes,' he said. 'Sometimes, she would just leave me alone. One time a neighbor heard me crying in the apartment. They called the super who let them in. They found me climbing up on the counter, trying to find food in the cupboard. I was three years old.'

'Good lord, Peter. Did they do anything about it?'

'About me? No. My mother did manage to get the super fired, and the neighbor evicted. I found out about that much later.'

'Well, you've become a good parent in spite of all that neglect. You should be proud of yourself.'

'I have fought against it,' he corrected her. 'I won't allow history to repeat itself.'

Dena got up off the floor and went around the room, turning on table lamps. Then, she snapped off the weak, overhead light. 'There,' she said. 'That gets rid of the gloom a little bit.'

'Am I depressing you?' he asked.

'Oh no,' she said. 'I just got the urge to make it a little cozier.'

The girls emerged from their room, Megan carrying a stuffed dog in a protective embrace. 'I like it here,' said Tory. 'You can see the lake from my window.'

Inside her belly, the baby kicked, and Dena gasped, clutching a spot just below her breast.

Peter frowned. 'What's the matter?'

'Nothing,' said Dena, when she caught her breath. 'Just the baby kicking.' She smiled at the girls. 'He must like it here too.'

THIRTY-ONE

Regina Bluefield, still dressed from work in a tight-fitting gray suit and fake python-skin pumps, sat in the police station, staring numbly ahead, sipping on the can of diet soda which had been bought for her from the lunchroom machine. They had returned twenty minutes earlier from the morgue, where Regina had identified the body of her mother after nearly collapsing at the sight.

'How're ya doin' there?' Heath Van Brunt asked solicitously. 'Any better?'

Tears ran down Regina's carefully made-up face and dripped off her jaw. She didn't seem to notice them. She shook her head. 'Not really. Oh, God, what am I gonna do?'

'Is there somebody we can call for you, Mrs Bluefield?'

Regina shook her head. 'No. I'm on my own now.'

Van Brunt reflected, as he waited for her to collect herself, that it was never easy to lose your mother, no matter how old you were. This woman seated beside his desk was in the process of discovering that harsh fact of life.

Nonetheless, there were questions to be answered and no time to waste. His men had discovered something very odd. The trunk of Mrs Kelly's car was wet. The guys from the lab were examining the fabric which lined the trunk to try and find out how it got that way, but Van Brunt already had his theories. He just wished he had someone experienced on whom to try out his theories. He almost wished the chief were here.

Almost, but not quite. He liked being in charge.

'Mrs Bluefield, I need to ask you a couple of questions. Just to clear up a few things.'

'Sure,' she said dully. 'What do you want to know?'

'Do you know what your mother was doing here in Monroe?

Regina looked around the police station with a dazed expression, as if she could not remember what she herself was doing in Monroe. Then, she looked back at the captain and seemed to remember. 'Mom . . . she used to live here. She had an apartment in a house on Bigelow Street.'

'Was she in the habit of coming back to visit?'

Regina shook her head and reached in her pocketbook. 'She didn't have time. She looked after my kids for me. Do you mind if I smoke?' she asked.

Van Brunt shook his head. 'I'd prefer you didn't. We found a receipt in her car for the Endicott Hotel where she spent the night. Did she have a . . . romantic interest here perhaps?'

Regina had to laugh. 'My mother? No,' she said flatly.

'Well, why would she spend the night here when you live half an hour away?'

'She wouldn't have driven home at night. She had cataracts, so her night vision was bad. She was afraid to drive on the highway at night.'

Van Brunt nodded. 'They remembered seeing your mother at

the hotel, but she didn't speak to anyone. Did she tell you she was coming down here?'

Regina shook her head wearily and wiped away the tears that were rolling down her cheeks. 'She didn't tell me anything. I was at work. She brought my kids over to my husband's . . . my ex, and she told him she had to go out of town for some reason. That's all I know.'

'Did she have a job here? Friends?'

'She had some friends. Some women in her church group. She used to . . . to baby-sit for the guy who lived in the same house she did. He was a widower. Had a couple of kids.'

'Name?' asked the captain.

'I forget. Wait a minute.' Regina rummaged in her purse and pulled out an address book. She looked up a number and then pointed it out to the captain. 'That's him. Peter Ward. She might have stopped by to see the kids. She loved those kids. She was always talking about them . . .'

Van Brunt jotted down the number and then hailed Ken McCarthy, who was passing. He handed him the number, instructing him to call Peter Ward at that number. He turned back to Regina. 'So, you had no idea she was planning to come down here?'

'No,' Regina wailed. 'She wasn't planning it. I'm telling you.'

'Could she swim?' Van Brunt asked.

'Swim? No way. She never went into the water. Even at the shore in the summer when we were kids. She stayed under the umbrella. She was deathly afraid of water. That's probably why she drowned. If my mother fell into a canal she'd be terrified.'

Van Brunt suspected it wasn't quite that simple, but he didn't say so. 'Would she be likely to have been taking a walk along that towpath?'

'I don't know,' Regina cried. 'I guess so. If she had nothing else to do. I never saw her with nothing to do. I guess she might take a walk. What else could have happened? There wasn't anybody who would deliberately . . .' Regina stopped and stared at the captain. 'She wasn't . . . you know, it wasn't a sexual thing, was it?'

'No, apparently not.'

'Thank God,' said Regina. 'Then it must have been an accident, right? She wasn't robbed. She had all her stuff . . .'

'Did you and your mother get along well?'

Regina sighed. 'She was always on me. She drove me crazy.

Didn't think I should get divorced. Didn't think I spent enough time with the kids. Didn't want me going out after work. I'm still young. I just can't sit home with the kids,' she complained.

Van Brunt looked at her with raised eyebrows.

'Wait a minute,' said Regina. 'Just because we didn't always get along . . . Don't look at me like that.'

Officer McCarthy returned, leaned over and spoke in a low voice to the captain. 'OK, thanks,' said Van Brunt. 'No one answered Mr Ward's phone. So my officer went to the apartment to check and apparently they have moved away.'

'I don't think she knew,' said Regina dully.

'Anyone else she might have visited?'

'I don't know,' Regina cried. 'Like I said, she had a couple of friends. She hardly ever talked to them.'

'OK, Mrs Bluefield. Can you give us a list?'

'I can look in her address book.'

'All right. I'm going to send you home for right now. I'll probably need to talk to you again, soon.'

Regina Bluefield looked at him vacantly. 'What do I do now, Captain? What do I do?'

'About what?' the captain asked.

Her abrupt dismissal seemed to fluster her. 'What will happen to her? To Mom?'

'Well, we will keep the body for a post-mortem. We'll know a lot more after that. And we are examining her car. We have some questions . . .'

'About what. She drowned, right?'

Captain Van Brunt stood up. 'After the post-mortem, the funeral home that you contact will make arrangements to come and get it . . . to come and pick up your mother's body.'

Regina sighed a shaky sigh. 'OK.'

'As for yourself, I really think,' said Van Brunt, glancing from her tear-streaked face to her trembling hands, 'that you should call a friend to drive you home.'

'I'm all right,' she said.

'I'm not sure that's true, Mrs Bluefield. I think you should call someone. People are usually pretty good about helping out at a time like this. If there's no one to call, one of my men can drive you.'

Not wanting to admit that without Bill Bluefield or her mother, there was no one who would care, Regina began trying to think of someone, neighbor or co-worker, she might impose on, to come and carry her home, just this one time.

Moonlight made a shimmering path across the surface of the lake. Dena stood beside Tory on the dock as the child threw little stones into the ladder-like reflection.

'Look,' Dena exclaimed. 'The stars are out.'

'Oh, I'm going to make a wish,' Tory cried. Then she looked solemnly up at Dena. 'I can't tell you what it is though.'

'No, of course not,' said Dena.

The child screwed up her face, her eyes squeezed shut, and communed with the stars while Dena looked around at the peaceful scene. Theirs were the only lights in the chain of cabins along the lakefront. She could see a few lights winking on the other side, but it seemed as if they had this side all to themselves. There was something undeniably pleasant about it. She looked forward to spending the next day with the children, here in this isolated, forest-like setting. There was something so appealing about being here where no one could find you, and no one knew where you were. Without wanting to, she thought of Brian. Perhaps he came back, searching for her, again today. She could not help but feel a certain satisfaction, imagining how frustrated and baffled he would be to find her gone. This trip to Chicago might have its drawbacks, but she felt no doubt that she had been right to leave. Right to take this baby far away from a father who couldn't control his jealousy and possessiveness. She would worry about Brian's legal rights later, when they were far removed from his everyday intrusions. They could discuss it at a distance.

'I did it. I made a wish,' said Tory. 'Do you want me to tell you what it was?'

'No, you can't,' said Dena. 'That would spoil it.'

'Do you want me to give you a hint?'

'Come on,' said Dena with a laugh. 'Let's go back inside. You need to get to bed.'

'Let me give you just one hint. It's about you.'

Dena put her hands over her ears and Tory laughed. 'Now scoot,' Dena said.

The child scampered along the dock and up the slight incline of the shore to the path which led to the cabin. Reaching the door, Tory pulled it open and went inside. Dena followed slowly behind her, conscious of her great weight, of the heaviness in her belly. The door to the cabin stood open, and the glow from inside seemed to beckon. She stopped on the path and looked up at the stars.

I wish for you, Dena thought, addressing her unborn baby, I wish that you arrive safely, and are healthy, and that you have a happy life. It was a lot to pack into one wish. Somehow she knew that this would be her wish from now on in her life. She would wish for the happiness of her child. She sighed and began to walk toward the glowing door. She'd wished on a million stars in her life, and usually she had wished for love and romance. Not any more, she thought. She was bad at that kind of love, she decided.

Besides, there would be no room in her life now for romance. Now she would have her child to wish for, and that would be plenty.

A dark silhouette appeared in the doorway, blocking much of the light. Peter looked around and then spotted her, coming up the path. 'Hey, what are you doing out there? It's dark. You could fall and hurt yourself.'

Dena smiled at his fretting. Now that they were settled in, and had eaten supper, he seemed more like himself. Concerned and caring. A good man. She came up to the door and waited for him to get out of the doorway. Then she went inside. The girls were already in their pajamas, and Tory was digging through her little duffel bag for a book.

Dena lowered herself into one of the chairs, under a paper lampshade strewn with ferns that topped a maple standing lamp. She felt comfortably relaxed and sleepy. She had a book to read, but she felt too tired to concentrate on it.

Peter took the book from Tory, examined it and then nodded. 'We're going to read in their room,' he said. 'Why don't you join us?'

'I don't think I can get out of this chair,' she said smiling. 'You girls have a good night's sleep.'

Tory rushed over to Dena and gave her an awkward hug. Dena hugged her back.

Megan peeked out from behind Peter's legs, her eyes wide and anxious-looking. 'Good night sweetie,' Dena said to her. Megan did not reply.

Dena could hear the soothing sound of their voices from the other room as she sat resting. She wished she had something to do. She glanced at the television which was on a little stand next to the fireplace. Why not, she thought? I'll keep the sound low. She knew that Peter did not want the girls to watch it, but they would soon be asleep.

Besides, it wasn't as if it were something immoral to watch TV. She picked up the remote control from the table beside her and switched it on, keeping the sound on mute and switched desultorily between channels. The reception was grainy at best, even on the few channels that were available. What was I expecting? she thought. Digital cable? She smiled and flipped past the game shows to the news programs. She stopped, by habit, at the local news that she and Brian used to watch, and gazed with detachment at the various snowy images on the screen. A fire, a picket line, some political thing that had residents lining up at a microphone to protest. She did not bother to turn on the sound for any of it.

All of a sudden, an image caught her eye that made her lean forward. Police and ambulances were clustered at the canal. It could have been anywhere along the canal, but the spot looked vaguely familiar. They were lifting a body bag and carrying it up the bank. Dena pushed the mute button and the sound blared forth.

'. . . found drowned today near the canal bridge in Monroe. The dead woman was identified as Brenda Kelly of Riverside. The police found her car a short distance from where the body was found.' At that, the image on the screen changed to a little purple Geo, parked near the water, the police looking it over carefully. 'A police spokesman said that Mrs Kelly, who could not swim, may have fallen into the canal while taking a walk. But acting Chief Van Brunt said they had not ruled out the possibility of—'

At that moment, Peter walked in front of her and turned off the television. Sound and picture disappeared in an instant.

Dena sat up as if he had slapped her. 'Hey, put that back on,' she demanded. 'I was watching that.'

Peter turned and held out his hand for the remote. 'You know perfectly well that we don't watch television.'

'Peter, if I want to watch it, I will,' she said.

'There can't be one rule for the children, and another for the adults,' he said patiently.

'That's ridiculous,' said Dena. 'Adults drink alcohol and children don't. What kind of a rule is that?'

'When we drink alcohol, it doesn't affect them. When you put the television on, they hear it, they see it, it seeps into their minds. And, let me remind you, that you don't drink alcohol right now for that very reason. That it would affect the child you are carrying.'

Dena stubbornly stuffed the remote into the chair beside her. She stood up, because she did not like the feeling of him looking down on her. 'Look Peter, I appreciate that you have these rules for the children and you want to stick to them. Heaven knows, I can go a few days without the TV. But . . .'

'But?' he asked.

'But I am an adult, Peter. You cannot tell me what to do. Even on this short trip, it's unacceptable.'

'I don't want to argue, Dena. It's not good for you. For your blood pressure.'

'That's what I mean, Peter. You're telling me what to do again. I'll decide what's good for me. Look, you've been on your own for a long time,' she said, trying to muster some understanding for his position. 'You've gotten out of the habit of having another adult to make decisions with. I'm sure you and your wife didn't agree on everything . . .'

'You are not my wife . . .' he said coldly.

'No, but as long as we're traveling together, we have to be able to make certain compromises.'

'No TV,' he said. 'That's final.' He turned away from her and rummaged around in his small bag until he found what he was looking for. She watched him, amazed at the way he had simply cut off the discussion. He seated himself at the card table with a sheaf of papers in his hand and began to study them.

'What are you doing?' she said.

'Just collecting the papers for the car, so I'll be prepared for tomorrow. Title, registration, all that.' He looked up at her. 'What's the matter?' he asked.

Dena shook her head. He clearly didn't feel troubled by the truncated conversation. And she was too exhausted to argue the point. Just ignore it, she told herself. It's only for a few days. 'Never mind,' she said. 'I think I will go to bed too.'

'Sleep well, Dena. I'll try not to disturb you when I come in the room.'

Dena frowned. He was calm as if they had never argued. She did not bother to thank him for his consideration. She turned her back on him and walked into the room they were sharing. Switching on the bedside lamp, she glanced at her book and thought she might read a while once she was under the covers. She turned back the bedspread and sheets, and began to search in her bag for her toothbrush.

All of a sudden, as she was changing into her nightclothes, a thought came to her.

She put on her slippers and walked out to where he was, still seated at the table. 'Peter,' she said. 'On the news, before you turned it off, they had a story about some woman who drowned in the canal. It said in the article that she had a purple Geo and that's what made me think of it.'

'Think of what?'

'Some woman came to see you the other night, and I forgot to tell you.'

'Came to see me?' Peter asked. He sat very still, and his face was pale beneath his beard.

'It was just before Brian broke in. I was so upset that it slipped my mind. What reminded me was that thing about the purple Geo. This woman had a purple Geo too.'

'I don't know anybody like that,' said Peter curtly.

Dena thought about it, remembering what the woman had said. 'She seemed to know you. She knew about the restaurant. She knew the kids. She said she'd come back.'

'Well, obviously, she didn't.'

Dena looked over at the blank screen. 'I wonder . . .' she said.

'What?' he asked, his gaze remaining on the papers in front of him.

'Well, I'm wondering if it was the same woman. Maybe that's why she didn't come back. Because she fell in the canal before she could come back.'

'I wouldn't know,' he said irritably.

'Her name was Kelly. Brenda Kelly.'

'I don't know who that is,' he said, in a tone that indicated that he wanted no more of this discussion.

'I know that name,' she said.

'I can't help you,' he said. He bundled up all the papers and put a rubber band around them. 'I'm going to put these out in the car,' he said. 'This way I'll be all ready to make a trade tomorrow. I'm really thinking about a van. Don't you think that would be more comfortable?'

'A van is practical,' she murmured, frowning at the feeling of something elusive, floating around at the edge of her memory.

'Well, I think that's what I'm going to do,' he said. 'See if I can get some kind of van for us.'

'That's good,' she said absently. She knew she had seen that name somewhere.

Brenda Kelly. She could picture it in her mind's eye, printed on a piece of paper. Somewhere, she thought. But where?

THIRTY-TWO

The gray light of dawn woke Ron Hubbell after a few minutes of sleep. He lay in his bed thinking about the night that had just passed. Not a single hour had gone by that Ron had not seen marked on his bedside digital alarm clock. Sometimes he would doze in between, but he had noted every hour. He looked around the hotel room in the Endicott where his father-in-law had put him up. It was a comfortable room, decorated in blues and grays. Jake had insisted that he stay there, and made sure that he had every convenience that the hotel could offer at his disposal. He took his meals in the dining room, had the odd drink at the bar. It was like living in some genteel men's club in the nineteenth century. Jake had treated him as if he were his own son. No one could have been kinder or more thoughtful.

Ron got out of bed and walked into his bathroom. He had to pee, so he did that. As for the rest, he had to think about it. Wash his face, shave, comb his hair? It didn't really seem necessary. Brush his teeth? No, that certainly wasn't necessary. He stared into the mirror on the old-fashioned medicine cabinet for a moment. It was a good mirror, not the kind you found these days. It had a clarity to the reflection, a depth somehow that you didn't get in one of those prefab bathroom cabinets from Home Depot. Ron stared at the face he saw. The mirror spared no detail. The skin was yellowish, with gray patches in the hollows of his cheeks and under the eyes. His beard, which was growing in gray, was a stubble. His eyes were already lifeless.

Ron opened the cabinet, and took out the little orange plastic vial with the white plastic lid and a label on it. Two each night, the label read, to sleep. The doctor had only given him a two-week supply, and then he wanted to see him again. Ron knew why, of course. It was to prevent this very thing. It hadn't been easy to resist these pills some nights, when he was in that pit of sleepless, torturous grief. But he had managed. He had hoarded every last one. The thought of how it was going to be scared him a little bit. But, after so many nights and days wracked by sleeplessness, there was undeniably a part of him that looked forward to sinking into it, to those first few moments when it would feel like falling asleep.

Ron took the vial in his hand and left the bathroom. A newspaper came sliding under his door, and he jumped as he saw it out of the corner of his eye. Then he recognized it. All part of the many kindnesses of the Endicott. He thought about bending down to pick it up, but then he thought, why? What did it matter to him what went on in the world yesterday? He didn't even care anymore if there was news about Jennifer's murder from the police. When he found Jennifer, she would tell him everything.

Leaving the paper lying in the little hallway off the bathroom, he returned to his bed, and sat down on the side. He placed the pills beside the clock and picked up the etched glass carafe of water with its matching tumbler. He poured out a few inches of the stale water, and the splash in the glass sounded loud in the silent room. He set the tumbler down, reached for the vial, and poured the pills out into his palm.

He had never seen himself as the kind of person who would do this. A quitter, or a person who was self-destructive. It was just too hard to continue. His mother had finally insisted that he go no further on the house until he was less distraught. He had agreed, just to get her to leave. To go home to his dad. He thought of his parents and he worried briefly about how they would feel. They had each other, though, and his younger brother in Hawaii, and their grandchildren. Maybe they would move there to be closer to them. That would be best. Ron thought briefly of his father-in-law, Jake Smith, who was kind, although they didn't know each other all that well. He knew Jake would be upset, but he would understand. He, of all people, would understand.

Ron glanced again at the clock. It was early. Not even six o'clock. Most of the world was still asleep. A good time to leave. He didn't want to disturb anybody. He'd spent most of last night trying to compose a note, but then he had decided, what for? It was self-explanatory. The only one he would have written to was gone. Ron took a deep breath, felt the fear, and willed it back. He willed it back by looking ahead. His life stretched out before him, empty and dim. He reached for the glass.

His phone rang, startling him so that he knocked the tumbler onto the floor and the pills scattered in his sheets. The ringing seemed infernally loud in the silent room. Ron picked up the phone and barked into it, 'Hello.'

'Ron. It's Skip.'

Skip. Ron felt exasperated and fond at once.

'I just had the worst nightmare about you, man. I woke up crying and I can't get it out of my mind. Laura said never mind the time, that I should call. That I wouldn't have a moment's peace unless I called.'

Ron didn't say anything. He felt somewhat amazed by what his old friend said. Was there really such a thing as ESP?

'I woke you up, didn't I?' Skip said. He sounded anxious and apologetic.

Ron said, 'No. I was up.'

'Are you . . . you're not all right, are you?' Skip demanded.

Ron held the phone to his face, but he couldn't think of what to say. 'Talk to me, Ron. I woke up thinking . . . *Are* you all right?'

A little voice inside him, a voice he would later swear was Jennifer's, said, 'Tell him.'

Ron remained silent.

'I can hear you crying, man,' said Skip.

Ron was surprised. He hadn't realized he was crying. But sure enough, tears were splashing onto his pajamas. In the background, at Skip's end, Ron could hear Laura's voice saying, 'Tell him we're coming. Tell him we're on our way there. We're going to bring him home.'

'Did you hear that, buddy? We're going to come down there and get you. Nobody's going to stop us this time. You hang in there. Laura's already getting dressed. Do I need to call Jake Smith? Can I trust you to wait for me?'

Ron nodded.

'Ron?'

'Yes,' he said.

*   *   *

Dena had not slept well, though the cabin had been quiet, and the bed reasonably comfortable. Despite the fact that she was tired when she went to bed, she had not fallen asleep easily. She pretended to be sleeping when Peter finally came into the room. She had heard him stop as he entered the room, but she couldn't say if he was looking at her or not. Then, he had quietly climbed into the other bed. She felt as if she had been awake much of the night, listening to the hooting of owls and the rustling of pine trees outside the window. Her baby had been still, making no movement, but she felt a shift in her belly, as if the baby were suddenly weighing more heavily on her than it had before, making it difficult to breathe. She didn't know when she had fallen asleep, but when she awoke in the morning, the room was empty, Peter's bed neatly made. She saw through the window that the day was gloomy, not warm, as the children had hoped. She pulled her clothes on without much thought to her appearance and went out into the main room.

The two girls were sitting at the table. Tory was coloring in a coloring book, and Megan was crooning a soft, disjointed tune to a baby doll.

'Ah,' said Peter glancing at his watch. 'I was just about to wake you. I have to go and see about trading the car.'

'Right,' said Dena. 'I'm sorry I overslept. I didn't sleep well last night.'

'Oh, really,' said Peter. 'You seemed to be fast asleep when I came to bed.'

'Well, I slept on and off. You know how that is.' Even as she said it, she wondered why she felt the need to make an excuse. Somehow, she didn't want to tell him that she was awake when he went to bed. In any case, he didn't seem to notice. He was busily collecting his papers and his keys in preparation for leaving.

'The girls have eaten,' he reported. 'Help yourself to what's here. I don't know how long this will take. I may have to try a few places. I'll be back as soon as I can.'

'We'll be fine,' said Dena.

'Goodbye girls,' he said.

Both children jumped up and ran to embrace him at the door, hanging on him as if he were leaving forever. 'You stay here at the cabin. Do what Dena tells you.'

'We will,' said Tory. She was the first to resume her activity. Megan, as usual, clung desperately to her father, and Dena had to help to extricate her from him. As he started the car and pulled away, Megan pressed herself up against the screen door and began to sob.

Tory regarded her sister with a long-suffering expression. 'I don't know how she's ever going to go to first grade,' she said to Dena. 'She always does this.'

Sometimes Dena wondered the same thing. She and Peter had discussed it a little.

She knew that he blamed the preschool teacher in Monroe for Megan's poor adjustment to preschool, but the child was undeniably more tense and frightened than other children her age that Dena had seen. Of course, she had lost her mother in infancy. That could account for much of it. Well, Dena thought, a little positive reinforcement can't hurt.

She walked over, knelt down beside her, and rubbed the miserable toddler on her back. 'It'll be OK,' Dena said kindly. Megan stiffened, and stopped crying, but kept her face pressed to the screen.

Dena could feel that Megan was frozen beneath her massaging palm. Best not to draw attention to it, Dena thought. 'What's that you're drawing, Tory?' she asked.

Tory sighed and looked at her picture. 'Santa and his reindeer,' she said.

'That's good. You're getting a little jump on the season,' Dena observed. She continued to rub Megan's back, but the child's stiffened spine did not relax.

'I don't know why I'm doing this,' said Tory. 'I hate Christmas.'

'You hate Christmas!' Dena protested. 'I thought all children loved Christmas.'

'Not me,' said Tory. She closed the book on her picture and sat back clutching her knees to her chest. She gazed out at the bleak sky. 'It didn't turn out to be a nice day,' she said.

'Not too nice,' Dena admitted. 'But we can still go for a walk. We can throw pebbles in the water. Would that be fun, Megan?'

Megan said nothing, but shook her head. Tory stood up and paced restlessly around the room. Dena watched her sympathetically. It had to be hard on these kids, moving around, no mother to help them get organized in a new place. Of course, Peter did everything he could to make it easier for them. But still. She wondered just how much they enjoyed the 'adventure' of moving.

'Do you wonder about your new home?' Dena asked. 'What it will be like?'

Tory folded her arms on the windowsill and put her chin on her hands. 'No. Not really,' she said. 'Oh no, it's starting to rain. Now we can't even go outside.'

Dena glanced at the window and saw the raindrops begin to bead on the glass. 'You're right,' she said. She thought for a minute and then she said, 'Why don't we play a game?'

'How about Candyland?'

'OK,' said Dena. 'Can you go get it?'

'Megan, come on,' Tory cried. She scampered to her room, followed by Megan, as Dena got up and went over to the table. The children returned in a few moments with a dejected air. 'It's in the car,' Tory said. 'It's in that box in the back.'

Dena pretended to share her disappointment. In fact, she *was* disappointed, for their sake. Then she had an idea. Yesterday, at a gas station, she had picked up a deck of cards for them to play games on the road. 'I've got a pack of cards. Do you know how to play hearts?'

Tory's eyes lit up again. 'I know how to play gin.'

'Gin rummy?'

'Yeah. Where are the cards? I'll go get them.'

'OK. Great. They're in my pocketbook.'

The child vanished into Dena's room and came back, triumphantly holding the cards aloft. 'Got 'em,' she said. In spite of herself, Megan lifted her head and looked at them curiously. She sidled toward the table and climbed up on a chair.

Dena offered to open the new deck but Tory insisted on doing it. Then, to Dena's surprise, Tory divided the stiff new cards in two, and began to shuffle them with an inexpert, but deliberate technique.

'Hey,' said Dena playfully. 'Where'd you learn to shuffle like that? Did your dad teach you that?'

'No,' said the child gravely. 'He doesn't know I can shuffle. Miss Kay taught me. She taught me to play gin, too.'

'Miss Kay?' Dena asked absently, picking up the cards that Tory dealt.

'Our old baby-sitter. Mrs Kelly.'

The name hit Dena like a jolt of electricity. At the same moment, Megan let out a wail. 'Miss Kay,' she shrieked.

Tory covered her ears. 'Stop that.' She looked at Dena. 'We always called her Miss Kay because Megan couldn't say Mrs Kelly.'

'Miss Kay,' Megan sobbed, and Dena reached for her and scooped her up, cradling the stiff, shrieking child in her arms.

Miss Kay, Dena thought. She remembered now. The flyers and charity appeals that would accumulate on the hall table in the duplex. She started to shiver. Mrs Kelly. Mrs Brenda Kelly.

THIRTY-THREE

B ouquets and arrangements of every shape and size were arrayed around Lou Potter's hospital room. One of the arrangements had a teddy bear vase, and three helium balloons floating over it.

The man lying in the bed did not seem to be cheered by the floral tributes. He lay facing the window, his face pasty, his eyes dull and sad.

Tyrell did not want to startle the chief. He cleared his throat as he entered the room, and Lou turned to look at his visitor. Tyrell gave the older man's shoulder an affectionate squeeze, and then folded himself into the visitor's chair at the foot of the bed. 'Good to see you off that machine,' he said. 'How you feeling?'

An oxygen tube ran out of Lou's nose. He shrugged. 'Not worth a damn. But, at least I'm still here. They're going to ambulance me up to Philly this week for bypass surgery.'

'That's what Kim said. You ought to feel better after that,' Tyrell said.

'I hope so,' he said. 'Thanks for helping Kim out. She told me you took Jeff to the ball game yesterday.'

Tyrell waved off his gratitude. 'I took him and my brother, Cletus. We had a good time.' Thinking of Cletus, Tyrell had to smile. He had been, to Tyrell's surprise, supportive after the suspension. He seemed almost relieved that the problem was in Tyrell's court for a change. It was funny how roles could shift sometimes.

'Well, it was a help to Kim,' said Lou. 'Bernie's working all hours trying to finish up that construction job, and she's got her hands full because of me.'

'I was glad to do it. I got time on my hands these days.'

Lou frowned. 'I guess that's my fault,' he said.

'Ah, you know Van Brunt. We don't see eye to eye.'

'It's my fault, for telling you not to file that report on Brian,' Lou admitted.

'If it wasn't that, it would have been something else. I needed the vacation.' It was a lie and they both knew it, but Tyrell had come to cheer his old boss up, not to lay his problems on him.

Lou seemed determined to shoulder the blame. 'You heard they fired me, right?'

'I . . . heard something about early retirement . . .' Tyrell dissembled.

'It was the letters,' said Lou. 'When they found out about the letters.'

'Look, Chief, you don't owe me any explanations. I could have filed that report and I didn't. It wasn't your fault.'

'Yes, it was,' he said. He turned his head and looked out the window again. Tyrell wasn't sure whether to stay or go. 'You tired?' he said.

Lou shook his head slightly. 'You're probably wondering . . .' he said.

'No, Chief, it's OK. You don't have to . . .'

Lou continued as if he hadn't heard him. 'I just hate it that Kimmy has to know. And the kids. But, everybody's gonna know, sooner or later.'

'You had your reasons, Chief. That's good enough for me.'

'He's my son, Tyrell.'

'Who is?' Tyrell asked, confused.

'Brian. He's my son.'

Tyrell shook his head, not understanding.

'His father . . . Matt and I were the best of friends. When he brought his new wife home, Hattie and I gave them both a party. I had no idea. When I met her, when I met Janine, it was like . . . I don't know. It wasn't love. It was a . . . passion. I'd never felt that way before. I resisted it for a long time and then, I gave in . . . Matt couldn't have children. When she got pregnant, obviously he knew she'd been unfaithful. She never told him who . . . I think he always took it out on Brian. Even though I was to blame. And I was too much of a coward to admit it. Then Janine left him. Left all of us. She wasn't a good woman. Anyway, Matt never knew it was me. Brian, either.'

'Well, you tried to make it up to them,' said Tyrell. He felt uneasy to have the chief confessing to him. They had never been close in that way.

'Yeah,' said Lou. 'It was a royal fuck-up. My Hattie figured it out. Women know things sometimes that men have no idea of. She forgave me. Took a while, but she did. I was the lucky one.'

'I'm sure you were a good husband,' said Tyrell loyally. 'Everybody makes mistakes.'

Lou turned his head and looked at him. 'Yeah, but my mistakes ended up ruining people's lives. That's why I never filed those reports. It's not Brian's fault that he's the way he is. I felt like I *had* to do it for him. Even though he didn't know the real reason why. It wasn't so much that I loved him, although I guess I do, as that I had fucked his life up good and well. I owed him, you know. And now, I owe you. It's my fault you were suspended.'

'Not the same thing at all,' said Tyrell. 'No big deal. Besides, this will all blow over. Van Brunt will always give me a hard time. But I can take it. To tell you the truth, I guess I deserved it a little bit. I knew what the right thing was, and I didn't do it.'

Lou turned his head back to the window. An uneasy silence fell over the two men. Tyrell thought about leaving, wished he could leave, and get away from the chief's sorry revelations, but there was no way. They were like two people up a tree. They couldn't jump down. They'd have to ease back down to solid ground.

'You're a good boy, Tyrell,' said Lou. And Tyrell knew the older man didn't mean it in the racist, pejorative sense. 'I'll bet Van Brunt wishes he had you now.'

Tyrell was skeptical. 'Oh yeah.'

'Really. He's shorthanded and he's got another murder on his hands. Kenny stopped by to tell me this morning.'

'The floater?' Tyrell asked. Both men were relieved to have the conversation turn away from the personal, however necessary, and back to police business. Tyrell had read the paper while he was eating breakfast at the Main Diner. His grandmother had offered to cook for him, but he didn't want to hang around the house all day. Being suspended was depressing enough. 'I thought she drowned?'

Lou looked around, just to make sure there was no one in the doorway before he confided in Tyrell. He knew Tyrell would be interested. Being suspended didn't make him any less a cop. 'The trunk of her car was all wet, so they figured she'd been transported. Then they got the ME's report this morning.' Lou's pallor was relieved by a faint color in his cheeks at the news he had to impart.

'What? She didn't drown?'

'Oh, she drowned all right,' said Lou.

'So, what's the deal?'

'She didn't drown in the canal. She drowned in tap water.'

'Like a bathtub? And then they moved her?'

Lou nodded. 'Guess what they found in her lungs?'

'You said, tap water.'

Lou shook his head. 'Something was in the tap water. Shampoo.'

'She drowned while she was washing her hair?'

'Not *her* hair. *Her* hair had traces of dandruff shampoo. The water in her lungs contained baby shampoo.'

'Jesus,' Tyrell yelped, and squirmed in the chair. 'I don't even want to think about how that happened. Has Van Brunt got a line on the perp?'

Lou shook his head and sipped from the straw in his water glass. 'They're not even sure why the lady was in town. She used to live here – someplace over on Bigelow Street. But nobody around here had seen her since she moved to Riverside.'

'Bigelow Street,' said Tyrell, instantly alert. 'Where on Bigelow Street?'

'I don't know,' said Lou. 'Why? You know somebody on Bigelow Street?'

Tyrell thought of Dena Russell, and her little second-floor apartment on Bigelow Street. He'd been tempted to stop by, to make sure she was all right, but then he thought it might seem strange, since he was suspended . . . It was just that since they'd let Riley go, he found himself worrying about her. Wondering if she was OK.

It's not your concern, he reminded himself. Your duties are suspended. Stop thinking about her.

'I used to,' he said.

'Gin!' cried the child, carefully setting down her last fan of cards. 'I beat you again. You aren't very good at this game.'

'I know it,' said Dena absently, staring at Megan, who huddled in the chair, rocking herself and sucking her thumb, once in a while letting out with a gusty sob.

'I'm really good at it,' Tory announced. 'I win every time I play.'

'Yes, you are good,' Dena agreed.

'Your deal,' said Tory, pushing the cards across the table at her.

Dena gathered up the cards and shuffled them in a desultory manner, her thoughts far away from the card game. Why did Peter lie about Brenda Kelly? Why did he pretend not to know who she was?

'You're taking a long time to shuffle,' Tory observed.

'Sorry,' Dena murmured, and began to deal the cards. Why did he snap the TV off when the story of Brenda Kelly's drowning came on? He didn't like the TV. She knew that. But even the most adamant opponent of television would surely make an exception to hear about the death of someone they knew well. Someone who had lived in the same house. Cared for your children. Could there be some mistake? Did she have the name wrong?

'Tory,' she asked casually as the child studied her cards, 'you know Mrs Kelly who taught you gin?'

Megan's rocking and moaning instantly ceased. The child froze, still and alert, on the edge of her chair.

'Of course I know her,' said Tory.

'Have you seen her lately?'

'Nope,' said the child. She set down a run on the table.

'What was . . . what's her first name?'

'I don't know,' the child said. 'Ask Dad.'

'Was her first name Brenda?' Dena asked.

'I go first,' said Tory. She discarded a ten of clubs.

'Was it Brenda?' Dena persisted.

Tory frowned at her hand. 'Yeah. That was it. Brenda. Your turn.'

'How do you know?' Dena asked, suspicious that she was being placated in the interests of the game.

'It was printed on the front of her Bible,' the child replied. Then she looked up at Dena. 'Sometimes she read me stories from the Bible. But don't tell Dad, OK?'

'OK,' said Dena faintly. She picked up the ten and slowly discarded a seven of hearts.

Tory hurried to grab it up, and threw down a queen, looking at Dena exultantly. 'I needed that one,' she said.

Dena was too distracted to react. She stared, unseeing, into her cards, thinking. She felt someone watching her and she looked over at the child on the chair.

Megan was looking at her, her eyes wide and fearful. 'Miss Kay,' the child whispered.

Dena held her gaze. 'Have you seen Miss Kay?' she asked.

Megan's eyes swam with tears. 'No,' she cried. 'I didn't. I didn't.'

Tory lowered her cards in exasperation. 'You're not playing,' she complained.

'Right,' said Dena. 'Let's just finish this game.'

She forced herself to hurriedly play her cards, and congratulated Tory on another win. Then, she got up from her chair and walked over to the window, her arms around her belly. The rain was stopping but the sky still rumbled and remained a gloomy gray.

There had to be some explanation, she thought. There had to be some reason why Peter had lied about Brenda Kelly. Maybe he didn't want the children to know, to be upset. But the children were already in bed when she turned on the TV. He could have discussed it with her. Or was he just treating her like a child again, not trusting her to keep the information to herself? That would be just like him. That explanation was annoying, but, for the moment, reassuring somehow.

And yet she knew, even as she thought it, that her worry went deeper. He had not been curious. He had not seemed surprised. When the news of Brenda Kelly's death was broadcast on TV, he had simply pretended not to know her.

She tried to remember what the woman had said when she came to the door.

Going over it in her mind, she had to admit that it was nothing special. The woman, Mrs Kelly, she told herself firmly, had asked to see Peter. She had inquired about the children. That was all. Dena looked around the cabin, the girls peacefully playing. Then she looked back out at the wide spot in front of the cabin that served as a parking space and wondered anxiously when Peter would be returning with the car.

The new car. Now, suddenly, that seemed strange to her too. Why did they leave so abruptly that he couldn't trade the car in Monroe? Why was he trading it now?

Stop it, she thought. Just stop. You're getting yourself into a state over nothing. She forced herself to exhale, to relax her tensed muscles. She bent her head against the windowpane and, as she did, she felt the cold glass soothing her knotted forehead. There was probably some simple explanation. There had to be. She was in a fragile state, so she was exaggerating everything out of proportion. There was some reason why he had denied his relationship with Brenda Kelly, and if she questioned him tactfully, and persistently, he might eventually tell her what it was.

He had some problem. She was sure of that. Maybe he had an argument with Brenda Kelly. Maybe she jumped into that canal over Peter. Dena tried to picture strait-laced Peter and that middle-aged lady in some sort of tempestuous entanglement.

The thought was rather fascinating. She wished she knew. Then, she realized the answer might be close at hand. Surely, she thought, they'll have something more about it on the TV. They were always having local news on. Or news bulletins. She could just check.

Dena walked over to the little stand where the TV sat and picked up the remote control. She pressed the button and the TV switched on, but this time there was no reception, not on any channel.

'Uh uh,' Tory chided her from across the room. 'No TV.'

'Oh, Tory, shush,' Dena said. She ran the channels again but there was nothing but station after station of static.

'You're not going to get anything,' said Tory.

'How do you know?' Dena said irritably.

'Cause Dad took that thing on the top. The bunny ears? He took it with him. He didn't want us watching just because he wasn't here.'

Dena switched off the set and turned to look at the child. The antennae, the rabbit ears, had brought in what little reception they could get. 'He took it?' she said incredulously.

Tory nodded. 'He said you would turn it on. He was right.'

Dena felt a hot flush spread through her.

'Are you mad?' Tory asked worriedly.

Dena's breath got short and suddenly she felt wobbly. She sat down in one of the cushioned chairs. Don't get crazy, she told herself. This could just be Peter being the universal parent again. She wondered, for a second, why she had admired his style of fathering so much. He was unbelievably overbearing.

But that's all, she told herself. It had nothing to do with the news. Him not wanting you to watch. But no matter how much she said it, she couldn't convince herself. What is going on here, she wondered?

'Dena, are you mad?' Tory asked.

'No, no, it's all right,' Dena said, trying to think what to do. All right. The first thing you have to do is find out. For a moment she felt panicky, wondering how, and then it came to her. It was so simple. So blessedly simple. Her phone.

'You girls play,' she said, getting up from the chair. 'I'll be right back.'

She smiled at them, so they wouldn't worry, and then she went into the bedroom.

Her purse was lying on the bed, where Tory had rifled it for the cards. With a sigh of relief she went over to it, not even sure, at that moment, whom she was going to call. She could call the television station or the newspaper. Just to find out. There was no need to go any farther than that. She thought, for a second, of Sergeant Watkins, but he was not, she reminded herself, going to be at the police station. He was, for some unknown reason, suspended. And she didn't want to involve the police anyway. Surely it wasn't necessary.

All the time she thought these things she was searching. Pushing things from side to side in her bag with no luck until, in frustration, she dumped the entire contents on the bed. She gazed at the jumble of her things – makeup case, brush, address book, pencils.

Everything she had put into the bag was there. Everything but her phone. The phone was gone.

THIRTY-FOUR

Eric Schultz drizzled a pale-yellow stream of extra-virgin olive oil onto some eggs in a copper bowl, then wedged the bowl under his arm and proceeded to whip its contents into a froth with a wire whisk. 'Why don't you just use a CD player?' he asked his life partner, who was standing, hands on his hips, on the other side of the restaurant's huge island. 'You can use our collections. We've got enough music to last a year and never play the same track twice.'

Albert regarded his stocky, balding companion with exasperation and rolled his eyes to heaven, as if to plead for patience.

Eric looked up from the emulsion he was creating and saw Albert's expression of disdain and disbelief. 'What? It would be one less salary we'd have to pay, and a whole lot less headaches.

You're the one who's always complaining about the payroll and disability and unemployment benefits and all that.'

'That's not the point,' said Albert.

'What is the point?' Eric asked irritably, glancing around the huge kitchen which was starting to buzz with waiters and sous-chefs. 'Because I've got work to do.'

'The point is, that if we have that piano in the foyer, and no one there to play it, we will have groups of conventioneers and their mates sitting down to begin a singalong while customers are trying to enjoy their meal.'

'So, we'll get rid of it.'

'And put it where? And put what in its place?' Albert demanded. 'Have you ever looked at the size of that foyer?'

'Excuse me,' said a voice from behind him.

Albert turned around and saw a tall, broad-shouldered black man dressed in a dark knit sport shirt and a leather coat. Albert, forever a connoisseur of masculine good looks, could not help but smile graciously. The man looked strangely familiar, although he wasn't instantly able to place him. 'How may I help you?' he asked.

It was Eric's turn to roll his eyes. 'A distraction. Thank heavens. I have sauces to finish.'

'A waiter sent me down here. Are you the owner?' Tyrell asked Albert.

'Guilty. Along with my partner,' Albert said, gesturing toward Eric.

'My name is Tyrell Watkins. I'm a sergeant on the Monroe police force.' Technically true, Tyrell thought. Although his badge had been seized for the time being.

Fortunately, Albert didn't need the identification. 'Oh, yes,' he said, recognizing Tyrell. 'You were here the other night. I asked you to move your car.'

Tyrell nodded. 'Could we talk in private?' Tyrell asked.

Albert raised his eyebrows. 'Certainly,' he said. He turned to Eric. 'I'll be in my office.' Gesturing with one manicured finger for Tyrell to follow him, Albert led the way from the kitchen up the stairs to an office in the back.

Heavenly smells followed them up the staircase, but Tyrell only felt a growing queasiness in the pit of his stomach. On his way home from the hospital, he had stopped by Dena Russell's place on Bigelow Street. Instead of Dena, he found a vacant apartment with a broken door, and a patrolman there, who had recognized him. The patrolman told him that he had been sent to look the place over because Dena's apartment was the very apartment where the drowned woman, Mrs Brenda Kelly, had once lived.

Albert unlocked the door to the office, and gestured for Tyrell to go in. It was a spacious room, furnished with French antiques of a slightly more formal nature than the furniture in the dining room. He offered Tyrell a seat, and then seated himself behind his tidy, gilt-edged desk.

Tyrell sat gingerly on the silk-upholstered seat. 'I'm here about one of your employees, Miss Russell.'

'Former employees,' said Albert significantly.

'So the waiter told me. I've just come from her house. There was no one there. I mean the place was empty and the door had been broken in.'

Albert shook his head, and folded his delicate hands in front of him on the desk. 'Miss Russell has left town. She left very abruptly. Accepted a ride from the man who used to play piano for me. He lived downstairs from her. In fact, the two of them left me with a slew of headaches. But . . .' said Albert, sighing, 'after my initial feeling of . . . annoyance with her, I have to admit I can understand it. Her boyfriend broke the door in. He was getting out of control. She didn't feel that you people were protecting her.'

Tyrell ignored the criticism. 'It was the boyfriend who broke down the door?'

'Yes, the other night. Didn't she call you?'

Tyrell was confused, and then realized that Albert meant the police. And he didn't know whether or not Dena had called the police. 'I may have been off-duty,' he said, evading the question.

'Well, she decided it was too dangerous to stay here any longer. And Peter was leaving town anyway, so she went with him. I believe he was going to drive her to her sister's house out in Chicago.' As he recounted this, Albert was suddenly overcome with the thought of all the problems he was now forced to deal with. 'Good riddance to both of them, I say.'

Tyrell thought about the man he had seen when he went to Dena's apartment. 'Is he a guy with a beard?' he asked.

'Peter? Yes.'

'And where was he going?' Tyrell asked. 'Was it a sudden departure?'

'Not really. I'd known for a few weeks that he was leaving. Going out to work for some place in Minneapolis. Of all places.' Albert opened the drawer of his desk, and extracted a slip of paper. 'Here it is. This is the number. Retro is the name of the place. What kind of a place could it be? They never even called me for a reference. It's probably some dive. It would serve him right.'

Tyrell studied the slip of paper. 'Did you know Mrs Brenda Kelly by any chance?'

'Who?' Albert asked.

'That was the name of the woman they found in the canal . . .'

'Oh, the one that drowned. Right. No. I'm afraid not.'

'It's an odd coincidence. She used to live in the same apartment Dena lived in.'

'Oh, my God. That's right. Mrs Kelly. She used to baby-sit Peter's kids. Oh, he bitched and moaned when she left. He relied on her.'

'Really?' said Tyrell.

'Yes,' said Albert, suddenly concerned. 'Why?'

'She didn't just drown. She was murdered.'

'Murdered?' Albert's mouth fell open.

'The same day this fellow left town,' said Tyrell. 'With Miss Russell.'

'Oh my God,' said Albert. 'But, what does it mean? Do you think these things are connected somehow?'

Tyrell shook his head. 'I don't know, but a coincidence like that . . . It's . . . troubling,' he said.

Albert shuddered. 'Indeed, it is.'

Tyrell pulled out his phone and punched in the number on the slip of paper. He held the receiver against his ear, and sat back, pressing his lips together as if in readiness for a conversation. After a minute, he frowned and pressed a few keys on the screen.

'What's the matter?' asked Albert.

Tyrell shook his head and punched in a few numbers. Albert watched him quizzically.

'Yes,' said Tyrell. 'For Minneapolis. The number for a restaurant called Retro. No, I don't have the address.'

Tyrell waited for a moment. 'You don't?' he asked. 'Are you sure? How about unpublished? I'll wait.'

Albert watched Tyrell closely.

'No. I see. OK, thank you,' said Tyrell. He replaced the phone in his pocket.

'It's not listed?' Albert asked. 'What kind of a restaurant isn't listed?'

'A restaurant,' said Tyrell, 'that doesn't exist.'

Albert stared at him.

'It's not unlisted. There is no such place.'

'Well, then why would he say that?' Albert wondered aloud.

'I don't know. Are you sure you got the name right?' Tyrell asked.

'He wrote it down,' said Albert. 'But why? Why make it up? Why not just tell me where he was really going?'

'Maybe,' said Tyrell, staring at the paper in his hand, 'he didn't want anyone to find him.'

'Girls,' said Dena, trying to sound casual, 'the rain has stopped. Let's go out for a walk. I want to find a phone. And then, *we* can walk by the lake later.' She had gone through everything, her purse and her suitcase, but she knew she wasn't going to find the phone, and she hadn't. She'd asked Tory if she might have seen it when she got the cards, but the child didn't know anything about it. No, Dena thought, I'm sure you don't. 'Come on, now,' she said. 'Let's get a move on . . .'

Reluctantly, with some grumbling, the girls agreed to put away their toys and put on their hooded sweatshirts, in case the rain started again. Once they were ready, Dena thought about where to go.

Surely someone in the office would have a phone she could use. She shepherded the girls up the path and then down the dirt road toward the cabin near the entrance which had the 'Hideaway Cabins. Register Here' sign. But when they arrived, the door to the office was locked with a cardboard clock in the window that read, 'Back at 5 p.m.'

Oh no, Dena thought. Five o'clock was too long to wait. She knew what she wanted to do, and she wasn't going to put it off any longer. When Peter came back, she would already have enlisted some aid. If she was wrong about this, and there was nothing to it, well then, no harm done. But, the sooner they got this over with, the better.

'How about if we walk to the Wawa?' Dena asked brightly.

'The Wawa?' Tory exclaimed. 'That's far from here.'

'I'll get you both some candy,' Dena wheedled.

'Yes, candy,' said Megan, brightening. She began to scamper up the dirt road.

'We don't eat candy,' said Tory stubbornly.

'There must be something else you want. Come on, Tory. If I can make it, you can make it. There's not that much else to do.'

'All right,' the child agreed glumly.

'I wish we had that little red wagon of yours. We could pull Megan,' Dena said.

'She won't ride in it anymore anyway. She goes ballistic if you try to put her in it. Dad left it behind.'

'I thought your dad always pulled her around in that thing.'

'He did. Then, one day she decided to get hysterical whenever she saw the wagon. Right, Megan?' Tory called to her sister, who was retracing her steps from her modest trailblazing mission. 'You don't like your wagon anymore.'

Megan froze, staring at Tory, and tears filled her eyes. 'No wagon,' she begged. 'The lady's house. I hate the wagon.'

'Tory, stop that,' said Dena, who could see that Tory saw it as a kind of parlor trick to make her sister break down. 'The wagon's not here, honey. No more wagon. Come on, we'll walk.'

The three of them began to walk under the canopy of pines, making their way out to the highway. The Wawa sign was visible very far down the road. That is a long walk, Dena thought, but she didn't say so to the children. Instead, she took Megan's hand and led the way, warning Tory, who was walking ahead of them, to stay far inside the white line that served as a shoulder. There wasn't much traffic along this road, but it only took one careless driver to create a tragedy.

As they walked, Tory offered a running commentary on their surroundings. All Dena had to do was murmur agreeably, which gave her a little opportunity to think. She could dial the local police, but what could she actually tell them? That Peter had taken her phone with him, and pretended not to know the drowning victim? That wasn't exactly an indictment. Still, she was sure there was something wrong. She needed to know more about the woman who had drowned. What she really needed at this point was some information and advice from someone she could trust.

A truck whizzed by, perilously close to the shoulder, and Dena jerked Tory over into the brown grass. Once the truck was past, they resumed their walk.

'Are we there?' Megan pleaded.

'Almost,' said Dena. Her belly felt uncomfortable, and all her organs felt squashed. She hadn't found walking quite this difficult in the past. She could see the sign not far ahead now. 'Let's cross here,' she said, finding a safe spot. She held both girls by the hand and made sure there was no traffic in view before she led them across the old, cracked, two-lane highway.

'I'm going to get a comic book,' Tory announced, having finally made up her mind.

'OK,' said Dena. 'That sounds good.'

Her legs were aching by the time they reached the parking lot of the little oasis of convenience set among the trees. Several cars were parked outside. There was a gas station on the other side of the intersection, and a couple of houses in a row, just beyond the gas station. Otherwise, it was a desolate area. But inside, the Wawa was brightly lit and well stocked. A young woman wearing khakis, a red visor and a red apron was behind the counter, stacking packs of cigarettes in the overhead dispenser.

Dena accompanied the children around the store, patiently looking over the goodies with them as they made their selections. She couldn't expect them to wait until she was done to make their choices. Tory pondered over the revolving rack of comics, while Megan picked up and put down every piece of candy she could reach, studying the wrappers as if she could read them, or see through them to the candy inside. Finally, having settled, with difficulty, on their selections, the girls brought them up to the counter and placed them in front of the clerk. She was a fresh-faced teenager with a blonde ponytail, a shadow of acne on her chin, and a name tag which read, Brittany. The clerk smiled warmly at the children and engaged them in conversation about their goodies, while Dena looked around the store. Then she turned back to the girls. She pointed to the bench just outside the glass-front wall of the store. 'Can you take Megan out to that bench?' she asked Tory.

'Where will you be?' Tory asked suspiciously.

'Right here. I have to get one more thing. I'll be out in one minute. Just make sure she doesn't move from the bench, you hear me.'

Tory nodded. 'I'll read her my comic.'

'Remember,' said Dena. 'The minute one of you girls gets off that bench, I'm going to come out there and take those treats away. OK?'

'OK,' said Tory obediently. She took her sister by the hand and led her out to the bench. Once they were settled side by side, Tory looked through the plate-glass window and waved at Dena.

Dena waved back and then turned to the clerk behind the counter. 'OK, miss. I would not bother you if I didn't have to, but this is kind of an emergency. The girls' father accidentally went off with my cell phone and I have to make a call. Could you, by any chance . . . Just let me make a call on your phone. I'll stay right here where you can see me. I'll pay you for it.'

The ponytailed teenager smiled and waved off Dena's concerns. She reached in her pants pocket and handed the phone to Dena.

'I'll only be a few minutes,' Dena said. 'Thank you so much.'

'No problem,' said the girl.

OK, Dena thought. Let me do this. Keeping her eyes on the girls on the bench outside, she took the phone and dialed the familiar number. Her lips felt dry and she licked them. It rang three times as she waited anxiously. Finally, someone picked up.

'La Petite Auberge,' he said.

'Albert, it's Dena.'

'Dena, my God,' he said.

She could hear the alarm in his voice. 'What?'

'Where are you?'

'I'm at a Wawa somewhere in Western Pennsylvania.'

'Where exactly?' Albert demanded.

Dena looked at the clerk, but she suddenly had a line of two other customers. 'We're staying on a lake, at some dive called the Hideaway Cabins.'

'Oh, my God,' Albert said. 'I've been worried sick. Listen to me, that guy you are with, Peter, is in big trouble. The police were just here. The woman who used to live in your apartment was murdered.'

'Murdered,' Dena whispered, her stomach doing a sickening flip.

'And Peter . . . Well, let's just say he is not headed to Minneapolis. You've got to get away from him. Right now. Listen to me, wait. Let me get Sergeant Watkins. Maybe he hasn't left yet. Hang on. I'm going to run outside. Just hang on.'

Dena felt her heart starting to thump in her chest. Murdered, she thought. Brenda Kelly had been murdered. And Peter had pretended, denied knowing her . . . No, it wasn't possible. Dena had a million questions, and she was afraid of the answers. But at least Tyrell would have the answers. Oh, let Sergeant Watkins still be there, she thought, a little embarrassed that she was even thinking of him by his first name. But somehow that name was comforting to her. Despite the fear inside of her, she felt suddenly easier, as if a knot had been untied, deep inside her. He was there. He would help her. She pictured his face, serious and thoughtful, and she knew she could trust him. Hurry, Albert, she thought. Find him . . .

At that moment, the phone was jerked from her hands.

She turned around, too shocked to protest, and looked into the blazing eyes of Peter Ward.

THIRTY-FIVE

'What do you think you're doing?' Dena demanded.
'Where did you get this?' Peter asked, holding up the phone.

'It belongs to the clerk,' said Dena, gesturing toward the girl behind the counter.

Peter walked over and slammed the phone down on the countertop. 'Let's go,' he said. 'We're leaving.'

'I was talking on the phone,' Dena said indignantly. 'How dare you?'

'You left my children alone out there.'

'I was watching them. I could see them from here,' she said.

'You could see them being hit by a car. It's a parking lot, for God's sake.'

Dena looked out at the children on the bench. Her face flamed, but she did not shrink from him. 'They promised to stay put,' she said angrily.

Peter shook his head. 'I thought so,' he said. 'I knew I couldn't trust you. How is it that you all think you can treat the minding of children so casually? Is this how you intend to bring up that baby you're carrying?'

Dena looked at him in amazement. It took her a moment to find her voice. She did not want to antagonize him. 'Peter, I don't know why you are so upset. We went for a walk. I bought them each a treat and I wanted to make a phone call. They didn't want to wait inside.'

'You bought them candy,' he said accusingly.

'Oh, forgive me,' she cried. 'I wanted them to have a treat.' She was shaken by his anger, but she didn't want him to know it. She tried to keep her voice calm. 'We wouldn't even be here if you hadn't taken my phone with you.'

'Your phone?' he said. 'I didn't take your phone.'

'I suppose it just walked out of my purse,' she said.

Peter shook his head in disgust. 'You probably lost it. You're obviously not very good at keeping your eye on things.' He looked out at the children. 'Come on. I don't want them out there alone.'

She didn't believe him about the phone, but what was the use of saying it? She looked with distaste at the set of his jaw. 'I'm sure it looked that way to you, but they were perfectly all right. I had my eye on them the whole time.'

'Ha. You didn't even see them get in the van.'

Dena looked out and saw the red van parked near the door. 'Is that the van you got for the trade-in?' she asked.

'Yes. I was driving by on my way home to show you and I saw them, sitting out there alone,' he said, 'while you were in here on the phone. How long do you think it takes for children to be abducted? A minute, a split second,' he cried.

'All right,' she said in exasperation. 'All right. I shouldn't have let them sit there.'

'You're not fit to have a child,' he said disgustedly.

'Hey, wait a damn minute,' she said. And then she stopped herself. She told herself he was just lashing out because he was upset. You might do the same thing if it were your child, she thought. She didn't want to get into a fight. It might be a dangerous thing to do. 'I'm sorry, Peter,' she said, 'for being distracted like that.'

'Sorry doesn't cut it,' he said icily. 'You've risked the lives of my children and you've lost my respect. Now, let's go. We have to get on the road.'

With an effort, she held her temper and spoke calmly. 'No, I don't think so,' she said. 'I'm going to call my friend back.'

The expression on Peter's face became stony. 'What friend? Who was that?'

'That's really none of your business,' she said, trying not to sound panicky.

There was something intimidating in the way he was looking at her. She kept thinking of what Albert had said on the phone – there was no restaurant in Minneapolis. Mrs Kelly had been murdered. For whatever reason, Peter had been lying about everything. She was reluctant to make him any angrier. Tread lightly, she thought.

'As a matter of fact,' she went on, 'if you want to go back to the cabins with the girls, just go ahead.' Go, and keep on going, she thought. I'm giving you a chance to get away. I don't want to be a hero here. I just want to be left alone with my baby. Just leave us in peace. I'll get a bus ticket. I'll make my own way.

'Who was that you were talking to?' he demanded.

'No one you know,' she said.

'Who?' he snapped.

'My sister,' she lied.

'Did you tell her where we were?'

'No,' she said, trying to be reassuring. 'I didn't have a chance to.'

'Why did you call her?' Peter asked, peering at her.

'I . . . I wanted to let her know I was on my way,' she lied.

'I don't believe you,' he said. 'You wouldn't walk all this way just to let her know that.'

'The children were restless. I thought a walk would be good.'

'They don't like to walk,' he said. 'They like to play.'

'Well, then, don't believe me. I don't care. I don't have to account to you for everything I do or say . . .'

'I don't even think it was your sister,' he said.

Dena turned away from him. Act normal, she thought, as if you don't find his behavior alarming. 'I don't care what you think. I'm going to call her back,' she said firmly.

'No, you're not,' he said, grabbing her by her upper arm. 'Now, come on.'

His action shocked her. Dena tried to shake her arm free. 'Let go of me. Get your hands off me.'

Brittany, the clerk at the counter, glanced worriedly over at them. She took a step toward them, and then was ordered away by the manager, a scrawny, irritable-looking guy in a tie with his sleeves rolled up. Glancing back, Brittany headed back to refill the coffee makers as she had been instructed.

'Come on, honey,' Peter said in a loud voice. 'You don't want to have that baby right here.'

The manager stiffened and approached them. 'Can I help?' he asked Peter.

'I need to get my wife out of here.'

'Your wife? Peter, what are you talking about? That's not true. I'm not his wife,' Dena cried. 'Peter, stop it.'

The manager looked in amazement at the very pregnant woman who seemed to have temporarily lost her senses.

'Come on, sweetheart,' Peter pleaded. 'The kids are waiting in the van.'

Dena stared at him in disbelief. 'Peter, stop this. Let go of me.'

'Now honey, I know you're not thinking clearly. But once we get you home . . .' He tightened his grip on her arm, almost lifting her along.

Dena struggled furiously against his grasp. 'Are you insane? Let me go.'

'We'll get you all settled down and feeling better,' Peter crooned.

Dena looked helplessly at the manager. 'Look sir, please. I'm not his wife and these are not my kids and I just want to make a phone call. Can't you help me?'

The manager grimaced in discomfort at being a party to the whole scene. 'I don't . . . I'm not . . .'

At that moment, the door to the store opened and Tory came in with a weary look on her face. 'Come on, you two. Can't we go?'

Dena stared at the child's small, white face and for a moment she felt utterly trapped. She realized how this must look to the manager. She couldn't pretend not to know the child. She didn't want Tory to know how frightened she felt by all this. But she couldn't just go along with Peter. 'He's forcing me,' Dena pleaded in a low voice to the manager.

Peter shook his head sadly. 'She's always like this just before . . .' he confided.

The man nodded. 'My wife's had four of 'em,' he said. 'Look, ma'am, it's going to be OK.'

The manager was not going to help her. It was clear. He saw her advanced pregnancy as being responsible for her behavior. He preferred to think that. She glared at the man who stood there, refusing to listen. He looked back at her pityingly. Then he turned away.

For a minute she didn't know what to do. Part of her mind said, just go along.

You can reason with Peter outside. But the pressure of his fingers on her arm was threatening, infuriating. Peter was lying about where they were going. He was lying about Brenda Kelly . . . a woman who had been murdered. He was not going to just let her walk away, that was for sure.

Once he gets you in that van . . . She didn't know what was going to happen. She only knew that she wasn't going to go with him. Then it came to her. I'll throw something, she thought. I'll break the window. I'll make such a fuss they'll have to call the police. She hated to do it in front of Tory, but suddenly she felt as if she were being abducted. Dena looked around desperately. She searched wildly around the front of the store for something she could pick up and throw. Everything was small, or light.

Cigarettes, candies, newspapers. Her gaze grazed, and then halted at the headline of the afternoon edition that was displayed beneath her eye level. 'Drowning Ruled a Homicide', it said. There was a photo of the woman in the checkered coat, who had come looking for Peter that last night in Monroe.

Dena stared down at the picture. She looked up to see Peter looking at it too, impassively, as if it were announcing a change in the weather. Peter met her gaze indifferently.

'You lied to me about Brenda Kelly,' she said. 'When I told you she came to see you. When I asked you last night, you said you didn't know her. She was your baby-sitter.'

'I don't know what you're talking about,' he said.

'Let's ask Tory,' Dena said defiantly. Her heart was thudding like a drumbeat.

'I think you'd better just come along,' he said. There was no mistaking the determination in his eyes.

'I'm not going another step,' she said. And then, all of a sudden, she felt it. From deep within her body, a wave of pain undulated through her like a distant but undeniable warning, a faraway rumble of thunder. Oh God, she thought. No.

Peter saw the expression on her face and he stared at her. 'What is it?' he asked. Dena's face turned white, and she gripped her belly with both hands.

'It's time, isn't it?' Peter said. His eyes were alight. He saw his chance and propelled her a few halting steps toward the door, where the manager stood, holding it open.

'Time for what?' Tory asked, tugging at her hand.

Oh God, Dena thought. No. I'm not due for six weeks. And at the very moment she thought it, she felt something inside of her give way, and there was a gush of water that soaked her legs and spilled out across the floor of the convenience store.

The manager gave a yelp of distaste, and then cried out, 'Brittany, get out here with a mop.'

'What is that?' Tory cried. 'What's the matter?'

'I'm sorry about all this,' Peter said to the manager, as he forced her through the door. 'I have to get her to the hospital.'

'Yes, the hospital,' Dena said in a hoarse whisper. 'Hurry.'

Six weeks early, she thought. The baby couldn't be born yet. It was too dangerous.

The manager backed up against the door and murmured, 'There you go. Good luck.' He could not get them out of the store fast enough. He quickly shut the door against them.

'That's right,' said Peter. 'We'll just go along to the hospital.'

In spite of herself, Dena gripped his hand. He led her to the van and helped her inside. Her clothes were wet. Her legs, her shoes.

'Dad, what happened to Dena?' Tory cried as he hustled her into the van. 'Is she going to die?'

Peter's eyes were bright. 'No, no. Nothing happened, sweetie. Everything is just fine now.' He bent down and whispered in her ear. 'She's going to have our baby.'

Regina Bluefield was pulling the last of her mother's shoeboxes from out of the back of her closet when she thought she heard a car rolling over the gravel in her driveway. She didn't get up. There was nobody she wanted to see. Maybe they're just turning around, she thought. She opened up the shoebox on the now-cluttered floor of Brenda Kelly's room. Regina pulled an old pair of Hush Puppies from the box, looked them over with an expression of distaste, and deposited them in a black garbage bag beside the bed.

Sondra Bluefield, Regina's eleven-year-old daughter, who had inherited her sandy hair and blue eyes from her father, stood in the doorway of her grandmother's room with her hands on her hips and tears in her eyes. 'I don't believe you, Mother,' she wailed. 'Grandma isn't even buried yet and you're throwing away all her things.'

Regina looked up defiantly from her task. 'I am not throwing away all her things. This bag is going to Goodwill. Somebody can wear these shoes. You're not going to wear them. I'm not wearing them.'

'Don't you have any feelings?' Sondra cried. 'How can you be so cold-hearted? No wonder Daddy left you.'

Regina looked up at her daughter with narrowed eyes. 'Daddy left me for that bimbo, and don't you ever forget it,' she said angrily.

'He did not. He left you because you're so mean,' Sondra insisted, stamping her foot. 'I can't even look at Grandma's things without crying.' As if to prove her point, Sondra picked up a paperweight from her grandmother's bureau; it held a tiny bouquet preserved forever in glass, and tears filled her eyes.

'All right, all right, have it your way. I'm mean,' said Regina wearily. 'Look Sondra, when the funeral is over I've got to go back to work. When am I going to get this job done? We need this space, and if I don't do it now, when am I going to do it?'

The doorbell rang, interrupting their quarrel. 'I'll get it,' said Sondra. 'Probably another casserole.'

Chad Bluefield, Sondra's eight-year-old brother, who was playing across the hall with some trucks said, 'Maybe it's a cake. A chocolate cake.'

'Go and get the door,' Regina ordered. 'And try not to be so rude. People are just trying to be nice.'

Breaking up the empty shoebox for the recycling bag, Regina scrambled to her feet and prepared to go out and greet whoever it was before Sondra had a chance to grab the covered dish and slam the door in their face. Kids, she thought wearily.

As she brushed the dust from the back of the closet off her clothes, she heard Sondra return to the door of the room. She looked at her daughter and saw that she was wide-eyed.

'It's the cops,' Sondra whispered.

'All right. So?' Regina said, walking past her into the living room. Captain Van Brunt was there with the young patrolman, McCarthy. Regina greeted them politely and offered them a seat. They both wore solemn expressions.

'Mrs Bluefield,' Van Brunt began. 'I wanted to tell you in person that we got the report back this morning from the medical examiner. It seems your mother's death was not an accident, as we first thought.'

Regina stared at them. Sondra and Chad crept into the dining room and were standing in the doorway, eavesdropping with unabashed curiosity.

Regina shook her head. 'I don't . . . I don't understand. You said she drowned.'

Van Brunt looked at the children and cleared his throat, but Regina paid no attention. This is a rather hard woman, he thought. She didn't seem to care that the children weren't out of earshot.

'She . . . apparently . . . drowned somewhere else, and her body was moved to the canal.'

'What?' Regina looked stupefied by this idea. In the dining room doorway, the older child gasped in shock. 'What do you mean, she drowned somewhere else?'

Van Brunt preferred not to discuss it further in front of the children, but their mother did not seem to notice their presence. 'It's very important, Mrs Bluefield, that we find out why your mother went to Monroe in the first place. Who she intended to see.'

Regina raised her hands as if in surrender. 'I told you everything I know already. My hus . . . my ex-husband said that she called to say she had some errand she had to do and would he take the kids. Something she saw on TV reminded her of it. I have no idea what. She didn't tell him, or me, what it was. She didn't call me. Why are you asking me all this again? I don't know. I told you . . .'

Suddenly the adolescent girl in the doorway spoke up in a voice that was squeaky with nervousness. 'I know what it was . . .' she said.

The two policemen swiveled around to look at her, and then, at each other. Ken waited for the captain to speak.

'What is it that you know, honey?' Van Brunt asked in his most avuncular voice.

'Why Grandma went. She was watching her show and she saw something that got her all upset.'

'What was her show, honey?'

'Oprah,' said Sondra.

'Oh yeah,' said Regina with a sigh. 'She never missed Oprah.'

'And what was it she saw?'

'Well, I was doing my homework in the dining room and she

was watching and all of a sudden she said, "I know that guy. I used to take care of those kids." And when I asked her what she meant she said never mind, and to get my stuff together 'cause she was taking us to Dad's.'

Regina turned angrily on her daughter. 'Why didn't you say any of this before?'

'She told me not to say anything.'

'Well, she's dead now. You could have said something,' Regina cried. 'You told me she fell in the canal and drowned.'

Van Brunt whispered something to Ken, who jumped up and headed outside for the car. Then the captain stood up and cleared his throat again. 'Sondra, you've been very helpful.'

'I have?' the child asked.

'Don't let it go to your head,' said Regina unkindly.

Van Brunt addressed Regina. 'The man downstairs in the duplex. Peter Ward. Did you know him?'

'I met him once. He was . . . a widower. I remember that. His wife had a brain tumor.'

'Was there anybody else she baby-sat for?'

'I don't think so. Are you saying you think Peter Ward had something to do with her death?'

'Right now, all we have are questions . . .' he said. 'But, thanks to Sondra, we have a strong lead. If we have more questions . . .'

'We'll be here,' said Regina without enthusiasm.

Van Brunt adjusted his hat back as he left the house. Ken was leaning against the car, talking on the cell phone.

'What did you find out?' Van Brunt asked.

'I called the network affiliate in Philly,' said Ken. 'They looked it up. It was a show about men who kidnap their own children.'

'There's our connection. The neighbor in the duplex,' said Van Brunt. 'She used to baby-sit his kids.' Then he frowned. 'Find out when he moved. Or if he came back. I think this is our guy.'

'Good chance, I bet,' said Ken. 'They're going to messenger a tape to the station.'

'I hope you impressed on them the urgency of this. That guy could be miles away by now.

'Do we put out an APB on him?' Ken asked.

'Let's look at the tape first. Meanwhile, let's get back and run down everything we can on this guy,' said the captain. 'Do we know where he worked? Who he associated with?'

Heath Van Brunt was beginning to feel a little excited. This case was cracking like an egg. Could it be he was going to find himself a killer? 'Let's get going,' he said. 'I'll start making calls from the car.'

THIRTY-SIX

Tyrell stared at the phone in Albert's hand. 'What happened?' he said to Albert.

'I don't know,' Albert cried. 'I told her to hang on, that I was running to get you.'

'What did she say? Did she say where they were?' Tyrell asked.

'No,' Albert admitted. 'Something about the Hideaway Cabins. She said she was worried about Ward. And then I was so busy trying to warn her . . . I'm sorry.'

Tyrell tapped his fingers on the desktop. 'I'll bet she had to hang up,' he said. 'He might have walked in on her and so she had to end the call.'

'Oh God, this is my fault,' Albert wailed.

While Albert fretted over what he had done, Tyrell tried to think. She hadn't called back. He was willing to bet that meant she couldn't call back. At least he could check the number. He held the phone, pressed the number from the last call and waited.

'What are you doing?' Albert demanded.

'I'm trying to find out where she called from,' said Tyrell.

Albert wrung his hands. 'I've got to get out there and deal with a delivery. Please let me know what you find out.'

Tyrell nodded as Albert, worrying aloud, left the office. The minutes crawled by while Tyrell waited. The number was not Dena's. Whoever she borrowed this phone from was not picking up. On about the tenth ringing signal, he heard a click and then, to his shock, a voice.

'Hello?' It was a young female voice.

Tyrell gripped the phone. 'Excuse me,' he said politely. 'Who is this?'

'This is Brittany.'

'I'm sorry,' said Tyrell. He thought about identifying himself as a police officer, but then decided it would raise more questions than it would help the situation. 'Maybe you could help me. Someone just called me from this number and we were . . . cut off.'

'Oh, they're gone now,' said the girl.

'Who's gone?' asked Tyrell. 'From where?'

'The family that was here. I'm at work in the Wawa. What do you want anyway?' the girl asked suspiciously

'I'm sorry. I just want to know the location – the town where you're located.'

The manager gave Brittany a signal not to be talking on the phone. There was work to do. He was finishing up the mopping in the front, unsatisfied with the job she'd done.

Brittany hesitated a moment. The man sounded nice and sincere. Besides, what difference did it make if she told him where the store was. 'Redmark,' she said. 'On Route 27.' Then, before she could get into trouble, she hung up.

Tyrell repeated it aloud. 'Redmark, Route 27.' He placed Albert's phone on his desk and pulled out his own phone. He pressed a few buttons on his phone and got the location. It wasn't that far. He just had to hope that they had stopped there for the night. He left the office, headed for his car, when he thought maybe he needed some help on this. He punched in the police station number and asked for Captain Van Brunt.

Peg said, 'Is that you, Tyrell?'

'Yeah, is he in? Tell him it's important.'

'He's in the car, hold on.'

Tyrell waited, looking at his watch. After a moment, Peg got back on the line. 'I'm sorry, Tyrell,' she said, sounding sheepish. 'I can't find him right now.'

'Never mind,' he said grimly, knowing that Van Brunt had refused his call. 'I'll take care of it myself.'

No one in the van made a peep on the way back to the cabin. The children, sensing that something was wrong, did not say a word. When they arrived at the end of the dirt road and Peter stopped in front of the little cabin, Peter ordered the girls to get out. They scrambled to comply.

'Why are we stopping here?' Dena asked.

Peter did not reply to her question, but demanded the room key from Dena, who reached into her pocket and gave it to him without a word. Peter handed it out the window to Tory, and told her to go and open the door and to take Megan inside.

When the two girls had disappeared through the door, Peter turned to Dena. 'How are you feeling?' he asked pleasantly. 'Still have the pains?'

'Yes,' she said. 'I just had another contraction. I think we'd better hurry.'

Peter gazed calmly through the windshield. 'No hurry,' he said. 'We just have to let nature take its course.'

Dena felt infuriated by his arrogance, but she didn't want to antagonize him. 'I realize this is normal and natural and all that, but I still will feel a lot more comfortable when we get to the hospital,' she said.

'Don't be silly,' said Peter. 'There's absolutely no need for that. You'll be perfectly fine right here.'

For a moment, Dena thought she must have misunderstood. She stared at his placid, opaque countenance with a growing sense of alarm. For a minute she thought of Brian. This was even worse. How could it be that she had ended up worse off than she had been with Brian? She wanted to scream, only partly from pain. 'Peter, this baby is not due yet,' said Dena. 'Don't you understand? It might be small. It might need help to breathe.'

'Oh, that's a lot of medico-feminist nonsense. Your body is built for giving birth, and babies are built to survive. Women gave birth for years without all those doctors and hospitals. Now, just relax and put yourself in my hands. I won't let anything happen to this baby.'

Dena turned and looked at him, fighting back the tears that were rising to her eyes. 'Peter,' she said, 'why are you doing this?'

An expression of irritation crossed his face. He pocketed the keys, opened the driver's side door on the van and climbed down. Then he walked around and opened the door on her side.

'Come on,' he said. 'Hop down. We'll get you all settled inside.'

'I'm not getting out of this van,' she said. 'I'm going to a hospital.'

'Don't fight me on this. I know what I'm doing,' he said.

Dena tried to think, although her mind was reeling with the possibilities of disaster for her baby. Calm down, she thought. Try and be reasonable. 'Peter,' she said carefully. 'I . . . I know . . . I realize that you might be . . . in some sort of trouble.' She tried to make her voice sound casual, as if the trouble were a minor traffic violation. She tried not to think about Brenda Kelly, and what it all might mean.

'Trouble? What do you mean trouble?' he demanded.

'Look, I don't have time to be . . . coy here,' she said. 'This thing about Brenda Kelly . . .'

'I don't know anything about that,' he said.

'Peter, I know there is no restaurant in Minneapolis. I don't know why you said there was. I'm assuming you might be trying to get away from something . . .' she said.

'I have my reasons,' he said. 'You would never understand.'

'Whatever your reasons are, I don't care. I just want to be sure my baby is safe. You don't have to take me to the hospital. Just give me the keys and I'll find it myself. Or drop me off at the door, and keep on going. I swear to you, I won't tell anybody. I promise you I won't. I owe you that.'

'Come on,' he said. 'Chop, chop. We're wasting time.'

Dena was trembling all over but she willed herself to speak quietly and forcefully. 'This is my baby,' she said. 'And we are going to do it my way.'

Peter gave her a long-suffering look. 'Dena, try to think rationally. There is nothing dangerous about having a baby at home. Women have been doing it for centuries. You know I'm right. Now come along.'

His self-satisfied smile made her want to reach out and smack him. It was frightening too, but she wasn't going to think about that. The only thing she could think of was her baby. Stay calm, she thought. For your baby. Change your tack.

'Peter,' she pleaded. 'I know how much you care for children. There is no one who is more concerned about children than you. This is my child and I'm appealing to you as a parent. Can't we just go to the hospital and bring this baby safely into the world?'

Peter sighed. 'Dena, I am thinking about the baby. That's all I'm thinking about. The baby is the only one worth thinking about. He's an innocent. A brand-new life who needs to be brought into this world in the right way.'

'That's what I'm trying to do. I'm trying to make sure that he is safe from birth. And I will take good care of him. Believe me, I will.'

Peter snorted and shook his head. 'I doubt that,' he said. 'Look how stubborn you're being. Now come on, get out of there.'

She knew what he said about home births was true. Most children had been born that way throughout history. But that wasn't the point. The point was that he didn't give a damn for what she wanted. He was making a life-threatening decision for her baby as if this was his child, not hers. And, without knowing exactly what his intentions were, she knew that she and her baby were in danger from him. He was deaf to her pleas. There was no use in pretending or hoping. She had to try something.

'OK, OK,' she said. She shifted around in the passenger seat so that her whole body was facing the open doorway. Peter lifted a hand as if to take hers, and help her out. She hesitated, remembering how he had been her friend. He had taken her side, tried to protect her from Brian. It couldn't have come to this. But it has, she reminded herself.

You have to think only of the baby. His upraised arm exposed his ribs. She had no room to pull her lower leg back, to give it some heft, but she did her best. She kicked her leg forward and hit him in the chest. Traveling upward, her foot hit his chin and he staggered back. She slid down off the seat, hitting the ground with a thud that jarred her up to the top of her head. What now, she thought? Run? She had seen a light on in the office when they came in.

She had a momentary head-start on him. She wondered if it was dangerous to the baby to run. What did it matter? she thought. It was dangerous not to. She had run on and off for years, for exercise. She knew how. She clutched her belly and headed up the path, crying out for help. She did not get as far as the dirt road when the pain hit.

It was not a sharp pain. It was a cramp. Just a bad cramp, but it doubled her up and stopped her short. Oh God, she said. Oh God, please help me. She breathed deeply and tried to start again. By then he had caught up with her.

He grabbed her arm and twisted it behind her, so that it felt as if it would break.

She could feel all the color draining from her face. 'Come on,' he said soothingly. 'Let's go back now, and I'll put a cold cloth on your head.' Then he patted her stomach fondly. 'And I'll take good care of you until we get this little fellow delivered.'

THIRTY-SEVEN

The door to Heath Van Brunt's office opened, and a patrolman stuck his head in and held up a package. 'Sorry to interrupt, sir. The disc you've been waiting for just arrived.'

Ken McCarthy, who was sitting in the visitor's chair, jumped up and took it from the patrolman.

'Pop it in,' said the captain, indicating the screen on his computer. Ken tore open the package and pushed the DVD into the slot. As Oprah's music and introductions of her guests began, Ken and the captain conferred.

'The guy who owned the restaurant didn't have a picture of him,' said Ken. 'He never had his picture taken. Always had an excuse to miss the photo session. This gay guy never pushed it. Told me he considered it rather,' Ken consulted his notebook, '"*déclassé*" to post a picture of your piano player anyway.'

'That figures,' Van Brunt said, shaking his head. 'Queens.'

'Anyway,' Ken continued, 'he was all in a lather because Tyrell had been there, claiming he was on duty, and asking questions . . .'

'Watkins,' the captain exploded, 'what business did he have going over there? That suspension is going to be permanent.'

Ken decided not to tell the captain that Tyrell had gone off in search of Ward and Miss Russell. He hadn't wanted to admit that Tyrell was involved at all, but the gay guy, Mr Gelman, had made such a fuss about him being there. 'He let us borrow his phone. We'll be able to trace where she was calling from. I'm expecting that information any minute.'

Captain Van Brunt was still fuming about Tyrell. 'Technically, he was impersonating a police officer. There are laws against that.'

'Hey, look, sir,' said Ken, pointing to the television. 'Is this the one? Ward has two daughters. This guy had two daughters . . .'

Ken and the captain turned their attention to the screen. Oprah's first guest, a trim, dark-haired woman in her thirties, sat tensely in her seat as photos of her ex-husband and missing children were projected on the screen. The man was clean-shaven and was holding a baby in his arms. A toddler with little blonde braids clung to his leg.

'And that photo was taken just before they disappeared,' said Oprah sympathetically.

The woman nodded. 'After the judge heard testimony about his irrationality, and his controlling behavior, she awarded me full custody. She referred to him as emotionally abusive. That was all he needed to hear. He was an abused child himself. His mother was . . . involved in the legal system, so had utter contempt for the law. His visits were supposed to be supervised, but he managed to charm his way around that. He could be charming when he wanted to be . . . The third visit . . .' The woman choked.

'He took the girls and disappeared . . .' Oprah finished her sentence for her. 'And you haven't seen him, or your daughters, since?'

The woman shook her head. Oprah said something soothing to her, and then cut to a commercial.

'That's got to be our guy,' said Van Brunt. 'The ages of the children would be about right.'

'He's got a beard now,' said Ken.

'So, Mrs Kelly recognized him from this program and decided to go and speak to him about it. That's what I'm figuring,' said Van Brunt. 'Have we got a match on the fingerprints?'

'They're running his music sheets that the restaurant guy gave me right now.'

'Good,' said Van Brunt.

The patrolman stuck his head in the door and apologized again. 'Captain,' he said, 'Jennifer Hubbell's husband is here.'

Heath Van Brunt grimaced. He knew what the man wanted. He wanted new developments. But there were no new developments. At least, not at the moment.

'Ken,' he said. 'Go out there and put him off. Nicely. Tell him I'll get back to him ASAP.'

Ken nodded, and walked out of the captain's office, and went over to where Ron Hubbell stood waiting with a nicely dressed couple. He felt sorry for Ron, who looked like nine kinds of Hell. He wished there was something encouraging he could tell him about their investigation.

'Mr Hubbell,' he said warmly, 'how are you doing?'

'Not too well, I'm afraid.'

Ken could see that. 'What can I do for you? The captain's tied up at the moment but he promises to get back to you ASAP.'

Ron ran a hand through his unkempt hair. 'I . . . um . . . I had a bad night.'

Ken folded his arms over his chest. He had a feeling that he knew what that meant. A bad night. He glanced questioningly at Ron's friend, who returned his look gravely and nodded.

'My friends here, think I should go up to Boston with them. I'm finding it kind of difficult . . .' His voice trailed off.

'Officer,' said the other man, extending his hand. Ken shook it. 'I'm Skip Lanman. I'm an old friend of Ron's. Laura and I are just concerned about him sitting around this town, not being able to work, with all these terrible memories. It's my understanding that you've eliminated him as a suspect, so we were wondering if it would be all right—'

Laura, who was squeezing Ron's hand in her own, blurted out, 'We just feel he'd be a lot better off if he came with us . . . What purpose can be served by keeping him here?'

Ken stared at her.

Laura automatically reached for the buttons on her blouse, wondering if she'd forgotten to fasten something critical in her haste to reach Ron. Early this morning, Skip had dreamed that Ron had hung himself, and he woke up, thrashing and wailing. As it turned out, he had not been far off the mark. When they arrived at the hotel in Monroe, Ron had confessed to considering suicide. Getting so far as to take the pills in hand. Laura felt she would always be grateful that they had decided to call. The rush to get a flight here had been worthwhile. But she did feel slightly discombobulated. Still, her buttons checked out. Everything felt as if it were in place. But the officer continued to stare.

Faltering a little, she continued. 'It's a simple matter to reach him. And we can have him back here anytime you need him . . . Officer . . .?' she asked.

'It's you,' said Ken. 'The woman on Oprah. It's you.'

Laura and Skip exchanged a glance.

Then Laura nodded. 'Yeah. I was on Oprah's show this week.'

'Your husband . . .'

'My ex-husband kidnapped our children three years ago. Oprah is very good about giving people like me a chance to tell our stories. To try to reach people.'

'Oh Lord,' said Ken. 'Wait a minute.' Then he put a hand up. 'Don't move. Don't go anywhere.'

Ken disappeared back into Van Brunt's office. Laura looked from Skip to Ron. Then she noticed how pale Ron looked. 'You'd better sit down, honey,' she said, pulling out a nearby chair. Ron sat, and Skip leaned against a desk. Laura stood, twitching. Not daring to hope for anything because after all this time, she tried not to get her hopes up. These appearances always occasioned leads and phone calls. And none of them had ever led her back to her girls. She bit her lip and rocked.

In a few minutes, Ken emerged from Van Brunt's office, followed by the captain. Van Brunt came over to them, and greeted the trio somberly. Then, he frowned at a paper he had in his hand, and cleared his throat.

'Mrs Mallory,' he said.

'Yes.'

'Your ex-husband is Clifford Mallory?'

'That's right,' she said. In spite of her determination not to entertain false hope, her heart was in her throat.

'He kidnapped your daughters three and a half years ago?'

'That's right,' she said. Her mouth was dry. Her pulse was a drumbeat in her ear.

Van Brunt handed her a photo. It had been taken in the restaurant during an anniversary party when Peter was at the piano. 'Is this your ex-husband?'

Laura let out a cry and staggered back. Skip rushed to hold her up.

'This is Clifford Mallory?'

Laura nodded, her face white.

'Mrs Mallory, it would appear that your ex-husband, and your daughters were living in Monroe for the last two years under an alias.'

Laura gasped. And then panicked. 'What do you mean, "were living." Where are they?' she cried. 'Are my girls all right?'

'Yes, as far as we know. Though they have left Monroe. They moved out of the house they were living in and headed for . . . well, they said they were heading to Minneapolis but apparently that's not true. Fortunately, they only left yesterday. They can't have gotten too far. I've just this minute issued an APB on them . . .'

Laura's eyes lit up wildly, with a kind of dizzy combination of joy and fear. 'They're that close. Oh God, this is the most hope

I've had in three years.' Her eyes filled with tears. She wiped them away impatiently. 'They might be . . . they were in Monroe. Oh my God, I don't believe it. Oh, Skip.' She turned to him and he crushed her in his arms, his face mirroring her joy.

'They'll find him now,' he whispered. 'You'll have them back. We'll have them back.'

'Oh, how can I ever thank you? And God bless Oprah. My babies. My darling girls. Are they healthy? Do you have a picture of them?'

Captain Van Brunt and Ken McCarthy exchanged a glance. Laura saw it and froze. 'What's going on? What's the matter?'

Van Brunt cleared his throat again. 'This is kind of tricky. We have to move carefully. Your . . . ex is in a rather desperate situation. I'm afraid your husband – ex-husband – is suspected of killing a woman who baby-sat for him. Apparently, she recognized him and the girls from the Oprah show. We think she confronted him.'

'Oh God, no.' Laura sagged against Skip. 'It's not possible. Tell me that's not possible.'

'I'm afraid so, ma'am,' said Van Brunt. He hoped she would not ask how Brenda Kelly had died. He didn't want to tell her about the bathtub, the baby shampoo. He didn't want to acknowledge, even to himself, the possibility that one of the children was in the tub when it happened.

'He was always crazy,' she said bitterly. 'He seemed normal when I met him, but in time . . . I knew. And then he took the children. But murder. Not murder. Could it be a mistake?'

'It seems pretty certain.'

'A coincidence, maybe.'

'I don't think so. There's something else, Mrs Mallory.' Van Brunt grimaced. Laura waited. What could be worse? She was afraid to know.

'Was your ex-husband acquainted with Jennifer Hubbell?'

'Well, yes. They knew each other, although they were certainly not friends. I was in the process of getting a divorce when I met Jenn. I was attending a support group for domestic abuse victims and their families. She'd started coming because of her sister's death. We became close friends. She helped me to move out.' And then, suddenly, she realized what he was saying. She looked over at Ron, who had covered his face with his trembling hands. She looked back at the two policemen.

The sickening sensation in her stomach as they returned her gaze confirmed her fears. 'You think . . . Jennifer.'

'We don't know that. But, it begins to seem . . . It's possible that they had an accidental encounter. In a town as small as Monroe, it was probably inevitable. There was a connection. He is . . . was . . . friendly with a woman who was staying at the Hubbells' house. It's possible that Jennifer recognized him, threatened to expose him, and he acted on impulse. He didn't want to be caught. Lose the children. The killer obviously did not have a weapon with him. Which leads us to think . . .'

Laura glanced at Ron. 'Oh God,' she breathed. 'Oh Ron. I'm so sorry. Our Jenn . . .' She began to weep.

Van Brunt watched them, moved by their pain. Why was it that the people who were not to blame suffered more than the criminals themselves? They rarely cared that much about the destruction they caused.

'Mrs Mallory,' he said gently. 'All of this is speculation right now . . .'

Laura shook her head with the certainly of one who is doomed. 'That's what happened,' she said. 'I know it. If Jennifer had seen him . . .'

'One thing is certain,' said Van Brunt. 'We are going to locate this man. And your children. I promise you. I think you might want to stay put, so that you can accompany us to them.'

'Wild horses couldn't stop me,' she said through her tears. She hesitated, wiping her eyes. Then, she walked over to Ron and knelt down in front of him. 'This is my fault,' she said. 'Because of my mistake, you've lost Jenn . . .'

Ron shook his head. 'No. Don't think of it that way.'

'I have to,' she said. 'When the girls and I first left, we stayed with her. At her apartment. Peter was furious. Jenn wouldn't let him in the door. We were all cramped in her place – the four of us. It was the first time I had slept easily in years.'

Ron squeezed her hands. 'That's the way she was. She wanted to help. She would have done anything to help you get those children back.' He tried to smile at her through his tears. 'Maybe now, she has.'

THIRTY-EIGHT

I t was nearly dark when Tyrell arrived in Redmark, though he had driven as fast as he could, keeping a sharp eye out for troopers. His heart had lifted when he saw the exit for Route 27, also known as the Redmark County Road. He rolled off the highway, wondering whether to turn right or left, and then he saw the little roadside advertisement for the Wawa, six miles to the left. Tyrell turned and headed in that direction.

A short way down the road, after passing a cluster of fast food restaurants, a Kmart and an automotive supply shop, he came to the main street of Redmark. It was a shabby boulevard with an empty town square; only a smattering of businesses seemed to be operating there.

Now that he was here, Tyrell felt a little foolish, and frustrated at the vagueness of his own plans. Maybe they weren't stopping here in Redmark. Maybe they were just passing through and made a pit stop at the Wawa. No, no, he could not allow himself to think that. They were stopping. They had to be. He drove slowly down the main street, looking side to side. At one point he spotted a gray station wagon, like the one described by Albert as Peter Ward's, and he pulled into a nearby parking lot. He was about to get out of his car and investigate when an old guy in a baseball cap came out of the hardware store, opened the door to the station wagon and slid into the driver's seat. Tyrell waited until the old guy pulled out and then he followed suit.

It did not take him long to arrive at the other end of Redmark. He continued along Route 27 in the direction of the Wawa. Every time he saw a motel sign he slowed, and drove into the parking lot, looking for the gray station wagon or a sign that said Hideaway Cabins.

This is partly your fault, he chided himself. She asked for help, and you gave her only the minimum. What was she supposed to do? He thought of her as he had first seen her, with blood on her face, in that bathroom, when he thought she was a child. You have to find her. Maybe, he thought, I'll go over to that Wawa and see if I can talk to that clerk in person. Maybe there's something she remembers that she didn't tell me.

He pulled out of the El Dorado parking lot and continued down the road toward the Wawa. There was very little to be seen on this road. It was really a country road, the road out of town. Oh God, he thought. What do I do next? Coming up on his right, he suddenly saw a sign that read, Hideaway Cabins. He slowed down until he had it in his headlights. Cabins for rent, day or week, it said.

All right, he thought. He could see the sign for the Wawa in the distance. That would be where they might stop for supplies if they were staying here. He turned into the dirt road and rolled slowly down under the pines, glad he had four-wheel drive on his car. It was pitch dark under the evergreens, and the road was rutted. He was surprised when the road opened out on a pretty lake, and the sky seemed to lighten accordingly. But, as for his search, it seemed he had struck out again. There was only one cabin occupied, and that had a red van parked out in front of it. The office wasn't even open.

He felt a nagging sense of hopelessness, but he was not about to give in to it. He turned his car around and drove back out to the highway. Turning right, he headed on down to the convenience store, which was, itself, in an isolated spot. He parked in front, where there were nothing but free spaces, got out of his car and went inside.

A gawky young guy in a khaki shirt, red vest, and red visor was leaning on the counter, reading a wrestling magazine. Tyrell quickly picked out a quart of orange juice and a pack of gum to buy, and set it down on the counter. Without bothering to look up at him, the young man shifted his gaze from his magazine to the items Tyrell had set down. He rang it up and mumbled the price. Tyrell paid up, and then put most of his change in a charity box with a sign that it was for a local child burned in a fire.

The young man glanced at him then, and gave him a brief smile, before returning to his article.

'Hey man,' said Tyrell. 'I wonder if you could help me.'

The boy looked up at him.

'Is there a girl about your age who works here?'

'I'm on my own here,' the boy said.

'I'm looking for a girl I spoke to this afternoon who works here. Her name is Brittany.'

The lanky boy rubbed his pale, fuzzy chin. 'Brittany was working here this afternoon.'

'Is she on a break? Is she coming back?'

The boy shook his head. 'No man, she's gone. I don't think she works again until the weekend.' Suddenly, the boy looked at him suspiciously. His pleasant expression faded away. 'Why do you want to know?' he said.

Tyrell understood. A black guy, looking for a young white chick. What was he thinking? 'Was there anybody else here this afternoon who might be able to help me?'

'I don't know, man,' said the clerk. 'The manager was probably here. But he's gone home.'

'Can you call him?' Tyrell asked.

The boy looked at him skeptically. 'Not unless it's an emergency. I'd lose my job.'

Tyrell hated to do it, but he had to try. 'Look son, I'm a police officer. I need this information.'

'Oh yeah?' said the kid. 'Where's your badge?'

'I'm not carrying my badge. Actually, I'm working undercover.'

'You'd still need a badge,' the kid said stubbornly.

Tyrell had to admire the kid's balls. Some kids would be afraid to defy a black guy when he was all alone in a store like that. I had to get a brave one, he thought.

'Come on, mister. I don't want any trouble,' said the boy.

Tyrell heard the anxious note in the boy's voice and raised his hands in a placating manner. The kid was doing the right thing. Playing by the rules. There has to be another way, Tyrell thought. Another way. He walked toward the door and then stopped.

'Do you have a men's room?' he asked.

The boy frowned, but gestured toward the back. 'Next to the stockroom.'

'Do I need a key?'

'It's open,' said the boy.

'Thanks,' said Tyrell. He headed to the back, and out of sight.

Dena lay on the narrow bed, a cold scratchy washcloth on her forehead, as the latest cramp subsided. Her head was aching, and the veins in her legs throbbed. She looked at the darkening sky through the window in the little bedroom. Peter sat on a chair beside the bed, looking at his watch and nodding amiably. 'The little one will be here soon.' He held up a small, plastic cup. 'Ice chips?' he asked.

Dena turned her head and stared at him. The sleeves of his pinstriped shirt were neatly folded back, and he hummed to himself as if this were the most pleasant, natural thing in the world. 'Peter,' she said. 'I know you are not a bad person. I've seen how you care for these girls and I know you would never want any harm to come to a child.'

He continued to hum, as if he didn't hear her. He simply increased the volume of his humming, trying to drown her out.

'I'm so frightened for my baby,' she said and, in spite of her intentions, her words came out in a sob. 'I need to get to a hospital.'

'You are going to be so surprised,' he said. 'I am right about this. The baby will be perfectly healthy and fine. Now, I don't want to argue about this anymore. You're wearing yourself out and you need your strength for the delivery. You just have to trust me. Besides, it will be a beautiful experience for the girls to be here when their . . . when the baby is born.'

'You realize,' said Dena, 'that you are holding me against my will. I can press charges against you.'

Her turned on her and there was fury in his eyes. 'Don't you dare. Don't you threaten me with legal double-speak. You keep your mouth shut or you will end up like Jennifer.'

'Jennifer?' she whispered. 'What about Jennifer?'

Peter struggled to compose himself. If there was one thing he could not tolerate, it was a woman threatening him with all her legal options. That unfortunate day, when he took Megan out for a ride in her wagon, they stopped to see if Dena was home. And who had answered the door but Jennifer. He couldn't recall who was more shocked, once they recognized each other. And then, almost immediately, she had started with the threats.

When he thought back on it now, all he could remember were her eyes, her voice, that russet hair, her icy fury. What did she think he was going to do? Back down? Walk away? After all he'd sacrificed? All he'd been through?

As Peter sat staring, lost in some violent memory, Dena closed her eyes to blot out his distorted features. She realized with a sense of despair engulfing her, that there would be no reasoning with him. No threatening him, no talking him out of this, and she was too physically incapacitated to resist his will. She felt a burning hatred for him forming deep inside of her, but, more persistent than that, was a sense of her own foolishness – stupidity, really.

What have I done to you? she thought, addressing in her mind the baby that was now trying to be born before it was ready for this world. If anything happens to you, it is my fault for going with him. Why did I trust him? Don't I have any judgment at all? I was so busy trying to get away from Brian that I turned to someone even worse . . . What in the world have I done?

No, she told herself. You can't give in to this. Until this baby is actually born, there is still time. You have to try to talk to him, cajole him, anything. You can wallow in your misery later. You have no physical card to play, she thought. Try and work on his mind. How to appeal to him? she wondered. There had to be a way.

'Peter,' she said, but he had shaken off the memory, and resumed humming. He didn't seem to hear her. She reached over toward the night table and tried to grasp the cup of ice. He pushed her hand away and picked up the cup. Then he shook out a chunk of ice into his hand, and shoved it between her teeth. The ice slid down her tongue and back into her throat, making her gag. She began to retch.

All of a sudden, outside, there was a thrum of a car's engine nearing the little cabin. 'Quiet,' he said, putting a hand over her mouth and a finger to his lips. Her head was shoved back against the pillow. She tried to cry out around his hand, but her voice was muffled. She couldn't breathe. She heard the thrum change tempo, as if the car had paused, and started again, and then the sound began to fade away.

Tears formed in her eyes and ran down the sides of her face. He took his hand off her mouth, reached over for a tissue and dabbed at her tears. Dena gasped. Still time, she tried to tell herself. Still time. Don't give up. She swallowed hard, and tried again. 'Peter.' Her voice was raspy, from the retching. He looked coldly at her, a cheerful smile on his lips.

'Was Tory born . . . at home?' she whispered.

The expression in his eyes became . . . not soft exactly, but anxiously reminiscent. 'No,' he said. 'She insisted on the whole medical claptrap. Doctor this and Doctor that. With Megan too.'

'Your wife?' Dena whispered timidly, surprised at the criticism in his tone. He rarely spoke of his wife, but in the past, when he did, it was always in the pained, respectful tone of the bereaved.

A fleeting look of guilt, as if he'd been caught out at something, crossed his face. 'I always wanted to do it this way,' he said. 'The right way.'

She was amazed at this change in attitude to his wife's memory, but she couldn't afford to dwell on it. She didn't have much time before the next contraction. And how many more would there be? Stay in there, she thought, trying to send her baby a psychic message. Rest inside Mommy. Don't be in such a hurry. She tried to regain her thready train of thought.

'Well, it certainly turned out all right for those two. You couldn't find two healthier, more beautiful girls.'

He was too proud of them to resist such an observation. In spite of himself, he smiled. 'They are beautiful,' he said. He lifted the cloth from her forehead, dunked it in a bowl of cold water and squeezed it out. Then he patted it carefully back on her forehead. 'No thanks to . . . anyone else,' he said.

'I guess you wanted them to be born at home,' she said.

'If you call that a home,' he said.

'I don't understand,' said Dena.

'You don't need to understand,' he said. 'Tory,' he called out.

The older child came rushing into the room. 'Is the baby here?' she cried.

'Not yet,' he said. 'But soon. Soon you'll have a little brother or sister. I think a brother. What do you think?'

'I think a brother,' Tory agreed automatically.

Peter handed her the bowl. 'Go and empty this out, and refill it with cold water.'

A brother or a sister, Dena thought. It made her feel almost dizzy. How could he even say such a thing? As if the moment she was back on her feet she wouldn't take her baby and leave. 'You know, you shouldn't encourage them to think that. I don't want them to get too attached to the baby,' she said.

'Why not?' he asked.

'You know why,' she said.

'No, I don't. Tell me,' he said.

'Well, I mean, obviously, after I give birth, the baby and I will be . . . making our home together. I mean, I'm sure we'd always love to see the girls . . .'

'Giving birth,' he said. 'That's such a phony expression. You're not giving that baby anything. If anyone's giving it birth, it's me. You're just going to lie there, like a pig in a sty. I mean, they let you take it home just because you carried it, but what do you really know about raising children? Nothing. You're ignorant. You don't have any idea what it takes, what responsibility, what vigilance is required . . .'

'I'll soon find out,' she said, trying to placate him.

'I doubt it,' he said.

She didn't want to know what he meant by that. She had to keep thinking that she and her baby were going to be all right. Get back to the girls, she thought. His favorite subject. Try and arouse a little sympathy in him. There had to be some. 'You are such a devoted father to your girls,' she said. 'You always put them first. You and your wife wanted to do everything you could for your children. You just had different ideas about how they should come into the world. Obviously, your wife thought a hospital would be the best place . . .'

'My wife was a lazy cow. She wanted to be in the hospital so she wouldn't have to do anything. She had no standards. She cut every corner. I mean, that's something she would do. Leave the kids out there on that bench like that. You know, I've yet to meet the woman you can trust with kids. I put up with Brenda for almost a year for want of anybody else, but if ever there was a woman with slovenly habits . . .'

'Brenda Kelly,' Dena whispered.

He suddenly became guarded again. He looked at his watch. 'Should be another contraction any minute now,' he said calmly.

Everything about you is a lie, Dena thought. I was fooled by the children. Their presence lulled me into thinking you were someone else. Dena tried not to think about Brenda Kelly. She tried only to think of her baby, and how she could get her baby to safety. 'Peter, I thought you were on my side,' she said. 'I thought you understood how important this baby is to me. You agreed with me that I should get away from Brian. You knew I wanted to love and take care of my baby and protect my baby from harm.'

'You are the harm,' he said.

She stared up at him, trying not to let her worst fears form in her mind. She swallowed hard and spoke in an urgent tone. 'I'm sure I have a lot to learn, but I won't be like your mom was. Believe me. I'm going to take him to the park every day and bundle him up when it's cold and sing to him and give him lots of love . . .'

'And have no father for him, and feed him candy, and leave him outside of stores on benches where anyone could come along and snatch him. Oh, no, I don't think so. What the world doesn't need is another child raised by a hopelessly inadequate mother like you.'

She couldn't pretend she didn't know what he was saying. She tried to struggle up off the bed, but he pressed her down with his forearm. 'Mustn't get up,' he said.

And then the next contraction came, knocking her back with all its force. Peter smiled at the sight of her frightened face. 'Here we go,' he said. 'All right. Focus and breathe.'

THIRTY-NINE

Once he was out of sight, Tyrell was able to explore the rear of the store. Across from the rest room he saw that the door leading to the manager's office was slightly ajar, the light on. Maybe the guy comes back to lock up for the night, he thought. Tyrell peered down between the aisles. The kid at the counter was absorbed in his wrestling magazine. Tyrell slipped across into the office and looked around. There on the wall was a chart of the week's hours, with names marked in the times they worked. He could easily read Brittany's name, written in red marker on the plastic overlay.

Brittany. That wasn't much help. He looked down at the man's desk, which was covered with piles of invoices, coupons and price lists. Behind the desk was a computer and a telephone with a fax machine. Her address and phone number were probably in the computer. There were neon-colored fish swimming around on the screen saver. Tyrell came around behind the desk and punched up the list of files. The list was large, but the files for employees was clearly marked. Checking the door again, Tyrell called up the employee file and began to scroll down the names which emerged on the screen.

Brittany, he said to himself. Brittany, Brittany. Brittany Guicide. He had it. He memorized her address and pressed the sleep button on the computer. Neon fish swam back into view.

Tyrell slipped out of the office, and made his way down an aisle crammed with breakfast staples. He emerged briefly near the doorway, where he was visible to the clerk. The boy looked up from his magazine. 'Take it easy,' said Tyrell, and pushed the doors open, stepping out into the crisp air of the evening. He didn't have far to go but he decided to drive anyway. He didn't want to leave his car behind and make the young man behind the counter suspicious.

Tyrell took a swig of the orange juice he had bought, and climbed into the driver's seat of his car. OK, he thought. Next stop, Brittany's house. He backed up, made a left turn onto the highway and then, after he crossed the intersection and passed the gas station, he signaled for another left. I'll bet she's hardly ever late to work, Tyrell thought. He pulled across the highway and into the asphalt driveway beside a tiny house with asbestos shingles that badly needed a fresh coat of paint. He parked behind a dusty little black Ford Festiva and got out of his car. Lights were burning in the house. Come on, he thought. Be home.

A burly guy, with a bulldog face and a gray athletic department T-shirt stretched across his large belly, opened the door and looked out at him.

'Mr Guidice?' Tyrell asked.

The man peered at him suspiciously. 'Who wants to know?'

'My name is Tyrell Watkins. I'm a police officer with the Monroe police department in Bucks County. I wanted to speak to Brittany?'

This man did not ask for a badge. As soon as he saw him, Tyrell had been betting he wouldn't. Among men of a certain age, that would be like asking for directions at a gas station. You didn't want to appear to be a poor judge of things.

'Is she in any kind of trouble?' the man asked, in a tone that would not have accepted 'yes' for an answer.

'No sir, not at all. She works at the Wawa and I wanted to ask her one or two questions about a customer who was in there today.'

The man looked down and then back at Tyrell. 'OK. Come on in. I thought you were one of them Watchtower people at first. Brittany,' he bellowed. 'You got company.'

A Jehovah's Witness, Tyrell thought. Why else would a black man be knocking on your door?

Brittany's father settled back down in his recliner. Tyrell glanced at the TV set.

The Philadelphia 76ers were tearing up and down the basketball court, holding their own against the Orlando Magic. 'What's the score?' Tyrell asked.

'It's 23-20,' said the man. 'Just started.'

'Who do you like?' Tyrell asked.

'I like Philly. That Embiid's a heck of a player.'

'Yeah,' said Tyrell. 'He's kind of a punk, but he's the real deal.'

The two men nodded in agreement. At that moment, Brittany came into the tiny living room, her blonde hair combed out long over her shoulders, wearing an oversized T-shirt over her jeans and some sort of flesh-toned cream caked around her jaw.

'Brittany?' asked Tyrell.

'Yeah,' she said warily.

'This is Officer Watkins,' said her father, respectful of the police.

'I spoke to you today at the Wawa.'

Brittany looked puzzled. She would have remembered this guy, she thought. 'About a customer who borrowed your phone.'

'Oh yeah,' she said. 'I remember.' She had been a little suspicious of the caller. She could tell by his voice that he was black. But now that she saw him in person, he looked like a nice guy. Besides, he was a cop.

'Can we go in the other room to talk? I don't want to disturb your father's game.'

'Oh, sure,' said Brittany, and led Tyrell into a cheerful yellow kitchen with plaid curtains. He could see the moon through the back-door window. He sat down on a plastic-covered chair cushion and Brittany leaned against the sink. 'What did you want to know?' she said.

'OK,' he said. 'The woman, today, in the Wawa. The pregnant woman. The man she's with is wanted for questioning about a homicide in Monroe.

'A homicide. Wow. You mean he killed someone?'

'We need to question him,' Tyrell said calmly. 'The woman was trying to give us her location but we were cut off. We need to find these people.'

'He did seem kind of mean and bossy,' Brittany admitted. 'I didn't think she wanted to go with him.'

'You didn't?' Tyrell's heart began to race. 'Did you hear them say anything about where they were going, or anything like that?'

Brittany shook her head. 'No, the man was just insisting that she go with him, and she was saying she didn't want to go.'

Tyrell squeezed his own wrist. 'That's it. Nothing else you can remember?'

'Yeah, well then . . . you know . . .'

Tyrell looked at her in confusion. 'Then what?'

Brittany made a face. 'Well, you know how when a woman is pregnant. When she's going to have a baby . . . you know how they say her water breaks?' The girl was clearly embarrassed to mention it.

Tyrell felt his skin go clammy. 'Her water broke?'

Brittany nodded and grimaced. 'Out in the vestibule. I had to get a mop and mop it up.'

'That means she's about to have the baby,' said Tyrell.

'I guess so,' said Brittany.

'So . . .'

All at once he saw a ray of hope. 'They must have gone to a hospital. Where's the nearest hospital?'

'There's only two hospitals for miles around here. Mercy and County General.'

Tyrell pulled his cell phone from his jacket and began to call the hospitals, making his way through patient information, emergency and admissions. By the time he was done, and put his phone away, Brittany's father had joined her in the kitchen, watching Tyrell curiously.

Tyrell shook his head. 'Nothing,' he said. 'Nothing. Everyone I talked to swore up and down that no women in labor were even admitted today.'

Brittany looked worried. 'Do you think they kept going?'

Her father snorted derisively. 'With a woman in the car whose water broke, already. I don't think so. She'd have the baby right there in the car.'

'Minivan,' said Brittany.

'Minivan, car, whatever,' said her father impatiently.

It took a moment to register on Tyrell. 'They were driving a gray station wagon,' he said.

Brittany shook her head. 'A red minivan,' she said. 'I saw them get into it.'

It took a moment to register. Then, Tyrell saw it in his mind's eye. The red minivan. Parked beside a cabin on a lake. Tyrell leapt up, grabbed Brittany's hands and squeezed them. 'Thank you, Brittany,' he said. 'Thank you so much.'

'You're welcome,' Brittany laughed, glad to be a part of this exciting search. 'Watch out for that guy,' she called after him, as Tyrell thanked her father and then rushed out to his car.

Tyrell waved as he backed out of the driveway. How they could still be in those cabins with Dena in labor, he didn't know. But he was going to find out. As he pulled out on the highway, he nearly swerved across the lane as the cell phone in his pocket rang. He pulled it out and pressed the button.

'Yeah,' he asked, all the while straining his eyes to look for the sign for the lakeside cabins.

'Tyrell?'

Tyrell nearly dropped the phone at the sound of Van Brunt's voice. 'Captain?' There was a crackling in the receiver and the signal was fading in and out.

'I know you're out searching for Peter Ward and the Russell woman . . .'

'Right,' he said. He wasn't going to listen to some kind of scolding. He had better things to do. But he could hear a conciliatory note in the captain's voice.

'Officially, of course, I can't tell you what to do.'

You got that right, Tyrell thought.

'But this is no time to stand on ceremony. I want you to know what you're dealing with. We have an APB out on Ward. We think he may have killed both Jennifer Hubbell and Mrs Kelly . . . If you have any idea of their whereabouts . . .'

'Jesus Christ,' Tyrell breathed. He was thinking of Dena. Thinking about Brittany saying that she didn't want to go with the man. He wondered, for a moment, if she was still alive. The thought sent a chill through him.

'Tyrell, do you hear me? Don't try to be a hero. This man is extremely dangerous.'

'Yessir.'

'Do you have any information on their whereabouts?' the captain asked. His voice was faint. It sounded like someone was balling up cellophane inside the receiver.

Tyrell hesitated. He spotted the Hideaway Cabins sign and slowed down to make a turn. He switched on his signal. Part of him wanted to just hang up, but the sensible part of him knew that he needed the help. More than that, Dena and her baby needed the help. 'I think I've found them, sir. I have information that the Russell woman is in labor and her baby may need some kind of special attention. I'm in Redmark on Route 27. Hideaway Cabins. About half a mile from the Wawa. Have you got that?' There was no response. Only the crackle of static on the line. 'Captain?'

There was nothing. He pressed a few buttons. There was no response. For a minute he felt panicky, thinking of what he might be confronting. He forced himself to stay calm. All right, he thought. I have to keep going. No turning back now. She was alone in there with those two kids, and a killer. Tyrell hung up the phone and turned the wheel. Switching off his headlights, he rolled slowly down the rutted road.

FORTY

Tory stood in the doorway and looked worriedly into the room. 'Why is Dena crying?' she asked.

'Well, it's painful to have a baby,' Peter said calmly. 'Now close the door and go into the other room with your sister.'

'Why don't you tell her the truth?' Dena asked.

'I did,' he said. 'I have to concede that it seems to pain you women, although I doubt it's half as bad as you make it out to be.'

'I meant, why don't you tell her that you are risking my child's life by having him born here. And threatening to take him from me, if by some miracle he manages to be born safely.'

Peter seemed shocked. 'Risking *his* life? Don't be ridiculous. I'm risking *my* life to stay here and see you through this thing. Believe me, if it weren't for that baby, I'd have left you by the side of the road somewhere and kept on going. I am the one with everything to lose here. But, I'm willing to take the chance, for the baby's sake.'

'Do you think,' she said, 'for one minute that I will ever let you get near this baby of mine? I will never let you have anything to do with my baby.'

'Oh, you're raving,' he said. 'Women do that in your condition. They start yelling things. I remember how pitiful Laura was. No guts at all.'

Dena looked at his placid face and wondered how she could ever have mistaken him for a friend. Sweat dripped off her forehead and mixed with the tears on her cheeks. But she did not feel sad. She felt furious. She had been able to keep it hidden before the labor had started in earnest. But now, it felt as if something had been released in her, and she had no energy left to pretend. 'You are kidding yourself,' she said. 'I would rather die than let you put a hand on my baby.'

'So be it,' he said calmly.

Dena heard the words and realized what he was saying. I have to get up, she thought. I have to get away from him. But even as she thought it, another contraction began. It stirred, and started to emerge, like some hideous dragon, lying in wait in a cave of pain hidden deep inside her. She knew she was supposed to breathe, to focus, to keep calm, but all she could see was Peter. Another dragon, beside her, also lying in wait.

Lying in wait for her baby, who was insisting on emerging, though she did not push, would not push. The monster pain roared within her, and she trembled from the force of it, the fear of it, sweat popping out all over her as she sat up, and tried to ride it out. Peter offered her his hand to grip, but she refused to take it, clutching the edges of the bed instead. Now, she knew the meaning of the words, holding on for dear life.

After what seemed an interminable assault, the dragon began to retreat, back into the cave. Her arms felt limp from holding the edges of the bed, but she didn't dare let go. He could turn at any moment, more ferocious than before.

'Daddy,' Tory pleaded, opening the door.

'I told you to stay in the other room, until I call you,' Peter commanded.

'I hear something. Someone outside. You have to come and look.'

'It's your imagination,' Peter said. 'I'm busy now.'

'I heard it,' Tory insisted.

Peter looked narrowly at Dena and then back at his daughter. 'All right. Just a minute,' he said. 'I don't think I have to tell you to stay there, do I?' he asked.

Dena, still gasping from the last contraction, gave him a foul look. She couldn't move, didn't dare. If she had been bound with steel, she could not have been any more immobilized.

'Remember to breathe,' he said. 'You're not doing well at all.' Peter walked over to the doorway and looked back at her, shaking his head. 'You would have made a terrible mother.'

Peter went out into the living room where Tory was standing alone, looking around her. 'Where is Megan?' he said.

'She's in her bed. She threw up,' Tory said.

'Did you clean it up?' he demanded.

'I did,' she said.

'Good. Now, let me check.' Peter walked out the front door of the cabin and looked out at the lake in the moonlight. The little motorboat lay tilted on the ground, beside the dock; the moon glittered on the lake's surface, and there was not another soul in sight. He looked around. No cars, no people, nothing. Probably an animal passing by, he thought. Tory was always imagining things. Always thinking someone was after her. It came from those years of being on the run, he suspected. He wasn't sure how much she knew. They never talked about it. But she knew enough to fear the police, to feel threatened by new people coming around. Sometimes, like tonight, she was a little overly cautious. But that made her a good sentinel when all was said and done. Nobody would ever sneak up on them.

It was the last thought he had before he heard a crunch of leaves, a whoosh, and felt something whack him on the head. Then, he lost consciousness.

In the bedroom Dena wept, without sobbing, and fell back against the pillows. I am a terrible mother, she thought. You're not even born, and I haven't taken good care of you. You're already condemned. He will kill me, and take you, and your whole life, if you survive at all, will be spent paying for my stupid mistakes. Oh, God, I've done everything wrong, but why does my innocent baby have to suffer for it? Couldn't you find some way to protect him?'

'Dena?'

She turned her head, and couldn't believe her eyes. 'Tyrell?' she said, for she had been thinking of him that way. Then she mumbled, 'I mean, Sergeant . . .'

He came over and sat down beside the bed, smiling wryly. 'Tyrell is fine,' he said.

She let her damp head fall against his chest and rest there. 'Oh, thank God,' she breathed.

He put an arm gingerly around her, and let his hand rest lightly on hers. 'It's all right,' he crooned. 'It's all right now.' She was shaking from head to toe.

She lifted her head and looked frantically into his eyes. 'The baby is coming and it's too soon and I'm afraid it's going to die. It might need an incubator. Its lungs might be too small to breathe without help. That's what happens when babies are premature.' She was babbling, clutching the lapels of his leather coat.

'OK, calm down.' He was talking to her, but also to himself. His heart was hammering, although he didn't want her to see his anxiety.

'Where is he?' she said. 'Where's Peter?'

'I knocked him out and tied him up with some rope I had in my trunk.'

'Oh, thank God. How did you find me? How did you know?'

Tyrell looked at her delicate face and smiled. 'I just got worried about you. I figured I better come looking for you.'

She laughed, but tears came to her eyes.

'Now look,' he said. 'We have to get you to the hospital. I tried to get an ambulance but my cell phone is out. But don't be afraid. We can do it.'

'I don't know,' she said, swallowing hard.

'Sure we can,' he said, smiling at her a little. 'Trust me.'

Dena sighed. 'Oh, you know me. I trust everybody.'

He heard the bitterness in her voice, and he couldn't contradict her. She had trusted two men and both of them had endangered her. No wonder she was bitter. 'Hey,' he said. 'Give it one more try.'

Dena nodded.

'Here. Put your arm around me and I'll lift you up.'

It didn't seem possible to her to get up, to walk out. But then again, five minutes ago she never would have believed that Tyrell would find her. She wrapped one thin white arm around his neck. He leaned down to get his arms around her and she could feel the warmth of his skin, soothing against her own. 'I'm sorry about this,' she said.

'You're sorry,' he said and, in spite of everything, they both laughed.

The dragon inside her heard them laughing and stirred. Dena was not quite to her feet when he struck again. 'Oh no,' she groaned. 'Let me down.'

Instantly, Tyrell lowered her back to the bed, as her eyes widened with the pain. 'It's bad,' he said.

'Help me, Tyrell.'

'I'm going to,' he assured her. She gripped his hands so hard he thought she would break the bones in them. It surprised him, the amount of strength in those narrow fingers.

'It's too late,' she cried.

'No, don't say that. Don't be afraid. We can do this.'

She closed her eyes, her face white as death, and tried to hold back the scream that was rising within her. From faraway she could hear his voice, reassuring her, promising her. She felt as if someone was disemboweling her while she was still alive.

'Daddy,' Tory whispered. She had been hiding in their room, waiting for him to come back. Megan was lying on her bed, with her back to the center of the room, making little noises, but otherwise not moving. Tory had waited and waited, but her father had not returned. She heard someone coming into the house, but it was not him. She knew his step. She knew it like her own. Finally, she had gotten up the courage to peep out of her room. There was no one in the living room. She tiptoed out the front door and looked around fearfully.

At first, everything looked OK. The lake, the moon, the little boat. Then, suddenly, she saw something big and dark on the ground, beginning to move. 'A bear,' she whimpered. 'A bear.' She wanted to start yelling but it was no use. Her voice had frozen in her throat.

'Tory,' a voice whispered.

It was coming from the mound on the ground. The bear knew her name. She was paralyzed with fear. It moved again.

'Tory,' said the voice. 'It's Daddy. I'm over here.' She squeezed her eyes shut, and then looked again. 'I'm on the ground,' he said. 'I can't move.'

'Daddy!' Relief flooded her voice as she realized that it wasn't really a bear. It was her father. She ran over to the bundle on the ground and then looked at him in amazement. 'Daddy. What happened to you? Why are you lying there?'

She came carefully around through the leaves to where she could see his face. He gave her a smile that was half a grimace. 'A bad man hit me,' he said. 'And then he tied me up.'

Tory looked fearfully around her. 'Where is the bad man?'

'Tory, listen to me. He went in the house. I need you to be very brave and help me.'

Tory began to shake. 'Why did he go in the house? What will happen to Megan?'

'Nothing. Listen, Tory, listen to me. Nothing will happen if you do what I say.'

The child's chin trembled and tears filled her eyes as she stared at the little cabin. 'Why is the bad man here, Daddy?'

'Tory,' he barked at her.

Reluctantly she looked away from the cabin and back at her father.

'In my pocket,' he said. 'My pants, on this side. I have a knife. I want you to reach in my pocket and pull it out for me.'

'It will cut me,' she cried.

'No, it won't. It isn't open. It's shut right now.'

'What if it's not?' she cried.

'It is. It's shut. It can't open in my pocket. That's how it's made. Now, do you want me to get rid of the bad man, or not?' he demanded.

'I want you to.'

'Then do as I say. Reach in my pocket.'

Timidly she approached him. He rolled on his side and lay still as her little hand hovered over the side pocket on his pants. 'That's the one,' he said. 'Reach in.'

The child fished around and pulled out the car keys. 'Put those down,' he said. 'Keep looking.'

She put the keys down in the leaves and reached in again. This time she pulled out a heavy silver, oblong-shaped object.

'There we go,' he breathed.

'Where's the sharp part?' she asked.

'I'm going to tell you,' he said. 'Now, this is important. Do you see that little button in it?'

The child nodded.

'OK, now hold it in your fist, and make sure you keep all your fingers, both hands, underneath that button. Show me how you're doing it.'

The child crouched down beside him and dutifully showed him her grip on the switchblade.

'OK, now. When I say so, you push the button and hold on tight. Don't let it go or move your fingers. Can you do that?'

Tory nodded, but there was a reluctant expression on her face.

'OK,' he said. 'Now, point it away from you, right, like that, and now, hold tight and push the button.'

Tory followed his instructions and pushed. The glinting, silver blade shot out with such force that it leapt from the child's hand. Tory yelped, but Peter soothed her. 'Good girl,' he said. 'Good girl.'

'I'm scared,' she said, looking at the knife as if it were alive.

'Stop it,' he said. 'Now you have to cut these ropes, and not cut Daddy.'

Cutting ropes seemed almost like fun to her. Peter decided to try feet first. That was safer than a seven-year-old wielding a switchblade in the vicinity of his wrists. At least until she got the feel for it. The child sawed away while he warned her repeatedly to keep her fingers out of the way.

'Is the rope breaking, Tory?' he asked.

She bore down on the knife and then yelped as she cut her own finger. But Peter felt the rope slacken, and pulled it apart easily with his feet. 'Good girl,' he cried. He scrambled up to a sitting position and held his hands behind him, away from his body. 'Now,' he said. 'You have to cut these.'

'I'm bleeding, Daddy,' she wailed.

Peter gave the cut a cursory look. 'You'll be OK. Now, it's very important that you do as I say.'

'I need a Band-Aid,' she insisted.

'You'll get a Band-Aid when I am free,' he growled. 'Now stop whining and listen to me. Do you want that bad man to kill Megan and the new baby? If he does it will be your fault.'

The child looked miserably at the knife, and her bleeding finger. Peter jerked his head back, indicating his bound hands. 'Now Tory,' he said. 'Start cutting. Be careful.'

The child began to saw at the roped space between his hands. He held his hands as far apart as he could, trying to avoid the veering blade. She nicked him a few times, but he pretended not to feel it. 'A little more,' he said. 'A little more.'

Tory pressed down and suddenly the rope gave way and the knife sliced down into the padding of his thumb. 'Ahh,' he cried.

She jumped back, dropping the knife, and began to cry, 'I'm sorry, I'm sorry.'

Peter jerked the severed rope off his hands, picked up the bloody knife and closed it. He put it back in his pocket. 'OK,' he said in a grim voice. 'Good job.'

'I need a Band-Aid,' Tory repeated.

'I'll get you a Band-Aid when I'm done,' he said. He glanced around at the peaceful setting and then he began to skulk toward the house.

Tory scampered after him. 'I want to come with you,' she said.

'No,' he barked. 'I don't want you in there.'

'Let's get in our car and run away from the bad man,' she pleaded.

'Oh no,' he said. He pulled the switchblade out of his pocket and pressed the button so that it shot open. 'First I'll get the bad man. And then the baby. And then we can leave.'

FORTY-ONE

She watched Tyrell as he brought towels, hot water and a knife into the room. He had removed his jacket, and he moved easily, gracefully around the small room, deciding what to do next.

'You act like you know what you're doing,' she observed.

Tyrell smiled. 'I try to look that way,' he said.

'You don't?' she asked anxiously.

'Well, I learned how to do this at the Academy. Though I can't say I ever had any hands-on practice, if you know what I mean.' He glanced at her tired face and shook his head. 'Don't worry. I remember what to do.'

He sat back down beside her, and she reached for his hand again. 'Do you mind?' she asked.

He smiled, and covered her hand with his. 'Not at all.'

Dena sighed and closed her eyes. 'I have been a fool, haven't I?'

'Aw, don't say that.'

'Are you kidding? I live with a man who hits me, so, in order to get away from him, I leave town with a man who wants to kill me.'

'You do have terrible taste in men,' he said. 'I'll give you that.'

Dena turned her head on the pillow to face him, and tears rolled down the sides of her face. 'I thought I was doing the right thing,' she said.

Tyrell frowned. 'I feel a little bit like I'm to blame for this whole mess. I didn't do enough to protect you when you asked me to. Even after I found out about Riley's . . . history.'

'Jennifer's sister,' she said.

Tyrell nodded. 'And he told me you were having an affair with this guy.' Tyrell angled his head toward the door. 'I thought it might be true.'

'I appreciate your high opinion of me, Sergeant.'

'I'm not the best judge of people myself,' he said, thinking of Lou, in his hospital bed, revealing the ugly secrets of his life.

'So why did you come after me?' she asked.

Tyrell didn't know how much she knew. He decided not to tell her about Jennifer. Or any more about Mrs Kelly, for that matter. She had enough on her mind right now, just getting this baby safely brought into the world. But, if he was honest with himself, he'd have to admit that he hadn't just come after her as a policeman. There was more to it than that. And he wasn't quite ready to admit that right now.

'Let's just say . . . I was worried about you,' he said, wiping her forehead.

'Thanks for being worried about me,' she said.

'That's OK. Glad to do it,' he said.

She smiled at him, and they shared a glance that both quickly looked away from.

A glance that left Dena feeling both happy and nervous inside. 'Let's concentrate on Junior here,' he said.

Dena nodded, and then gasped. 'Oh, Tyrell.' Her eyes widened. 'I think this one is it. I have to push.'

'Go ahead,' he said. 'We're ready.'

In the frightening hectic minutes that followed, he strove to help her, to help her baby be born. It was the first glimpse of the baby's hair that he would always remember. It was not bald, as he subconsciously expected it to be. The baby had hair on its tiny scalp. Hair, soft and wheat-colored, like his mother's. As if he was already claiming his individuality. Such a fragile thing, a baby, but resilient as well, like a silky strand of hair.

'Is he all right?' Dena was crying. 'Is he breathing? He's so tiny,' she worried aloud, the blueprint of her life to come.

Tyrell did his clumsy best to clean up the slippery creature and swaddled him for his mother to hold. When he released the baby to his mother's arms, Tyrell felt a pang of regret and, at the same moment, a fierce sense of responsibility for his life. Up until that moment, he had never imagined himself wanting children, being a father. It had always seemed a thankless, confusing chore. Suddenly, he had a glimmer of something rapturous in it. The surprise of it was humbling. It made him feel . . . grateful for this moment.

Dena cradled her baby and studied his face. 'He's perfect.' She looked up at Tyrell and gave him a radiant smile. 'Thank you, Tyrell. How will I ever thank you?'

Tyrell could hardly stand to look at her face, it was so bright. He pressed his lips together and tried to think logically. 'We need to get him to a hospital,' he said.

'OK,' she said. 'I'm getting up. Let's go.'

'You can't get up,' he said, awed by the amount of blood and fluid in the heap of towels around her.

'Watch me,' she said. 'Let's go.'

'Are you sure?' Tyrell asked, helping her as she started to rise. He knew she was not going to be dissuaded.

'Positive,' she said.

'Negative,' said a voice from the doorway.

They both looked up and saw him. Peter stood watching them, an open switchblade glinting in his hand. 'I'll take that,' he said, pointing to the baby Dena had pressed against her chest.

'Are you crazy?' Dena demanded.

'I'll take care of it from now on,' he said. 'You're unfit.'

Looking at the man's cruel, selfish face, Tyrell felt a fury that was overwhelming.

This murderer, this kidnapper had the audacity to stand in the doorway and waste precious moments of this baby's fragile life. To try to prevent them from carrying a newborn to safety. It occurred to Tyrell that he would kill this man in front of him, without hesitation, for the sake of this still nameless infant. He knew it was bad to go into a fight with too much emotion. He couldn't help it. He saw the knife in Peter's hand, but it might as well have been a crackerjack toy for all he cared. He didn't think any further. He lunged at Peter, and seized his wrist as if to tear it off his arm.

Tyrell's furious assault took Peter by surprise. He fell backward into the living room and hit the floor with a thud. Tyrell landed on top of him and they rolled on the floor in a vicious embrace, each grasping and pounding the other, for the advantage.

Tory and Megan, huddled together in the doorway, started to scream. Dena was crying out also, although her voice was weak.

All of a sudden, there were the sounds of sirens piercing the air, and the thump of vehicles coming quickly down the road outside. In that minute, the room was filled with the reflection of blinking, red lights.

They all froze, momentarily stunned by the arrival of the outside world into their struggle. Then Tyrell whooped in triumph. He looked down at Peter who was struggling frantically to free himself from Tyrell's grasp. 'Oh no you don't,' said Tyrell. 'Got you now, you mother,' he said.

Their eyes met and Tyrell had to steel himself not to shrink from the venom in Peter's gaze. Tyrell was tempted to jump up and run out the door, to flag down the paramedics and direct them in, to urge them not to lose a second. But he did not dare to leave Peter, now pinned beneath him, alone in the house for a moment with Dena and the baby. Tyrell shouted out, 'Help, in here.'

'Police,' shouted a voice outside. 'We're coming in.' An instant later the door burst open, and two cops in bulletproof vests, their guns drawn, were in the doorway.

They looked in and saw Tyrell straddling Peter, pinning him to the floor. Since he wasn't in his uniform, Tyrell hoped they knew that the man they were looking for was a white man. One of the cops pointed his gun at Peter.

'Peter Ward,' he said.

'That's him,' said Tyrell, relieved. Then he looked up. 'Have you got an ambulance out there?'

'Just pulling in now,' said one of the cops.

'Get somebody in here quick. We've got a newborn, premature . . . how early?' he asked, looking back at Dena.

'Six weeks,' she said.

The first cop came in and the second went outside to pass the message to the EMTs. As Tyrell climbed off Peter, the armed officer held a gun on the wanted man. Before anyone could stop them, Tory and Megan ran shrieking to their father and buried themselves in his arms.

A woman carrying a medical bag and dressed in a blue coverall appeared in the doorway. Two men, similarly dressed, crowded in behind her. 'Someone here had a preemie?' asked the woman.

'In here,' said Tyrell, leaving Peter on the ground clutching his girls, while the cop held a gun on him. Tyrell followed the paramedics into the bedroom, where Dena sat on the edge of the bed, rocking her baby against her chest and crooning.

'Help my baby,' Dena cried. 'He wasn't due yet.'

'We're going to help you both, ma'am,' the woman said, gently taking the child from his mother as the EMTs began their work.

As the paramedic lifted the child from Dena's arms, Tyrell could see that the baby's skin had a sickly pallor, a faint bluish tinge. 'Is he all right?' Tyrell asked. 'Is he breathing?'

The woman did not respond directly to Tyrell. She turned to the man behind her, who was unpacking medical equipment. 'Breathing's shallow. Let's try to clear his lungs.'

'Is he going to be all right?' Dena cried, as Tyrell put a comforting arm around her shoulder.

The woman flashed a reassuring smile at them both. 'He's not too bad. I've seen much worse. Did you deliver him?'

Tyrell nodded, feeling at once proud and helpless.

'Take it easy,' said the other EMT as the woman and the first man obscured the child from view with their ministrations. 'How's your wife?'

For a second, Tyrell was confused. Then he realized that the man, seeing Tyrell in his civilian clothes, had made a mistake. It didn't seem like a natural assumption, given the color of the baby's skin, but the man was looking at him with a disarming openness.

Tyrell realized, in that moment, that Dena was leaning into him as if she had always been there. At the man's words, she looked at Tyrell, apprehensively. He smiled, embarrassed, and she smiled back.

'I'm OK,' she insisted. 'It's the baby I'm worried about. What are you doing to him?'

'First, we'll make sure he's stable. Then we'll transport him to the hospital.'

'Can I go with him in the ambulance?' she asked.

'Of course.'

'I'll be right back,' Tyrell said. Dena nodded and looked back at her baby.

Outside there were two Redmark police cruisers idling beside the ambulance and waiting for the officers inside to herd Peter out the door. It was a difficult process because the girls had thrown themselves on Peter's neck, while he was still on the floor, and refused to let go of their father. One cop had crouched down and was trying to reason with them to let go, while the other cop held a gun nervously on the wanted man.

All of a sudden, over them, was a deafening, thudding noise, as if something huge was about to fall on the house. Tory and Megan began to scream at the sound, and everyone looked up as lights flashed from above.

A helicopter, carrying Captain Van Brunt, Laura Mallory and Skip Lanman was coming in low, preparing to land in a field across the highway from the lake. Laura saw the shimmering surface of the lake, and the flashing lights of emergency vehicles below her, but it was impossible to see what her gaze sought. Two little girls, even blonde-headed girls, were not visible from that height in the dark of night.

Van Brunt, sitting behind her, watched her leaning against the window, shredding, in her lap, a Kleenex she had wept into on the way. She had begged, like a small child, to sit next to the pilot, so that she could look out and try to spot them. At least someone would come out of this nightmare with their heart's desire, he thought.

He wondered if the Russell woman was all right. It was ironic that she had been trapped here with Clifford Mallory while the man she fled, Brian Riley, had been kicked to death by a horse. Word of his death had come in around dinnertime. Some rich guy who boarded his horse with Riley had found him there when he went in to pay his bill.

Van Brunt wondered how Dena Russell would react to that news. Or even if she had lived to hear it. It was entirely possible by now that Peter – Clifford Mallory, he corrected himself – had put an untimely end to her and her pregnancy. He wondered about Tyrell, too. Van Brunt didn't approve of hot-dogging, grandstanding and all the rest. He believed in doing things by the book, and this was most certainly not by the book. Still, he didn't like to see harm come to one of his officers. Even Tyrell Watkins.

The pilot shouted at Van Brunt that they were about to descend. The so-called field looked like little more than a clearing, surrounded by trees. The pilot did not seem to be nonplussed by the lack of elbow room.

Van Brunt leaned forward, toward Laura. 'Almost there,' he shouted.

She nodded, but did not look back at him. Her gaze swept like a searchlight over the earth below.

FORTY-TWO

Distracted by what sounded like a spaceship landing, the crouching cop stood up, and the one who had been holding the gun on Peter glanced back at the window. Peter was not distracted. As Tyrell emerged from the bedroom, he saw Peter reach down and retrieve the switchblade which had been kicked beneath the rug in their scuffle. Tyrell shouted, but it was too late. In a swift motion, Peter grabbed Tory and Megan to him and held the switchblade to Megan's neck. The others turned, too late, to see the results of their momentary inattention.

'Put the knife down, Mr Mallory,' said the cop with the gun. 'You can't get away. Let the children go.'

Peter saw that it was hopeless, knew it in his head, but he had not come this far just to give in. 'Let them go for what?' he cried. 'So Laura can get them back? Never.'

'Let's just all calm down,' said the cop soothingly.

'No, I won't give them back to her,' Peter said. 'Nothing could make me. They'd be better off dead than with her. I'll kill them first.'

Tory let out a shriek, but her father squeezed her tighter.

Peter began to back out the door while the police watched help-lessly. Once outside, he dragged the girls down the path, just as another van pulled up and two more officers – one in plainclothes, the other in uniform – got out. They came rushing toward him, but stopped when they saw the girls being threatened.

The plainclothes officer held up a badge. 'Mr Mallory, I'm the

Redmark police chief. Please, let go of the children. Let's talk this over.'

'Stay away from me or I'll kill them,' Peter repeated.

Another squad car came roaring up the bumpy road, red lights flashing, and there was the sound of doors slamming and men shouting in the dark. The chief quickly conferred with his officers. They knew this was no idle threat. Children had been killed before in the name of their parents' great love for them – slaughtered like the front line of foot soldiers in a war they could never understand.

Peter looked madly around. The police would never let him get back to his minivan. It was surrounded by cops. By the time he got the girls inside, they would shoot him down. And Laura would win. The thought of her, the image of her face made his stomach turn. She, who had turned on him. She who, at first, he had hoped would be the perfect mother, had proved to be shoddy, like all women. No, she would never win. She could win in every court in America and that would not stop him. They were his. It was only an accident of nature that they had been born to her. They were his. And he would keep them to the end.

His frantic gaze fell on the motorboat pulled up alongside the dock. He tightened his grip on the children, the knife still hovering near Megan's throat, and began to back down toward it. He hauled Megan, while Tory shuffled along beside him, white-faced. 'Don't try to come after us,' he said. 'Don't come a step closer.'

'You can't get away on the lake, Mr Mallory,' the chief tried to reason with him. 'Wherever you come ashore, we'll intercept you.'

Peter ignored him. Making sure he was always shielded by the children, Peter managed to push the boat into the water and drag the children in after him. On the shore, the chief warned his men not to fire. It was too dark. The children could be easily hit.

Peter pulled the engine cord and the engine started on the second try. The little skiff began to move.

The Pennsylvania Highway patrol had arrived and the chief conferred with the ranking officer. Then he called his headquarters. 'Get some divers and the police launch out on the lake,' he said. 'Stand by for orders.'

As his skiff began its steady cruise across the water in the dark, Peter felt a moment of peace in his heart. It was almost as if they were on a little excursion. All they needed was a basket of food and it would be a moonlight picnic. He looked at the two small girls, huddled together in the bow of the boat, whimpering. Tory had her arm around her sister. Megan's head was buried under Tory's arm. 'Hey, you two,' he whispered softly. 'Cheer up.'

'Where are we going, Dad?' Tory asked.

'We are going to get away from these terrible people,' he said, and his voice sounded confident, but a note of alarm was sounding in his heart. The boat was beginning to take on water.

'My feet are wet,' said Tory.

'It's all right,' he said distractedly. He had brought nothing along. Not even a paper cup that he could bail with. It was as if the floor of the boat was an invisible sieve. The water level in the boat began to climb.

'I'm cold, Daddy,' Tory said.

Peter looked back to the shore. The lights were still flashing, ruining the tranquil scene. The men were standing on the shore, watching him escape. For a minute he thought maybe they had put the invisible holes in the boat. The engine on the skiff dipped low in the water and sputtered to a halt. Peter looked around. They were out near the middle, where it would be deepest. In the distance he saw a boat coming toward them. It wasn't a boat in his view yet, just a searchlight on the water. But the sound of its engine was coming closer, heading toward them. There were no life preservers in this boat. Not even a cushion to cling to. The launch steaming in their direction had a bullhorn on it and, through it, someone was shouting incomprehensible commands to him. It was questionable, however, if the boat would reach them before they sank.

Peter crawled across the waterlogged craft to his children, and the two of them came willingly into his arms. 'My precious girls,' he said. He wondered to himself how people could be so cruel to children. They were just innocent beings, who never tried to hurt you or betray you or contradict what you said.

Perhaps it's best this way, he thought. He was not going back with the police, and he was not giving these children up to Laura Mallory. That was not an option. He thought of the three of them, sinking below the water's surface, intertwined. Never to be separated, or grow a day older. Kissing the soft, shiny hair on their heads, he marveled that if none of this had happened, these girls would someday grow up to be women. He couldn't picture that. They were nothing like the duplicitous, dishonest women he had always had the misfortune to know. These two were perfectly gentle. Now they would always stay that way. He wondered for a minute about the knife. It would be kinder than drowning. He could use it on them this minute, while they were here in his arms. It would be quick and painless, and they wouldn't have to be frightened. He thought of it, and then he hesitated. He wanted to hold them, alive, for just a minute more.

Fleeing the cold, rising water, Tory and Megan tried to climb higher up on him.

The water in the boat was so deep now that their movement was all it took. The starboard side dipped, and a rush of black water poured in, turning them over. The girls began to shriek, and cling to him. He reached out for them and his knife left his hand, and drifted down to the lake bottom. Peter and the children sank, but came up again, the girls thrashing wildly, sputtering and shrieking in fear. Peter saw the police launch approaching. He could see the eyes of the men on board, their arms reaching out.

Don't cry, he tried to tell the girls. Don't cry. Their little arms were around his throat, choking him. Let it be over, he thought. Let it be over. He was blinded by the searchlight of the boat, shining inexorably on him. He could hear the sound of the bullhorn. Now, he thought. Do it. It was the best thing for them. For all of them. Hold them tight and go down. Always together. He turned his head, and his gaze met Tory's. Her face was glowing in the merciless searchlight. Her eyes were crazed with fear. She knew they were going to drown.

'Daddy, save me,' she whispered. And, despite their thrashing in the water and the cruel light and the noise of the bullhorn and the idling of the launch's engine, he could not help but hear her plea. No matter the hell it would be, she wanted her life. Her heart, her poor little heart, trusted him. His peace of mind vanished, and his will, and his plan. Gulping in a breath, he forced them up, above his head, above the water line, and felt them being lifted. Now that it was too late, he understood the truth. He should have used the knife.

Dena and Tyrell emerged from the cabin. He was holding her up on one side, while one of the EMTs supported her other arm. The baby was already in the ambulance, in a portable incubator, connected to breathing equipment. Dena looked at the horrible scene unfolding on the lake.

'Tyrell,' called a voice in the dark, and they both turned to look as Captain Van Brunt strode up and clapped Tyrell in a brief hug.

'I guess you heard me before the phone went dead,' said Tyrell. Van Brunt nodded. 'Thank God.'

The two men spoke together in low voices. Dena could see two small children in the back of the police launch. They were huddled together, wrapped in blankets, as the boat headed to shore, while divers searched for their father who had disappeared beneath the surface of the lake.

'Oh, those poor babies,' Dena said. And her heart ached for them. But her gaze was drawn irresistibly back to the ambulance, and her own son, needing her in there.

Tyrell excused himself from the captain and returned to Dena's side. 'The girls' mother is here,' he said, nodding toward Laura Mallory, who stood at the edge of the lake, kneading her hands. It wasn't the blonde woman in the picture that sat on Peter's mantel. That was some mother he had invented for the girls. This woman had long, dark hair in ringleted curls. And a face that was at once a vision of dread and hope.

Dena stared at Laura, the woman who Peter had said was dead. Her eyes were blazing in the dark.

'Come along, miss,' said one of the men to Dena.

The EMTs opened the back doors of the ambulance, and Dena and Tyrell climbed in. They closed the doors behind them.

As the siren began to sound, Dena looked out the back window, and saw the woman on the shore, fully dressed, begin to wade into the lake, oblivious to the water and the cold, her arms outstretched, toward the launch. Dena caught a last glimpse of two white triangles in the dark, the children's small faces, fixed on this stranger, their mother, reaching out for them, as the ambulance began to bump up the road.

Lightning Source UK Ltd.
Milton Keynes UK
UKHW011810130819
347844UK00002B/127/P